A FAR WAY TO RUN

TURNAROUND IN TEXAS
BOOK 2

LORI ALTEBAUMER

Scripture quotations taken from New International Version® and New King James Version®.
Scripture is taken from the Holy Bible, New International Version®. NIV®. Copyright ©
1973, 1978, 1984 by International Bible Society. Used by permission of Zondervan. All rights reserved.
Scripture taken from New King James Version®. Copyright © 1982 by Thomas Nelson. Used by permission. All rights reserved.

Copyright © 2022 Lori Altebaumer
One Thousand Hills Publishing
All rights reserved.
Print ISBN: 979-8-9885764-9-5
eBook ISBN: 979-8-9885764-7-1

TO JOE
"Husbands, love your wives, just as Christ loved the church..."
Ephesians 5:25
Thank you for continuing to be the example of this kind of love in my life.

Who knows, perhaps you have come to your royal position for such a time as this.

Esther 5:14

CHAPTER ONE

There is more than one way to bury a person.

The smell of damp earth and the funeral sprays made of freshly cut flowers drifted to the parking area as a wintery wind tussled the white daisies and yellow roses surrounding the soon-to-be occupied hole in the ground. Unseasonably cold air chilled her. The words rattling like bones in Shayne Wright's head chilled her more.

Her legs—bare beneath the tailored dress she wore—refused to move her away from the vehicle she'd exited. She stared at the crowd of mourners—men and women wearing starched denim jeans and polished boots mingling with suited business executives and the ragtag rabble of the down-and-out or barely-getting-by. They came together as one in the small country cemetery, each here to pay their last respects to Peg Moreland.

She didn't often find such diversity gathered in unity of purpose in the facelessness of the city she now called home.

That was the beauty of Peg's life and the blessing of community.

Or so she had once believed.

But coming here was a mistake. Why had she?

The wind carried Reverend Mack Stapleton's voice across the cemetery, bringing bits and pieces of the eulogy to where she stood.

News of Peg's passing had come to her the same day Nick Turner had asked her to marry him. The same day the word *yes* had refused to attach itself to his proposal.

And the day before she awoke from the nightmare, tangled in sweat dampened sheets and fighting to fill her lungs. In her troubled subconscious, she'd stood at the edge of a grave watching herself being buried alive. The gritty sensation of the dirt covering her skin as she suffocated beneath the weight of an encroaching darkness—although only a dream—clung to her long after she'd risen.

That's why she'd come.

But it was a mistake.

The afternoon sun shone through the bare limbs of the massive oak trees surrounding the cemetery, its light casting skeleton-like shadows that came for her.

She swung the driver's side door open and ducked back into the safety of the Ford Escape.

Turning the key in the ignition, she relaxed in the soothing comfort of the engine's vibration.

Out of habit, she reached for her cell phone. Nick would have an answer. He always did. He knew how to help her see what was real. Not the bucolic life of a rural West Texas town. The incorruptibility she'd believed in growing up here was a lie. Wickedness was a disease without boundaries.

She pressed the speed dial and waited for him to answer. Instead, it went to voice mail. *Hey there. This is Nick. If you've reached my voice mail, it's because I am busy doing kingdom work. But your call matters to me, so please leave a message, and I'll get back to you as soon as the Lord allows.*

At the sound of the beep, her thoughts failed. He had

been against her coming. His expression when she'd left this morning to make the four-hour drive told her they were both startled by her determination. For three years, she'd trusted every decision he'd made. Until his marriage proposal had paralyzed her with an inability to answer. Soon after came their first real disagreement over a funeral she didn't have to attend, suggesting something to her subconscious she didn't want to explore.

Sometimes he worried too much, but that was what love did. Right?

The image of the clean-cut Nick Turner standing at her door on their first date, holding three white roses, swept into her thoughts. He'd looked so ... innocuous. Nothing more, nothing less. He hadn't taken her breath away or made her weak in the knees. But the roses reached into her chest, touching a long-forgotten place in her heart.

When a dozen long stem white roses arrived on her doorstep the next day, she'd opened herself to the possibility her life might be normal. Red roses wouldn't have done it, but the white ones awakened within her the hope that with Nick Turner, the up-and-coming young pastor, perhaps she'd be redeemable. Most importantly, she'd be sheltered. Or was the truth more that she'd be hidden?

Had she fallen in love with the roses instead of the man? She sighed, expelling the troublesome thought. *Say yes,* her brain advised. But still the word stuck in her throat.

"Just calling to hear your voice and let you know I'm okay. I'll try again later." The words came out sounding awkward and uncertain.

She wasn't okay, and Nick's recorded voice hadn't brought the assurance she'd hoped for. Ending the call, she stared at the phone as though it were the portal between two worlds.

Between two worlds—the revelation rang true. She existed

in a place belonging to neither, yet holding on to both. She had to let go of one.

That was why she'd come, wasn't it?

The thin slice of space in between too closely resembled a stifling, lifeless tomb, when what she craved was a breath of fresh air.

I came that you might have life and have it more abundantly. The old familiar words bubbled up from a well of hidden truth deep within her, drenching a soul she hadn't recognized thirsted.

She dropped the phone back in her purse, then drove away from the rows of weathered gravestones, a reminder the day would come when she joined their ranks.

That day didn't bother her. What troubled her was the pressing question concerning the days in between. She needed a better answer than waiting out what life was left like a potted plant.

She left the cemetery behind, but a melancholy mood clung to her thoughts with the tenacity of a spider's web. Entangled in the threads of indecision, she spent the next hour driving in circles on the backroads of Turnaround, Texas, getting no further from her past and no closer to her future.

There is more than one way to bury a person. The words persisted in her thoughts.

The realm outside her windshield blurred. Her eyes cut to the speedometer. The orange needle pointed to a number that sucked the wind from her lungs, snatching her back to reality.

She was driving too fast, but even worse, she was driving scared. Her heart raced in rhythm with the hum of her tires skimming across the asphalt.

She jerked her foot from the accelerator, not ready to take her place among tombstones just yet.

The vehicle slowed. Her gaze flickered from the gray strip of pavement that sliced through the terrain in front of her. The open field of dried grass the color of aged parchment and the rocky, juniper and oak-covered slope of the limestone hill came into focus. The view provided a touchstone for her heart, drawing her back to her roots.

Drawing her back to truth.

Her attention shifted to the diamond engagement ring encircling her finger. The ring didn't sparkle beneath the thick gray blanket of clouds now hiding the sun in advance of the predicted storm. Freezing rain was forecasted to fall during the night. The increasingly sullen sky gave Shayne no reason to hope otherwise.

Perhaps the sparkle was missing because the ring was a lie. It wasn't Nick's fault the word *yes* had hung in her throat like a bur, refusing to be spoken. She'd been faithfully by his side for the past three years. Of course, Nick expected her to say yes. She'd expected it too.

But that wasn't the way it happened. Instead, she'd asked for time to think. She'd been too unsure of herself to resist when he suggested she wear the ring until she had her answer. An answer he clearly believed would be yes.

Peg's funeral had lifted a veil on Shayne's life. She wasn't sure she liked what she saw. A sense of loss for more than the life of a friend pressed against her.

The rigorously constructed armor she lived in felt no thicker than an eggshell, fragile and ready to crack with the slightest pressure.

Maybe that's what she wanted.

The asphalt stretched out straight for another quarter mile before taking a sharp left. She stared up at the cloud covered sky, closing the door on thoughts of a future she didn't want to contemplate today.

A decision solidified in her head. She'd stay at the farm

tonight. One night for a final goodbye. She'd collect a few sentimental items and leave as soon as everything cleared in the morning. The sooner she got back to Austin, the sooner she could slip back into the life she'd chosen.

Wrapped in a threadbare sense of peace, she glanced at the ring again.

A motorcycle swung around the bend in the road ahead. Taking the curve too fast, it swerved farther into her lane. The driver leaned hard. The machine wobbled before the rider regained control.

Shayne jerked the wheel to the right as the motorcycle careened straight toward her, missing her SUV with only inches to spare.

Her tires bounced off the jagged edge of pavement, causing the seatbelt to yank her hard against the seat. She clutched the steering wheel, wrestling the car to a stop. Her heart thrummed in her ears while the voice of Johnny Cash crooned from her radio about the dangers of falling into a burning ring of fire. Pinned in place, she fumbled to release the nylon strap holding her tight.

Did this person know how close they'd just come to death? Understanding she could have hurt someone hollowed her out—even if the fault wasn't hers.

Despite the plunging temperature and angry wind outside, the air inside the SUV pressed against her, warm and clingy, turning her skin clammy. The claustrophobic sensation pulled her back into that black moment when everything she believed about herself ripped away. In her mind, she was alone in the dark again. Only she hadn't been truly alone. The memory of each touch still burned her flesh.

Tearing at the cashmere scarf she wore, she unwound it from her neck. Air brushed against her damp skin, bringing a small measure of relief.

She adjusted the car's temperature control and waited for

an unheated blast of air. She needed the air to move, to blow against her skin and remind her she wasn't trapped in the stagnant vapor of that old stone building.

The feeble, tepid puff that met her fell short of the bracing touch for which she hungered.

Lowering the window, she welcomed the winter storm in as she watched rust-colored leaves being tossed and driven by the gale. The same wind swept the haunting memories away with the hurrying leaves. Several minutes ticked by before she rolled the window up and maneuvered the car back onto the road.

The trees on the hillside thrashed in the brutal wind, sending more leaves scattering in front of her. The premature cold front bore down on a landscape unready to let go of fall. The darkening lip of sky on the western horizon announced the brunt of the winter squall was almost here.

She switched on the wipers as a fine mist blew against the windshield, blurring her sight. She could still beat the storm out, forget the sentimentality, and be safe back in the city tonight. But if that's what she wanted, she should leave now.

If that's what she wanted ...

There were a hundred reasons she should leave this town and return to her life in Austin.

Yes, a hundred reasons to go, but it only took one to make her stay.

She checked her watch. Enough time to pick up something to eat in Turnaround before the roads turned dangerous. If there was anything open. The entire town had attended Peg's funeral, and with the threat of icy roads overnight, most people would be making sure the hay was out, the pipes wrapped, the wood stacked, and the livestock tended before hunkering down somewhere warm and safe themselves.

Safe. Nick was her security. Yet sometimes his protection gave her the smothering sense of too little air to breathe.

Like being buried alive. Her grip tightened, her knuckles turning white as she squeezed the steering wheel.

But the morbid thought persisted.

Then fight.

Fight? She could barely catch her breath. Her entire world teetered on the brink of something she couldn't yet see, but terrified her just the same. But the idea of fighting came at her like the release on a pressure cooker. She didn't just want to hit something, she wanted to *destroy* something. The absurdity of the thought was laughable. Unexpectedly, the idea also carried a cleansing sensation that appealed to her.

But fighting wasn't in her. Not anymore. There was only the rigid need for self-control, keeping the facade from falling away and exposing the truth. Her truth. Her shameful secret.

But one night away—a single night to slip into the past and remember the time *before*. She could do that. She needed to do that.

Reaching into her purse, she rehearsed what she should say to Nick.

Her fingers never found the phone.

CHAPTER TWO

Ethan McGregor slung his duffel bag onto the back seat of his truck and turned to retrieve a box of blueprints from the porch of the McGregor and Sons Construction office building. Not that he was looking forward to crunching numbers during his time away, but the work provided a focus for his thoughts when his mind refused to let go of the memories.

"You sure you want to do this?" Cameron leaned against a porch post in front of the office.

Ethan gave his brother a sharp glance and continued loading boxes into his back seat. "Yep."

"Going to be a pretty lonely gig out there."

"You worried I won't get the job done?"

"Not at all." Cameron took a long sip from the coffee cup in his hand. "No one reads blueprints and manages a job site like you, man. I swear you were born with construction in your blood."

Ethan faced his brother, pinching the shamrock green hoodie to pull the fabric tight, drawing attention to the McGregor and Sons logo printed across his chest. "Still wearing the family name. Although why you couldn't keep your wife from choosing this awful color makes me question your manhood a little. I look like an overgrown leprechaun."

Cameron chuckled and shook his head, looking away. "Yeah, well, Krissy can be persistent, and you know what they say. A happy wife is a happy life."

Ethan failed to stop the muscles in his jaw from clenching.

"Aww dang it, Ethan, I'm sorry. I didn't mean to say that." Cameron looked at him with a regret Ethan knew was sincere. He despised it.

"No big deal. The past is the past." He shifted his back to his brother as he shuffled the boxes under the pretense of making room for more. "Besides, I know Krissy's the one behind this brotherly bonding moment you're trying to have." He angled so Cameron could see his smile. He loved his brother more than he loved himself, but Cameron didn't need to know that.

"She's a worrier. But hey, man, I'm worried about you too. I mean, what're you going to do out there in the middle of nowhere?"

Ethan studied the ground for a minute. Here, he was surrounded by family and a few good friends, and he'd never felt lonelier in his life. Not at boot camp, not in a sniper's nest in the middle of some god-forsaken desert, not even when he lay for a week in a state of semi consciousness after the IED that blew up their Hummer nearly took his life.

"It's only for a few weeks. I'll be fine." He picked up the last box and shoved it in the back seat. "Besides, you got it all wrong. It might just be the middle of everywhere."

"Ty's going to miss his Uncle Ethan. Who'll take him fishing with you gone?"

Ethan gave his brother a look that said he knew what he was trying to pull. He'd miss his nephew more than he wanted to contemplate. But looking into the child's innocent eyes gutted him. Ty didn't yet know the truth about his Uncle Ethan. Only four years old, he wouldn't understand. But one day he would.

Ethan didn't want to be here to see the light of adoration replaced by fear when he did.

He clamped his eyes closed, turning his back to his brother, as something hot and corrosive churned through his veins. "I doubt Krissy's going to let me take him fishing in the middle of winter. I'll be back by the time it warms up again."

"It wasn't your fault, you know. That Alexa left. She never was right for you."

Ethan opened his eyes to watch cars speeding past the construction yard on the adjacent highway. His hands gripped the bed of his truck as he worked to cover the gaping wound in his heart that refused to heal. "It is what it is. I'm over it."

He suspected that was one of the biggest lies he'd ever told himself. Not that he wasn't over her. She'd burned that bridge when she slept with his best friend. But everything that had gone into creating that disaster still haunted him. The question of his own guilt, how maybe he'd driven her to it because he couldn't handle the memories—the ones that still raked across his conscience, keeping the wounds open and chafed. The bleeding may have stopped, but his soul still oozed out, revealing his lack of humanity. Something Alexa had discovered only after she'd married him.

Cameron came to stand behind him. His voice was husky as he gripped Ethan's shoulder. "Don't do this to yourself, man."

Ethan moved away from his touch, turning to face him. "I'm good. Really. Looking forward to a little fresh air and time away from the city." He retrieved his rifle case from the porch and slid it behind the back seat. "Besides, time to do a little hunting and fishing won't hurt either."

Nope. *That* was the biggest lie he'd ever told himself. The very thought of looking through a scope at an unsuspecting target, deciding when to pull the trigger, when to take a life or grant a life, left him so cold it felt as though his bones might shatter. He schooled his face into the emotionless blank he'd perfected. It wouldn't help for Cameron to suspect the real reason he was taking his gun—one he wouldn't need the scope for.

This trip wasn't about needing time away to do some hunting and fishing in between working on quotes for construction projects. It was a mission to find redemption.

Or die trying.

CHAPTER THREE

Levi Hollingsworth beat his fist on the dashboard, more in frustration than expectation of change. He'd meant to get the gas gauge fixed weeks ago, but like everything else in his life, it had taken a back seat to the good times.

Good times. Even that was a joke. He punched the dashboard one last time as the truck coughed its way into the ditch lining the narrow country road.

The indicator crept to the left of the gauge, confirming what he already knew. The red E that stared at him stood for more than just an empty gas tank right now. He uttered a string of words that would've had his grandmother washing his mouth out with soap.

He'd left his cell phone behind when he'd slipped away. He didn't really understand how that tracking stuff worked, but he'd watched enough cop shows to know better than to risk it.

The stiff wind shook the old Ford, snaking wintery air in around his feet. He let loose one more word that would have called down the wrath of Grandma Hazel.

Five miles. That's how much farther he had to go. Farther than he wanted to endure in this freak winter storm.

Think. He closed his eyes and drummed his fist against the steering wheel. If memory served him correctly, it was less than a mile to the old Tackmore Ranch. The Tackmores leaned toward the category of visionaries known as preppers. He had no doubt he could find something useful, like a can of gas. If not, it would still be a warmer place to spend the night than his pickup.

Anger burned through his veins, heating him up from the inside. He couldn't get it right even when he tried.

Resigned to the miserable state of his current circumstances, he climbed out, zipped up his coat, and began the cold walk over the ridge. Now, if only what he expected to find hadn't changed in the past ten years.

————

An hour later, he had his answer. A lot had changed in ten years, not the least of which was that the Tackmore ranch was under new ownership.

New owners doing dirty business.

He couldn't stop the shivering that wracked his soaked body as he dragged himself out of the deep river channel and into the rocky shallows. How many times had he thrown himself off the same bluff for the pure enjoyment of it after a hot summer day in the hay field?

Never once had he contemplated using it in the winter as a means to escape being shot.

The wet shale was slippery and sharp, digging into his fingers so frozen and stiff they were almost useless. The only place on his body that registered anything besides numbness was the gash in his side where his blood flowed in a warmth that didn't last.

The image burned into his eyes inflicted more pain than the cut on his side, though.

He lifted his head, gauging the distance to the cover of brush growing up from the riverbank. Would they come looking for him? The current hadn't carried him far enough downriver to be safe. If he could believe any place would be safe now.

What had he really seen? Stuff like that existed in the movies, but not here. Not in his quiet hometown of Turnaround. Things like that didn't—correction—shouldn't ever happen here.

He tucked his head and gritted his chattering teeth. He'd find help. She—whoever she was—needed him.

Correction again. She didn't need him. Nobody had ever needed him. He'd lived his life in such a way as to make sure of that. But someone had to know she was out there and in danger.

She was in danger, right?

Maybe she wasn't. Maybe this was her choice, a willing participant. Some women were, right?

He ground his teeth together. Not a chance. There was no way he'd ever believe any woman would consent to be treated like that.

Besides, if that were the case, why would the Rocky Balboa wannabe try to kill him?

His fingers sank into the sand lining the river above the outcropping of shale. Not that he could feel the wet earth. He only knew that whatever his hands grabbed for now gave way beneath them as he continued to work himself away from the water.

Once out, he rolled onto his back, the dead, brittle grass jabbing into his flesh. Curling onto his side, he drew himself into a tight knot to conserve what warmth he had left, ignoring the searing pain that shot through him. He'd take that over the numbing cold deadening his body.

You always wanted to be famous. Well congratulations, buddy, you're going to be the first person ever to freeze to death in Turn-around, Texas. The irony would have made him laugh if he'd had the energy to spare. Not a single person would know about it because no one knew to look for him.

The gray sky overhead held the promise of a winter storm, convincing him he'd better find the energy to keep moving.

"Hey, Country Boy!" the voice echoed down the river-banks. It was the same voice attached to the fists that had sought to beat him senseless before taking potshots at him as he ran. Levi pictured the man standing on top of the bluff he'd jumped from in his escape. "Or maybe we should say Country *Music* Boy. The famous Levi Hollingsworth. You think you're a tough man? A hero? You're getting in over your head here. But don't worry, you will not get far."

Great. The one fan he had was a psychotic killer. The tall grass and dim light might hide him for now, but this guy—whoever he was—would be coming for him.

"I know you can hear me! It's not over. You can't interfere and think you get to walk away. And just so we have an under-standing, if you tell anyone what you saw here I will cut her up into tiny pieces and send them to you one by one."

The shivering in his body stopped. Nothing like cold, honest terror to heat a man up. A few more minutes and the dark would give him enough cover to get into the trees. And then what? The forecast predicted temperatures below freezing tonight.

The walk back to his truck was too far, and he couldn't be sure this maniac wouldn't be there waiting to cut him up into tiny pieces too. Going there wouldn't be an option. It would be a death wish—especially since the vehicle wasn't about to magically fill with gas or sprout wings.

He needed to find shelter and lie low for the night. A fire was out of the question, especially since he got kicked out of the Boy Scouts before they'd gotten to the part where you learned how to rub two sticks together to start one. Some form of protection from the vicious cold sweeping in from the north would be a necessity, though.

There was only one place he could go. He'd been headed there anyway. It'd be a long walk, but properly motivated—which he most certainly was—he could probably make it to the old farmhouse before he froze to death.

He pressed his hand to his side. The thick, sticky patch of blood mingled with the wetness of his clothes. He must have gashed himself on the glass when he jumped out the window. His icy fingers found the warmth of the blood strangely comforting.

Crawling into the trees was a slow process, but he wouldn't risk standing and being seen. If he could make it to the top of the riverbank, he'd find an open field on the other side of the trees or something similar that would help restore his bearings.

It'd been a few years since he'd walked these woods, but he hadn't forgotten.

The wind picked up, bringing with it a cold that bit into his bones. It wasn't going to be a good night for him, but a measure of empathy unfamiliar of late assured him his would still be better than that of the girl he'd just seen.

There had been a time when his heart had been soft. Life had done a bit of work hardening it up, but it would never be so hard that what he'd just seen wouldn't appall him.

Please, Lord, keep her safe until I can find help. It was a prayer he wasn't sure God would bother listening to. Broad was the gate and wide the way that led to destruction. That was the path he'd chosen.

Childhood memories crowded into his thoughts. Better days before he'd let the world put its mark on him. For the millionth time, he thought of Shayne and wondered what had happened that night. He'd tried for years to recall something, anything.

She'd always run from his every effort to reach out to her, giving him the darkest idea he didn't really want to know.

CHAPTER FOUR

A scarlet swath of blood smeared across the asphalt in the wake of a tangled mass of flesh, entrails, and cowhide.

Shayne swerved to the right, missing the bulk of the unfortunate beast, but not its entirety. The bump of her tire rolling over an extended hindquarter caused her teeth to grind.

She'd already come to one jarring stop just minutes before. This time she eased the SUV into the grass bordering the pavement, working to recall the correct procedure for reporting a dead cow in the road. Should she call nine-one-one, the Sheriff's Office, or County Services?

Skid marks interrupted her thoughts, directing her attention to an open field.

Thirty yards to her right, a truck rested upside down in the yellow grass. A perforated line of freshly turned soil told her the vehicle had rolled more than once on its way to where it now resided.

Great arcing loops of barbed wire, like a knitting project gone awry, curled amid bent and twisted metal posts where the out-of-control vehicle had broken through the fence.

Shoving the gear into park, she bolted out of the vehicle before her mind fully processed the scene. The chilling wind snapped her to attention, clearing her head and stilling her.

There was little chance anyone might have survived. *But what if...*

She took a step toward the wreckage, then stopped again. Her brain reasoned with her saying, *Don't go. There's nothing you can do. You shouldn't see this.*

Her heart thumped against her sternum as indecision hammered conflicting emotions within. *Miracles still happen.* To remain standing at a distance would be to say she doubted that truth.

Like the needle on a compass, Shayne's true north was pain. The suffering of others—whether friend or stranger—was something she was compelled to pour herself into. She couldn't turn away from it, even when she couldn't take it away.

Unless it was her own.

That pain she'd learn to bury. *Right along with yourself.*

With one hand gripping the open car door while the other clutched at hair whipped wildly by the wind, she stood frozen in place. What if she only made it worse?

But miracles...

The person on the motorcycle had looked the other way.

That wouldn't be her. Ever.

She killed the engine. With a newfound sense of urgency, she retrieved her phone. Her fingers tapped in the passcode as she hurried down the slope. Unsteady steps over the rough ground covered in falling mist forced her to slow.

A heel of her black leather pumps snagged by a hidden piece of mangled fence made her stumble. The phone flew from her grip as she fought to keep from falling amid the tangled barbed wire. She paused her prayers to chastise her vanity again for wearing these shoes on a day like today. Or ever. She hated these shoes. Only it wasn't vanity that made her wear them. They were all a part of the hiding.

Jerking her leg free, she winced as the barbs dug into her flesh. Blood trickled in a thin trail along her calf as she stooped to pick up the phone.

The wind moaned over the ridge and down through the river bottom, but that wasn't the sound that made her scalp prickle. A distinctly human sound resonated over the growl of the gale. In the tall grass several yards from the truck, someone was alive, although the guttural cry emanating from their broken body said they must wish otherwise.

Searching, she found a young man lying face up, a patch of red growing on his torn t-shirt as his limbs stretched, bent in too many places.

She turned away. His suffering wasn't something she wanted to look upon, knowing his pain would flow through some unconscious connection into her soul. The suffocating grip of inadequacy had already begun squeezing against her chest.

But fear must not win. She wouldn't let it. Squaring her shoulders with more readiness than she felt, she forced her attention back to his crushed body.

His eyes opened, his features twisting in agony as he mumbled words she knew were Spanish.

"I don't understand," Shayne said as she knelt beside him. Serpent tattoos circled his neck. She recoiled.

Don't look away. Focus on his face. As she did, she found her gaze met by the pain-filled, frightened expression of a man who believed he was dying.

Eyes rimmed in suffering told a different story than that of the fierce and wicked images inked on his face and body. Compassion flooded her heart. This wasn't a condition she would wish on anyone—with maybe the exception of a handful of monsters from that horrific night. Monsters without faces or names.

His lips moved, and she leaned closer to hear words whispered in as much fear as pain. "Help me."

The words rasped out as though wrenched from somewhere deep within his broken body, gripping her heart.

"I'm calling nine-one-one." Hands shaking, she lifted the phone. His bloody fingers pressed against her forearm, stopping her.

"No. No *bueno*." He licked his lips, smearing blood across them.

"What's your name?" Shayne fought the urge to flinch away from his touch, or vomit. She could only guess what kind of person he might have been minutes ago, before gravity had thrown him from the truck, then ground him beneath its weight. But right now he was a mother's son, someone's brother or friend. A once innocent child who had somehow turned down a path that led to tattoos shaped like serpents and teardrops.

"No. *It's ... el escorpi* ..." A moan escaped, turning into a cough that sent a trickle of blood trailing from his mouth down his cheek. "*Escorpion* ... he has her ... the money. Take the money." He stilled, eyes closed. Shayne waited, pressing her palm across her mouth to stifle a sob.

Heavy lids lifted slowly. He stared at her through the haze of death. His bloodied fingers now reached toward her face, latching on a stray lock of hair that blew against her cheek.

"*Por favor*, save her."

"Please don't give up. We'll get help." The forgotten phone dropped from her fingers as she reached for the icy hand that slid weakly from her hair, squeezing it in her own as though by doing so she could impart life.

His gaze held hers as he pled one last time, his eyes

draining of life but his voice desperate. "Tell them it's *El Scorpion. Por favor*, promise me you'll help them find her."

Shayne held tight to his hand, but his hold on life seemed to recede with the light of day as the dark clouds swept over them. His words made no sense, but the torment in his eyes left her convicted of a need to say something that might offer him comfort. "I'll try. I promise."

A sharp crack ripped through the howling wind. Something sliced across the flesh of her right shoulder, tearing her grip from his hand and sending her reeling against the ground. Fire raced down her arm.

A second object exploded the dirt near her head. Bits of cold earth struck her cheek as truth ricocheted in her thoughts. Someone had shot her.

And apparently they weren't through.

Survival instinct more than thought process propelled her response. She rolled to her side as another blast struck the ground where she'd been. She grabbed her phone from where she'd dropped it, then half crouching, half running, she headed for the wrecked vehicle, keenly aware it offered the only cover in the open field.

It wouldn't be enough if the shooter came looking. Another round screeched through the metal somewhere farther back on the truck.

Then nothing. No more shots. No approaching footsteps.

The silence terrified her more than the whine of the bullets. Where had the shooter gone, and what were they doing?

This wasn't the day she wanted to die. And it certainly wasn't the way.

The burning discomfort in her shoulder dimmed as the rush of adrenaline heightened her other senses. She reached to touch the open wound, only then remembering the phone she held. It slid from her fingers as she looked down at the growing blotch of red. The shot had ripped open her sleeve to expose her now bloody arm.

Breathe in, hold, breathe out. Think. Be able to state your location.

She picked up the phone, repeating the words as her trembling fingers pushed the keys. Her gaze landed on the face of a second man—the driver—still trapped in the vehicle, his dead eyes staring at her from a head no longer properly attached to his body.

"Nine-one-one. What's your emergency?" The voice of the operator cut through her panic.

"I ..." Shayne doubled over and retched.

"Caller, can you hear me? Please state your emergency."

Shayne swallowed against the knot of emotion swelling inside her. "Someone's trying to kill me."

CHAPTER FIVE

That someone was using her for target practice made the pain in her arm pale compared to the rage burning through Shayne. Anger held her together, pushing back the shock that hovered one shallow breath away. The bullet had only grazed her shoulder, but its impact sent a throbbing, aching wave down her arm and through her upper body.

The world around her spun like a kaleidoscope of vivid and distinct sensations.

The smell of the still warm engine—hot oil and diesel fumes—hung heavy in the moist air, mixing with the musty, sweet scent of the freshly turned soil clinging to the bumper. The sharp stubble of dead grass stabbed at her bare knees while the smooth, solid curve of metal pressed against her side. The blood seeping from her shoulder left a thick warmth that soon morphed into an icy wetness that numbed her skin.

As though it meant to pull the world apart, the wind raged across the landscape. Its steady roar silenced every sound except the thunderous pounding of her heart.

She might have marveled at the amount of detail the

mind registered under such horrific circumstances if fear of dying hadn't been her most urgent concern.

Drawing herself into a tight ball, she knelt in front of the only thing between her and a potentially fatal bullet. She could ponder the mysteries of the human brain later.

If there was a later.

At last, the wail of sirens rose through the growling storm.

Only then did she let herself shiver, the moments-ago sharpness of her surroundings dimming into a haze of gray. Once the shaking started, she couldn't stop. The surrounding scene smudged as though it were a watercolor painting touched by too much moisture. The world spiraled into a long, dark tunnel threatening to pull her into its depth. She clung to the edge with a tenacious determination, refusing to fall into the black abyss of a panic attack.

Other sounds became distinct, each one existing in its own separate vacuum, registering in her consciousness with exquisite clarity—the squeak of a truck chassis bouncing over rough ground, slamming doors, urgent voices.

The metallic zing of zippers.

She couldn't move, couldn't speak. The line between reality and nightmare was eggshell thin, and maybe if she didn't so much as twitch, it wouldn't crack.

A swirl of unfamiliar faces surrounded her. Latex gloves, tiny lights, fingers pressed against her wrist—touching her. Voices asking questions.

She wanted to answer, but her mouth refused. She nodded, trying not to flinch beneath their touch.

For whatever reason, the shooter hadn't wanted her dead enough to finish the job. She was safe now, right?

Strangers ushered her to the shelter of the waiting ambulance. She recoiled under lights that were too bright. A fresh jolt of alarm shot through her. They planned to examine her. Her fingers went to her right hand, where she twisted the silver ring—a simple band with the outline of a compass stamped in it. The smooth way it rotated on her finger soothed her, reminding her to breathe.

They were asking about her injuries, their gloved fingers already clipping away the torn fabric over her wound.

"Just my shoulder." The words came out tight and defensive.

Lord, please help me be okay. She held back the sob that rose in her chest.

Her fears ebbed as they cut away the sleeve of her dress where her blood saturated the expensive black fabric. Surrounded by people doing their best to protect her, she let herself calm. Their compassion helped pull her away from that thin line between reality and hysteria. The shivering stopped.

Two EMTs moved around her with trained efficiency. The atmosphere inside the ambulance soothed her raw nerves. No wind, no bullets, no dead faces staring at her through cracked windshields. Rational thinking returned in slow, steady waves. Physical pain she could withstand. It was emotional pain that was her greatest nemesis.

A deputy joined her. Tipping his tan Stetson hat, he introduced himself as Deputy Harmon and asked if she might be able to answer a few questions. Shayne nodded, knowing there wasn't much she could tell. She hadn't understood most of what the injured man said, and she hadn't seen the shooter.

After several rounds of disappointing "I don't know" answers, the deputy must have decided to give up.

"Well ... thank you." He closed his notepad and slid his pen back into his uniform pocket in defeat. "You'll probably hear from an investigator soon, but I'll let you know if I have any more questions." The resignation in his voice said he figured asking them would be just as pointless as asking the previous ones.

She couldn't tell him what she didn't know.

The EMT finished his assessment and left her as the next round of questioning walked over wrapped in the rugged, crusty form of Sheriff Rock Griger. He was the same mixture of intimidation and begrudging compassion she'd always known him to be. Someone you wanted in an emergency, but not a social gathering.

"Miss Wright," he lifted his hat, but quickly jammed it back onto his head in the biting wind. "They taking good care of you?"

"Yes, sir." Surprised that he recognized her after all this time—and all she'd done to remake herself—Shayne avoided eye contact, focusing on the plain brown boots he wore instead. Though they shone as if subjected to a rigorous polishing, numerous scuff marks told a story of hard use.

Sheriff Griger had always been serious about taking care of the people in his county—apparently even when they ran as fast and far as they were able to leave said county.

"Exactly the answer I expected from one of Frank and Hazel Hickory's offspring. My deputy briefed me on what you were able to tell him. Not exactly an abundance of information to go on, but I reckon that's understandable, considering. You think of anything else you'd like to add? Any reason why someone might have taken a potshot at you?"

Shayne bristled, trying not to let her offense show. No one had taken a potshot at her. They'd tried to kill her. There was a significant difference.

"Deputy Harmon said you mentioned some money. Any indication where or how much?"

"No. I couldn't make sense of what he was saying." Shayne's gaze focused on the upper right corner of the ambulance interior as she struggled to recall any other details. "He said something about a girl, but none of it made sense."

"Well, there's no money or girl in the vehicle. And the

only other person we've found so far is the driver, and he won't be talking." His eyes darted to her as though he realized the callousness of his comment, but wouldn't point it out unless her reaction told him it was necessary. "A bit surprised to find you on this side of the county. Taking the long way home, I suppose." He stared at her. "The road to your grandparents' place is on the other side of town. And the road out of town ... well, you're familiar with that too, aren't ya?"

She hesitated to believe his jab was intentional, but it hinted at a truth that made her tuck her hands beneath her legs, looking down like a scolded child. "Reminiscing, I guess. There's something about driving down the old roads that reminds you who you are." Or were, anyway. She wished that wasn't how she'd answered. Her words revealed too much of her heart, but there was no way to take them back.

A short, wiry man rushed toward them, clipboard pressed against his chest as the wind tugged his bushy hair in wayward directions. "Sheriff, is it true? Tell me it's not. You aren't seriously asking me to do an autopsy on a cow."

Sheriff Griger rolled his jaw as though his answer had to be kneaded a bit to soften it. "Nice to see you too, Hughie. First of all, it's a steer, not a cow. And yes, that's exactly what I'm asking."

"I ..." the man shook his head with a look of both disbelief and displeasure. His mouth hung open, but apparently he had nothing more he was willing to say to the sheriff.

"Just want to confirm how it died."

Hughie snorted then said, "Kind of obvious, don't ya think?"

"I want to know if someone shot it, too," Sheriff Griger responded. Hughie might have been oblivious to the impatience in the sheriff's voice, but Shayne was not. Under other circumstances, she might have found it humorous. "Just asking you to take a look at what's left of Buster, and tell me what you find. You can do that, can't you?"

Hughie's expression said he could do a lot of things, but preferred to stick to those he deemed more important than the death of a steer. His answer squeezed out between lips pressed into a thin line. "Yes, sir."

Sheriff Griger stared after Hughie as the man stomped away, then he turned back to study Shayne.

News the dead animal was Buster the Longhorn steer, the unofficial town mascot, somehow made the scene around her even more unbelievable. A bizarre dream she might wake up from at any moment.

The sheriff's request unsettled her. The possibility someone shot her at random wasn't nearly as distressing as the possibility there was a lunatic out to kill everything he could. Someone still roaming freely among the people she loved in the place that had been her home, and maybe still was.

"The men in the truck ... were they shot too?" she asked.

"No signs that they were, but we'll see what Hughie can find." He looked at the scene playing out across the field. Men scattered through the grass, the beams of their flashlights moving methodically over the ground in the fading light. Another deputy walked along the road, apparently assessing the angle from which the shooter might have positioned himself, searching for something Shayne hoped he found.

A sleek black and white SUV pulled to a stop on the opposite side of the road, the distinctive Texas State Trooper emblem unmistakable on its side. A Trooper in the equally distinct tan uniform, blue stripes bordered in red piping down the pants leg, stepped out, securing his Stetson on his head as he stood. An aura of competency and legacy came with him.

Deputy Harmon moved up beside the sheriff. "DPS is here. What do you want me to tell them?"

"With Miss Wright being shot, we'll need to work the scene as an aggravated assault first, so we'll take the lead. Unless we tie the wreck and the assault together as part of the same event, he can have the wreck as soon as we're done. Tell Trooper Hernandez I'll be right over. Until then, give him whatever he needs."

Griger looked at Shayne. "We'll find out who did this and why. For now, I'm gonna release you under one condition."

"And that is?" She would agree to just about anything if it got her away from here.

"You let the ambulance take you to get properly checked out at the hospital. I'll send a deputy behind with your car. And after that I don't want you out on the roads by yourself tonight." He scratched his chin with rough, thick fingers. "You came alone to the funeral. You got someone you can stay with tonight?"

Shayne didn't point out that those were two conditions, not one. "I'll stay at the farm. You know they keep it ready for when Grandpa comes home."

He lowered his eyes, and Shayne looked away. They could let the lie hang between them if they didn't make eye contact, acknowledging what they both understood. Her grandpa wasn't coming home. The circle of life on the Hickory family farm had already been broken.

Sheriff Griger cleared his throat. "That's not what I asked."

She rolled her bottom lip between her teeth and kept her gaze directed at her feet. "I'll reach out to a friend."

His eyes narrowed as though he didn't trust her answer.

"I haven't forgotten the muleheaded streak in your family. Given the circumstances, I don't think they meant this to be an attack specifically on you. You were probably just in the wrong place at the wrong time. But until we know something for sure, we aren't going to take any chances. If I find out you do something reckless by being too stubborn to ask for help, you'll answer to me."

In the wrong place at the wrong time. Again.

"Understood." Which was true whether she chose to comply or not.

"All right then." Sheriff Griger nodded to the ambulance personnel, then reached out to stay the closing door. "And Shayne, glad you made it back for Peg's funeral. It's good to see you back in Turnaround."

The ambulance doors closed, sealing her off from one nightmare as she drifted into the grips of another—that of memories she couldn't stop.

CHAPTER SIX

Being shot had first of all terrified her, then it had really ticked her off. Shayne tugged at the flimsy hospital gown, stretching it over her bare knees as though it were armor to protect her against the onslaught of unwanted thoughts.

All it had taken was one word. She'd sensed its presence behind the concerned looks and cautious utterances.

Victim.

She hated the word. A victim is one who is injured, mistreated, or tricked—or most crushing of all ... one who is sacrificed.

The truth burned like a glowing ember in her soul. She hated that label because it fit her.

And it was the label the EMT had used as he handed her off to the emergency room staff.

Closing her eyes, she inhaled, held, exhaled just as she'd learned to do when her control slipped toward the edge of hysteria.

But this time, the circumstances were different. She couldn't have foreseen the possibility someone might shoot her when she stopped for the wreck. No rational person would have considered what had happened to her a reasonable concern. And no one with an ounce of compassion would have driven on without stopping.

So where did that leave her?

The slow, steady cadence of footsteps coming from the tile hallway made her clutch the side of the bed, breath held, until they passed.

The eggshell thin armor had cracked.

Too much excitement and trauma to her body, coupled with fatigue and a growing hunger, made her edgy.

She should call Nick even though she'd only gotten his voicemail earlier. And by now he'd be at the Annual Shelter House Volunteer Appreciation Dinner and wouldn't answer his phone.

Nick had been the first man she'd allowed to catch her eye after she came out of that season of suffocating despair.

The clean-cut, mild-mannered Nick Taylor had inserted himself into her life before she had a chance to object. There was nothing threatening about him, nothing risky. Filled with life and fueled by ambitious plans for the future, he cast a wide shadow where she was content to hide.

The son of a pastor who had founded a growing, although not quite mega, church, Nick was determined and optimistic. She might occasionally wonder if his aspirations drove him more than his desire to serve the Lord did, but mild-mannered Nick could also be intensely determined when there was something he wanted. Maybe they were meant to balance each other out.

Whatever God's purpose in bringing them together, with Nick's single-minded focus on his dreams of planting and pastoring a church, he was exactly what she needed.

He made no demands on her physically. In fact, their relationship might qualify as platonic if it weren't for the random kiss on the cheek or squeeze of her shoulder. He told her he wanted to keep their relationship pure. Sometimes he'd hold her hand or put his palm on her back when they were in front of a crowd, a gesture that felt territorial to Shayne, but also gave her the sense of being protected.

And he didn't mind being the one making decisions, requiring little input or vulnerability on her part. Life with Nick would be quiet. It would be safe. It would be shaped like the perfect cookie cutter family behind the white picket fence.

She'd never find another man like him who would be willing to spend his life with her. Nick was her chance at living life as a normal family—where ugly secrets stayed locked in closets no one cared to enter.

So why hadn't she said *yes* to his proposal?

Twisting the silver ring on her right hand, she refused to contemplate the blood covered diamond on her left. Her gaze went to the cell phone lying in the chair beside her purse.

Touching her bare feet to the cold tile floor, Shayne retrieved her phone, and reseated herself on the end of the hospital bed, tucking the gown snug around her body. The phone felt heavy in her hand as she stared at the screen, still smudged with blood. Her blood or the dying man's—she didn't know. Besides, what did it matter?

She drew another deep breath meant to somehow render confidence. It didn't. She felt like a balloon blown up too many times, its rubber too thin and old to pop, left instead to succumb to the slow loss of air.

Exhaling, she hit the speed dial. As expected, the call went to voice mail. Relief shouldn't have been the first emotion she experienced, but there it was. She recorded a brief message saying she'd try again in the morning.

A soft rap sounded on the wall outside her curtained examination room. "Shayne Wright?"

She flinched, her body tensing until recognition eased her

nerves. She would recognize the smooth, comforting tenor of Reverend Mack Stapleton's voice, even if she hadn't just heard him speaking at Peg's funeral.

She adjusted the one-size-fits-few hospital gown for maximum coverage, trying not to think about the countless other naked bodies it had touched before her. After she'd done her best, she invited him to enter.

"Conner suggested I stop by and check on you. I hope you don't mind."

Conner. The man at the scene who'd covered her with the blanket. A friend of her brother's when they were teenagers growing up. Though it had been years since she'd seen him, this wasn't the side of the law where she'd expected to find him. The Turnaround Volunteer Fire Department was setting the bar low.

Mack chuckled, then said, "I see that look a lot when people hear about Conner these days."

"I'm sorry. No judgment intended." Shayne scrambled to cover the offense.

"No need to apologize. I won't argue he's earned it. But he's on a much better path these days. Even has a sweet, but feisty, girlfriend who's smoothing the rough edges." The warm, solicitous smile and sincere regard in his eyes touched her guarded heart. "But enough about him. How're you doing?"

"I'm fine." Lying to the reverend was bound to have eternal consequences that she wouldn't enjoy. Admitting to him an unexpected joy had overcome her at the sight of his familiar face was too much for her to handle. She wanted to dive into the fatherly safety and comfort of his arms, but more than the ill-fitting hospital gown held her back. The urge surprised her. "I hope you didn't go out of your way to come by."

"It's never out of the way when it comes to the well-being of one of the flock."

Her throat tightened at the revelation he still considered her a part of his flock, even after all she'd done to run as far and fast as she was able.

"You took off so quickly at the funeral, I didn't have an opportunity to speak. I hope you'll be merciful, but if I'm being honest, I'm thankful for the chance to say hello... which sounds terrible considering the circumstances."

"Thank you. Mercy granted. And I didn't realize anyone saw me."

"I would understand if you didn't share my sentiments when I say I'm happy you were able to make it today." He shook his head, laughing as he stepped aside from the opening, but leaving the curtain slightly parted.

"I didn't exactly stay for the service." Shayne looked away as tears of regret pooled in her eyes.

"Peg would say your presence was an added ray of sunshine on a day meant for celebration. And I wouldn't argue with her."

"No one ever argued with Peg." With a shaky hand, she swiped at her tears, then laughed. Other than a little more silver in his hair, little else had changed about the man she remembered as her grandparents' pastor. The laugh lines that crinkled around his eyes had always made him look at peace with the world. He'd gained a few wrinkles since she'd first met him. Or perhaps she'd learned to notice more, appreciate more. Perhaps this essence of peace was something she saw too little of in the life she now lived and the people who surrounded her.

"Not more than once, anyway." He arched an eyebrow. "Although I recall a precocious and strong-willed blonde-haired teenager who tried a time or two. As I recall, Peg wanted to influence her choice of college and career."

"If by influence you mean dictate." The hint of sarcasm in her words didn't hide the warmth the memory filled her with, drawing a smile—although there had been many times when it wasn't a smile Peg had drawn from her. Two strong-willed personalities in opposition to one another. One with the wise counsel of experience. The other with only the misguided wisdom of youth and the want to argue. Peg Moreland had been as sharp as a tack and tough as nails. She'd faced more than her share of adversity when a drunk driver took the life of her only son—a drunk driver that Peg had taken hold of, shaken sense into, and loved into the pastor who now stood before her. "I should have taken more of her advice."

"Hindsight is always the clearest view. Unfortunately, we can't move forward if we're always looking back," Mack said.

His words touched a strand of truth buried beyond where she was willing to go. "I did become a teacher, though. That part I'm glad I listened to."

"She was quite proud of that, and as I recall, she wasn't the only one. Your grandfather was incredibly proud of you." Mack directed his attention to the white board with the assortment of pain emojis peering back at them. She'd convinced the nurse to circle the one above the pain level of five, even though it was the number seven that stared at her with a knowing look. The less pain they knew about, the sooner they would release her.

"A five? Really?" Mack cast a sideways glance in her direction. "I'd go with at least a seven. You'll get more sympathy that way."

"I come from tough stock. We aren't known for seeking sympathy."

Mack laughed, the sound already becoming familiar to Shayne's ears. "That is an understatement. Few days have surprised me more than the day your mother finally talked your grandfather into leaving the farm."

Shayne studied the floor, a few black scuff marks marring the shiny white tiles laid out in straight lines. "I'm sure it was a hard time for him and Momma both."

Mack glanced down, looking up at her from his lowered brow. "I'm not certain I should tell you this, but I believe he always hoped that you'd come back here to teach. If he and Peg might have brought you back, they would have. You surprised a lot of people when you left, but I think they came to understand your return needed to be on your terms."

Shayne glanced away as more tears stung her eyes, her throat squeezing shut until she forced herself to swallow. They wanted her to come home.

But she chose not to. She'd never thought of it in these words before, but yes, coming home had to be on her terms. And her terms had been to bury the past and everyone in it.

"Well, you remember what the Good Book says ... Man may plan his path, but the Lord directs his steps. I'm certain you're right where God needs you to be."

A moment of silence opened between them. She didn't know what Mack might be thinking, but she welcomed the opportunity to adjust both her physical and emotional covering.

"You aren't worried about my salvation, are you, Reverend?" The words came out false in her forced effort to lift the mood or redirect their thoughts.

"No. I remember that day quite well. And I remember a few other days pretty well too, like those of a summer ten years ago. If there's anything you'd like to talk about, I'm yours for as long as you'd like me to stay." Mack lifted his hands. For a moment, it wouldn't have surprised her to find the scars of nails etched in his palms.

Shayne hesitated, fixing her attention on the gown that barely stretched to cover her knees. She smoothed nonexistent wrinkles from the fabric in her lap, trying to work the hem down as she flailed through her thoughts for anything that could change the subject. But it was more than her physical body she needed to cover. That Mack might know what had happened—even if he only suspected—sent a piercing cold through her veins that brought greater agony than anything she'd been through today. She grasped at any thought that moved them away from this path. "Did he ... the man on the ground ... did he die?"

Mack tilted his head and watched her, clearly understanding that she was avoiding his unspoken question. "I'm afraid so. Sheriff Griger told me what you did. It was brave and compassionate, but he said nothing but a miracle could have saved the young man."

Shayne nodded as if accepting absolution, but it wasn't guilt over her inability to save his life that knotted her middle. It was being so close to death itself. It was a ledge she had walked near more than once, letting her own toes touch the edge.

"Have you called your mother to tell her you're okay?" Mack held her gaze as if he suspected the answer.

"I didn't want to worry her. I'll call Mom after I leave." She picked at a piece of fuzz clinging to the rough fabric, wondering why her mother was the one she mentioned instead of Nick.

"It doesn't look like they plan to keep you overnight, and I'm pretty sure you came alone to the funeral today. Can I offer to help you find a place to stay tonight?"

The squeak of shoes and the clatter of a cart across the shiny tile floor echoed down the hall. She was safe here, right? In capable medical hands where no one would dare try to harm her. But how long could she hide in this sterile environment?

"I'll stay at the farm. They keep it ready to go just to ease Grandpa Frank's mind."

"I don't like the idea of you being alone out there. And I definitely wouldn't want to call your mother—or ever look your grandfather in the eye—and tell them I let further harm come to you." His expression was less gentle country preacher and more stern uncle right now.

"I promise I'll be fine."

"Are you sure you'll be comfortable staying out there alone?"

"I honestly can't think of anywhere else I'd rather be at the moment." That was the most truth she'd spoken in quite a while, and it surprised her.

"Then how about you let me drive you out there?"

"I'm fine. Really." Shayne wasn't up to any more company than she'd already had for the past two hours. "You'd just have to come in the morning to help me get to my car."

"I see city life hasn't lessened any of the family's stubborn streak." Mack rubbed his hands together. "Although, if I'm honest, I don't like this much." He held his hands up, palms out. "But I learned a long time ago not to argue."

He watched her, a puzzled glint in his eyes as though he recognized the inner turmoil churning in her head. "Is there anything at all I can do for you?"

"I'm good. Just ready to get to Grandpa Frank's house and get some sleep."

"Are you sure that's a good idea?" Mack frowned. "I know someone I could talk into sparing a bedroom for you tonight, so you wouldn't have to be alone."

"I'm sure." She hoped her words sounded more confident than she felt. But she didn't want the company of a stranger right now. The farm had always been a refuge from the troubles of life. The fact she'd left it had nothing to do with her true feelings for the place.

Mack dug around in his shirt pocket for a pen and a scrap of paper. He scribbled his number on it, but didn't immediately hand it to her. "I'm not sure I agree with you, but you're an adult, and I'm only your pastor, not a parent. I'll trust you to call if you need anything. Peg would come back from the grave if I let anything else happen to you."

Shayne laughed as tears crept into her eyes. "If only it were that easy to bring her back. I'd love to have one more conversation with her. I wish ..." She looked away. No sense wishing for things that couldn't happen.

Mack cocked his head to the side and studied her. "We can't undo the past, can we? But if you'll let him, God will show you he always has his hands on the details."

She didn't agree. If she did, it would mean that what happened that night had happened for a reason, and the only reason she could believe was too cruel to attribute to a loving God.

"How long will you stay?" His quiet, solicitous question asked for more than a timeline. He was suggesting a lifeline, whether or not he knew it. She suspected he did.

"I haven't decided. I should probably head back as soon as the roads clear tomorrow." She should, right? There was no reason to stay, so why didn't her answer sound more certain?

"Do me a favor, then. Allow me to buy your lunch tomorrow—provided the roads are clear by then—before you leave town?"

"You don't need to do that. I'm sure you're busy."

"It has nothing to do with need. I just want to catch up on your life. To be honest, I miss your grandparents and the conversations we used to have. It would be an honor for me to have a little time with you, too. What do you say? One lunch and I promise to keep it shorter than my sermons. Noon at Momma Mae's?"

A short, quick nod was all she offered. But it was still more of a yes than she'd been able to give Nick.

Thirty minutes later, Shayne only half listened as the

nurse recited a long list of discharge instructions she wouldn't remember. Her brain was on the verge of shutting down, and her interest in self-preservation was waning. Food, sleep, and time to put herself back together away from curious and sympathetic eyes were all she wanted.

When the oratory ended, the nurse gave Shayne a motherly pat on her uninjured shoulder. "Any questions?"

Shayne shook her head. *None you can answer.*

"Then you're good to go."

Ready to go? Yes. Good to go? Not so much. But that would all change once she got to the farm. Safely ensconced beneath a mound of patchwork quilts in her old bed, the world couldn't touch her.

At the soft swoosh of the curtain closing, she slid off the edge of the bed and reached for her bag.

The deputy who had driven her car from the accident scene to the hospital had brought her purse and keys in with him. Then he'd been gracious enough to retrieve her suitcase as well. She had options, and the blood-stained dress wasn't one of them. Neither were those hateful shoes she'd had to purchase on a payment plan, back when she'd defiantly refused financial help from her father or from Nick. She'd bought them to please Nick, but her stomach recoiled every time she recalled the cost.

She dug a pair of thick wool socks from the suitcase and tugged them on. Her hands froze as she touched the soft, worn flannel of a shirt, gripped by the realization someone expecting to stay more than one night had packed this suitcase. She closed her eyes and squeezed her hand into a fist. Was she losing her mind or was her subconscious trying to tell her something?

Or maybe this reflected a heightened sense of the need to always be prepared. After all, hadn't she learned the hard way that unexpected things happen? Unexpected and bad things.

Not a path she wanted to revisit today. She worked a pair of black leggings over her long legs using only one arm.

So much for being prepared. These leggings were an invitation for frostbite in this kind of weather, but she didn't plan to be out any longer than it took to get from her car to the restaurant and then the farm.

Next she pulled on the flannel shirt Nick didn't know she still owned and topped the outfit off with the worn Uggs she'd found buried in her closet. The fleece lining wasn't as fluffy as it should be, but the shoes comforted her in a way that wasn't physical.

As she reached for the black funeral dress, Nick's words echoed in her head, reminding her that appearance was important. She touched the smooth fabric, running her fingers over the tightly stitched seams. The seams held firm, but that hadn't kept the bullet from shredding the fabric. Appearance only mattered when you weren't taking on bullets.

The perfectly tailored cut of the dress had never failed to draw Nick's admiration when she wore it. She was never sure if it was her or the dress that garnered his admiration, though. She leaned on the side of the bed as understanding niggled at her thoughts.

This line of thinking was clearly the result of a traumatic day. She needed to reschedule all further life choice evaluations until she'd had food and sleep.

Her eyes settled on the torn sleeve—a ragged section of expensive fabric now surrounded by dried blood.

Her blood.

Even if the dress could be mended, it would never be the same.

The outfit she wore now could never measure up to the fashion standards of Nick's world. If she showed up in this at their church, they'd hand her one of the care bags they distributed to the homeless.

She removed the engagement ring from her finger, dropping it into her purse until she could clean it. The dress and heels she'd arrived in slid into the bin marked Biohazard with a thud.

Before leaving, she slipped into the hallway bathroom to splash water on her face. In the mirror over the sink, she recognized the person staring back at her for the first time in longer than she could remember.

Even with the paleness of a trauma filled day, the spark flickering in tired eyes told her there was a battle coming.

CHAPTER SEVEN

Ethan picked up the saltshaker, studied it from all angles, then set it back in place while he waited for his dinner-to-go. He drummed his fingers on the counter as though he might alter the tempo of time, speeding it forward until he obtained his goal. He'd never been good at shutting off his thoughts, quieting his mind. Idle time drove him to the verge of insanity on more than one occasion. His energy needed a release.

Or, more truthfully, his thoughts needed a target that demanded his focus.

The ding of the bell over the door pulled him from his contemplation of the condiment containers. Tension tightened his muscles, coiling them like a spring, a reflex he hadn't overcome and wasn't likely to anytime soon.

He didn't turn, but let his senses interpret the change in the environment as though he possessed some sort of internal barometer for danger. In a way, he did, which accounted for the fact he was still alive.

But the maddening inability to relax had him stretched tighter than a trip line. That needed to change before someone got hurt in his explosion. He snorted in derision. The chance of that was another thing not likely to happen anytime soon.

Although it was a small crowd seated around the rustic, no frills cafe, their collective inhale made the atmosphere frizzle with excitement as though the Queen of England had walked in wearing nothing but her crown. He sneered at the irony, doubting these yokels would recognize the Queen of England. Heck, he doubted he would, either. The silence that followed hung in the air like a smoke grenade on a breezeless day.

Curiosity pulled him around to see what caused such a mood swing among the natives. So much for using the internal barometer.

The sight turned his scowl into a charmed smile. It also stirred a hunger the menu in front of him wouldn't satisfy.

The pretty blonde frozen in the doorway was worth turning around for. That she looked terrified by the attention piqued his interest. He told himself the crowd's reaction caused his heightened enchantment and not the attractiveness of the girl standing like a marble statue—a marble statue with long, shapely, athletic legs.

The cafe's collectively held breath released, whooshing out in a buzz of hushed whispers.

Her eyes widened in a mortified sort of surprise. Crimson rose along the woman's neck onto cheeks already pinkened by the icy wind outside. The spotlight was clearly unwanted. Considering the gawking bunch of busybodies, he didn't blame her.

She ducked her head and rushed into an empty booth behind him. Amused, he swiveled back to face the counter, then tilted his head to peer over his shoulder, continuing to watch her. The blush deepened, contrasting with fair skin and hair the color of sunlight on corn silk.

Whatever the reason for this much scrutiny, it couldn't be for her fashion sense. She looked like she had a date with perdition and dressed appropriately.

And still it stirred feelings in him he'd rather not deal with tonight.

She appeared too timid for the kind of scandal needed to generate such enthusiastic notice. Must be a slow week in Turnaround—he looked at the swarm of gray-haired gossips —but then, out in the middle of nowhere, America wasn't every week?

Irritated, he used his tongue to move the toothpick he chewed on to the other side of his mouth. Hadn't he just told his brother this might be the middle of *everywhere?*

Coming here was probably a mistake. Sure, time off from the questioning looks and unwanted sympathy sounded good. He could still get his work for the family construction business done from here, even if the slow internet speed would likely be a serious source of frustration. As for the other assignment—the one his buddy had asked for as a favor and the reason this was the place he'd come to get away—it was sure to be a waste of effort.

This was a place where there were no secrets. The locals would have refined the skill of nosiness to a high art.

He let his gaze linger on the newcomer for the simple pleasure of enjoying the attraction. He'd almost forgotten how it felt. Almost.

Perhaps she sensed his attention. Her eyes cut to his, wariness replacing the embarrassment. Her breath hitched. A nervous tell, followed by an even more obvious one as she tucked a strand of hair behind her ear before tugging the collar of her over-sized shirt tight around her neck. But most honest of all was the blush. He hadn't thought it possible to become any more vivid. He stood corrected. A paint strip from the princess section at the hardware store wouldn't offer any more shades of pink.

She stared at her menu, but Ethan would have bet money she wasn't reading a word of it.

He smiled, letting his thoughts wander. He'd done nothing but work since he'd uncovered Alexa's little secret. Now he'd finagled some time away from the city and the faithless, self-centered hoard of backstabbing parasites there. Not that he was jaded or anything.

He sneaked another look, then chided himself. It wasn't like he was any better. He wasn't interested in a relationship, just a little warm company on an awfully chilly night. Yep ... just another faithless, self-centered parasite.

Besides, she wasn't the type. And therein lay his conundrum.

If he could believe there were women out there who weren't the type for one-night stands, why couldn't he believe there were women who believed in fidelity, love, faithfulness to one man—that happily ever-after garbage his brother seemed to have with Krissy and insisted he'd find one day?

The answer was pride. Ethan's wouldn't let him make the same mistake again.

Best to avoid them all.

He turned to the waitress as she set his to-go bag down in front of him. "What's up with Miss Popularity?" He nodded in the newcomer's direction.

"According to table number three, she's some sort of local athletic hero. According to the Baptist blue hairs in the booth by the door, she just up and disappeared the summer before her senior year, causing her grandma to die of a broken heart. And according to table number six, she got shot." The waitress, a young girl who couldn't be more than sixteen or seventeen, shrugged and chewed her gum in indifference.

"Shot?" Ethan asked, his interest spiking.

"Yeah, like it was probably a deer hunter, although this is only bow season, but around here that doesn't mean much." She paused, narrowing her eyes as she studied Ethan before cutting them to look at the woman. Her brow puckered as she peered at the new customer. "She doesn't look very heroic if you ask me. Just looks scared. And like a really bad dresser."

Ethan grinned as the girl faced him again. "I didn't know the fashion police patrolled in these parts. Thought a person could get away with wearing whatever they wanted around here."

"I'm not from *these parts*." She smirked, but it was the flirtatious spark in her eyes that set warning bells off in his skull.

"Well, thanks for the food and the information, uh ..." he looked at her name tag.

"It's Kindley, as in kind ... like as in kindness matters." A coy smile played across her features.

A petite, older woman with spikey bleached blond hair poked her head out of the kitchen. "Okay, Miss *Kindness Matters*, so does serving our customers their food while it's still hot."

Kindley rolled her eyes and started to speak.

Ethan reached for her hand and placed a fifty-dollar bill in it, silencing her with a wink. "For the hero's bill along with mine."

The girl's eyes widened, her jaw dropping when he pulled out a twenty and handed it to her as well. "For the tip." He moved it just out of her reach when she lifted her hand. "Under one condition."

Her eyebrows arched in question.

"Steer clear of boys and don't start dating until you're at least thirty." He extended the bill, relieved that she at least looked contrite as she took it.

Although the hypocrisy of his message brought him no small amount of self-condemnation, he hoped his words made an impression on the girl. He wasn't quite thirty himself and he'd certainly never encouraged any female his age to abstain from his company or turn down his romantic intentions.

He slipped his wallet back in his pocket, unsure of why he was doing this, other than the pleasure of knowing Miss Hometown Hero would probably blush again when she found out. Handing out fifty-dollar bills was not the way to keep a low profile in a town like this. And fifty dollars would have bought the entire right side of the menu, which he doubted she would order.

The older waitress glared at him, letting him know his welcome here was ending. He was pretty sure he knew why. Not his fault, but a problem he could solve by eliminating his presence from this place.

He pulled his jacket on, suddenly in a hurry to be gone. Picking up the paper bag that held his order, he walked away before he did anything else foolish.

Like wander over and introduce himself to the first woman he'd noticed since he'd discovered his ex-wife's affair. He wasn't going down that road again. And not with anyone as attractive as the local hero.

He took one last glance and caught her watching.

This time, he didn't smile when she looked away.

CHAPTER EIGHT

Shayne twisted the ring on her finger, her gaze captured by the world on the other side of the windowpane. A world of darkness broken only by the muted artificial light of the streetlamps struggling through the falling sleet. Maybe Nick was right. She shouldn't be here. She lacked the good judgment needed to avoid getting herself hurt. Today was proof enough of that.

No sense in pretending otherwise. She pulled her phone from her purse and retrieved the note Mack had given her with his number. One quick call to cancel their lunch date, and she would be free to leave as soon as the roads cleared in the morning. No obligations.

The same desire she'd experienced at the hospital—a longing for his fatherly comfort—stilled her fingers over the keypad. She set the phone on the vinyl seat beside her and tucked his number back into her pocket. Perhaps she'd have the emotional strength she needed if she ate first.

The icy rain had frozen into small chunks of ice that pelted the glass and gathered along the curb in a ribbon of grayish white. Already cars were moving slower as they drove by.

The stranger who stared at her was out there somewhere.

He was here before she came in, so reason said he wasn't following her. There was no way he'd have known she'd come here after she left the hospital. And the bright green hoodie he wore certainly didn't lend itself to inconspicuousness. The odds he wasn't the one who shot her were in her favor ... right?

The scrutiny of his stare burned into her thoughts. He'd been too mindful.

Chills covered her arms. Too wolfish, but not as if he were stalking prey. His look had been one of a desire to know more, not just to enjoy the view.

She pulled the sleeves of her shirt down to cover her fingers, tucked one leg underneath her, and attempted to shrink into the seat only because completely disappearing wasn't an option.

The events of the day ground her into a fine dust. Her thoughts refused to stick together sensibly. All except one.

She'd accepted living with the same question every time a man she didn't know crossed her path. *Was he one of them?*

That she'd never know was a frightening darkness to live within.

Besides, why wouldn't he stare after the grand entrance she'd made? This was a small town. News around here spread faster than the flu through the Kindercare.

Frank and Hazel's granddaughter, the one who up and left without a word, returns and gets used for target practice. The gray-haired grapevine thrived on fertilizer that rich. Especially since the only other time she'd returned was for her grandmother's funeral ... something Shayne blamed herself for.

"What can I get for you? Order whatever you want. It's

already been taken care of." Standing beside Shayne, the girl's messy bun flopped as she emphasized the word *whatever.* The look she wore was one of admiration, edged in envy.

"Taken care of? You must be mistaken."

"Not exactly a lot of shooting victims filling the place up tonight, so I'm pretty sure I got the right person." The girl rolled her eyes. "Your meal's been paid for. And trust me when I say order whatever you want."

"By whom?" Shayne cut her eyes to the table full of locals on the far side of the cafe, her browed furrowed, face pinching in displeasure.

"That incredibly fine-looking man who just left," the girl said, shaking her head as though that much well-formed masculinity walking out the door without her number in his phone was a disappointment she wouldn't recover from for days.

Shayne's frown grew. He looked old enough to be this girl's father. "There must be a mistake. I don't know him."

"Well, he thought you were some sort of celebrity hero and left enough to cover your bill along with his."

"He was mistaken, then. Please return it to him the next time he comes in. I can pay for my meal."

"Can't. He's not from around here. Just enjoy your dinner and accept your blessings." Again the girl wagged her head in regret, then mumbled, "Even if it didn't come with a phone number."

Shayne held her tongue, although there were things she'd like to say. This girl was too young to be mooning after a man of his age and life experience. But if he really wasn't from around here, perhaps it didn't need to be said. It would most likely fall on deaf ears, anyway.

It wasn't a passion for grammar and literature that had drawn Shayne to teaching. The opportunity to influence girls like this was the real reason.

She looked at the menu and hesitated, her appetite now uncertain. However, if she was going to die tonight, she might as well have the works—chicken fried steak with extra cream gravy and Mae's famous warm blackberry cobbler topped with Blue Bell ice cream for dessert.

But she didn't plan to die tonight. Instead, she ordered the grilled chicken salad with oil and vinegar dressing and a side of fried pickles.

She ate it without tasting and was back in her car in less than half an hour, eager for home and not just because the roads were icing over already.

As the streetlights faded behind her, she glanced at the rearview mirror for the hundredth time. Nothing.

No *incredibly fine-looking men* lurking in the shadows, waiting to assault the person whose meal they'd just paid for.

Stopping for supper had been a mistake. Too late, it occurred to her that one does not get shot and then drive to an empty house alone in the dark no matter how brave one pretended to be.

She ordered her breaths, working to stop her pulse from taking off like a frightened colt. Inhaling, she forced the air into the deepest part of her lungs, filling them until they ached. *Inhale for four, hold for seven, exhale for eight.* Again. Again. *It's just a panic attack. You can make it stop. Resist the devil and he will flee. There's no one behind you. Focus on your happy place.*

The fear faded, a sense of calm settling over her.

Her happy place. She was almost there.

The rain had turned to ice and the windshield wipers scraped a steady rhythm that blended with the staccato of the sleet striking the car. She drove slower than she wanted, watching for patches of hidden ice already forming on the road's surface. She didn't need the light to find the road home. No matter how preoccupied or confused her thoughts might be, her heart knew the way. Once there, nothing bad would find her.

The weather the past week had been in the seventies, so the ice wouldn't stick around after the storm passed through. Texas weather tended toward the schizophrenic side.

Being trapped at the farm for an extended stay wouldn't bother her, but the hazardous road conditions were unlikely to give her an excuse for more than a night.

Fatigue emptied her just as the entry into the long driveway materialized through the haze of falling sleet. Tension seeped from her shoulders as she turned into the Hickory farm, like shedding a heavy coat and leaving it on a coatrack. In a few more minutes, she'd be secure. If she loosened her grip on reality, the day's events receded like nothing more than the vague remnants of a dream she might soon forget. A day that had happened to someone else.

Almost.

The gravel drive passed through a grove of live oak trees, then angled down, curving its way around the base of a small hill that hid the homestead. The sleet fell harder as she rounded the sheltering knoll. Her headlights only reached a few feet into the night before meeting the solid resistance of Mother Nature's icy tantrum, leaving her unable to see farther than a few feet in front of the SUV.

Unexpected emotions fluttered through her. What if the place had changed? What if it was exactly the same, and she was the only thing different?

Which would be harder to face?

Her grandfather had been gone for nearly a year, but the promise her mother had made in persuading him to leave was that they would keep the house ready for his return. Thanks to that, Shayne hadn't felt the need to let anyone know a stay was possible.

Her grandfather's going away only had to be temporary,

her mother had told him. He could return as soon as he was able. Shayne wondered if it pained her mother to lie to him that way.

She might wonder, but she certainly wouldn't be casting the first stone. Sometimes, lying was just what family did when they loved each other. Right?

Everyone knew her grandpa wasn't coming back. Probably even he knew it. But Shayne suddenly understood why he needed to hold on to the hope that he could return home.

She squinted and leaned closer to the windshield. The dark crew cab pickup shouldn't be sitting in the exact place her grandfather's faded ivy green 1974 Ford always parked. She stepped hard on the brakes and realized too late her tires had found ice.

The Ford Escape slid, the weight of the rear end pulling it sideways. Unable to stop the skid, she waited for tires to find traction again.

Stop. Stop. Stop. She braced as the truck loomed nearer. Her front bumper connected with the truck's back bumper, pulling the Escape further around until its side was pressed firmly against the truck. The impact jerked the seat belt tight against her shoulder for the second time today.

With more hope than expectation, she eased her foot down on the accelerator. The car skated further backwards, raking itself along the side of the truck. The screech of metal scraping against metal clamped her teeth together.

She sat, breath held, afraid to move lest her vehicle inflict more damage.

There was no way this oversized, fancy looking vehicle ever belonged to Grandpa Frank.

Tears of both defeat and anger stung her eyes. This day was not what she'd expected and certainly not what she hoped for.

The urge to punch something overwhelmed her. But in

spite of her recent thoughts of destroying something, punching things wasn't her way. Instead, she killed the engine and contemplated her options.

The house was dark. Other than the truck, there was no sign anyone was here.

She opened her purse and dug for her phone, her search intensifying as her fingers failed to find it. Queasiness pitched through her midsection. She'd left her phone on the seat next to her at the cafe.

The cold bit at her nose and fingertips. She couldn't sit here all night. Unbuckling, she twisted in the seat to study the house. There were plenty of reasonable explanations for why a strange truck might be parked at an empty house where it didn't belong, right?

She sighed.

Nope. Not a single reasonable explanation came to mind.

But the house looked so unoccupied. No hint of light slipped from the curtained windows.

Her hand gingerly touched the bandage over her gunshot wound as a cold that had nothing to do with the weather chilled her from the inside. What if he was here, waiting?

With his big shiny truck parked where she couldn't miss it —literally. A murderer would have better sense, right?

Think logically, Shayne, instead of letting fear make you do something foolish.

Even if she could drive away, which wasn't going to happen on this ice, at best she could go to the sheriff's office and report—what? That someone had left too nice of a truck at the farm? It would mean additional questions, and that was more attention than she wanted today.

It was possible the truck really was Grandpa Frank's— some sort of post-midlife crisis. The onset of dementia had necessitated his move to an assisted care facility. Maybe this was one indication he hadn't been himself.

Which might have been a plausible explanation if her grandpa hadn't left a year ago. This truck looked too new for that.

She could use the phone in the house. There were few other options, anyway. And by few, she meant none. A trek back to town in this weather was out of the question. Even the closest neighbor was several miles away.

The old Shayne would go for it. The voice she heard was hers, but she didn't appreciate the mocking tone. She had to live with the consequences of the old Shayne's lack of good judgment for the rest of her life.

She opened the side pocket in her purse and retrieved the key. There'd been many purses over the years, but the key always remained stashed away in a safe pocket. Not on her key ring as a constant reminder, but close by, just in case. In case of what, she couldn't say, but she'd never been able to part with it.

Her fingers brushed against the diamond ring. The irony nipped her heart. Two objects, side by side, but the life they represented was as far apart as the feelings each elicited.

Next, she found the pepper spray. She winced as pain shot through her arm. No surprise the bullet had connected with her dominant arm instead of taking out something less useful.

The driver's side door pressed against the truck, forcing her to climb out the passenger side.

The winter wind numbed her cheeks as soon as it touched her skin, carrying shards of ice like sharp arrows, biting at her exposed flesh. She tested the ground's surface tentatively before setting her feet. Her shoulders hunched against the wintery night as her left hand came up to shield her eyes from the blowing ice.

She studied her car, and her stomach sank. She wasn't going anywhere until the ice melted. A sound resembling a growl of frustration and a sigh of surrender escaped to be devoured by the pelting rattle of sleet.

Maybe if the truck didn't look so pristine—and expensive.

If it really wasn't Grandpa Frank's, then someone would definitely not be overjoyed to hear from her.

Unable to withstand the cold any longer, she took a last wary survey of the house, then headed to the porch, concentrating on not falling instead of overthinking who or what she might find in the house.

Her house. Determination steeled through her.

She could do this. She would check the house out like a reasonably sane person before giving in to the panic picking at the edges of her confidence.

Knock first or use the key? She had a key and a rightful sense of ownership to a house that should be empty. And she was growing desperately cold without her coat.

Slipping the key into the lock as smoothly as if it hadn't been ten years since she last used it, she opened the door and listened to the familiar squeak that always greeted her entry. Other than the storm, there was only silence. Not that she would have heard anything over the noise of the ice plinking against the tin roof like a maraca convention had kicked off in the attic.

A profound sense of emptiness met her as she closed the door. She didn't bother reaching for the light, preferring instead to let the harsh reality of an empty house reveal itself to her slowly. Ten-year-old grief shouldn't be this painful. She should've prepared herself for this moment, standing in the home where her family no longer lived.

But then, there was no way anyone could have prepared for this day.

Most notably absent from the house was the comforting smell of her grandmother's kitchen.

Grandma Hazel had possessed the gift of hospitality.

There was always a simmering pot or baking bread filling the warm kitchen with the thick aroma of home cooking.

Biscuits browning in the oven, fresh black-eyed peas simmering with slabs of salt pork, or Shayne's favorite, bread pudding with a whiskey sauce Grandma Hazel swore everyone to secrecy for out of fear the preacher would find out. All the Baptists became a bit Lutheran when Hazel Hickory had a bread pudding in the oven.

The smell of Grandma Hazel's kitchen alone had been enough to make the staunchest of dieters ditch their calorie counting and seize the moment.

While she nourished their bodies with food, she fortified their souls with truth, mending their hearts and covering their wounds in the salve of love. Grandma Hazel's kitchen had done more for Shayne's faith than a church sanctuary ever had.

Swept up in emotion, her thoughts of an intruder vanished as Shayne headed to the first place she, and everyone else, always went when they entered this house—the kitchen.

Her hand went to the wall where she knew she'd find the light switch. The same kitchen she'd always known greeted her. Same, yet not.

The same plain white Frigidaire covered in pictures and notes containing important phone numbers, dates, and Bible verses all held in place by colorful plastic fruit-shaped magnets. The chipped blue and white speckled enamel tea kettle on the middle of the stove and the orderly row of ancient metal canisters. Once white as snow with bright red cherries painted in the center, the canisters now held an aged yellowish tint that the cherries seemed to fade into.

Everything neat and in its place, but devoid of life.

Except for the paper bag and large Styrofoam drink cup on the table.

Her pulse tripped, stumbling through her veins, and making her skin tingle. Brown paper bags weren't exactly rare, but finding one sitting on a kitchen table in an unoccupied house wasn't a comforting discovery.

The fact the generic paper bag might have come from anywhere didn't ease the gut feeling she'd seen a bag like this all too recently walking out the door of Momma Mae's in the hands of the man who'd paid for her meal.

Her fingers set about twisting the ring on her finger.

Don't overreact. Don't panic.

Her gaze locked on the coat draped over the back of the chair. Again, the tan work coat wasn't exactly an anomaly in these parts. But the last one she'd seen had been across the broad shoulders of the stranger at the cafe.

Ripples of electricity zinged through her, igniting a buzzing in her ears.

He was here.

Alarm raced in to fill the hollow cavity that formed in the center of her being. Her vision swam.

Not this time.

She attempted to remove the safety latch on the pepper spray. *Why hadn't she done that before entering the house.* Her left hand moved clumsily, and the canister slipped from her shaking fingers to rattle across the floor.

Indecision paralyzed her. She had to get out, even if she had nowhere to go. She'd hide until morning. Hide and not freeze to death ... probably.

There were, of course, alternatives worse than freezing to death.

She knelt to retrieve the spray, reaching under the table where it rolled.

"Can I help you?" The deep masculine voice rumbled like distant thunder in the small space behind her.

A thick numbness clamped around her, robbing her of her senses.

Breathe in. Hold. Breathe out. It won't happen again. Don't give in. Or up.

With her back still to him, she ignored the pain shooting up her injured arm as she squeezed the pepper spray in her palm, this time successfully releasing the safety.

She risked a glance behind her and caught sight of bare feet. Odd choice for a stalker. She realized no one ever discussed footwear in the news of violent crimes. They should.

"Stand up slowly and turn around," he said.

With slow, deliberate movements, she did as he ordered, forcing herself to make eye contact. This time, she'd see the face of her attacker.

The man from the cafe, only half dressed, scowled at her.

Drops of water trickled from his wet hair and beard down his bare torso. Every feature of his face furrowed into an angry V.

The expression carved into his features intimidated her as much as the gun he held.

Training taught her she was too close to use the pepper spray. What it hadn't taught her was which would be faster—the spray or the bullet.

"I ..." She fought the hysteria racing through her. She had to get out. Without thinking, she glanced down at the hand holding the canister she'd slipped inside her shirt sleeve.

She cried out as vice like fingers seized her wrist, sending a white-hot pain up her injured arm. The pepper spray clattered to the floor again.

Don't cry. You've survived before. Convince him not to kill you and you'll survive again.

Only this time, she wasn't sure she wanted to.

CHAPTER NINE

What in the blazes was this woman doing in his house? Well, not his house exactly, but legally, if only temporarily. Her watery eyes riveted to the gun he still steadied in his right hand. Unfortunately for her, Ethan's reflexes were equally keen from both his right and left sides. It was a quality that had made him a fierce competitor on the pitcher's mound in high school, and a deadly adversary in his subsequent career.

Great. He really knew how to pick 'em. Why had he needed to play the big shot and pay for her dinner? He'd let an attractive face fool him again and now here she was, breaking into his house to steal from him.

Or possibly she was looking to hook up for the night.

Either way, following him from the cafe was a bold move, but breaking into the house was a little too psychotic for his preference. There was a fine line between attracted and bunny-in-the-pot crazy. No thanks, he'd pass.

Despite his original interest, she wasn't all that appealing from a physical aspect. Plain would be an accurate description. Ethan preferred a little sparkle and a lot of curves. His attraction must have resulted from too much time avoiding women altogether.

He surveyed the tall, thin woman now facing him. A distinctly antiseptic smell wafted from her. The waitress had said she'd been shot. The way she'd cried out when he grabbed her arm told him where.

Remorse pricked his conscience, but he shoved it aside. He wanted her gone and nothing else. If the pain helped convince her she shouldn't be here, well, that wasn't really his fault, now was it? She'd brought it on herself.

"Look, babe, I paid for your dinner. I'm not interested in anything else." He released her wrist. It wasn't a completely honest statement, but prudence won out ... at least for the moment.

Her eyes narrowed as confusion mixed with pain in her expression. Then she straightened, her left hand squeezing her right forearm, as she looked him nearly dead even in the eye. The legs didn't lie. She was tall.

And in obvious pain.

He should apologize. A part of him almost wanted to. But a better part of him wanted to make sure she understood just how dangerous and painful life could be. Breaking into a man's home in the middle of the night was a sure way to get hurt.

"What?" The bewildered tone of her question matched the growing uncertainty on her face.

He felt the same. The gut sensation he relied on in confrontations whirred that something wasn't right.

Still, her presence here irritated him. He didn't need this.

"This is going a bit far just to say thank you, so I'm guessing you have another reason to follow me and break into my house?" He ran his eyes up and down the length of her, trying to register more indifference than he honestly felt. "If you're here to seduce me, I'm offended that you came looking like this. So what is it? Robbery? Did I not leave enough to cover your bill?"

Tears that probably weren't completely from pain alone trailed along her ashen cheeks. She wasn't blushing now. In fact, every ounce of color had drained from her face, further evidence she was in more pain than she wanted to admit.

"What are you talking about?" Her eyes darted from his face to his gun and back again. "Would you please put down the gun ... or at least point it at something besides me?"

Her words triggered a memory he tried to forget. "Is anyone else with you?"

"No." She drug her bottom lip between her teeth, a telltale sign she didn't like the taste of her answer. Was it because it was a lie or because she feared telling him the truth? Judging by the dilation of her pupils, he'd lean toward the second, but wouldn't completely rule out the first.

From what he'd heard, there were a lot of unanswered questions about who shot her and why. He lowered the gun in a trust-building move. "How about you tell me what you're doing here?"

"It's my house."

He shook his head. "Afraid not. This house belongs to an old man named Hickory, and I currently have a lease with my name on it. That makes you ... a trespasser. Now that I think about it, you broke into my house armed with a weapon. That's a bit more significant than just trespassing."

If she didn't leave soon, she'd be stuck here all night. He worked his jaw. What was he thinking?

There was no way the roads were drivable, and she clearly wasn't in the mental condition to be sent out on a night like this. She'd end up freezing to death in a ditch somewhere.

She was already stuck here. Whether she was crazy or not, he wasn't willing to risk adding her death to his already overburdened conscience.

Plus, he didn't know who she might tell. He had his cover story, but he'd rather not have any attention just yet. A goal he'd failed at miserably when he handed a teenager a fifty-dollar bill to pay for a stranger's dinner.

His buddy Reuben was wrong. This would not be the career path he needed.

She swiped the tears that slid from her eyes with stiff fingers and attempted to appear defiant. But the truth in her eyes revealed something much different.

Sighing, he tucked the gun into the back of his jeans, then held his palms out, hoping to lower her anxiety. No sense scaring her witless if he wanted her cooperation. "Better?"

"I ..." She swayed, bracing herself against the table. A physical agony radiated off her like heat waves over hot asphalt. But her internal angst came out like a sonic boom ... felt as much as seen.

He resisted the urge to reach out and steady her.

"I didn't follow you, and this isn't your house." She blinked as though surprised by her own words.

He'd seen the effects of shock before. If she lost any more color, the white Formica tabletop would appear to have a sun-kissed copper tan compared to her complexion. "Perhaps you'd better sit down."

"No, I just need you to leave. I won't call the sheriff or tell anyone you were here."

Shock could also make a person hallucinate and delusional.

Or maybe she was simply crazy.

"Why should I leave? You're the one who broke in."

"I didn't break in. I used my key." Her voice rose, a determined quality sneaking past her fear. Supported by the kitchen table with nowhere to go, she worked her eyes up to meet his. When she got them there, to his surprise, she held his gaze.

She might try to look brave, but her effort fell short of convincing. Her fear was practically palpable. Of course, that didn't make her any less crazy, and frightened crazy people, when given a chance, could be exponentially more dangerous. He kicked a chair out from the table with his bare foot. "Sit."

"I'd rather not." She held her ground.

"It wasn't a suggestion." He gave her a look that said it wasn't open for debate.

She hesitated before complying.

"Now let's start over. Who are you and what are you doing here?" Ethan asked after she was seated.

"This is not your house. That old man is my grandfather and if ... if you ... have a lease, it's a fake." Her eyes traveled to his still wet torso. She averted her eyes. "Why are you wet?"

"It happens when I take a shower. I wasn't expecting company, or I'd have waited for you to join me. Water conservation is important, you know?" For the devilment of it, he winked, then seated himself in a chair across from her. He knew the look he was giving her. Much stronger men than this frightened woman before him had been broken by the expression he now wore. "Now who are you, Miss ...?"

She blushed, visibly shrinking, but the color was coming back. Good. Maybe she wasn't going to pass out after all.

He looked away, running his tongue over tight lips as though it might help soften his words. But he didn't want them softened. He wanted them hard enough they sent her running—tomorrow when the roads cleared again. He sighed. This woman wasn't the enemy—yet. She certainly couldn't be much of a threat. He could always pat her down to check for concealed weapons. The idea appealed to him in a way it shouldn't have, but one glance at her frightened face dampened those thoughts. If she was the guy's granddaughter, then he could lower her assumed level of crazy a notch or two.

"My name is Shayne Wright. And you're the one who is

trespassing." Her voice was thin but no longer shaky. Her chin tilted up defiantly. He'd done a decent job of scaring her, but apparently she had a fighting streak, too. He admired her for it. In the choice of fight or flight, she'd picked the only one available. Fight.

He could handle a woman willing to fight better than one who shattered in hysterics.

"Okay, Miss Wright, there's a signed lease in the inside pocket of my coat. You're welcome to check."

She hesitated, then reached for the coat.

"And my name is Ethan McGregor. Thanks for asking."

The look she shot him revealed how much she cared. He smiled despite himself. Apparently, they wouldn't be exchanging phone numbers.

She unfolded the paper and read. Her eyes—dark caramel eyes he was trying not to notice—darted back and forth as she scanned the documents. They stilled over something that must have bothered her, judging by how quickly her eyebrows drew together. "It says the lease is with McGregor and Sons Construction."

"That's right."

"There's no construction ..." Her voice trailed off as the color emptied from her face again. There was that hitch in her breathing. Her voice had caught on the word construction, although he had no idea why that would be a problem. Unless ... Great, a tree hugger. He cranked the level of crazy back up a notch.

"I don't understand," she said, her mumbled words barely discernable. Her expression told him she did. She just didn't like it.

Those eyes. Something in those flecks of brown and gold vexed him, igniting his protective nature. There was a depth of vulnerability in them that hadn't been there a moment ago, as though a guard had come down, albeit unintentionally.

Behind it, he sensed a woundedness that sought to awaken the decency in him he'd just as soon deny existed. Twice in his life he'd tried to go that route. Both times ended in an utter failure.

"It's not rocket science, darlin.'" Frustrated as much at himself as with her, he folded his arms in front of him, making his face an unreadable mask.

Let's just shut this down right now.

He might not put a stop to his wayward thoughts, but he could make her off limits. She didn't need to get the idea he'd be her friend, and especially not her savior.

Getting ahead of yourself there, buddy. Just because a pretty face looks at you as though she's hanging over the edge of a cliff doesn't mean she needs or wants your help up.

His eyes swept over the woman across from him, her long hair spilling forward to touch the table as she studied the papers in her hands. The attraction he experienced was unwelcomed and more than a little frustrating. Not only was she not his type, but he had no wish to entertain even the slightest sensation of attraction. "That document says I have a legal right to be here, while you, on the other hand, do not."

Her lips parted as she glanced across the table to study him, as though trying to determine if he was serious. He didn't miss the fact that her eyes skimmed over his chest like bare feet on hot coals. It returned the pink to her cheeks double fold. He'd clearly misjudged her when he wondered if she was here to seduce him. Her obvious innocence confounded him almost as brutally as it intrigued him, even more so when she requested he put a shirt on.

"And give you a chance to arm yourself in the utensil drawer while I'm distracted? No thanks, I'm good."

"You're afraid I might get my hands on a spatula?" Her eyebrow arched in cynicism.

She had more sass in her than she'd first let on. He kept his face blank, though his lips itched to smile.

"This looks like the kind of place one might find a rolling pin and a cast-iron skillet. Who knows what kind a danger you'd be then?" He bit down on the corner of his mouth. Not grinning when he said it took more effort than he expected.

But no matter how much effort it took, he couldn't let her know there was anything more to him than the angry, unsympathetic jerk he insisted she take him for.

The problem was, when he looked into her eyes, he was starting to believe it himself.

CHAPTER TEN

The longer she spent in his presence, the less her skin prickled with alarm. That alone should scare her. Trust was not something Shayne doled out like Halloween candy.

She was completely at his mercy. They both knew it, but he had done nothing other than seat her at the kitchen table to discuss who had the rights to occupy this house tonight.

She'd experienced wickedness. That wasn't what she sensed here. Animosity, antisocial behavior, and an unwarranted hostility, but not evil. If he'd wanted to harm her, he would've done something by now.

Of course, he didn't know about his truck yet, either.

Shayne shifted in her chair, then placed the papers on the table, running her hands over them as though flattening the creases might change the wording.

"That's not going to change what's written there."

She dropped her hands to her lap, clenching them so tight she winced at the pain in her arm.

This had to be a bad dream. She stared at her mother's signature. "You can't stay here. I'll call my mother and tell her to cancel this."

He reached over and tapped the papers. "This says I can, and there's nothing you can do to change it."

She leaned away from the nearness of his hand. "Isn't there some sort of ... what is it called ... free look period?"

"Yeah, for my protection, not yours."

Her eyes narrowed. *As if you need protecting.* "We can't both stay here."

"Surely you can control yourself for one night. Besides, you're not my type."

His words stung more than they should have, and the smirk he wore sent her pulse thrumming with offense. Which made no sense, since *not being his type* was exactly what she wanted. It wasn't experience but intuition that made her doubt the truthfulness of his statement. The clearly unintended message in his expression was less *get away* than *don't leave.*

"I can only imagine." *That's just what the old Shayne would've said.* The voice inside her head wasn't helping.

"Want to know why I paid for your dinner?" He pinned her in place with his glare as certainly as if he'd duct taped her to the chair.

The answer to his question was no, but she didn't bother stating it. He was going to tell her, anyway.

"For one, I was told you'd been shot trying to help an accident victim, but you clearly didn't want any special treatment for it. I respect bravery and humility when I see it." He leaned toward her and lowered his voice as he spoke. She caught herself inclining toward him. Her back went ramrod straight, causing his eyes to sparkle with awareness. "Honestly, I just like the way you blush. I don't see many girls who can pull that off anymore. Buying your dinner was my way of thanking you for the pleasure."

An internal heat source scorched up her neck like mercury rising in a thermometer suddenly dropped into a pot of boiling jam. She watched him smile, and knew he thought it was her modesty that caused her discomfort. He couldn't know it was shame and the bitter truth of her deceit.

"Oh, hold on there, darlin.' I'm all out of fifties now."

Like a tea kettle left on the flame too long, anger boiled inside. She would not sit in the sacred space of her grandmother's kitchen and allow him to speak to her this way. He couldn't just waltz into this house and ... and what? Make her feel like the damaged goods she was?

Ignoring the ache, she placed her palms solidly against the table and met his stare. "Leave."

Regret pinged inside her the moment the word came out. No good would come from him seeing his truck.

Well, as soon as he stepped out, she'd lock the door, and ... then what? Wait for him to bust it down or break a window? He looked like someone who would have no problem—physically or morally—letting himself in by whatever means necessary.

"Not happening." He leaned back and folded his arms across his chest.

Her stare was no match for his, especially since her eyes were filling with the telltale moisture of raw emotion. Whether from fear, anger, or utter defeat, she didn't know. Either way, it said he'd already won.

"Did you shoot me?" She hadn't planned to ask, but there it was.

"No." He squinted as though her question surprised him.

"Why should I believe you?" Her eyebrow arched in challenge, her chin jutting out. She wanted an accounting for his actions, not simply a denial.

"Because you're alive." Storm clouds burst, rolling over his features, a haunting that was gone as quickly as it came.

Unable to watch the tempest that both frightened her and caused an oppressive anguish in her soul, she dropped her gaze to the table. The hardness of his words pierced her heart more painfully than the bullet had pierced her flesh. But the storm in his eyes touched something deeper.

Ethan's voice brought her attention back to the present. "I suggest we get comfortable for the night. We can sort this out in the morning. And by sorting it out, I mean you're leaving."

"I can't stay here—with you tonight." The indignation in her words rang with a melodramatic air that made her feel childish.

"Can and will. The roads won't be safe."

"And staying here is?" Staying or not was a pointless argument to engage in. Just poking the ant pile, her grandmother would've said. But she couldn't stop herself. If he only realized just how unsafe that little patch of ground beside his vehicle had become. But maybe now wasn't the time to mention it.

"That's up to you. If needed, I can detain you physically."

"Then I'm a ... a prisoner?" Shayne swallowed with the terrible distaste of the word on her tongue.

"I'm not a terrorist, Miss Wright. I don't take prisoners. Let's use the term guest. Voluntary or involuntary is your choice."

"I refuse to be an *involuntary guest* in my home, Mr. McGregor." Sarcasm thickened her words.

"Call yourself whatever you want. It's your choice."

"But you're saying that you won't *let* me leave?" *Breathe in, hold, breathe out. You are not being held against your will.*

"Correct."

"Then I don't really have a choice, do I?" She looked away, afraid he might see too much if she held his gaze any longer. She knew there was no other option, but she didn't have to like it. She could, however, stop poking the ant pile just to make a point.

"It's like everything else in life—all about perspective,"

Ethan said. He winked, and added, "And it eases my conscience."

Emotionally spent, she sank back into the chair and rested her head in her palms.

"Keys?" He held out his hand. "So you don't try something stupid like driving off."

"You don't need them. I'm not going anywhere." She recognized the skepticism written on his face. "You have my word."

"All right then, how about I check that arm? You're bleeding."

Shayne looked at her shoulder and the fresh red stain soaking into the flannel. "You shouldn't have twisted my arm."

"That's the consequence of trying to pepper spray me." He shook his head. "And by the way, next time you plan to pepper spray someone, don't give them a heads up first."

He was right. She'd learned the hard way one has to be prepared to face the consequences for one's choices. She'd forgotten her lesson too soon.

"A heads up?"

"You probably shouldn't play poker. Your face isn't good at keeping secrets."

Shayne glared at him. His arrogance in thinking he could read her mind goaded her. She could only hope he never saw what truly lived there.

"Hoping for me to drop dead right now won't help."

"Lucky guess."

"How about we call a truce? If I can trust you to stay put, I'll grab a shirt. I assume you have a suitcase I can bring in, then I'll look at that arm." He rose and half turned, pausing when he caught sight of her staring at his bare chest. A wistful look danced over his face before vanishing beneath a mask of stoicism.

He wouldn't understand it was the cross tattooed over his heart that had caught her attention. If she could have found her voice, she would have told him so.

"I believe our hometown hero is blushing again." His expression remained stoic, not smirking as she expected. But his eyes darkened with a regret she didn't understand. A sorrow lingered behind the arrogance and machismo. When she'd first felt his stare at the cafe, and even when he had a gun aimed at her, his eyes constantly radiated a soul deep sadness.

He turned abruptly and disappeared down the hall without waiting for her response.

Shayne wasted no time shooting out of the kitchen and through the front door. There was no way he was touching her arm again, and certainly no way she wanted to confront her car's complicated relationship with his truck tonight. She'd carry her own baggage.

She always had.

CHAPTER ELEVEN

Silence hung in the air like cotton candy—sticky and fragile. Her subconscious pushed against the deep sleep that gripped her.

Shayne groaned, shoving herself from the comfortable warmth of the quilt where she snuggled as alarm ballooned within her. What was her sleep-heavy brain trying to say?

The stranger downstairs.

The injury to her arm forgotten, she bolted upright and received a painful reminder.

She'd heard a noise. She was certain of it, though identification of what she'd heard eluded her.

Details of the day spun her in a cyclone of detached impressions.

Startled from her sleep, her heart thrummed as she strained to hear. The chair she'd jammed under the doorknob remained exactly as she'd left it. She reached for the pepper spray on her nightstand. The small canister now held a dubious status in regard to how much protection it offered.

"You know this stuff won't stop everyone, right?" His

words replayed in her head as the memory of his touch when he'd handed it to her replayed somewhere closer to her heart. Had his touch lingered a moment longer than necessary? Had she wanted it to?

The warning hadn't held a threat, but a word of caution that somehow brushed against her soul with a tenderness she didn't think he intended.

Don't be stupid. She flounced under the covers, tugging the quilt back in place.

If she were lucky, she would go down the stairs and discover Ethan McGregor was nothing more than a bad dream—a consequence of consuming too many fried pickles. She chose not to risk it yet. There'd been enough disappointment for one day.

She twisted the silver ring. Ethan was not like the men she associated with these days. Nor was he exactly like the men she'd grown up around. His was a strange mixture of confident strength and measured compassion camouflaged beneath a thick veneer of forced animosity and roguish innuendo.

He was not a nice man, but that didn't mean he wasn't a good man.

His irritation with her had been obvious when she'd refused to let him check the bandage covering her wound. Concern that a few stitches might have burst when he grabbed her arm paled in comparison to the idea of his fingers playing across her bare shoulder—even if he might handle the situation in a strictly professional and impersonal way, which she doubted he would.

Besides, she didn't owe him the opportunity to ease his conscience by helping her now.

The physical stitches to her wound held, but the threads holding her together elsewhere were proving less secure.

He'd given up his quest to help by crossing his arms over his puffed-up chest, telling her to suit herself. The expression on his face had been pure don't-say-I-didn't-offer ... and definitely don't-come-crying-to-me-when-it-hurts.

He could put his worries to rest on that one. She planned to keep all of her crying to herself. Another thing she was skilled at.

The telltale creak of the front door opening shot her upright again. Panic ping ponged through her body. Had Ethan gone outside and discovered his truck?

She braced herself for the sound of angry steps charging up the stairs.

Instead, it was the sound of scuffling that met her ears.

She reached for the pepper spray again.

"What the—ease up, man." A slurred voice—not Ethan's —tripped her pulse into overdrive. "I'm not doing anything wrong."

"Sneaking around in the dark suggests differently."

"Hey, I just want to warm up for a bit. Didn't know anyone was here."

The voice lacked its usual cockiness, but it was unmistakable. Shayne's left hand pressed against her chest as though she needed reassurance that she was still breathing. That she hadn't died and stepped into purgatory. The ring twisted beneath her fingers while her brain spun in circles, grasping for options.

She could stay in her room and pray Ethan forgot her presence. He could handle this situation—probably every situation—without her input.

The reminder of his gun compelled her otherwise. As much as she might have wished for this new guest to suffer, she couldn't let Ethan shoot him.

She set aside the pepper spray and slipped into the fleece jacket she'd pulled from her bag before going to bed. She removed the safety chair from beneath the doorknob and stepped quietly from her room. The longer it took them to notice her, the longer retreat remained an option.

Anxiety stiffened her movement as she crept down the creaky wooden steps, arresting her completely on the bottom step with a view of the gaunt, lanky frame of someone she never wanted to see again. Hunched and shivering, he stood facing the gun in Ethan's steady grip.

Ethan, an angry madman, just waiting for a reason to pull the trigger.

"Levi!" The surprise in her voice competed with the bitterness surging through her veins. How many nightmares would God force upon her in one night?

He looked over, his face a canvas of black and blue blotches, harsh against unnaturally pale skin. "Shayne?"

Part of her hated him for what had happened ten years ago, but her tender heart couldn't ignore, much less enjoy, his misery. Brushing past Ethan and his gun, she hurried to Levi. She maneuvered him to the sofa. Then she tugged the quilt that rested across it down and tucked it around his shivering body.

"You two know each other." More of a statement than a question, Ethan remained unmoved.

Straightening, she turned to meet Ethan's fierce stare and the suspicion that sparked in his eyes. Shayne's annoyance rose beneath his glare. "Obviously."

He threw his hands out, palms up. "Of course you do." The sarcasm in his sharp laugh made his words rake against her soul. "Only one reason people sneak around for secret meetings. And to think I thought—" His gaze cut to Shayne with a disappointed light she didn't understand. "Never mind what I thought."

Shayne tucked a loose strand of hair behind her ear, shoving her confusion at his comments aside before turning her attention to Levi. "He's freezing. See if there's any coffee in the kitchen."

Ethan didn't move.

"Please." Shayne placed her palm against Levi's ashen forehead. The touch was brief, her hand lingering no longer than necessary.

"Don't need to check. There's coffee. *My* coffee."

She spun back to face Ethan, her words hard and unflinching as frustration and fear for Levi upended her other emotions. "If it's so precious to you, I will pay you back." Her lips pressed together as her chin tipped upward. "And you can put your gun up now. You're not in danger."

Ethan stared, his thoughts unreadable, but his lack of response spoke volumes. Finally, he tucked the gun away, then folded his arms over his chest, no less belligerent.

Shayne's eyes narrowed. "Either go make him something hot to drink or go back to bed." She jabbed her finger in the air to emphasize her instructions in case her tone didn't speak for itself. She wouldn't defend herself against his insulting assumption about what was going on here. What he thought didn't matter. She had a more urgent dilemma than navigating through his messed-up mind.

At least, that's what she told herself for now. The boldness of her speech startled her. The release of something hostile sparked a memory. For the first time in a long time, her feelings didn't frighten her, they freed her.

Levi moaned, his eyelids fluttering as his gaze went from Shayne to Ethan and back. "Who's he?"

"He's not important. What happened? You need a doctor." Shayne raked her hair to secure it behind her ears. Getting him to a doctor would be a problem.

He brushed his stiff fingers against her sleeve. "No. He'll find me. Just let me rest and warm up so I can think." His hand dropped to his side. He seemed to melt into the cushions, his next words little more than a whisper. "I need your help, Shayne."

Anger flared, turning the last of her tolerance to ash. For the second time in the past twenty-four hours, a man placed his hand on her and asked for help.

What was he high on this time? She'd avoided him as much as possible, keeping every conversation brief for the past ten years, but she heard the stories. His life was a well-publicized train wreck. And now he had the nerve to ask for her help. She might choose to offer it, but he had no right to ask for it.

"Trust me, please." His last word faded as sleep pulled him away.

Trust him? Helping him would be one thing, but trusting him would be impossible. Of all the people who had hurt her, his betrayal left the deepest cut.

The first time she'd seen him after that summer, she stopped wondering how it would feel to face him. It brought out a wicked side of her that horrified and shamed her. How would others view her if they knew the thoughts of which she was capable?

She should revel in his suffering, not fret about easing it. To see him in this beaten and half frozen condition triggered a sympathy she didn't like, but couldn't ignore. Unable to consign herself to a single emotion, she bounced between the extremes.

Why couldn't she just hate him and be done with it?

Memories danced into her thoughts, memories of the times *before*, when laughter was innocent, dreams were limitless, and trials only strengthened the cords that bound them.

Miracles still happen. She took a step back, as if needing to place more distance between them, afraid to entertain that hope. Some cords could never be retied.

"Who is he?" Ethan's irritation was clear. He hadn't

budged, but held his position like a Secret Service agent waiting on the president to appear.

Shayne didn't respond.

"You realize this isn't normal, right? Getting the life beat out of you and wandering around in an ice storm. If you aren't going to call an ambulance for your boyfriend, then call the sheriff." The anger in Ethan's voice wasn't helping.

"I can't." *Why can't you?* The fact he had the audacity to ask her to trust him should have made the call easy. She stared at his bloodied face. There had been days when she'd imagined doing that very thing to the man who now slumped on the sofa, appearing as if death wouldn't be too far of a journey. Her eyes stung at the bitter reminder she hadn't made the call then, and she still couldn't. "I just can't."

"There's a difference between can't and won't." Ethan wasn't bothering to hide his annoyance or distrust. He snorted in derision. "I guess that answers all my questions, though. Wouldn't want to get caught red handed in your little secret, would you?"

His remark struck Shayne like a fist, tightening her inside until everything about her felt hard and flintlike. Yes, she had a secret, but he couldn't possibly know.

"Would you see to the coffee, please?" she asked, failing to keep the snappishness she felt from tainting her words. If he didn't know, then what he was implying sparked a new level of indignation. He could make a fool of himself if he wanted. She refused to argue over such a stupid assumption.

"You *can* make coffee, can't you?" Somehow lashing out at Ethan seemed to release the pressure building inside her.

He didn't budge, an uncooperative wall of refusal.

The dark red stain on Levi's shirt captured her attention. In an instant she was back at his side, lifting his shirt to find a ragged gash across his ribs. "This doesn't look good."

"We—and by we, I mean you—need to get him to the

hospital. Or better still, call the cops." Ethan's tone remained unmoved by the sight of Levi's injury.

"You're the one who said the roads are too dangerous tonight." She stood, facing him with her hands on her hips, elbows wide, refusing to acknowledge the pain screaming down her arm. "So we—and by we, I mean you—need to either help or get out of the way."

His self-righteous scowl disappeared for a moment, replaced by a flash of surprise. Then he clamped the disapproval back in place without a word.

Ignoring him, she turned back to Levi, studying the wound on his side. "This looks really bad."

Shayne felt Ethan's nearness as he moved closer to lean over her shoulder. She moved away, shifting, so he was no longer behind her. He didn't need to touch her. His body radiated ... what? Animosity? Yes. But something else, like an aura of security her soul seemed to gravitate toward.

But standing behind her was never an option.

He bent closer to Levi, his words indifferent and unfeeling. "Yep. Gonna need stitching."

She tugged a corner of fabric clinging to the dried blood.

Levi grunted as the fabric separated from his skin. "No hospital. He'll be watching there."

"Who'll check?" Shayne asked, her expression filled with doubt. What kind of trouble might follow Levi? What kind of danger was he bringing down on her again?

"Don't know," Levi answered, fatigue slurring his words.

"All right then. Time to call the cops." Ethan snatched her hand, then thrust his phone into her upturned palm. "Make the call or I will. And trust me, it'll sound a lot better if you do the talking."

She took the phone, then lowered her head. What could she trust right now? Once she had thought she knew Levi, maybe better than he knew himself. But she'd been wrong. Hadn't she?

"I can't. Not until I give him a chance to explain." She reexamined the wound. Surely it wasn't life threatening. "Something isn't right here."

"You're kidding me?" Ethan shook his head in pretend astonishment, throwing his arms wide as he leaned back to speak to the ceiling. "I'm the only one here without a hole in him and you're telling me something isn't right? First, you broke into my house. Now your boyfriend's bleeding all over the place. From the looks of it, both of you have people who want to hurt you. I can only imagine who and why that might be."

"He wouldn't ask for my help unless he really had nowhere else to go." Her words sounded less certain than she wished, whispered more to her heart than for Ethan's ears.

Ethan appeared unmoved by either the words or the emotion.

"He came here seeking shelter ... and my grandparents would want—expect—him to get it." She looked at Ethan, resolve steeling through her despite her doubts. "In this house, we live with grace and mercy."

"Grace and mercy? Well, in this house it sounds like there's a good chance of getting yourself killed."

"Or saved. You said it wasn't safe to be out on the roads. How many lives do you want to put in danger because you'd rather be right than righteous?" She inhaled, biting her lip, knowing where the words came from but surprised they'd found their way out. She shook her head, softening. "Levi's not a danger to you, I promise."

"Look, lady," Ethan said as he thrust a finger in her direction. "I don't know what sort of game you two are playing here, but I know it can't be a coincidence that you're both here. And clearly you both have enemies."

Shayne sank into a chair as Ethan's words swept her feet out from under her. What he said made no sense. No one could have known they'd both be in town, even if someone had a reason to want to hurt them. She rubbed her forehead.

Did they have enemies? Had Levi made enemies that were just as willing to exact revenge from her as from him? She spun the ring, unable to buy the idea that what had happened to her had any connection to whatever was going on with Levi.

Ethan moved his head in a slow nod. "I knew when I first saw you there was something different about you. I should have realized it's because you're certifiably insane. There are some people who just attract problems everywhere they go, and you must be one of them. Gotta save every stray puppy that comes along. Sacrifice yourself so someone else can have it easy. Is being a hero not enough? Now you need to be a martyr too?"

Shayne flinched at his harsh speech. He couldn't recognize the truth that lay buried there, but it rose like a sharp knife to cut her. Tears welled in her eyes, and she knew that, yes, she'd have to save this lost puppy again. "Please."

It was the only word she could muster, and it killed her to let him see her tears.

He paced a few steps and spun back, shaking his head. "Suit yourself. If we're not all dead in the morning, I'll decide what to do with both of you then."

Something inside Shayne snapped at the thought of Levi dying. "That's not a decision for you to make. You aren't going to tell me who I can help in a house that doesn't even belong to you."

"It doesn't belong to you either, Hero."

"My family. Same thing. And why do you keep calling me that?"

"Because ..." He ran his fingers through his hair before shaking his head in frustration. "Yeah, I have no idea."

"Well, stop! I don't need you belittling me in addition to everything else. So just stop, please, and help me take care of him."

Ethan froze. Even his breathing appeared paralyzed by her words.

"He's cold, and his cut is still bleeding." She looked at Ethan, ashamed of her tears but too tired to stop them.

He rolled his head in exasperation as if she'd just asked him to take out last week's garbage. Then, rubbing the back of his neck, he turned and headed for the door.

"Where are you going?"

"I'm not leaving, if that's what you're hoping." The door slammed behind him but not before she heard, "But you can make your own coffee."

She might have hoped for his departure before, but now she wasn't so sure. Alone with Levi wasn't something she wanted no matter what condition he was in. Especially if he was bringing trouble here with him.

Ethan returned with a medic bag over his shoulder. She didn't miss the sharp look he gave her, but he didn't say a word about the parking situation either.

"You're a medic?" Shayne asked. The prolonged pause before he answered, as though he wasn't sure how to answer, mystified her.

"No." He knelt beside the couch and began examining Levi's wound. He must have noticed her confusion. "It's handy on a construction site. Now, bring me some warm water and clean towels. Looks like your boyfriend here has a nasty, but not life-threatening, wound that needs stitching."

"He's not my ..." Shayne stopped. Would knowing the truth make Ethan even more suspicious? "He's my brother."

He paused with his hand buried in the nylon bag, then

resumed pulling out a bottle of antiseptic, gauze, and a black nylon pouch. Opening the pouch, he extracted a needle and a length of filament.

"You're not going to ..."

"Stab him to death with a needle? No." He stopped and stared at her. "Are you going to help me or stand there wondering when we'll get around to discussing what happened to my truck?"

CHAPTER TWELVE

Her brother? With the way she'd paused before she'd said it, Ethan wasn't sure it was information he fully trusted. Even if it was the truth, she'd taken her time confessing it. Lies of omission earned distrust just as soon as spoken deceit. Deception of any form was not a quality he tolerated.

He scratched at his beard, thankful there was at least one itch he could tend to.

Belittling her? Is that what she thought he was doing? He sighed.

Well, wasn't it?

No, it wasn't. She possessed more strength than she let on, maybe even to herself. Yeah, perhaps there was an element of teasing in calling her a Hero. Or perhaps, subconsciously he was just calling it like he saw it.

Ethan settled into the recliner across from where his unwanted patient slept on the couch. He'd refused to give Levi any painkiller before stitching him up. He felt a little guilty about that, not for Levi's sake, but seeing what his pain did to Shayne.

Without knowing what other drugs Levi might have in his

system, Ethan wasn't about to put anything else in him. The wound was deep, and Levi had probably lost a decent amount of blood, but the only real threat would be from infection and the concussion he was sure Levi had. A drug overdose on a night like this would be dangerous at best.

He rolled his head and stretched neck muscles that had grown progressively tight since Levi's arrival.

He'd interrogated Shayne about her own injury while he tended to Levi. Then he'd sent her upstairs with fresh bandages for her own wound. It had been an effective ruse to get her out of his presence. Her nearness had unsettled him somehow. It was also clear that she was about spent from the events of the past twenty-four hours. That she'd complied without argument surprised him. She'd seemed determined to fight since Levi showed up.

He appreciated the spunk—a woman who would stand up for herself—just not when it went against common sense. If he was honest, not when it went against him.

If he were really honest, not when it fed his undesired attraction instead of repulsing him.

She'd even exhibited a bit of a command presence as she dealt with Levi. It certainly wasn't what he'd seen in the cafe and only glimpsed in the kitchen earlier, which drove him to consider there might be far more to Shayne Wright than a man could figure out in a day or two. Not that he aimed to try.

She might not be a damsel in distress, but she was definitely a damsel in leave-me-alone. An unspoken request with which he intended to comply.

There was still the question of delayed honesty to contend with.

Of course, the fact she didn't want to discuss his truck might have influenced her willingness to comply with his dismissal. Another bit of deceit. She might not come out and tell lies directly, but hiding the truth was just as bad in Ethan's opinion. Trust wasn't something he doled out like dry socks at the commissary.

He shook out the quilt covered in patterns of looping circles, spreading it over himself, and wondering if the house doubled as some sort of quilt museum. How many quilts did these people own?

He also wondered if he'd catch any sleep tonight, or if he dared try.

There was a perfectly comfortable bed he'd paid for right down the hall. Instead, he was stuck here playing nurse to some jerk he didn't know.

And who likely had trouble trailing not too far behind him.

Kicking the recliner back as far as it would go, he rested his gun across his chest. He planned to guard their patient, not to ensure Levi's health or comfort, but to safeguard theirs. There was something odd in the way Shayne acted around him. Protective, almost defensive of him, but shrinking away from him at the same time. She said he wasn't a threat, but her words and her body language didn't match. More deception.

Whatever the relationship, he was pretty sure that, despite how she stood up for him, Levi rattled her.

And that bothered Ethan more than it should.

A yawn broke free, reminding him he wasn't immune to exhaustion either. He'd do some house cleaning tomorrow. Then he could finally get on with what he had come here for —something that hopefully didn't require the need to feel.

His eyelids dropped like heavy curtains he wouldn't bother lifting.

Shayne. The Hometown Hero. Supergirl. The woman who had captured his attention when he first saw her at the cafe and most of his thoughts since. That wasn't a good thing. For him or for her. He didn't have a place in his life, much less his heart, for anyone who practiced duplicity of any kind. Alexa had taught him well to avoid attractive women with the talent for treachery.

Tomorrow she'd grab her bag and leave, and that would be the end of it. He'd make sure of it.

After they had a talk about his truck.

The winter air seeped in around the window frames of the old house. The cold front had finally pushed through and left a silence almost as deafening as the noise of the storm had been.

He huffed an annoyed breath and stretched his legs. Then he growled in aggravation as his feet dangled off the edge of the footrest and told himself not to think about the comfortable bed going unused a few feet away.

This was the sort of place where people lived a simple life, planted gardens, tended fruit trees, baled hay, milked cows— did people even really do that anymore? Perhaps the Amish. Maybe he should look into that way of life.

He'd lived in worse conditions, but if this house was ever going to hold life again, there were some maintenance issues that needed tending. He pulled the blanket higher. Some caulk around the windows and a bit of insulation would make this place almost inhabitable.

He engaged his mind with the remodeling plans he would implement if it were up to him, and let the tension seep from his muscles. Remaking, restoring, remodeling. Ethan thankful his drug of choice was a hammer and a tape measure. Some weren't so lucky.

His imagination wandered until he realized it had strayed into something a little too steamy with the fascinating woman sleeping upstairs. She wasn't for him, and neither was the kind of life where people settled down in old farmhouses to raise a family. If that had ever really existed, anyway.

The way she acted led him to believe she thought it had.

When sleep finally came, he couldn't keep Shayne Wright from making herself at home in his dreams, until the nightmare came. The one that always came. He awoke soaked in sweat with the image of Shayne as seen through the scope of his rifle.

CHAPTER THIRTEEN

Unless Shayne could scale down the side of the house from her second-story window, avoiding the scene that awaited her downstairs wasn't an option. She rotated her injured arm and winced. No wall scaling today.

The aroma of freshly brewing coffee wafted from the kitchen, stirring old memories and triggering the faint hope nothing had changed—that the calendar had simply rolled back ten years, and she could pick up and carry on with life from that place of innocence.

She placed her palm against the cold windowpane. Outside lay a world suspended in time, as though life had hit a giant pause button. The thick layer of ice coated the landscape in a blanket of dazzling white. An unsoiled canvas for a new day, possibly even a new beginning.

The morning sun glanced off the ice crystals with a light so bright it hurt. She turned away.

Ice seemed to cover her heart as well, but it wasn't nearly so dazzling there.

We can't move forward if we're always looking back. Mack's words drifted into her thoughts as smoothly as the scent from the kitchen floated up the stairs.

As a child, the day after an ice storm had always suggested to Shayne a land for a fairy princess. A world made of pure crystal. Well, the world she lived in was no land for fairy princesses.

And fear made looking back the only thing she dared to do. But was it all she wanted?

With a gentle touch, she ran a hand over the bandage that covered her wound. Life shouldn't be this way.

Understatement.

The misfortune of having Levi show up fueled her simmering anger. It didn't help that her heart kept insisting he needed her. He had no right. When she needed him, he'd been stoned out of his mind, oblivious to the viper's den he'd thrown her into. He owed her, not the other way around.

But seeing him like this hurt in ways she didn't understand.

For such a time as this. Again, Mack's words from Peg's service echoed in her head. She'd not given any thought to the words he'd spoken during the funeral, but they'd planted themselves in her subconscious. He'd used the story of Esther as he told of the life Peg had lived—a life she hadn't chosen but had used for a greater good.

Perhaps understanding wasn't the point.

She looked to the top of the dresser where her phone should be, then remembered her mistake. Huge mistake.

She wanted to call her mother and find out what was up with Ethan and the lease he possessed. But her mother would ask if she'd heard from Levi lately, and that was a conversation she wasn't up to having. She couldn't answer in a way that wouldn't hurt her mother's already-shattered heart. It was a question that found its way into all their conversations. Her mother believed one day they'd reconcile. She also carried a mother's angst and guilt for both her children and the way their lives had come undone.

After the divorce, her mother had depended on Levi, probably more than she should have. Those were hard days for them all. Perhaps she'd meant to offset the damage done by their father by building Levi up in every way she could.

Shame had made Shayne run, but it was the adoration both her grandparents and her mother bestowed on Levi that had convinced her to keep her secret. She wouldn't be the one to hand them the proof that all their prayers to set him on the right path had been for nothing.

And she couldn't be sure they wouldn't blame her. After all, she did.

If Ethan had a legitimate right to be here, it would horrify her mother to know Shayne had spent the night in a house with a stranger. There were a lot of things her mother didn't know. If Shayne had her way, she never would.

Then there was Nick. Another conversation she was okay with postponing.

With one arm, she worked her way into a pair of jeans and pulled on a fresh, unbloodied flannel shirt she'd pulled from the closet still filled with her old life.

Appearance wasn't high on her list of priorities today. Navigating the disaster downstairs ranked near the top, but so did maneuvering through the minefield of emotions battering around inside her.

Of course, there was also a visit to Momma Mae's, first for her phone, and second because she hadn't canceled her lunch with Reverend Stapleton. Guilt that she wasn't more eager to have her phone again took a seat on her emotional roller coaster ride.

Poor analogy. A roller coaster had fewer ups and downs than her emotions had gone through in the last twenty-four hours.

Is this what it feels like to have an identity crisis? She paused mid-buttoning. Maybe it wasn't an identity crisis but a remembrance. Who she was wrestled with who she'd tried to become.

Who do you want to be, Shayne?

She resumed working the round buttons through the narrow slits. Was it possible she'd been given a glimpse of the answer last night? A piece of her former self resurrected to life in her grandmother's kitchen?

Searching for a distraction, it was Ethan's face that came to mind.

Recalling the feel of his stare at the cafe, she tugged the oversized shirt tight across her chest. Hollywood standards might not consider Ethan McGregor handsome, but theirs weren't the standards that mattered. Shayne's above-average height had him standing not much taller than she. And if not for the contradictory expression in his eyes, the semi-permanent scowl he wore beneath his copper-tinted mustache and beard would leave him looking devoid of much warmth.

Yet there was a quality about him that drew her to him, like a flower following the trail of the sun's light. His masculinity radiated off him in waves of confidence.

But his physical strength didn't provoke her interest as much as the strength she sensed from within. She had no doubt about his physical strength judging by the broadness of his shoulders and the ... well ... she cleared her throat and the images in her head. She'd seen his bare chest and abdomen. He was strong. She'd just take her wayward thoughts captive and leave it at that.

She hadn't been around a man like him in a long time. That was her choice, though. Men like him ran on too much adrenaline and testosterone. They were prideful and dangerous.

But Ethan also emitted a strength of character. A stubborn, arrogant character that had been merciful about her and Levi's presence here and even more merciful—so far—about his truck.

He reminded Shayne of something she'd forgotten.

Not all strength was physical and not all powerful men were egotistical predators. Like her grandfather, for one. Strong enough for every task the farm required, but it was the quiet, humble steadfastness of his character that revealed his greatest strength.

She sat on the edge of her bed and let her brain process the emotions oozing from her soul. Masculine strength didn't equate to moral weakness. Ethan had tended to Levi's wound with practiced skill even if it had been begrudgingly. He hadn't thrown a fit about his truck—yet.

That said a lot.

And he hadn't sent her packing out into the storm on dangerous roads. Surely, that was evidence of something decent within him.

She inhaled, filling her lungs until they could hold no more, then held the breath until her chest ached.

That could all change soon.

Still, the thing that captivated her the most about Ethan McGregor was the picture on the home screen of his phone. She'd seen it when he handed it to her last night. Ethan and a little boy, around four years old perhaps. In the photo, Ethan knelt beside the boy who held up a fishing pole with a perch half the size of Ethan's hand. The smiles they both wore, though, more than compensated for the pitifully small fish.

She didn't know if the child was a son or nephew or just a friend. What she did know was Ethan had a tender side he worked hard not to let her see.

She stood, ready to get on with whatever awaited. She'd survived worse, right?

The familiar warmth of the kitchen greeted her as she

descended the stairs, but the temperature was the only thing familiar about the scene.

A strange emotion—a mixture of offense, anger, and curiosity—bubbled up at the sight of Ethan at her grandmother's stove, cooking with her grandmother's pans. Shayne froze on the bottom step to watch him maneuvering around the space like someone who didn't consider the kitchen solely a woman's domain.

The smell hit her as he lifted thick strips of bacon and settled them into the cast iron skillet.

Her stomach revolted. She swallowed the rush of nausea that rose in her throat. The odor of smoke cured meat unsettled her insides and sent her memories straight down a black hole.

Breathe in, hold, breathe out. You're in Grandma Hazel's kitchen, not the old smokehouse.

She repeated the process until the nausea abated. With one final step, she planted her feet firmly on the kitchen floor.

Shayne wasn't willing to share this house—especially not with someone making himself far too at home. Whatever he was paying to rent it, she'd offer double just to get him out.

She chewed her bottom lip. With no savings and a job Nick had gotten her, financial independence was only a dream. A more upsetting notion niggled into her concerns. Working in the administration office for his father's church had been Nick's doing. Relieving her of that position would be just as easy for him if she gave him a reason. Would he stoop that low if she didn't say yes? And if so, did he even deserve her yes?

She gave the ring a quick twist, then brushed her hair over her shoulder.

Now was not the time to delve into that concern. She had a home to defend.

Perhaps she could tell Ethan the house was haunted, though she doubted he would let a little thing like ghosts in the attic change his course of action.

Just when she thought him determined to ignore her, he picked up the pot of coffee, filled an empty cup with steaming black liquid, then turned to hand it to her. No smile, but the mocking in his eyes made his message clear. "I made coffee."

Not commenting took effort, but the hint of disappointment on his face when she didn't made it worth it.

With the mug held close against her body, she savored the sensation of the steam dampening her cheeks as the rich aroma awakened her senses.

She took a tentative sip, then forced herself not to flinch as the thick black substance assaulted her taste buds. Much too strong, no surprise.

The liquid fought its way down her throat as she forced herself to swallow, unwilling to tell him it was anything but perfect. Especially when she caught the twinkle in his eye as he watched her take the first sip.

"Problem?"

"Nope." She glared at him through narrowed eyes. "How much do I owe you?"

"I'll settle for another one of those famous blushes," he said. His answer was accompanied by a taunting wink.

Against her will, she obliged, reminding herself that when she chose to square up with him, she needed to brace for the punch.

Her gaze traveled to the living room where Levi still stretched on the sofa.

"He's alive," Ethan stated before she could ask. "For however much that's worth."

"That's ... good." She took another agonizing sip of coffee, ignoring the antagonism in his words. In fact, maybe it would be best to ignore Ethan altogether.

What she couldn't ignore were her own mixed feelings about Levi's condition. Being relieved he was alive didn't mean she had to be happy about his presence.

Ethan's expression said he found her hesitation interesting. That he watched her now as though he expected to unlock all of her inner oddities by observing her facial twitches, pupil dilation, and pulse rate grated through her. She was not an experiment to be decoded for entertainment. But if she were honest, her annoyance stemmed more from the worry he might get it right than the indignation of being treated like a lab rat.

She took another drink, hoping her tastebuds would forgive her for the abuse.

His mustache twitched in what might have been mirth, proving she did a poor job of hiding her opinion of his coffee.

Once again, the glint in his eyes sent unnerving sensations through her midsection. What was going on behind them was more than she could guess, but she sensed more than a casual scrutiny—whether or not he intended it. His inspection wasn't cruel or judgmental, yet it still felt hungry. Hungry for what, she didn't know. Only that it wasn't the kind of hunger that devoured innocence.

"Maybe you can get your *brother* to come clean with whatever he has going on." Ethan nodded his head toward Levi, then returned to cooking. "Before whatever trouble he's in finds us all."

He emphasized brother as though he questioned the title. Shayne didn't care about that, but his last words made her hesitate. *Finds us all* ... as if they might all still be here at the end of the day. Clearly he wasn't planning to go anywhere, but did that mean he considered she'd be staying as well? She took another sip of coffee without thinking of the consequences.

Because the more she thought about it, the less willing she was to leave the house with these two in it. If this was the end, the last time she'd visit, then it deserved a more fitting farewell than her running away in defeat. Maybe running had been the wrong thing to do ten years ago as well.

And if it's not the last time? If you never go back to Austin?

She snuffed the ridiculous notion from her thoughts.

Levi was the only thing keeping her here now. She couldn't leave him in this condition. If anything terrible happened to him ...

Watching him self-destruct from afar was one thing. To see it firsthand was something altogether different.

She stared at the man sprawled across the sofa, rolling her bottom lip between her teeth before setting the cup on the table with hands she hadn't realized were shaking. If she didn't do this, then Ethan would. There were too many unwanted things that might be exposed if that happened.

She approached with soft steps, as if he were a sleeping newborn she didn't want to wake. More like a sleeping cougar with the power to shred her.

"The goal is to wake him up. Stop tiptoeing in there like it's not." Ethan rattled the cast iron skillet onto the burner, causing more noise than necessary. Shayne stiffened. He'd done exactly what Grandma Hazel used to do when she wanted to express her disapproval without saying a word.

And he was right. She was approaching Levi as though she didn't want to disturb him. She paused, quietly studying his battered and bruised face.

As though Ethan's coffee hadn't already taken care of it, she cleared her throat, then spoke his name, feeling the tight way it slipped over her lips.

He moaned without opening his eyes. "Is it morning

already? The drill sergeant you're with woke me up a thousand times last night."

Ethan came to lean against the opening separating the two rooms, arms crossed. "Signs of a concussion. Just keeping you alive, buddy. Believe me, it wasn't my first choice." He gave Shayne a look that said the blame for any compassion on his part was fully her responsibility.

"Can we have a moment, please?" She didn't need Ethan's scrutinizing gaze or judgmental ears for the conversation she had to have. He shrugged and returned to the stove. Not that he couldn't still hear everything that was said, but she could think better without the heat of his animosity hovering in the air around her like a toxic fume.

"We have to talk," Shayne said. She crossed the room, picking up the quilt Ethan had left tossed in the recliner—the double wedding ring patterned one that was her favorite. She bristled. First her grandmother's kitchen, now Shayne's quilt. Ethan was taking liberties with parts of her life he wasn't entitled to.

She discreetly sniffed in Ethan's scent, then folded it and draped it over the chair he'd slept in. She was stalling, not ready to have this conversation with someone she had worked hard to avoid for almost ten years.

Levi tried to sit, but gave up with a tortured groan. His hand drifted to the bandage on his side. "I ache all over."

"Then be still, before you hurt yourself."

He raised his swollen eyelids just enough to say he wasn't amused, but she hadn't intended it to be a joke.

"Who's he?" Levi nodded toward Ethan, his voice a dry whisper.

"Who he is doesn't matter. What matters is that he took care of you. And I'm guessing loaned you a clean shirt." She studied the gray t-shirt that hung too loosely on Levi's lanky frame. Admitting Ethan was a stranger would only add to the vulnerable feeling she didn't like.

Warmth flushed her cheeks again. She spun the silver ring. Thoughts of Ethan might warm her skin, but her heart must remain off limits.

"I see. So your boyfriend saved my life. Quite the hero. Aren't I the lucky one?" His face contorted as he attempted to shift his position, the pain he expressed overriding the sarcasm in his words.

"He's not my boyfriend, and he did more for you than I would have." She didn't need a mirror to know the look she gave him was as icy as the morning. Her statement wasn't exactly the truth since she'd begged Ethan to help. But in the daylight, Levi looked a lot less likely to die, and her empathy drained from her heart like water through a tow sack.

A haunted wounding flickered over his face and cut through the apathy protecting her soul. His next words sliced even deeper.

"So that's it? You still hate me. When are you going to tell me what happened? What went wrong back then?"

Numbness crept from the hard wood floor along her legs and up her spine to settle around her heart as she retreated into the imaginary walls that kept her safe.

"Coffee. Do you need some coffee?" Without waiting for his answer, she turned and headed to the kitchen, her fingers twisting the silver ring.

Ethan reached for a cup before she asked, confirming his eavesdropping skills were decently accurate. He gave her a look that conveyed he wasn't feeling gracious about it as he handed it to her. She filled it half full, pouring slowly as she composed herself. She knew he was staring at her, but she refused to make eye contact.

Levi had worked up to a seated position when she returned. Sweat beaded his forehead, and he grimaced as he coughed. In the condition he'd been in last night, pneumonia was a strong possibility. He needed a doctor.

She sighed. And she'd have to be the one to get him there.

He reached for the cup, and she placed it in his hands.

"I need to know what happened to you," she said.

"Not with G.I. Joe in there listening. Does he know who I am?"

"I have no idea what he knows." She resisted the urge to say she hoped Ethan had better taste. "Why'd you call him G.I. Joe?" she whispered.

"Obviously military. You need to get out more."

Shayne hadn't considered the details of Ethan's life, and now wasn't the time to start. "What's going on Levi?" Her eyes narrowed. "The truth."

He stared into his cup, moisture clouding his eyes. His voice was coarse when he answered. "I don't know. I wish I did, but I don't." He pounded his forehead with his fisted hand, as though it might help him think. "I saw a girl."

CHAPTER FOURTEEN

"You saw a girl?" Shayne asked, as a familiar bitterness crept up her throat.

"In the hangar on the old Tackmore ranch, but ..." He shook his head as though he'd only watched the movie in bits and pieces. "I don't know. I wanted to help her, but this guy jumped me. He knocked me out. After that, everything is fuzzy." The intensity of his anguish caught Shayne off guard.

"Sounds like everything before it is, too. What were you doing there?"

"Looking for gas. I ran out and didn't want to walk the rest of the way in the cold."

"The Tackmores sold that ranch years ago." She offered no sympathy despite his obvious discomfort.

"I remember that now." His words were snappish, and he mumbled a tired apology.

"So instead of going to the house to ask for help, you went to the barn to steal gas?" Nonplussed, Shayne's tone conveyed her opinion of his integrity.

He looked at her with an anger that mirrored her own. "I went to the house, but no one was there. I would've left some cash or gone back later to repay them. But thanks for thinking so little of me."

Yep. Same old Levi. Rules, boundaries, and other people never mattered if they stood in the way of what he wanted. At one time, she had thought she was the exception to his selfishness. She'd learned the hard way there were no exceptions.

Still, her response at this moment was too harsh, and she knew it.

Because what if ...

What if one night had been a horrific and devastating mistake they'd both undo if given the chance? Levi never meant to harm others with his selfishness. He just never considered the price others might pay for his good times.

Shayne knew that. She just couldn't absolve him.

"It wasn't like I was eager to see the place again. The last time I was there wasn't such a great memory for me. Not that it's much of a memory at all." His eyes came to hers, the heat of his anger visibly dissipating into an expression filled with questions. Questions he didn't voice, but to which he seemed to want her answer.

She looked away, unwilling to ease his burden, even though she knew what he sought from her. If she allowed her heart to soften, the pain would consume her.

The building he spoke of—the old hangar—occupied a space at the bottom of an oak covered hill, separate from the barns and riding pens erected on the ridge above where the main house stood. The barn stood tucked out of sight unless you looked for it. The Tackmores had transformed it into a hangar for the experimental aircraft they toyed with. Beside it stood an old one-room stone structure once used as a smokehouse in the late 1800s. The prepper-minded Tackmores had installed a bunker few people knew about beneath the building.

Shayne knew.

On summer nights, teenagers had used the barn-turned-hangar to host clandestine keg parties and smoke pot. The Tackmores had willingly turned a blind eye under the misguided thinking that letting the kids have a place to blow off steam was the safer thing to do. Shayne had only gone there once at Levi's insistence to experience one of these parties, a sort of rite of passage.

It had proved to be a rite of passage alright. Only the passage for her was a long, dark tunnel she'd yet to emerge from.

"She was chained to the bed in that room in the loft," Levi said. He whispered out the words as though he didn't want Ethan to hear, then slid a hand up to cover his eyes.

"Who?" Shayne's attention returned to the present.

The room had been a crash pad for visiting pilots. Shayne had only seen it once. A strong inclination to doubt his story hardened her inside, but when he lowered his hands, his eyes were glassy with tears.

"I'd never seen her before." A sob broke loose, ragged and raw. "She looked so ... terrified. I've never seen anything like it. Not in real life, anyway."

His voice faded to a distant hum, as memories and emotions sucked Shayne backwards into the dark tunnel.

Not in real life? She wanted to scream at him that if he believed that, then he had no idea what real life was like.

Breathe in. Hold. Breathe out. Focus on where you are. She pinched the tender area between her thumb and forefinger until the pain pulled her back, grounding her again.

Each breath became a footstep, moving her away from the terror as she searched for the shelter of her current reality. "So all of this ..." she lifted her hand to indicate the cuts and bruises on his face, "this stranger did that to you?"

"I didn't even have a chance to take a swing. He just

started pounding me, and saying things that sounded like Russian or something. The next thing I remember, he's gone, and I'm lying on the floor. I told her I was going to help her." A short, derisive laugh broke from his lips.

"Some joke, right? I don't know what I was planning to do. I had just started out the door when I saw him coming back with a gun. He hadn't seen me yet, so I ran. I jumped out the window onto the roof of the old smokehouse, then took off through the field toward the river. Run. That's all I could think. I heard gunshots, but I just kept running. I wanted to help her, though. I did."

He tried to stand, but wobbled back onto the couch. A flash of failure clouded his eyes. He doubled over, sobbing into fisted hands. "I do. I have to go back. I have to find her, save her."

Loathing wormed through her insides. There was a girl in danger, and he left her. But then, wasn't that what Levi did best, abandon those who needed him the most in order to save himself?

"How'd you get cut?"

"Must've happened when I jumped through the window."

As mad as she was, she couldn't deny the terrified feeling that Levi could have died. "We have to call the sheriff."

His eyes snapped open. The hard glint of obstinance left no room for opposition. "No."

"What do you mean, *no*? Or is the part about a girl merely another one of your lies?" The cyclone of emotions Levi stirred in her carried her to the edge of her self-control.

"I swear I'm not making this up. But the man who attacked me threatened to kill her if I go to the sheriff. And … the guy may have had a badge." Levi swallowed and locked eyes with Shayne. "And he knows who I am."

"You said he was speaking in Russian."

"I said something that *sounded* like Russian. And apparently, he's bilingual." His typical cockiness returned.

"How does he know who you are? What ... did you try to impress him with your fame, offer him an autographed t-shirt in exchange for not punching you?" Sarcasm gave her words a hard edge. If he knew who Levi was, then he must be someone familiar to them, so why didn't Levi recognize him. Was this all one big story to hide another of his poor decisions?

Suddenly drained, Shayne sank into the recliner. "What makes you think he won't kill her anyway?"

"I don't know. Hope, I guess." His voice was hoarse.

Miracles still happen. Wasn't that what had driven her actions yesterday?

Too many unexplainable occurrences threw her world off kilter, but something toyed with the fringe of her understanding.

"You said the guy jumped you from behind, that you didn't see anything. But now you're saying you had a conversation, and oh yeah ... he might have had a badge." Her words slowed, as tiredness crept over her. The needling impression there was something she was missing frustrated her. Something hovered on the fringes of her memory, but refused to step out of the shadows.

"We didn't have a conversation. He was yelling at me after I took off." He raked his fingers through matted hair. "All I'm saying is *I don't remember*. After I saw the girl, all I have are random images."

Shayne closed her eyes, then opened them slowly, fearing the answer to the question she would ask. "Were you—I mean, did you ... take anything yesterday?"

"Was I high? Is that what you're asking?"

Shayne studied her hands in her lap, running her index finger over the band of silver. The memory of receiving the ring as a gift from Peg captured her thoughts. The small, simple ring with an engraved compass, the unexpected gift had come with a brief note containing the words: *Trust in the Lord with all your heart and lean not on your own understanding. In all your ways acknowledge Him and He shall direct your paths. Proverbs 3:5-6.*

In this simple message, Peg had thrown her a lifeline though Shayne hadn't been able to grasp it at the time. Not until this moment had the truth begun to soak in.

She put the thought aside and returned her attention to the problem in front of her now.

That Levi felt condemned by her question was obvious, but she didn't relent. "It's not an unreasonable question, is it?"

He exhaled and ran his tongue around the inside of his cheek. "No, I guess it isn't. I'm sure it's hard for some people to believe, but I'm not some deadbeat addict. I was completely clean and sober last night."

Shayne flinched at his words *some people*. He meant her. Once, she'd been his biggest fan, and he'd been her superhero.

"I've screwed up my whole life. I get that. My career is in the toilet. I got no one and nothing." He paused, the words choking in his throat.

"That's not true. You still have family. You'll always have us."

His laugh stung, even before the words that followed reached her ears. "Says the girl who abandoned hers without even so much as a goodbye. Save the platitudes, Shayne. You checked out on us, and you certainly didn't want us there for you."

"Don't you dare." All the wrath and condemnation boiling inside her spewed out in those three words.

Something flickered in Levi's eyes, a small spark of understanding. Whatever the thought was, he snuffed it out.

As much as she needed him to feel the pain she lived with, if he really didn't know, then it was better to leave it that way.

His gaze moved around the room. "I want things to change. That's why I came back here—to clear my head, sort stuff out." He scowled, his hand gingerly touching the place where the outline of Ethan's bandage was evident beneath the t-shirt. His breathing was heavier now. "I can't get her face out of my mind. That's the only thing I remember. You can hate me all you want, but what about her? Are you going to help *her* or not?"

Shayne looked away to hide the tears. He hadn't come to her rescue that night ten years ago. Now he wanted her help saving someone he didn't even know. The familiar sense of sacrifice settled over her. Ethan had been partially right. Shayne was always the sacrifice. The strength she'd felt earlier crumbled to her feet.

The smell of burning bacon intruded, and she glanced at the kitchen to see Ethan shifting the skillet away from the burner as a cloud of smoke hovered over the stove. She would have cautioned him about the perils of sticking his nose in someone else's business, but the harsh aroma was probably enough to remind him. Grandma Hazel was certain to be turning over in her grave. She didn't tolerate smoke in her house, whether it be from the kitchen or a cigarette.

The moment sparked a memory, reminding her of her grandmother's resilience and determination. Self-pity didn't fit her. *I come from tough stock. We aren't known for seeking sympathy.* That's what she'd told Reverend Stapleton yesterday. Maybe she needed to live as if it were true, especially if someone might be in danger.

"How do you think you're going to help her? You can't even help yourself. Look at you. What's it going to take, Levi? How far do you have to fall? Even now, you think you know best. Levi Wright—correction, Hollingsworth—doesn't need the sheriff. He'll take care of it. If this man—whoever he is—knows who you are, then we're all in danger here. So what if someone else gets hurt, as long as Levi gets to be the big man?" The outburst drained the last of her energy.

Raw emotion swept her from the room, hurrying her out the front door into the biting cold. The icy touch of morning air brought relief to skin that seemed far too hot. She rested against the porch post. Was coming home a mistake? If not, then she would have to deal with the question of who she was and who she wished to be.

Her breath puffed out in thick white clouds, and she wished she'd grabbed a coat. Awareness that the chill she felt wasn't entirely from the cold temperature caused a soul-deep shaking.

Her car—her only way out—still sat partially lodged beneath Ethan's truck.

She'd come back to find what was right, but instead, she found everything wrong. She seated herself on the porch swing and looked out over a view she knew better than any place in the world. It had turned out to be an illusion, but she let herself sink back, running from the present, hoping to capture the past. As always, it slipped from her grasp.

Mack was right. The past wasn't coming back, and she couldn't move forward if that was the direction she insisted on looking.

A couple of male cardinals flitted in the branches of a tree, their bright red feathers startling in front of the backdrop of white blanketing the landscape. A vision of winsome beauty against a hard, harsh world.

She wasn't here to claim a few sentimental keepsakes. There was a much deeper longing at play. Was it peace? Closure? Healing? Whatever it was, she was unlikely to find it now.

Shayne had taught herself to dig her grave deep and bury her pain out of sight. Peg's funeral uncovered the truth she was slowly dying inside. Now she understood one thing for certain—she wasn't ready.

Memory of Peg hummed through her heart as she thought about a long-forgotten conversation. On a summer evening filled with the chorus of tree frogs and cicadas, Shayne had learned the story of how Peg's only son had died. Peg had sent him out that night because she had forgotten to turn off the coffee pot at the church. If Peg had only remembered it herself before she left the ladies bible study, or if she'd insisted on being the one to go back, he wouldn't have been in the path of that drunk driver.

Against the backdrop of a peaceful summer evening, the harshness of Peg's story had unsettled Shayne. But over the ugliness of that story, Peg had painted a masterpiece of grace and mercy. It was in that moment Shayne saw that life comes at us in layers.

The remembrance of her friend's touch, as gentle and warm as that of the evening breeze, came back to Shayne.

Holding Shayne's hand in her aged and wrinkled ones, Peg told her the secret to life was accepting that it wasn't meant to be fair. *Everyone lives within a story*, she'd said. *The question we must answer is, will it be a story about ourselves, or will it be a story about something much bigger?*

That was the moment Shayne knew she wanted the story to be about something bigger.

Less than a week later, her world shattered. And she'd been living in the same chapter of a story she hated ever since.

She pulled her knees up to her chest, clenching herself into a tight ball, partly to hold on to the warmth and partly to hold on to herself.

Soon the sun's heat would melt the ice. The icicles would

drip until they were too weak to hold on. Then they'd let go, and the air would fill with a desperate, grating sound as sheets of ice slid from the roof, building speed as they raced over the edge to smack against the wet ground. A moment of silence and peace, always followed by the messiness of life breaking apart and moving on.

If she thawed just a little, there'd be no going back.

Even if she wanted to leave, she was stuck until the thawing occurred. In more ways than one, maybe she'd been stuck for a long time. She shivered. The consequence of thawing out was too messy to contemplate.

She longed to feel the confident expectation that summer was coming, that season where life thrived, and good things could grow in abundance. To come in from a summer day spent in the garden or the hayfields to a kitchen table covered with a home-cooked meal. To hear the hum of the water cooler or the purr of the oscillating fan, and the farm report playing on the radio while the old windmill squeaked out its arrhythmic but unceasing song.

One more summer evening spent on the riverbank fishing with Peg to the music of the frogs and cicadas, watching as the fireflies flickered in the growing darkness. Listening while Peg told the truth about life.

Her leaving had been an act of love, though. After the devastating divorce her parents had gone through, knowing the truth about what had happened that night would have been too much. She couldn't impose that on so many hearts still trying to heal.

She'd done it for them, right? She had done what she did to protect them from the pain, not out of a fear that in their brokenness, they would have nothing left for her, right?

Memories of her family breached the dam and more tears fell.

It wasn't all about protecting them, was it? It was about

protecting yourself from the shame, and from having to see they couldn't—or wouldn't—be able to fix it.

The door opened, and she averted her face, pressing her cheek into her denim clad knees, trying to erase the tears. Why couldn't Levi leave her alone?

She swiped at her cheeks, her fingertips lingering against the damp skin, attempting to conceal the emotions she couldn't wipe away as easily as she did the tears.

"Breakfast is ready." Not Levi's, but Ethan's voice surprised her. His thick, strong fingers materialized in front of her, holding out the wedding ring quilt. His voice had softened, a note of concern mingling in his simple statement. Unwinding herself, Shayne took the quilt and wrapped herself in a warmth that resonated deeper than her flesh, thawing her soul.

Ethan stuffed his hands in his pocket, fidgeting uncomfortably as men do at the sight of a woman's tears.

"Thanks," Shayne said, her words a murmur as she stared into the distance, looking anywhere but into the dark eyes that refused to leave her.

"She won't be there," he said. He crossed his arms and leaned against the rail. "If she ever was to start with."

Shayne sniffed and wiped her nose. Guilt settled over her. So wrapped up in her own pain, she'd forgotten the possibility there might be someone else in grave danger. "How can you be sure?"

"If we're to believe his story, then for one, they've been discovered. Not likely they'll take a chance waiting around to see what happens."

She traced the pattern of swirling stitches that bound the quilt together, knowing there was never a beginning or an end to be found.

"So you think there could be a girl in danger?" Her voice

came out as a whisper, as though saying it too loudly might make the worst come true.

"The world's a wicked place. Anything's possible." Ethan looked away and shrugged. "You didn't tell me last night your brother is Levi Hollingsworth, the famous, or at least notorious, country music star?"

"I didn't realize it mattered."

Ethan laughed. "Shayne, listen to me. No one is looking for him. He's got himself in trouble, and now he needs time to lick his wounds and recover. That's what men do. He's only trying to avoid some bad publicity."

Licking his wounds. That's what men do. Does that include you, Ethan? The truth whispered in her ear. Ethan was here to lick his wounds, too. The pain in his eyes confirmed it. If she was honest, so was she. But not Levi. "I don't think so. Not this time."

"Oh, really?" Skepticism hardened the lines of his face.

Shayne struggled through the war of emotions tearing her inside. But deep within was the swirling stitch of hope that this time, Levi really wanted to rescue someone. And she didn't believe he was here to *lick his wounds* as Ethan put it. Something told her there had to be more.

Levi had begun the practice years ago. When he couldn't gain their father's attention with good behavior, he was just as happy to gain it with bad.

She looked at Ethan. "Levi's been licking his wounds with bad publicity all his life."

CHAPTER FIFTEEN

Physical beauty no longer had any effect on him. Short, tall, amply endowed, or raw-boned. Blond hair or raven black. None of that mattered.

Only one thing aroused his excitement and fed his hunger —fear. That infinitesimal yet indelible splinter of time when understanding sparked terror in their eyes. The ones who thought they were brave would try to hide it. The rest fell to pieces in a variety of ways he found altogether uninspiring and more than a little repulsive. But for one brief instant, the look of terror in their eyes was undeniable. One might miss that delicious moment if one wasn't paying attention.

The tip of his tongue trailed along his upper row of teeth. Vito Slavin always paid attention.

He snapped the laptop closed and pushed back from the desk. Tilting his head from side to side, he stretched thick, corded neck muscles. He could think of such things later. Today, he had a large quantity of missing money to locate, and a man to kill.

Doing so would be a pleasure. An accident would be a

simple thing to sell, given Levi Hollingsworth's propensity for hazardous living.

Like prowling around where he wasn't welcomed.

Leaving the door unlocked last night was a serious oversight someone would have to pay for. But not until Vito had his money.

Were the missing money and the unwelcome guest connected? He didn't think so. Not yet.

Discerning what might have brought the man to Vito's hangar was troublesome, but not enough to cause a great deal of worry. If the law suspected anything, he would have sensed it by now.

He rubbed his knuckles, tenderly soothing the scrape he'd gotten when he'd knocked Levi unconscious. It had only taken two blows to knock him out. He should have slit his throat right then, but dead bodies are harder to carry than people realized, not to mention all that blood to clean up. The arrival of the ex-con ranch hand had been an unfortunate interruption. The man had come around to check that everything was secured before the storm.

Everything but the lock on the door, Vito had wanted to say.

The hand in question, Jimmo Cleese, was a big man, burly and roughhewn. And if he hadn't made the mistake of "giving his life to the Lord" while he served his time at the state penitentiary, he might have made a respectable miscreant. But Vito didn't have time to *unsave* the blindly misled. He would talk to his foreman about managing the ranch and the men he employed with a more attentive care for details.

He hated it when things didn't go as planned. He took his planning seriously. Now there were loose ends everywhere.

He cupped the fingers of his other hand over his fist and cracked the knuckles. The sound was not unlike the breaking of bones, only with the breaking of bones there came a satisfyingly distinct grating sound when done right.

Levi had regained consciousness while Vito had been dealing with the clueless ranch hand. He'd run, escaping his fate for now, but it wouldn't last. Vito wouldn't rest until he'd dispatched that concern.

He sneered, finding a rather providential irony that he had recognized Levi, but Levi hadn't a clue who he was. Drugs did that to a person. They were for fools who never played to win.

Vito moved to the small window that looked out over the repurposed hangar below. Some farming equipment and a few fencing supplies lent the legitimacy of a barn, without making it glaringly obvious there was another purpose for the structure. He frowned at the pallet of cardboard boxes containing tight spools of baling twine. His request that it be moved had not been obeyed. Preparation for the unexpected demanded this space be ready to secure the plane out of sight on short notice.

Hands clasped behind his back, he contemplated his options for damage control. The Cessna wasn't due back for almost a week. A long time to wait when one was dealing with a human commodity.

He smiled. She'd dared trying to escape once. She wouldn't try again. He didn't care for drugging his merchandise when there were so many more creative ways to ensure their compliance, but with his attention demanded elsewhere, he had made a concession this time.

The daughter of a prominent Mexican attorney, this job had been a special request. The anonymity that existed in these kinds of deals was a joke. He was pretty certain he knew exactly who the actual client was, no matter what agents the buyer worked through. Vito rarely accepted assignments like this. He had no cares for the messiness of politics or cartel power plays, and he liked to choose his own victims. Perhaps he'd made the decision in a moment of boredom. The money had been significant, but it was the challenge that lured him. Like playing chess with the lights off.

Now here he stood, out of a considerable amount of his own money to have brought her this far. He'd learned of the wreck fairly quickly. Reckless driving had put everything in jeopardy.

He had no tolerance for those who couldn't do their jobs well.

His fingers pressed against the diamond-encrusted gold ring he wore on his pinkie until the image of the scorpion inset pressed into his flesh. Too many unusual events all merging at one time. Could it be his luck was running out? A sardonic laugh escaped his lips. He didn't believe in luck any more than he did coincidence. The events of the past twelve hours were merely the gods testing his ability—a chess match meant for deities. Vito knew he'd pass. Even the gods were no match for him.

The door below opened and the man Vito employed under the guise of ranch foreman entered. Unlike the lumbering, bearish walk of the ranch hand from last night, this man moved with the fluid grace of a prowling leopard. The man crossed the open floor without looking up, before making his way up the stairs to knock on Vito's door.

Vito took his time answering. He didn't like to rush. He'd rushed too quickly at his visitor yesterday, and now he had a loose end.

"Enter."

The man Vito knew as Bryce Leech stepped through the door, but stopped just inside, waiting to be invited any further. As it should be, Vito smiled. A whiff of the man's cologne carried over, mingled with the smell of mornings at the cafe. Cheap coffee, over cooked bacon, and imitation syrup. The man had risked the treacherous roads because Vito had told him to.

Leech had potential. He was soulless. A useful quality, but it could also turn against him. Men without souls were also men without loyalty.

Leech was also something of a prodigy. Had he functioned with the normal range of human sensitivity, he would have, no doubt, settled into the lackluster life of a moral and ethical genius. There was little Vito had found that the man couldn't learn. Computers, aircraft, fluent Spanish, and an astounding array of chemical compounds. The only thing he held any empathy for were his horses.

And he was handsome. Vito was not. It was an ugly truth that men who looked like Vito could live a life of perfect piety and still be seen as a villain. Whereas men who looked like Leech might practice all sorts of darkness and never be suspected. Humans were such shallow creatures.

It amused Vito the man had actually come with the sale of property. He'd found the perfect piece of property, complete with its own Renaissance man and sociopath already employed and willing to stay on with the new ownership. Setting him up as a horse breeder on this remote ranch, four hundred and twenty acres conveniently situated for both ground and air transport, had been almost too good to be true. Which was why he knew it wouldn't last. What he didn't know was if it would be Leech or the property—this location—that failed him first.

Light glinting off the silver Texas star money clip Vito wore attached to his pocket reflected in the glass window, catching his attention. The persona he'd adopted in order to ensure his success here was becoming wearisome. Maybe it was time to move on.

"Learn anything?" Vito asked, turning to Leech as casually

as if they were discussing the proper way to treat hoof rot in horses.

"Not yet. The little son-of-a—"

Vito cut him off with a sharp look. Profanity was for the uneducated and base, and Vito was neither. Born into poverty and raised in a Ukrainian orphanage, Vito learned early on the only thing he had possession of was his ability to sound as though the opposite were true. From an early age, he had cultivated every characteristic he associated with the well-bred. Vito was a chameleon who could play whatever role was needed, but he was never to be taken as crass and ignorant unless it suited him to do so.

"I found an abandoned truck. Might have broken down or run out of gas. Could be what brought him here. This would be the closest place he might have found some."

"Why is Levi Hollingsworth in the area, and who would he go to for help?"

"He couldn't have gone far last night. From the looks of the blood I found, he must have cut himself rather significantly when he went through the window. More than likely, he's bleeding out or freezing to death in the brush by the river."

"I do not deal in *more than likely*. Find him." Vito stared at the man in front of him, an Adonis-like figure to which charm came naturally and deceit more easily than breathing. The women loved him. Vito knew he could count on him to use his ample talents to gather the information he needed. Things they might be reluctant to share with someone of Vito's appearance. "And has there been any mention of the money?"

"No, sir. But there was one interesting thing. Apparently, there was a woman at the scene of the accident. I hear someone shot her."

Vito's curiosity piqued. "Shot? By the local law enforcement—Turnaround's finest?"

The man grinned, but it was wickedness that dripped from his lips, not joy.

No, Vito deducted. For Leech, wickedness and joy were joined as one.

"No one knows. The only thing for certain is that they didn't kill her. Nothing more than a flesh wound."

With the palm of his hand, Vito rubbed his smooth-shaven jawline. "Interesting. And who is she?"

"A former resident who came back for the old ladies' funeral." He broke eye contact with Vito, his eyes drifting to the left.

Tiny prickles of misgiving registered on a visceral level. What was he hiding? "She is still in town?"

"Possibly. The roads were undrivable last night."

"Interesting coincidence, her being shot at the very accident from which my money disappeared. I think I should like to know more about this lady." Vito turned back to the window. *More about this lady and more about why you are lying to me now.* "Yes, while you are finding our unfortunate visitor from yesterday and the money, find me this woman. In fact, I am confident when we find her, we will find far more than we expect."

"And the girl?"

"I have given the original buyer a deadline. If he cannot take her off our hands by then, I'll sell her elsewhere. I've put out a few inquiries to see if we might find a backup buyer, but I am afraid I may have to take a substantial loss to part with her to anyone else. Until then, relocate her as a precaution. She is, of course, still off-limits so mind your manners around her."

The man smiled his soulless smile. "Not my type. I prefer blondes."

Had Vito possessed the human emotion of fear, he might have shuddered. He was well acquainted with his foreman's tastes, and with his fantasies. Whereas Vito harbored no misconceptions about how the objects of his attention actually felt about him, Leech lived with the delusion that they all loved him. He only needed to show them how much.

The money was a concern, more because it was missing than due to the amount. The buyer had paid half up front, but the other half was to be handed over when they exchanged the girl. The buyer had also hinted they blamed Vito for this, as though there had been a weakness in his organization. He turned to trail his finger along the edge of his desk, brushing away an unseen trace of dirt while studying his foreman from the corner of his eye. If Leech had crossed him, he'd pay. For the first time, he wondered if he might be wrong about Leech. Perhaps, the man played his role a little perfectly. But the madman standing before him gave him no sign anything was not as it should be.

Of course, the buyer was going to want the girl, whether Vito received the rest of his payment or not.

They were not gods. They couldn't harm Vito. But they could become an inconvenience to business.

He sighed, the sound laden with the tiresomeness that came from having to deal with those who were not his equal.

Vito once again clasped his hands behind his back before turning to face the man still stationed by the door. In all the details of the accident unearthed so far, there had been no mention of any money. Even in the most tight-lipped of departments, and small rural departments were rarely ever tight-lipped, that kind of cash was hard to keep a secret.

He wasn't concerned any of this would lead back to him. But Vito wanted what belonged to him, and he did not take well to having his plans upset.

One way or the other, he would exact his pay.

CHAPTER SIXTEEN

Sheriff Rock Griger downed the remaining cold coffee from his cup and looked at the bland plate of food in front of him. Today was chili day at Momma Mae's, but Cindy had refused to bring him any. Instead, he had a sorry-looking piece of baked chicken, mashed potatoes—no gravy—and green beans —no salt. How was a man supposed to fight crime and protect the public on food like this? For Pete's sake, he was the one paying for his meal. He ought to be able to order whatever he wanted.

He was going to have to make that doctor appointment for a check-up just to show that bossy waitress he was fine. What she was doing bordered on tyranny.

But it would mean she'd won. Headstrong, stubborn women were the bane of a man's existence. Let 'em start caring about ya and you'd have nothing but misery.

"Harmon." He called the young deputy into his office, then dug his wallet from his pocket and pinched out a few bills. "Run over to the cafe and get me a bowl of chili. And keep it to yourself who it's for." There was more than one way to skin a cat.

The deputy eyed him but didn't take the money. "No can-do, sir. Strict orders from Cindy."

"You don't work for Cindy. You work for me."

"Yes, but she scares me more."

Rock growled as he stuffed the money back into his pocket and looked down at his lunch. Truth was she scared him too. Although he was pretty sure for an entirely different reason. He poked at the food in the Styrofoam container. He was just about hungry enough to eat anything. Last night had been unprecedented in his years in Turnaround. Since Peg placed her ranch in a trust for the church with directions to turn it into a home for teenage girls, there had been a constant stream of unfamiliar faces in and out. It was hard to keep track of who belonged and who didn't.

The two deceased men in the truck last night did not. Their fake ID's—something Trooper Hernandez had spotted right away—had left him with nothing to go on until they got the fingerprint report back. The tattoos on the men told him more than he wanted to know. Gangbangers with a history of prison time.

Paperwork fanned out over the desktop. He could fill out and file the crash report, handing that part of the investigation to Trooper Hernandez and the DPS. He tapped his index finger on the paper, unable to ignore the notion the two events—a fatality accident and an aggravated assault—weren't as separate as logic would have him believe.

So far, the only fatality in the accident to be positively identified was Chubby Nuckols' pet steer, Buster. The spoiled geriatric Longhorn was known to stick close to the feed trough. He was probably the only overweight Longhorn Rock had ever seen. What he was doing out on the road was a mystery.

Buster was a local icon, appearing in the annual Fourth of July ceremony every year draped in red, white, and blue with streamers tied to his tail. But he'd be most missed at the school's yearly Rodeo Day, where he showed up to give kids rides across the lawn in front of the old stone building that housed the elementary.

Well, looked like the ol' fellow had his final hurrah last night right before he'd met up with that tool truck. A tool truck with an unregistered logo and no tools. The truck must have hit the corner at a pretty fast clip to have knocked a thousand-pound steer as far as it had.

Rock needed to walk the scene again, just to satisfy himself they hadn't missed anything. There had to be something somewhere that would give him a clue about who and why someone had taken shots at Shayne.

He stabbed a bite of the chicken and shoved it into his mouth. It sure wasn't a bowl of Cindy's chili.

He glanced down at the photos of the unidentified men from the accident. And these sure weren't good ol' boys out for the fun of running the backroads. He hated to think Shayne had found her way into the middle of some cartel's nasty business.

And he hated that it might be going on in his county.

He wouldn't jump to that conclusion—yet. Right now, he had an aggravated assault and a fatality accident. Two separate incidents that just happened to occur in the exact same spot and in proximity time wise. He dug a roll of antacids from his shirt pocket, flicked back the torn wrapper, and examined the next in line. Pink. He put it in his mouth and bit down, crumbling the small disk into grit. Maybe he didn't need the chili after all. His gut was already churning around the idea that this was bigger than it looked. And maybe not as random as it first appeared.

A half hour later, Sheriff Rock Griger parked his patrol SUV on the side of the road. He'd intentionally rolled up from the opposite direction today, following the path the doomed vehicle had taken.

He'd threatened to retire before cold weather had set in again this year, but nothing was ever as easy as he hoped it could be.

And if he was honest with no one but himself, losing a friend like Peg and walking away from the only job he'd ever loved all in the same year was too much to deal with.

He'd have to step away soon. There was too much change coming to his little country town. It'd take a younger man to keep up. The aches in his body confirmed it. But he couldn't let go just yet. While a younger body was needed, his old mind was still sharp, and he wasn't going to leave his people in the hands of anyone who wasn't capable—anyone who didn't harbor the same love for this rugged country and its eccentric band of citizens.

It pleased him to know Conner would leave for the academy in a matter of weeks. This was an unexpected career path for a man Griger had often worried he'd be sending in the opposite direction, proving once again that the Good Lord works in mysterious ways.

Getting him hired onto the force would be a challenge if no one left to create a job opening, but he had a plan for that as well. He was willing to forgo a portion of his pay to fund the salary of an extra deputy. It was money he didn't really have to spare, but he could sell his boat if necessary.

And he was certain he could convince the county commissioners of the need for another deputy while all the construction for the girl's home was going on.

He plucked the roll of antacids from his pocket and checked the next one in line. Purple. He popped it in and crunched, thinking over the photos from the accident scene in his mind again, wondering if something was missing, grudgingly thankful he'd eaten the chicken instead of the chili. A truth he'd never admit to his gastronomic nemesis. That waitress was the worst lunchroom bully he'd ever encountered.

He cleared his throat. She was also the most attractive bully he'd ever encountered.

Shaking his head, he shifted his attention back to the matter at hand. Gut feeling kept nagging him. There was more to this than the puzzle pieces he already held in his hands. He sighed and stepped out of the vehicle. He pressed his lips together in dissatisfaction as he zipped his overcoat, bracing himself to keep from shivering like a feeble old man.

The question of why someone had shot at Shayne pestered him, and the notion that there might be a connection between the accident and her being targeted hung on like a dog with a new bone, teeth clamped tight.

The blind corner where the road curved sharply to the left might have been fine in the days of the Model T, but it wasn't fit for the speeds people drove these days. That didn't excuse the fact that the driver of the tool truck must have been doing at least seventy when he hit it.

He might have wrecked even without the unfortunate fact that Buster the steer was standing just around the corner, smack dab in the middle of the road.

Rock rested his hands on his hips and frowned.

A battered old Ford pickup rattled alongside him as he chewed on his thoughts.

"Morning, Sheriff." Chubby Nuckols rolled his window down and the hot air blowing from his heater rushed out to remind Rock there were other options to standing out here in the cold. But not today, and not for him.

Rock nodded in greeting. "Morning."

Chubby was a giant brick wall of a man, a hefty girth but solid as a rock, inside of which beat the heart of a teddy bear. Chubby's red-rimmed eyes and downcast face attested to the grief he felt over the loss of Buster. A childless widower of many years, Chubby was also beyond the age of training a new steer. There would never be another Buster.

"It's terrible, Sheriff. That weren't no way for Buster to go." Chubby shook his head and turned to face out his front windshield as the tears collected in his eyes. "They're going to give him a proper goodbye, though. The mayor and the town council done agreed to bury him in the park. That way, he won't never have to miss another Fourth of July parade. We're going to have a funeral and everything. School's even letting the kiddies walk over to attend."

"That's nice, Chubby." Rock meant it, but it didn't erase the fact that there were also two dead men who no one was mourning yet because nobody knew. He was sure the men would show up in the criminal database and were probably up to no good, but as bad as they might have turned out, surely their lives had mattered to someone—their mothers, at least. One thing this life had taught him—every life was worth grieving, even if that person had taken the wrong road somewhere along the way.

Chubby scratched his jaw. "Something's puzzling me though, Sheriff. How'd Buster get out here on the road?"

Sheriff Griger leaned over and spit, working the last of the antacid taste from his mouth. "I was wondering the same thing. You find any downed wires or a hole in the fence? I know you'd never have accidentally left the gate open."

It was possible the man was starting to miss a few gears now and then, but the way he loved that steer, it didn't seem likely he'd overlook something like that. Chubby was more likely to forget to tend to himself than he was to neglect Buster.

"No, sir, I never would. And I checked it myself after I found out what happened. I don't think I could've forgiven myself if that'd been the case. But the gate's still shut tighter than Aunt Ethel's girdle. And there ain't no holes in the fence. I just don't see how he done it."

"I'm gonna have a look around. Let you know if I figure anything out."

"I'd shore appreciate it. It just feels so undone not knowing." Chubby put the truck in gear. "I best get going. Today's chili day at Momma Mae's and I don't want to miss out. I know it's beef and all, but you don't think Buster'd mind, do ya, Sheriff?"

"Not at all." Rock patted the side of the truck as a sendoff as the reminder made him scowl.

Chubby rolled a few feet and stopped again. "You going to come to the funeral on Monday, right Sheriff?"

"I'll do my best." Rock wasn't sure his best would get him there. It was more than enough to attend funerals for people he actually cared about. Attending one for a pet steer was pushing the boundaries of his compassion. But Chubby had always been a likable guy and an ally on more than one occasion. Rock sighed, knowing he'd be there.

But he wasn't sending flowers.

An hour later he'd walked the sides of the road from both directions and found nothing other than a set of indistinct tire marks left by a motorcycle. It had stopped farther down the road on the opposite side and spun the back tire as it took off. The melting ice had softened the ground, blurring the marks left by the tire. The width and singularity, along with the spray of gravel rooster tailing away, was all the reliable information he could gather.

Nothing unusual about that. And it had probably happened days ago. No sensible person would have been out on a motorcycle in yesterday's weather.

No convenience store receipt or junk food wrapper. None of the usual flotsam left behind at a crash scene, especially one with a rolling vehicle. The mangled service truck had been completely clean. It might have been a recent purchase on its way to be delivered to a new owner, but there was no paperwork for a change of registration. And the insurance and registration papers in the glove compartment were fakes.

That they were up to no good was a certainty. And though they might no longer be a threat, there had to be others in whatever business they had going here.

He crossed the highway and headed back to his vehicle, stopping when something caught his eye. He squatted and stared, then reached down to run his finger over the small, golden grain embedded in the asphalt. It wasn't alone. A two-foot circle in the center of the west bound lane was embedded with oats. He sniffed the slightly sticky kernel in his hand, letting his nose confirm what his fingers already told him. This was sweet feed, the molasses-covered grain that ranchers often fed their cattle.

Rock rose, grimacing at the crackling sounds that came from his joints. Could have spilled off the back of a truck. This time of year, nearly half the trucks in the county carried feed on their beds. But it wouldn't typically have fallen off in a circle in the middle of the highway.

He stared at the sharp curve in the road. If he'd wanted to put an obstacle in someone's path that would cause the greatest amount of damage, a steer feasting on sweet feed at this very spot would do it.

He tossed the grain into the wind, suddenly filled with a fresh round of questions. But one thing he felt certain he knew already.

Buster the steer had been murdered.

CHAPTER SEVENTEEN

A jagged line of black paint stretched along the front fender of her forest green SUV, bearing a frightening resemblance to the scowl on Ethan's face.

He had taken the accident better than expected, adding another layer of intrigue to the onion that was Ethan. Peeling the layers down to see what made him tick would be a long-term project she didn't plan to tackle.

The damage to her vehicle was superficial. Nothing to keep her from getting where she needed to go. But explaining it to Nick wouldn't be fun—at least not the part where she confessed to spending the night with a stranger. That would hit a nerve somewhat deeper than surface-level damage.

What are you doing, Shayne? The question persisted, unanswered.

She concentrated on navigating the roads, still harboring slushy patches of ice while contemplating how to tell Nick everything she needed to. The accident, the shooting, the stranger she'd shared the house with last night, and hardest of all, that her answer was no. Or at least, not yet.

Of course, first she'd have to find her phone, not that she

was worried about that. She knew it would be either on the seat where she'd left it or in the cardboard box behind the counter where all the lost and found items accumulated.

The warmth of the ground meant the ice had started melting as soon as it hit the ground. When the sun's rays had touched the surface this morning, the already slushy ice was quick to disappear.

By mid-morning, Ethan had her car extricated from his truck's fender and pointed in the direction she needed to move. Away.

Which was where she headed now.

He'd done it with an exasperated glance or two, but few words. And since most of his words tended toward angry, she took his lack of speech as a good sign.

That her suitcase wasn't sitting in the back seat was a concern. It meant that she'd have to return to the house at least one more time. She fostered a hope Ethan and his lease would disappear before she returned. But like the ice melting beneath the sun's heat, the lie she told herself dripped away against the backdrop of dismay she might never see him again.

Levi's presence complicated things. His story about a girl in danger added another tangle to the mess already knotting her insides. While she had no doubt he was in some kind of trouble, her conversation with Ethan had given her even less faith in Levi's story.

She'd hidden those misgivings from Ethan. Or at least, she thought she had.

But seriously injured and potentially ill, Levi needed her. Perhaps she should have stayed in case he required her assistance, instead of leaving him at the mercy of Ethan.

Beneath it all resided a nagging uneasiness that there was a purpose to her presence here. There was something she needed to find before she left for good. Something other than the double wedding ring quilt she'd come for.

In a few minutes, she'd sit down with Mack for lunch. It was a date she wasn't eager to keep. Not that she didn't want to see him, but the number of secrets she kept suggested she'd be better off avoiding her family pastor.

A white truck going in the opposite direction was the first vehicle she'd seen out besides hers. It slowed as it neared her, the driver staring, probably afraid she might plow into him. The truck was a King Ranch edition Ford that appeared to possess all the bells and whistles—she could practically smell the leather interior.

Emotion passed over the driver's face, flashing into and out of existence so fast she wasn't certain what she'd seen. Only that the impression it left her was one of surprise.

Perhaps he wasn't expecting to find anyone else out on the roads today, which would have been a misinformed expectation. If nothing else, the ranchers would be out to check on the livestock and bust ice on water troughs as needed.

Or maybe he thought he knew her, although the obligatory wave had been missing.

Maybe, like her, he wondered why she'd be out driving on a morning like this?

She could stop by the sheriff's office. Hearing they'd apprehended the shooter with a full confession would be helpful. Unlikely, but helpful. She could inquire about the men who died. She wasn't positive about what she'd promised to do for the man whose hand she had held. Likely, the dying man's plea had been from the traumatized delirium of his pain-wracked body. And everything before she'd been shot remained a blurry haze.

But she needed to believe she'd at least tried to fulfill whatever pledge she'd made.

Then there was the dilemma of Levi and his story. She

needed proof this wasn't some wild fabrication like Ethan said, just Levi trying to cover his own hide. If his story was a lie, nosing around it might risk exposing her own secret. Besides, how could what he told her actually happen way out here in simple ol' Turnaround? The people around here wouldn't allow it.

What she'd experienced years ago was different, and thanks to her, a secret.

And a secret she intended it to stay.

Shayne ruled out a visit with Sheriff Griger. When you're guarding as many secrets as she was, you don't just pop into the Sheriff's office for a chat.

If Levi was telling the truth, then she was wrong not to go. But what if his life really was in danger?

Still, wrong not to go. But if Levi had seen a badge, was it possible going to the sheriff would put Levi in danger?

A vice like pressure clamped around her temples.

For the love of Job, Levi, why did you have to make me doubt you? Shayne's annoyance found its way down her arm and into her fingers as she squeezed the steering wheel in anger, then flinched as pain from her injury followed the same path.

If there really was a girl in trouble, there was no way Shayne could look the other way. That there was nothing she could do right now to uncover the truth frustrated her.

She couldn't just wander out to investigate. If her fears didn't stop her, common sense should.

However, finding out who owned the ranch and how the residents of Turnaround felt about them shouldn't be difficult. That much she could do simply by choosing the right seat at the cafe and staying there for a half hour.

Levi's story about a captive woman wasn't all that had her bothered. Something else skittered around the edges of her mind. Some truth that banged on the door but couldn't get past the fatigue, confusion, and raw emotions bolting it shut. Time alone and away from Ethan and Levi would clear her head and give her perspective.

She parked and hurried across the street paved in red brick. Years of traffic and the shifting ground beneath the historic paving had made the street wavy and uneven. But it still held far more charm than the grimy asphalt of the city she was used to.

Little had changed in the fifty years that Momma Mae's had been open. The red checkered vinyl tablecloths draped over the mismatched tables surrounded by the same wobbly wooden chairs were just as she remembered. They might have borne a few more scuff marks than before, but that only added to the ambiance. The aged look of Momma Mae's was timeless.

The sugar packets jammed under uneven table legs might be the only thing that had changed. Probably.

Even the menu had moved through the passage of time with few alterations. Fried pickles were the only fresh addition she'd noticed last night.

This was the in between hour at the cafe, after most of the breakfast crowd—for whatever that might have amounted to on a morning like this—had gotten on with their day, and before the lunch crowd arrived.

Kindley leaned on the far end of the counter, flicking the edges of a stack of menus while talking to a boy about her age. He didn't seem to pay much attention to the girl, who seemed equally determined that he would. Head down, he bent over something in his palm.

At the sound of the shopkeeper's bell over the door, the girl glanced at Shayne. Her eyes widened, alarm replacing the coy doe eyes with which she'd watched the boy. In a motion that carried the impression of urgency and guilt, she elbowed the boy. He raised his head, then turned to follow Kindley's stare. The moment he shifted, Shayne understood the reason for the girl's distress.

It was her phone in the boy's hands. The purple phone case had been a custom-made gift from Nick.

"I see you found my phone," Shayne said.

"Collin's really good with this kind of stuff. He's just looking to see if we could figure out who it belongs to so we could get it back to them. I promise." Kindley's voice pitched higher as the words tumbled out.

"So you ..." Shayne's eyes narrowed, noting that the app open on her screen was her text messages.

"Yeah, it's not like your passcode sequence is all that secure. It was pretty easy to follow the pattern." The boy handed Shayne the phone and threw in a flippant and angry glare to go with it. He zipped up his coat. Without looking at either Shayne or Kindley, he spoke to the girl. "I got places to be. See ya tonight."

The surly attitude glanced off Shayne. After all ... teenagers. But the sense of violation his search of her phone stirred, even if he had done it with no other intention than helping Kindley find its owner, made her mouth dry. She twisted the ring, her mind a blank as to what she should say to the girl.

"Shayne Wright!"

She turned to find someone she hadn't seen since he was more boy than man waving at her. He motioned to her in the same way he had when they were in high school, and he'd wanted to copy her homework.

Conner Pierce waved at her from a booth by the front window. "Come join us."

"I'm meeting someone." Shayne took a step back, her gaze shifting from Conner to the woman sitting across from him. "And I don't want to intrude."

"In response to both your objections, you won't be. Mack sent me to find you. He's had a change of plans."

The disappointment that resonated within surprised her.

"His sister fell on the ice last night and broke her hip. He's gone to Fort Worth to be with her at the hospital." Already on his feet, he motioned her into the spot he'd vacated.

Shayne remained where she stood. She had no desire to reminisce about old times with Conner ... or anyone. She'd politely tell him no thanks and find somewhere else to eat.

"He said to tell you how sorry he is. He was looking forward to the visit. But I say his loss is our gain, so here we are," Conner said.

The woman still seated in the booth smiled, dimples appearing like exclamation points in a face framed in coppery red waves of hair. She didn't appear bothered by the idea of Shayne's company. In fact, she looked hopeful.

"Shayne, I'd like you to meet Maribel Montgomery," Conner continued. He didn't introduce Maribel as his girlfriend, but the connection between them was palpable. No matter how he introduced his friend, the smitten grin he wore told Shayne enough. Conner had made another conquest. Maybe she should warn the poor girl.

Conner Pierce had been the master of flirtation in high school. Shayne suspected the only reason she hadn't succumbed to his irresistible charm was because her brother kept Conner in his place. Levi hadn't always let her down. He'd just gone big the one time he did.

Conner still wore the look of a cowboy, right down to his slightly bowed legs and rider's hips. Everyone loved Conner, but Shayne had to admit it surprised her to see him serving as the reverend's messenger.

She contemplated the vacant seat. Returning to the farm before having some time to think wouldn't help. And trying to think on an empty stomach wouldn't do her any favors either. Plus, she had to be somewhere, and this might be as good as anywhere else.

Besides, if anyone knew who owned that ranch, Conner would.

Still, Shayne hesitated, because if anyone really knew what happened at that ranch ten years ago, Conner might be that person too.

"Maribel, this is Shayne Wright, the one I told you about from the accident last night," Conner said.

The warmth of Maribel's response as she seconded Conner's request for her to join them erased Shayne's reluctance.

Giving in, she slid into the seat Conner offered, while he scooted in across from her, sliding in close to Maribel.

"How're you feeling today?" The concern in his expression appeared genuine. "I saw you last night, but couldn't get to you. I was one of the First Responders, but they had me attending to the other guy."

"I'm okay. It really wasn't much of an injury." She studied Conner, someone she'd known since she was a little girl, but suddenly felt she didn't know at all.

"Praise God for that," Conner said.

It took a moment for Shayne to realize her mouth hung open.

He laughed. "It's okay. I'm not exactly the same person you knew in high school. Praise God for that as well. I'm sure Mack would have plenty to say on the subject if he were here."

Shayne contemplated the possibility Conner had gone from lost to saved, while she had gone from saved to nonexistent.

A petite waitress slid a glass of water and an empty coffee cup in front of her. She tipped the coffee pot she carried in the other hand over the cup, then paused. "I don't even know what I'm doing, Hun. I guess I'm assuming everyone had a night like mine, and we all need coffee today." She stopped and stared at Shayne. "So, do you?"

Shayne had forced down two cups of Ethan's bulletproof brew this morning and didn't want to contemplate what sort of heart arrythmia she might develop if she took in any more caffeine. But one glance at the haggard expression the waitress wore, and all she could do was nod.

The woman's spiky blond hairdo framed a countenance etched in lines of worry and exhaustion. She filled the empty cup, then slumped into the booth next to Shayne.

"If I never have another night like last night, that will be just fine by me. First Peg's funeral, then the cook calling in sick and then trying to keep Kindley from falling all over every man that came through the door. You should see the tips that child brought in, but still ... I swear that girl is going to be the death of me. I don't know how much longer I can handle her." She pressed her palms against her cheeks, shook her head, and continued.

"Then that terrible wreck had Rock working late. That poor man's heart don't ever let him get any rest. And on top of it all, now Mack's sister took a fall, and he's gone to take care of her. Feels like the whole town is caught up in a good old fashioned West Texas dust devil, dirt flying everywhere so you can't see what's coming. It just is, and it ain't gonna be pretty."

Conner and Maribel exchanged a bemused look.

"What?" A frown deepened the lines already etching her face.

"I just don't think we've ever seen you sit before," Maribel said. Although Shayne suspected the look she'd shared with Conner meant something else. She shifted in her seat and reached for the ring. Secrets—even good ones—were always uncomfortable.

"Well, I don't reckon it happens often." The waitress crossed her arms and leaned back, resting against the seat.

Maribel introduced Shayne, "Cindy, this is—"

"Oh, I know exactly who she is. Shayne Wright. Mack's told me all about you, and even if he hadn't, your Grandpa Frank made sure I knew. Your picture is still on the wall over in the far corner." Cindy smiled and patted Shayne's hand. "He used to eat here a lot after your grandmother passed. I think he was lonely."

Shayne hid her guilt beneath a smile.

"I'm really sorry about what happened," Cindy said. "I would have checked on you last night, but you were gone before I even knew you were here. Running the kitchen and keeping an eye on Kindley had me meeting myself coming and going."

"Kindley is Cindy's niece. She's staying with Cindy while her parents are in Japan on a temporary job assignment." Maribel was the only one who seemed to perceive a need to bring Shayne up to speed about Kindley and why there seemed to be an unusual level of angst in her regard.

"They thought her being in a small town might keep her out of trouble," Cindy said as she shook her head. "What'd keep her out of trouble would be a daddy who didn't spend all his time at work. I love my brother, but I wish he'd take a little less interest in climbing the ladder and a little more interest in being there for his daughter."

"I'm sorry she's giving you a hard time," Maribel said. "I know what it's like to be in her shoes, and you're right. Fathers make a huge difference in a daughter's life."

"From the perspective of a guy who knows, unfortunately, given the slightest opportunity trouble will always find a way," Conner said.

"Don't get me wrong. I love having her here. She's such a sweet thing ... just too boy crazy. Always looking for attention and approval in all the wrong places—which is why she should be with her father." Cindy inhaled and exhaled as though the act finished one topic and launched another. "I'm so happy for you though, Maribel, deciding to be baptized. The way you cared for Peg in her last days ..." Cindy's voice ground to a choking halt.

Silence settled around the booth, the death of Peg still too fresh. The news that Maribel had been close to Peg, had taken care of her, endeared her to Shayne.

"I wish I had done this while she was still alive. She should have been there to see." Maribel's whispered words were heavy with regret. Cindy leaned across the table to squeeze Maribel's hand.

"Hun, don't think she didn't know your heart. You were so busy trying to make her last days beautiful, and there ain't nothing in that to regret. What you are doing now is just the outward showing of what's on your inside. And girl, don't you doubt for a hot minute that Peg didn't know it."

The irony that the outward showing of Shayne's life was not a reflection of what she held inside twisted in her middle.

The conversation about Maribel's decision continued. Shayne felt like an intruder in their lives, hovering on the edge as though she didn't belong. But there was an ease to their conversation that reminded her once again of something she had forgotten. This was a kind of camaraderie she hadn't experienced in a long time.

"So, when's the big date?" Cindy clapped her hands together.

Conner's expression froze. He stammered, "I ... uh..."

"Not that date, you moron." Cindy laughed, a high scraping sort of sound. Had it been any less filled with amusement, it would have been offensive to the ears. "Although any day now would be fine with me. I'm talking about the baptism?"

He ducked his head, looking sheepish. "Well, that too is something we are having a small debate about." He turned to Maribel. The level of respect and adoration gripped Shayne's heart until a painful awareness oozed out. She'd never seen that look in Nick's eyes.

She also recognized a fear in Conner's eyes the other women didn't seem to notice, or ignored.

"I want to do it right away. Right now," Maribel said.

Conner sighed, thumping the red plastic glass in front of him. "And therein lies our problem."

"What problem? The woman wants to get baptized, so you baptize her."

"That's what I said!" Maribel's passion intensified now that she had an ally. "I want to go to the river, to the place where ... where I think God first reached out to take hold of me and wake me up."

"Oh ..." Cindy leaned toward Shayne and whispered, "Dead body in the river. Worst welcome to Turnaround ever —until you showed up yesterday and got shot. But here she is. I wonder what made her stay?" Mischief danced in the waitress's eyes. She winked at Conner as he slouched lower in his seat, as though distancing himself from the conversation. "But honey, isn't it a little cold to be getting into the river right now?"

Maribel was not easily dissuaded. "It'll be even more memorable. Besides, I doubt John the Baptist turned anyone away because the temperature of the water wasn't just right."

"Yeah, well my camel hair coat is at the dry cleaners," Conner said. "Besides, Mack needs to be the one to do it. It would just be—"

"Be what? More official?" Maribel arched an eyebrow, cutting Conner off mid-sentence.

His index finger continued thumping a steady rhythm on the plastic glass.

Maribel reached over and took his hand. "We don't know how long Mack will be away with his sister. I want to do this today. It's taken me a long time to make this decision. I've felt for a while I wanted to, but taking care of Peg kept me busy. Her funeral yesterday made me see how silly it was to keep waiting. And I want you to do it. Yes, Mack has taught me a lot and been the best mentor. But you ... you're the one who taught me what forgiveness looks like. You're the one who caught my heart and gave it a safe place to heal while I learned to trust God. It just feels right to have you do this."

He leaned close and brushed a tender kiss across her forehead. "If you're sure, then."

Shayne picked up on the hesitancy in his words.

"What is it? Why don't you sound more excited?" Maribel must have sensed it, too. She pulled back, studying him, her face lined with concern.

Conner stared at the table, then shook his head. "I just don't want you to confuse me with Jesus."

A silence so thick it was tangible hung in the air over their corner of the cafe.

Then three women burst into laughter.

A flustered Conner tried for crowd control. "What's so funny?"

Maribel wiped the tears from her cheeks and tried to catch her breath. "Conner, sweetie, I don't really think that will be a problem ... ever." She clamped her lips together until she couldn't hold the laughter in any longer.

This time Conner acknowledged a certain amount of irony in his request with an eye roll and a sardonic smile. "All right, then. Y'all have made your point. What I meant was sometimes it's easy to see a person as something more than they are. Yes, I was there to help you, and I always want to be there. But I can't be your savior." Conner scanned the women seated around him with wary eyes as they covered their mouths and tried to hide their amusement.

Maribel composed herself, laying her hand on his shoulder. "I'm sorry. I'm not trying to be insulting. It's just so ... funny to think ... of you ..." She composed herself, sitting up straight, her face sobering. "Seriously now, I love you. You're the most incredible man I've ever known, and I know what you're trying to say. It's easy for women to make a man their god. Don't forget I lived a bit of that, and it did not end well."

She slid her hand down his shirt sleeve to claim his hand. "I promise you will never be my God, but you'll always be my best friend." She leaned in, her lips familiarly close to his ear.

Shayne didn't have to hear what Maribel whispered in his ear to guess the content of the message. The flame sparking in his blue eyes as he looked at the woman beside him said it all.

Shayne blushed, suddenly much too warm in the confines of the small booth. She leaned toward the window where chilly air filled the space close to the frosty windowpanes. But it was the idea of a safe place for her heart to heal—that maybe healing could be possible—that captivated her. Nick was a safe place, but there was no healing. Even if it had been unintentional, had she sought the wrong savior?

She watched out the window as the same white Ford she'd passed on the way in pulled into park behind her SUV. A tall, lean man in Levi's and a burnt orange sweatshirt got out. A navy-blue toboggan fit snug against his head, accentuating a face covered in stubble he hadn't bothered to shave this morning. There was something familiar about him. She stared as he walked alongside her vehicle, pausing as though he might reach for the door handle. She stiffened. He shifted, turning to face the cafe as though he were looking for her and knew exactly where she'd be.

Shayne shivered.

Glancing both ways, he stepped up to the sidewalk on the opposite side of the street. He held the door to the Buffalo Nickle Dime Store open for a young mother with a toddler in tow, winking as he said something that made the woman smile.

Recognition hit her. She'd never actually met him, but a girl never forgets a face that attractive. He worked for the Tackmores the summer she'd left.

CHAPTER EIGHTEEN

Shayne checked her watch. Lunchtime, but the cafe remained fairly empty. That wasn't what made her consider the time, though. It was the urge to return to the farm that prompted her. Unfortunately, it wasn't out of concern for Levi, and that was a problem.

In the pleasant fellowship that flowed around her in the comforting warmth of the cafe, her dormant roots experienced new growth.

Maribel turned to Shayne. "I hope you're planning to stay for a while. It's difficult being the outsider, not to mention just about the youngest person at any gathering around."

"Hey!" Cindy gave Maribel an offended look. "Don't let this tired old body fool you. I'm as young at heart as any of you hooligans." She sighed and heaved herself back to her feet, picking up the cooling pot of coffee.

"Maybe that's why Sheriff Griger looks like a deer caught in the headlights every time he sees you. I think you scare him," Conner said. He threw in a teasing wink for emphasis.

Cindy slapped at him in mock offense. "I don't have a clue what you're talking about. That old goat is determined to kill himself. I'm only trying to watch out for him. It's my civic duty to be concerned about our law enforcement officials."

"Uh huh. Do me a favor, then. If I ever become a law enforcement official, could you be a little less ... *concerned about your civic duty*?"

Cindy latched her hand onto a hip cocked obstinately to the side. "You better watch yourself, young man. You're not too big for me to tan your backside."

Which they all knew wasn't true, but he clearly had the waitress flustered.

"Back to you, Shayne. How long are you staying?" Maribel steered the conversation onto safer ground.

"It's not a good time for an extended stay," Shayne said. Ethan's face frowned into her mind. Staying would require keeping more secrets, and she already had a suitcase full of them.

"I understand. It's hard to get away when you have responsibilities."

Responsibilities? With her hands clasped beneath the table, Shayne twisted the silver ring around her finger. A job, yes, but she was pretty sure it was a gratuitous offering, a way to sort of work her into Nick's family's business. So far, all they'd done was shuffle what amounted to busy work in her direction. It was possible she was more needed here right now with Levi and Ethan at the house than she ever was in Austin. "It's not that so much. I mean, my responsibilities don't require my constant presence. I just ..."

Just what, Shayne? She spun the ring faster. The awakening roots seemed to dig in ever deeper.

"Ya know, I think I may have me a first-class idea." Conner leaned back, draping his arm over the seat behind Maribel, a pensive expression sitting unnaturally on his features. The twinkle dancing in his eyes belied the seriousness he feigned.

Three curious faces, eyebrows raised, all looked his way. "Shayne, did you know Cindy's niece has qualified for the state cross country meet?"

All heads swiveled Shayne's direction.

Conner continued, "Yes, I do feel I'm onto something here. If your responsibilities really don't require your constant presence, I think you might be able to help us out. Cindy, you may not realize it, but you are looking at the Turnaround High record holder for cross country."

"I believe her grandpa might have mentioned it once or twice." Cindy's eyes sparked with delight.

"That was years ago." Shayne shook her head.

Conner ignored her. "Of course, we may have another contender ready to challenge that record. Sad thing, though. Tragic really. Coach Klein went and got pregnant with twins and had to go on bed rest last Wednesday." He turned to Cindy. "When's the state meet?"

"Two weeks from yesterday, but that's just if I can keep the girl focused. Coach Klein was working her so hard she was too tired for shenanigans, but without the coach pushing her, she's lost some of that commitment."

"What do you say, Shayne? Can you spare us two weeks to help keep a girl out of trouble? You might even help her win the state championship and uphold the school's honor." His right eyebrow peaked in challenge. "Of course, if you're worried about losing your place in the high school's Athletic Hall of Fame, we'd understand."

Shayne pressed her rigid body against the vinyl covered seat. It was underhanded of Conner to play the pride card against her from both sides. They were asking her to help someone else win the championship she might have had ten years ago. The one she might have won if she hadn't left. She wished she could tell them how little that recognition would mean to a girl like Kindley in the grand scheme of a cruel world.

But her shift in posture wasn't from wanting to hold on to her place among the athletic elite of Turnaround. It was the crushing desire to help that made every fiber in her body tingle. A sense of purpose burned a hole in her heart.

For such a time as this. But did she really have anything to offer this girl?

And the housing situation was still a problem.

Cindy gave Shayne a wink. "The Lord provides."

Everyone was staring at her as though her thoughts were scrolling across a banner on her forehead. That she couldn't force a flat refusal from her lips surprised and excited her. "Possibly. I'll consider it."

"Well," Cindy gave the table a solid pat, "the chili is nice and warm today. Lunch is on me."

The waitress walked away with a renewed bounce in her step as the spicy aroma of chili filled the cafe.

"So Cindy and Sheriff Griger, huh?" Shayne moved to provide another topic for the conversation. She'd had a larger share than she wanted already, and now she had even more to contemplate.

"Yeah, I just don't think he knows it yet," Conner said. He chuckled and took a drink of iced tea.

Must be a common problem. Like, if all she wanted was to clear her head, then how was it possible Ethan appeared to be taking up residence in all her thoughts? Or better yet, if she really loved Nick, then what was Ethan doing in her thoughts at all?

Shayne traced a finger around the rim of the coffee cup. Perhaps God really did have his hands on the details. The question was, did she want them there?

CHAPTER NINETEEN

Ethan welcomed any activity that took his mind off the tall blonde who had wrecked his truck and his sleep last night. He wasn't here to make friends. Especially not those kinds of friends. The ones that mattered but left you trying to hold on to thin air.

When his old buddy had talked him into this little recon mission, Ethan half suspected Reuben was only doing it to keep Ethan busy and out of the downward spiral he headed toward. He still hadn't ruled that out.

If that was Reuben's angle, as underhanded as it felt, he'd done well in inserting Shayne into his life. Ethan McGregor was officially distracted.

But if he trusted that Reu wasn't setting him up for some kind of intervention or twisted practical joke, perhaps there was more to this.

After what he'd heard from Levi, as much as he wanted to doubt the loser, maybe there was some serious business going on. It coincided too closely with the reason why he was here.

Ethan's nerves fired super-charged energy through his

body the more he thought about it. His limbs hummed with an eager anticipation.

After he'd retired from the Special Forces, Reuben had joined up with a group that tracked down human traffickers and took them off the street. He'd tried to talk Ethan into doing the same.

At the time, Ethan had been making a last-ditch effort to save his marriage. That had been his excuse, but if he were honest, he just didn't know if he could handle the work. The ghosts from his past had to be held on a tight rein. Any involvement with something like that might hit too close to home.

So here he was, stalking over soggy ground and strips of ice still lingering in shadowy places untouched as yet by the sun. The juniper scented air was crisp, filled with a pungent woodsy scent that soothed his raw soul. Ethan inhaled, filling his lungs. He had no complaints about his current circumstances. What he had were doubts about trusting himself.

Yeah, if he were honest, he didn't trust himself. He didn't want to ask anybody else to trust him, either.

Reuben had told him they were looking for a location where a plane might land and take off without drawing much attention. Considering this was ranch land, and the type of planes they were watching could land in any smooth, clear field, they hadn't been able to pinpoint anything on satellite maps. Still, their computer surveillance convinced them there was something in the area. What they needed to find was a hangar or fuel storage tank—anything that might indicate aircraft activity—and go from there.

Even though this had the potential to be a lead in their search, Ethan hadn't called Reu with the new information yet. He'd check it out before he made a fool of himself like some gullible rookie fresh off the recruiting bus.

Shayne's involvement complicated things. Trying to

persuade her to buy into the probability that Levi's story was a pure fabrication took effort. He was pretty sure she was leaning toward seeing things that way herself. And he didn't quite believe her the type to play amateur detective, but her behavior left enough doubt to cause him concern for her safety if she got the notion to investigate on her own.

Finding an acceptable way to keep Shayne quiet required some creative thinking, and he wasn't sure it was needed. But if Reuben's team was on to something, they didn't need any attention until the details were all in place. If she went to the sheriff, or if she started talking to a friend in town, the entire operation might fall apart. All it would take was the wrong person to get wind that someone was poking around. Ethan didn't want to let his friend down, even if it meant finessing Shayne in the wrong direction.

He'd taken his time separating her SUV from his truck, trying to come up with a solution. In the end, he'd had to watch her drive away with only the hope she wouldn't talk. He'd been both annoyed and relieved that her suitcase hadn't gone with her.

She'd be back. He just hoped she didn't bring the sheriff with her. His biggest encouragement was that she seemed determined to keep Levi hidden and protected, and she certainly wasn't the type to want anyone to know she'd spent the night with a stranger—no matter how innocent it had been, unfortunately for Ethan.

With her out of the house, he'd had Levi to himself. He'd used his skills of persuasion to extract a few more details, sufficient to give him a focus for this wild goose chase. Levi didn't trust him, but that feeling was mutual. Ethan got enough out of him to know there was a hangar and where to look for it.

What he couldn't fathom, though, was Shayne's reaction

to the guy. She obviously didn't want to be around him, and yet she was willing to protect him.

That she would offer such devotion to someone like Levi irritated the perdition out of Ethan. And that took a lot of irritating.

He stopped his hike, hands on his hips. How much of this was he doing for her? And even more concerning, why?

Because brown eyes that held the promise of spring stirred something in him. The seed of a strange hope he'd buried long ago began to germinate. If it were true that something good and pure still existed in the world—someone good and pure—wasn't it natural for him to want to protect it? Wasn't he wired for just that very thing? Wasn't that what had him out in the cold, hiking through the brush in response to the questionable story of a total stranger? All because there might be a girl in danger.

It had encouraged him to find Levi's truck exactly where he'd said it would be. People under the influence rarely ever remembered where they left their vehicles. That was one he could attest to from personal, although not recent, experience. When his path in life had taken him into the realm of knowing exactly when another human took their last breath before a twitch of his finger took their next, he found inebriation to be a childish and selfish pursuit. He also knew that once he started dulling his memories, there'd be no stopping.

He swallowed, pushing the bitterness down and forcing the steps of his thoughts from the dark path they gravitated to.

The satellite images he'd pulled after getting details from Levi confirmed Levi's story so far and gave him a pretty clear picture of what he would find and where to find it. The images showed nothing other than horse barns, pens, and exercise arenas. From casual observation, there was no hangar. But Ethan knew just how deceiving looks could be.

A preponderance of caution made him hide his truck a distance away, but he didn't mind the hike. A tromp through the woods was cleansing to his soul.

The sky looked almost close enough to touch. A fresh blue expanse washed clean by last night's storm and purified by the arctic air. A stiff wind remained, but the thick cedar trees he passed through provided a break. Sweat dampened his t-shirt beneath the insulated camouflage coveralls he wore.

He reached the top of the last ridge and paused, then adjusted his course by angling to the right. Less than fifty yards later, he stared down at an open field. Most likely used as a hay field in the summer, its uniform surface was cut short, making it look like a carpet of pale yellow covering the valley floor. The moisture from last night gave it the color of thick, rich cream, with patches of ice still milky white scattered throughout. On the far side, nestled against an oak covered rise, stood a barn. He pulled out a pair of binoculars and studied the building.

A small stone building stood near the barn, matching the old smokehouse Levi had described.

The set of sliding doors on the long side of the barn drew his interest. He counted the ridges in the sheet metal walls and estimated the length of the building to be one hundred feet. The two twenty-foot sliding doors situated in the center would create a forty-foot opening. Ethan pulled out his cell phone and searched for wingspans. Reuben had said it was a Cessna 172 they were surveilling. His online search confirmed that the thirty-six-foot wingspan of this plane would fit through the opening these doors would create.

He directed his observations to the field where the barn stood. It might be a tight run for an aircraft, and he was no pilot, but he'd white knuckled it through takeoffs and landings that required less. He snapped a few pictures to send to Reuben, then dropped his phone back into his pocket.

Ethan stood, shutting off his thoughts while his instinct analyzed his environment. Stop, look, listen, smell ... like learning to ride a bicycle, SLLS—or sills—lessons learned in the Corps were permanent.

The tingling in his gut all but shot sparks from his fingertips.

A gravel road led up from the far side into trees where he made out the roofs of more barns. Levi had said that was where the main house was as well.

Crossing the open field wasn't an option. He looked at his watch. There were still a few hours of daylight left, but it would take him most of that to hike back to his truck.

But what if ...

The possibility someone might be in danger gave him no choice.

Two hundred yards below him to the left ran the river Levi must have used for his alleged escape. From there, it would be three hundred yards back to the barn on the opposite side of the field. The tree line would keep him hidden for most of the distance. Would it be sufficient to get him close enough without being seen?

He tucked the binoculars in his pack. Only one way to find out.

With his deer rifle slung over his shoulder, he could pass for a lost hunter. It would be a thin and risky cover. Levi's uninvited visit yesterday would have them on edge.

If the storm hadn't obliterated all signs, he might have found proof of Levi's run. He was no tracker, but he knew enough to spot whether a bleeding man had torn through the scrub running as though his life depended upon it.

A half hour later, he'd made it to the last of the tree cover. He'd have to move up the hill to stay hidden from the barn below, but that would expose him to whatever—or whoever—was up top.

Tall stalks of dead weeds occupied the pens near the building that was his focus, leaving the impression they hadn't been used for quite some time.

The smokehouse stood near the barn. From this angle, Ethan couldn't observe the exact distance between the two, but it was certainly close enough for the jump Levi claimed to have made. The broken window above it, now covered in a sheet of plywood, supported Levi's tale.

Moving slowly to avoid drawing attention, he eased himself to the ground. It had been over an hour since he'd first seen the barn and so far there had been no sign of movement. He gave himself another quarter hour, then rising, he headed into the open and jogged into the late day shadows stretching alongside the small stone house. It wasn't much more than a two-room hut, built of the red stone readily available all around. The acrid scent of wood smoke still seeped from the porous stone.

He eased his way around the front of the small building, noting the solid steel door covering the opening. It was out of place against the old stone walls.

A streak of dark red ran along the inner edge of the door-frame, away from where the weather might have washed it away. Levi's blood?

A partial imprint of a boot pressed into the soft earth, smearing mud near the base of the doorframe. He knelt to examine it. Levi had been wearing tennis shoes last night.

His skin prickled.

Ethan tested the lock on the door and found it secure. He hesitated, debating what might prompt the locking of a rundown old smokehouse. His objective was the bigger barn, however. That was where Levi claimed he'd seen the woman.

If there was still time after he'd done that, he'd come back here.

Stop, look, listen, smell ... he repeated the life-preserving technique before moving on. Covering the short distance of exposed ground, he paused again. The door leading into the barn from this end was locked. He wasn't surprised, although it did raise a few caution flags. In a place where people often didn't lock their doors at night, why were these all locked?

Perhaps to prevent people like Levi from breaking in and helping themselves.

The door Levi said he'd used was around the broad side facing uphill.

Ethan slid along the wall of the building, well aware his forest camo coveralls did not blend in with the dark brown metal side of the structure.

He grasped the metal knob and gave it a tentative twist. Locked. The discovery upped his curiosity and his vigilance. He pulled a lock pick set from his pocket and employed a skill he didn't advertise. Lock picking was more art than science, and his art paid off in a matter of seconds. The door grated across the cement floor as he slipped inside. He slid sideways in the black interior with his back to the wall, close enough he could sense its presence without actually touching it, once again observing with all of his senses.

Nothing but quiet, and the absence of the smells he expected. No horse manure, alfalfa hay, or leather tack lingered in this place. Instead, the air hinted at grease and aviation fuel. It was worth noting too that the air lacked the staleness of an unused building.

After a few minutes of silence, he pulled the small flashlight from his pack and began his exploration.

In front of him were two pallets stacked high with cardboard boxes. To his right, a couple of horse stalls now being used as storage areas for fencing supplies. To his left stood the wooden staircase leading to the loft where Levi said he'd found the girl.

He moved first to the storage areas, clearing each before moving to the next. He ran his light around each of the walls, then made his way to the staircase, slipping up the wooden planks with steps as soft as a sixteen-year-old sneaking in after curfew.

His light hit the large sheet of plywood nailed over the window Levi jumped through. So far, he'd found everything exactly as Levi said he would.

He flicked the beam into the rafter corners, checking for cameras or surveillance equipment. When he found none, Ethan moved to the door Levi indicated, aware of every creak beneath his feet. He was mildly surprised to find this door unlocked. He opened it with added caution, sliding in without the benefit of his flashlight. His eyes adjusted, and he found himself in what appeared to be a crash pad for pilots.

The space was unoccupied and sparsely furnished. That didn't mean it hadn't been empty last night. His small light only took in a few details at a time. He wouldn't risk turning on the overhead bulb, so he took his time moving along each wall. The rough unfinished wood used for the walls scratched against the thick material of his clothing. He froze. Stop, look, listen, smell. Nothing.

There was nothing particularly troublesome about the room. He was about to dismiss Levi's story when it hit him. The smell in this room was wrong. Too freshly cleaned, but that wasn't what drew his attention.

He sniffed, then aimed the light at the headboard and bent closer. Fresh paint.

The door below him scraped across the cement. Ethan clicked off the flashlight as the grating click of footsteps crossing the floor followed. Analyzing his options, with only one way in and out of this room, he knew they were few. He could rush out and take whoever it was by surprise.

Or he could wait and see what happened. He chose the latter.

Moving to the wall behind the door, he pressed himself into the corner. The footsteps had reached the staircase, the sound changing from the scratch of footfalls on concrete to the dull thump of feet striking the wooden steps.

A second swoosh came as the door below opened once again. The footsteps on the stairs halted.

"Oh, hey, boss. Didn't know you were here. Just checking to make sure everything is alright." A man's voice, one that held a note of deference—obligatory deference unless Ethan's ears deceived him—reverberated from the space below, telling Ethan this was the person who'd entered second.

"Is there any reason why it should not be?" The cool tones of the voice from the man on the stairs set Ethan's nerves on edge, his intuition sharpening his focus.

"Nope. Just checking to see there weren't no busted pipes after the freeze. But if everything looks good, I'll just be going."

"Well, Mr. Cleese, since you mentioned it, I did find the door unlocked again."

"Is that so?"

"It is. And it makes me curious to know how it is you knew you could come in."

Ethan heard a command, not a question, in the man's statement.

A chuckle rose from the guy farthest away. "Can't say as I even gave it nary a thought. Just turned the knob and came in."

"I see. Well, thank you for your attention to the care of these facilities. I'll be certain to let you know if I find anything amiss."

"Yes, sir. Evening to you."

The door clanked closed. After what seemed an unusually long pause, the footsteps resumed, sounding heavier than they had before. At the top of the stairs, they paused. Ethan held his breath. He'd unslung his rifle and held it tight against his chest, his trigger finger resting straight along the trigger guard. He'd use it as a club before having to shoot if he could.

Keys jingled softly, followed by the almost imperceptible sound of metal sliding into a lock, the sound so faint Ethan was certain it didn't come from the door he hid behind.

The door across the hall opened and then clicked shut. Ethan allowed himself an extended exhale.

He waited, listening. He'd noted the large plate-glass window facing over the space below from the other room. His departure would need a bit of tact if he wanted to remain unseen.

He could try to wait out whoever this was, but that held the possibility the man might eventually venture into the room where Ethan now hid. He had confidence in his ability to defend himself, but it would serve his purpose better to go unnoticed.

Easing the door open, he hesitated, sensing. A muffled conversation drifted from behind the closed door. He held his breath and listened, but the voice was too faint for him to understand what was being said. Plus, he was pretty sure the words were in Spanish.

His steps were as light as a two-hundred-and-fifty-pound man could make them as he moved to the edge of the stair-case, placing his feet at the far edges where they were least likely to creak and give away his presence. Descending as far as the window allowed him before giving his presence away, he crouched and lowered himself over the edge. He hung there, listening, then dropped to the concrete below, landing as stealthily as a cat.

There was only one practical way out—through the same door he'd entered. To get out the door would leave him exposed, but skirting the wall to get there would keep his presence hidden until then. If he was quiet, and his luck held, the man upstairs would never notice. With deliberation, he worked his way to the door, inched it open and let himself out, closing it as quietly as possible.

He ducked around the stone building and waited. The light of day was slipping away, both a good and a not-so-good thing without his night vision goggles.

He let the sun drift down past the horizon, then ran for the tree line.

As much as he would love to stay and see how things played out, he couldn't risk letting Reuben down by exposing the fact someone was watching.

Had he found enough to confirm any suspicions? Objectively, the best answer he could give was, maybe.

But instinctively, he knew the answer was yes.

CHAPTER TWENTY

Wandering the familiar streets of Turnaround had been like fitting a piece of a puzzle into a picture she'd forgotten how much she adored. A lingering sense of need to be a part of that puzzle, with a place and a purpose, stirred an unexplainable contentment. The picture wasn't complete without her in it. Like a giant jigsaw, life had shaped her into a part of the grander story with a specific place and purpose.

Right now, that place and purpose just might be helping Kindley avoid the danger she couldn't yet see.

Given a reason to stay, Shayne found she couldn't say no.

While discussing the possibility of helping Kindley prepare for her race, the opportunity for Shayne to spend some time in the classroom presented itself. Seems the cross-country coach doubled as the English teacher. Perhaps it was the other way around, but it didn't really matter to Shayne.

Her phone call with her mother had confirmed what she feared. Ethan's lease was legitimate. Thankfully, her mom had been on her way out the door to an appointment, and the conversation had been too brief for her to discover Shayne had already met Ethan, much less the circumstances of that meeting.

She still needed to call Nick, but hadn't yet. She needed to make her own decisions before she did.

Thoughts of Maribel's baptism niggled at her. Shayne had been thirteen when she'd given her life to God. But at thirteen, what had she really known about giving her life to anything? What she hadn't grasped at the innocent age of thirteen was the reality that giving one's life to God didn't exclude one from the horrors of a broken world and the pain it caused.

Was she mad at God? She didn't think so. To believe He was God meant to accept His sovereignty over all—the good and the bad.

Like nearly being shot to death yesterday.

She might not be mad at God, but that didn't mean she fully trusted Him, either. She'd used the walls she'd built around her heart to exclude Him along with everyone else. Superficial. That was the extent of all her relationships now, including the one with her Creator.

Perhaps that was the first thing that needed to change.

Because He'd certainly been whispering in her ear a lot lately. Or as Mack would say, showing her He had his hands on the details.

She parked in front of the house and stared. Staying wasn't something she should even consider. Unfortunately, packing her bags and driving back to a life she was unsure she wanted had no appeal. The life Nick had planned for them was a life she didn't really want. What if Nick was a husband she didn't really want, either?

Retrieving a bag containing cheeseburgers, French fries, onion rings, and crunchy tacos from the passenger seat, she headed in. The bag filled with food from the local Dairy

Queen wasn't a peace offering, but perhaps a statement of a willing truce.

And she couldn't just let him starve.

Levi stirred in the dark as she set the bag on the end table nearest the couch. Grandma Hazel didn't allow eating a meal anywhere but the kitchen table, but she also wouldn't have considered burgers from a fast-food establishment a meal. Shayne hoped to get by on the loophole this one time.

Grandma Hazel also wouldn't consider this a suitable meal for the sick, but Levi should be grateful she'd bothered at all.

"Sorry. Didn't mean to scare you. The lights are killing my head," Levi said. He picked up the bag and began exploring its contents. "Tacos still your favorite?"

Shayne shrugged.

"I'll take the cheeseburger then," Levi said.

It would have been easy to slip back into the past. Levi eating the cheeseburger and fries while Shayne ate the tacos and onion rings. And talking of all the things that no longer seemed to matter.

"I still think you should see the doctor." She looked around, a tendril of hope curling inside, only to be snuffed out by an unexpected nudge of disappointment. "Where's Ethan?"

"He's on a mission to prove I'm a liar. But don't worry, I drew him a map." One corner of his mouth lifted in a half smile. "He was appreciative enough he threatened to kill me if I didn't lie low and stay out of sight, so here I sit."

"What?" Shayne asked, not sure she wanted a deeper explanation, but even more afraid of not knowing.

"Hey, I didn't argue. Besides the point I have nowhere to go and no way to get there, he strikes me as someone with skills." He raised an eyebrow as he faced her. "If you know what I mean."

Shayne was afraid she did. She'd had the same thought. "I meant, what mission?"

"He decided to check out my story before kicking me out."

"I thought he didn't believe you. What made him decide to check it out?"

She'd learned the Tackmore ranch had sold to a corporation that used the place for an investment in cutting horses, or more likely, a tax write-off. A man named Bryce managed it. He kept to himself and spent a lot of time on the road traveling to horse shows around the country.

Levi shrugged. "I don't really want to know what goes on inside that angry head of his."

"Is it safe for him to go back there?"

"Safer for me." Levi leaned back and closed his eyes.

Yes, Levi, it's always about you. Her thoughts didn't linger long on Levi, moving instead to speculation on what Ethan was doing. The man who'd told her Levi's story was all a lie hadn't seemed inclined to actually explore the possibility it wasn't.

"How're you feeling?" Shayne changed the subject.

"Like I've been beat with a tire iron, but I'll live. Listen, Shayne, I'm sorry for busting in here like this, for dragging you into whatever is going on. I really have no one else and nowhere to go. I promise you, if I did, I wouldn't be here."

"Not even Mom?"

The look he shot her answered her question. Their mother still held an unwavering faith in Levi's goodness. She just might be the last person on earth to do so. Even Shayne could understand why he wouldn't want to lose that.

Still, his apology left her unmoved. "There must be someone you can call."

"I don't have my phone and memorizing numbers hasn't really been a priority, so no, there isn't. Besides the fact he threatened me—and I'm not talking about your boyfriend, Rambo." He grunted as pain tightened the lines of his face. A foul word slipped from his lips. "You shouldn't stay here. You could be in danger if you do."

"He's not my boyfriend."

"Oh yeah, I figured that out when I made the mistake of telling him he wasn't in charge around here. Turns out he is. Thanks for the heads up that we're guests in our own house, by the way."

"If you're so worried, why don't you go to the sheriff?" Shayne was nonplussed by his concern for her safety and miffed that he thought she should be the one to leave.

"Because he said he would kill me—and her—" he cut accusing eyes at her, "and I believe him. Whatever he was doing, it is the worst kind of bad, and I doubt he wanted it interrupted.

Look, I wasn't thinking right this morning, but I am now. There was a woman chained up and a man I didn't get much of a look at, but who seemed intent on killing me." Levi clawed at the top of his head. "I wouldn't recognize him now if I met him on the street, so how in Hell's teeth does he know me?"

Shayne swallowed. Every man she met, every new face that passed her in line at the grocery store or stopped next to her at a red light or seated themselves by her at the doctor's office or glanced her way in a restaurant—every single one could be one of them. He'd get no sympathy from her. "And you still think he had a badge?"

"Yeah."

"Kind of convenient, don't you think?"

"What?"

"That the man in your story had a badge. You're using that to justify not going to the sheriff."

"You know what? Just think what you want. That's what you've been doing for the past ten years, anyway."

Shayne seated herself in a chair across the room, picking up the wedding ring quilt to trace the stitches with her finger. While in town with Conner and Maribel, everything seemed doable, almost like an easy, possibly even logical, thing to pull off. Here, everything seemed much less clear. "So then you go to the sheriff, and he gives you protection."

"Yeah, Sheriff Griger isn't exactly one of my biggest fans."

"But you could still trust him."

"Except what if the guy did have a badge?"

"Surely you don't think it was Sheriff Griger."

"No, I would definitely have recognized him. Even without seeing him, a guy can tell he's entered a room. But if it was one of his deputies, whose word is he going to take? I assure you, it won't be mine."

"And whose fault is that? Besides, I don't remember Sheriff Griger being the kind to tolerate crooked cops."

Levi stared at her. No anger, no request for pity, just the honesty of a man who understood how little justification he had to ask for anyone's help, much less trust. A fit of coughing gripped him, and she reached over to press her hand against his forehead.

"You're burning up. You need to see a doctor."

"I just need a drink of water. Would you?"

Shayne went to the kitchen, carrying the tacos with her. Her phone rang just as she reached for a glass. It was Nick, again.

She'd ignored his call twice already. Somehow, facing this conversation was still more pleasant than extending the one she was having with Levi. His coughing had subsided, so he'd live until she got back with the water and the medicine she'd bought for him.

With a lack of enthusiastic anticipation, she hit receive. "Hey."

"Hey? That's all I get. I've been worried out of my mind. You haven't answered my calls. All I can picture is you dead in some car crash along the way. Do you have any idea what you are putting me through here?" Nick's tone held enough annoyance and frustration she knew her news wouldn't go well. That he hadn't bothered to ask her if she was okay stabbed at her heart.

The sharp edge under his smooth words, like syrup on the blade of a knife, had a hardening effect on her resolve. One night away, and she didn't want to go back.

She always found his driven nature—a by-product of his passion for serving others—an admirable quality, but she'd never stood in opposition to it before. She wasn't sure she found it as admirable now.

The fact he didn't ask how she was doing chafed because after being shot while holding a dying man's hand, spending the night trapped in a house with a stranger, and having a borderline traumatic conversation with an estranged family member, she was not okay. Pinching the skin between her thumb and forefinger, she winced. She wouldn't fall apart now. She'd lived through worse betrayals, after all.

"I assume you're on your way back now. We need to go over some stuff to get ready for the interview. I know how nervous you are around people. I want to make sure you understand what's expected—what to say and what not to say." He forged ahead in the one-sided conversation.

How nervous she was around people? After the past twenty-four hours, all she could do was try not to break down in a fit of mad laughter.

"Most of the questions will be for me, but in case someone asks you something, you'll want to be prepared," Nick continued.

Guilt nudged her back to reality. Her decision to stay here suddenly felt like a willful attempt to sabotage Nick's plans for their future. Or were they more plans for his future, and she was just a necessary and acceptable accessory?

But she didn't want to go back to Nick, back to her life in the city. Not yet anyway.

This moment of freedom was about more than retrieving a family heirloom or riding out a storm until the roads were no longer dangerous.

"I'm not coming back yet. I found some things I need to take care of before I leave." She sounded bolder than she felt. "The following seconds were heavy with what she knew was disapproval. Nick Turner had plans, after all. The resentful tone in her own thoughts surprised her. When had her attitude shifted?

Perhaps while watching the end of a life that mattered as they lowered her friend into the earth.

Or while hiding in an open field with an unknown someone shooting at her.

Either way, she shouldn't have to defend herself to the man who claimed to love her.

But she didn't tell him. She held onto the truth she could have died yesterday, guarding it. It felt too big and sacred a thing—as though she'd stepped to the edge of something too deep to fathom and glimpsed something too mysterious and powerful to entrust in lesser hands. Hands that couldn't grasp the significance of what she was feeling right now. Hands that might not bother trying. For the first time she could remember, Shayne felt cheated by the very attribute in Nick that had first drawn her to him. His unbending pursuit of what he wanted.

It had been her hiding place.

The silence grew heavier by the minute. She bit her lip,

waiting on him to speak first, refusing to cave into the power struggle his silence signified.

Although it seemed a childish thing, she allowed herself a small, fleeting smile when she won.

"We had an agreement. I let you go because you promised to be back last night. A promise you've failed to keep." Nick's voice was a little tighter than before. He was giving her a moment, one chance to change the trajectory this conversation would take.

Usually a patient, gentle man, Nick could also be stubborn when it came to getting his way.

Had she promised that? She knew the meeting was important to him. But had they argued so long over her coming to the funeral she'd given in and promised what he claimed? She retraced their conversations from the preceding days, trying to find the words she'd said that might have led him to this conclusion.

They weren't there. At least, she didn't think they were. Her steadfast determination flagged, her breath becoming shallower as she contemplated the possibility.

"I ... I'm just really exhausted. If I stay here, I can really rest." The words tumbled out too fast as she repeated her decision, not because she thought he hadn't heard, but because she needed to keep saying it until she convinced herself she meant it.

She should tell him she'd been shot.

She closed her eyes.

Tell him and what? Cause him to worry? Or find out he didn't?

Instead, she said, "I just need a little time to say goodbye."

"I know how it is when you go back home. You think you're seventeen again and ..." he paused.

The urge to tell him being seventeen wasn't something

she wanted to experience ever again was strong. But now wasn't the time to hash out that potential revelation.

"Listen, you attended a funeral. Funerals make people sad. I get it. What you're experiencing is natural. But you don't need to act on it. You don't belong in that place anymore. Come on home. You'll feel right when you're back with me."

She stared out the kitchen window, taking in the fields that stretched all the way to the river beyond.

Home. Maybe she was.

Or maybe she was being sentimental in a world where sentimental was foolishness.

There is more than one way to bury a person.

She needed to do this. Like trying on a pair of old jeans to prove to yourself they no longer fit, she had to try. If she didn't, she'd never know whether the girl she had been might have survived given the chance.

"Shay, are you there? Are you hearing me?"

Weariness pushed down on her shoulders in a heavy mantle.

"I'm tired, Nick. Too tired to make the drive home just yet." The fire that had raged in her earlier had nothing left to devour. Snuffed out, it left nothing but a parched soul. Too brittle to bend, too desiccated to care. She'd gone so long refusing to fight, it took little to drain her when she tried.

"I don't think you understand how important this meeting is for me. Everything I do is for our future, so I can take care of you. I'm working hard here. Most women would be thrilled to be marrying someone who was trying this hard to make them happy."

That's just it—I'm not happy. She hadn't known it until she got here. But she was forced to admit it now, even if only to herself.

Por favor, promise me ... Glad you made it back ... Are you going to help me, Shayne? Maybe you can help ... Scattered words and snatches of phrases ricocheted in her head.

"I know. It's just ... I really won't be much help if I'm exhausted. And I ... I just want to say goodbye." Her gaze traced the erratic path of a bright red cardinal, flitting from branch to branch in the leafless tree outside the window. Maybe this was the effect of exhaustion and fear and trauma and grief all mingled together. Maybe she would awake tomorrow with the overwhelming desire to run to Nick and put everything about this place—about the person she had been—behind her. She almost hoped it would be so.

Almost.

"Then say it. Good ... bye. See there. It only takes two seconds."

"That's not what I mean."

"No, you mean some dilapidated old house and a piece of dirt are more important to you than the man who is trying to build a better life for you."

"I'm sorry. That's not what I'm—"

"As your fiancé, I'm telling you to come home. I need you here where you belong. Honestly, I don't really know how you expect me to feel right now. You never even mention the old place. It can't be too important to you."

Shayne pressed her lips together to keep from reminding him he wasn't her fiancé until she said yes.

And as for this place, she loved it and always had. He just never wanted to hear.

A heavy sigh reached through the phone and pinched her throat with his displeasure. "Look, I don't have time for a pointless conversation right now. I have to get ready for this meeting. One of us has to be the adult and plan for our future. Don't say I didn't warn you when people question where your priorities are. Seriously, Shay, could you have picked a worse time for this little episode?"

She bit down on both lips, pressing them firmly between her teeth so no disagreeable words could slip out. If he couldn't be compassionate about the little things, what would he be like with the big ones? This was the farthest distance they'd been apart since their relationship became serious. And the biggest trial they'd faced.

The space was either clouding her perspective or clearing it. Nick was a good man with a bright future, right?

"I'm sorry. You're right. I'm just being overly emotional. It's just so much going on and ..."

He sighed again, a softer, more tolerant sound. "I know you love me. We can talk about it later. Right now, I gotta go." He clicked off without waiting for her goodbye, proving that it really didn't take any longer than two seconds to execute a goodbye.

Yes, she needed time to say goodbye, but who or what was she really saying goodbye to?

She turned to drop the phone in her purse and found Levi leaning against the doorframe.

"He seems nice," Levi said, his words as dry as Sahara desert.

"Were you listening? You have no right."

"The kitchen is free territory. Not my fault I was forced to hear that pathetic display of relationship dysfunction."

Shayne brushed past him and headed up the stairs.

"Turn the heater on in the bathroom when you stomp by. I need a shower after having to listen to all that bootlicking."

CHAPTER TWENTY-ONE

Too early to get up, Shayne stared at the ceiling, knowing sleep was over. She pulled the Bible from her nightstand, clicked on the light, then opened to the Book of Esther.

In her opinion, the story of Esther had been shamefully glossed over and romanticized by modern retellings. The only redeeming aspect of the story was Esther's strength of character, evidenced by her courage and willingness to sacrifice. It was something Shayne admired but didn't possess. Or did she?

For we have been sold, my people and I ... Esther was referring to the Jewish people when she made this statement to the king, but the words still resonated in Shayne's soul. They touched a tender nerve deep inside—*sold.*

Maybe no money had changed hands that night, but the sense of betrayal, as though her value amounted to nothing more than someone else's good time, left her with a crushed spirit and a ragged wound in her heart.

For if you remain silent at this time, relief and deliverance will arise ... but you and your father's house will perish. Esther's circumstances positioned her to save an entire nation of people. But only because she had the courage to act.

She understood something Shayne was only now grasping. Peg's words played through her mind. *We all live as part of a larger story. The question is, will it be about us or about something bigger?*

Climbing from the warmth beneath the thick covers, Shayne padded softly to the window. The cold hardwood floor creaked beneath her sock-clad feet, despite her attempt to avoid anything that might wake the sleeping bear below her.

Was she responsible for saving her brother despite the hurt he'd caused her? No, God alone could make that happen.

But God used Esther to save her family and her people. He'd allowed great tragedy to position her exactly where she needed to be in order to play a role in the rescue mission of her people. His hands had, indeed, been on the details even if His name was conspicuously absent from the story.

Wasn't the soul of a single person as precious to God as an entire nation? If Levi's story was true, then there were two lives that needed saving—his and that of the unknown girl he'd seen.

And what of her own?

Flicking back the edge of the curtain, Shayne studied the dark beyond. The waning moon cast a thin, shadowy light over the world outside.

The lonely desolation of the scene below sent her back to the sanctuary of her bed. This place was slipping through her fingers, the same as so many other things had. And there was no one to blame but herself.

She tugged the quilt over her shoulders, letting its weight press down against her.

Was it her fault? Like she believed her parent's divorce was somehow to be blamed on her as well. A small flicker of truth marched through her middle, demanding she follow. Even if she wasn't responsible for what had happened, she'd been responsible for what she'd let it do to her life.

Choices and consequences. She'd paid a high price for hers.

Levi. Why did he have to be here now?

Perhaps the question she needed to answer was why was she here when he needed help?

Resentment she hadn't expected soured her mood. But with it came awareness.

When she'd run, why had no one run after her?

This bitter root had been thriving in her heart for years, but she'd refused to name it until now.

When the sun finally cast its glow on Sunday morning, it found Shayne already dressed and ready. She slipped out of the house unnoticed and headed to church. She'd have some digging to do if she wanted to *"unbury"* herself. Now was a good day to start.

———

"What happened? Are you all right?" Maribel asked, her wide-eyed concern confirming for Shayne she'd done a poor job of hiding the dark circles beneath her eyes and the traces of emotions stealing her sleep.

"Is your arm bothering you? Should you have it checked again?" Maribel continued questioning without giving Shayne a chance to answer, her eyes narrowed in scrutiny.

"It's a little sore, but I'm okay." She had no problem blaming her unpolished appearance on the physical injury instead of the emotional storm destroying her from within. "And I had forgotten how much noise the old house makes at night."

All that was true. Her arm did ache, and her sleep these past nights had been troubled, to say the least.

It had been late in the night when the squeak of the front door announced Ethan's return. A part of her had wanted to rush down and demand to know what he'd found. She hadn't. Perhaps because the weaker part of her feared knowing.

He'd left again this morning before she'd finished dressing. *Where had he needed to go so early in the morning?* The unanswered question pulled the knot in her stomach even tighter.

"I hope you helping Kindley and taking over Coach Klein's class tomorrow isn't too soon. We should have made them wait another day or two," Maribel said, her frown in danger of becoming permanent if she held it much longer.

"Focusing on something besides my arm will probably help my recovery more than you know." Shayne leaned back on the wooden pew, inhaling the scent of furniture polish mingling with decades of Aqua Net hairspray and horse liniment—the local preferred remedy for everything from sore muscles to a toothache. Only arthritis avoided the liniment treatment. For that, they went straight to WD-40.

Dust particles floated on the sun's rays as it shone through the stained-glass windows. There was something enduringly unchanging about the atmosphere inside this old church. The painful ache in her shoulders loosened as the distance between her present and her past narrowed.

"Say a prayer for Conner. This is his first time filling in on a Sunday morning, and he's nervous. I saw him actually drinking a cup of coffee earlier." Maribel rolled her eyes. "If I had a nickel for every time he lectured me on my coffee drinking … bless his heart."

"I won't lie. Seeing the change in him was quite the surprise," Shayne said. She grinned at the unexpectedness and irony of Conner's current position.

Maribel laughed. "I hear that a lot. I'm kind of glad I

didn't know him back then." The love in her smile lit her face like the sunlight coming through the colored panes lining the sanctuary. "I'm really glad you're staying, even though it's only for a couple of weeks."

The sincerity in her voice wrapped Shayne in something hopeful.

And filled her with apprehension at the same time. Maybe she should start wearing a sign that said *'I'm not who you think I am.'* Her eyes traveled to the carpet beneath her feet. She wasn't even who *she* thought she was.

She'd been dishonest in wearing an engagement ring when she hadn't actually said yes. That was as good as lying to Nick when she should have been firmer with her request for time to think. But then, why should she have needed time? They'd been together for three years. Did she really think they could go on forever as platonic friends—each other's forever plus one? No, she'd really thought she wished to be his wife—that saying yes would be an easy thing. Until he asked and the word wouldn't come.

She'd been dishonest with the ring on and dishonest when she took it off. Her life was one big lie. It had been a lie for so long, maybe even she didn't know the truth anymore. She was going to need a really big shovel to dig herself out of the hole in which she'd buried herself.

Conner stepped into the pulpit. He fidgeted with his notes, tugged at his shirt sleeves, then cleared his throat. He'd turned his life around.

Levi hadn't turned his around but had set it on the fast track to destruction. And hers had simply stopped.

That didn't mean things couldn't change, though.

When Conner announced his message would be from John 11, Shayne understood why she was here.

And he who had died came out bound hand and foot with grave-

clothes ... then many of the Jews who had come to Mary, and had seen the things Jesus did, believed in Him.

A spontaneous and unhindered stream of tears flowed down Shayne's cheeks. Without taking her eyes off Conner, Maribel pressed a tissue into Shayne's hand.

Shayne's heart thrummed. It'd taken the events of the past two days for her to recognize the truth, but she was the one being called out of the grave now. This was why she was here. She wanted to be free. She wanted to live again. Now the question was, *how?*

Tangled in her thoughts, she didn't notice when the service ended. People were up moving about, saying goodbye before Shayne realized she was the only one still seated.

Maribel placed a hand on her arm. "You okay?"

Shayne nodded, appreciating that the look in Maribel's eyes said words weren't needed.

"I'm so glad you're here." She patted Shayne on the knee and smiled conspiratorially, then pulled a folder from her backpack and handed it to Shayne. "And I'm even more happy you're the one who will be reading those, and not me. Conner and I stopped by to tell Coach Klein the good news, and she asked if you'd mind grading these poems the kids wrote. She thought it might help you get to know the kids better."

Shayne slid the folder into the sleek black tote she carried, the one that proclaimed power and control in stark contrast to the emotional and slightly disheveled mess who carried it now.

Hitching her backpack onto her shoulder as she stood, Maribel sobered, her expression mellowing. "Kids these days deal with so much more than we did. Anything that gives us a window into their lives is valuable—even if it is terrible poetry. I'm just thankful they found someone to fill in who'll care."

Maribel's gaze went to the back of the church, her head cocked slightly to the side, reminding Shayne of a curious puppy.

Shayne followed her gaze to see the man from the white truck engaged in a conversation with an elderly woman who seemed like she might dance a jig over whatever he had said to her. He pulled an envelope from his pocket and pressed it into the woman's hand.

"Something wrong?" Shayne asked.

"Not at all. I've just never seen him in church before."

He shrugged into a fitted leather coat, then tipped his hat, giving Shayne and Maribel a quick nod, grinning as though he sensed they were talking about him. Then he turned and left.

"Well, can you imagine that?" The older woman hurried over with the envelope clutched in her hand. "Mr. Leech just made an extremely generous donation to our mission of the month—the new girl's home." The lady hurried off to share her excitement with others.

"That's interesting ... and fantastic," Maribel said. "The new girl's home is part of Peg's legacy. I'm sure you heard they are turning her ranch and the camp into a place for teenage girls."

Shayne hadn't heard, but it sounded like something Peg would do. With no heirs to her estate, she was gifting others through her generosity.

"That's where I work," Maribel said. "Although, even getting started has turned into a bigger challenge than I expected. There's a lot of paperwork and legalities to establishing a home for minors. Never mind that we're just trying to keep—or get—them off the streets and some place safe. Sorry. I can get wound up talking about this, especially since the construction company we hired fell through.

We're praying God sends us someone else soon. But for

now, how about we head to the cafe and get a table? Conner can meet us there."

There was a day when it had been her Grandma Hazel's kitchen where everyone headed after church. Shayne didn't mind the change too much. The cafe seemed to offer the safer alternative these days.

They took their seats in the same booth they always seemed to occupy, causing Shayne to wonder if they permanently reserved it for themselves.

"I wish I could cook, but I'm terrible in the kitchen," Maribel said as she worked her way out of her coat. "That's a problem because Conner loves to eat. I'm afraid I'll be a disappointment to him no matter how much he tells me it doesn't matter."

"So then ..." Shayne gave her a sly look, "it's true that the two of you are—"

"In a great big knot of cold feet and confusion," Maribel said. "I'm pretty sure we both know what we want, but we've both made such a wreck of our past that it's a little frightening trying to figure how to do it right."

Shayne eased into the booth, not sure if she should ask for an explanation.

"Conner says dating sober is the hardest thing he's ever done. I may not have been as messed up as he was, but I still won't argue. Doing a relationship the right way is hard ... but also so ... I don't know, easy." Maribel peered at Shayne. "I'm not making very much sense, am I?"

"I think I understand what you're saying," Shayne said. Did she? Shayne pulled the menus from the metal holder made of horseshoes and handed one to Maribel. Dating Nick had been easy, but she was pretty sure she'd never radiated the completely enamored look she saw on Maribel's face as she talked about Conner. "So it's pretty serious, then?"

"I think so ... I'm not really sure, though. When we first

met, I had some major issues to work through ... and I was being stalked. Note to self ... be careful who you choose to date.

"Anyway, that was kind of a buzzkill for starting a relationship. I definitely needed to get myself right before I could think about dragging someone else into my mess. It's funny. I always thought if I found the right guy, he would be there to fix me. Turns out, the only one who could fix me had been with me all the time." Maribel's gaze drifted as though pulled along by her thoughts. "Well, anyway, then Peg was sick. I worked for her, but it was more than that. A friendship. And I needed to be there for her. Conner and I agreed it wasn't the right time to start dating.

"At least I thought we agreed. I feel like he's avoiding the subject lately. Like maybe he's changed his mind." Maribel frowned, wrinkles once again digging into the space between her eyebrows. "Or maybe he never wanted to."

Her mouth fell open as she stared at Shayne. "I don't know why I just told you all of that. That was way more than you wanted to hear and way, way more than I ever share."

"I don't mind." Shayne relaxed. It had been a long time since she had a girlfriend who confided in her. Nick was almost always present. That put a damper on the girlfriend sharing thing.

She found it funny, though, that her new friend could doubt Conner's interest. "I assure you, he doesn't look at you like someone who has lost interest." Shayne picked up a plastic covered menu and fanned herself, making Maribel laugh.

Conner chose that moment to arrive, suspicion written on his face as he slid into the seat next to Maribel. He looked at Shayne. "You're never going to guess who's asking about you."

CHAPTER TWENTY-TWO

Ethan motioned to the waitress to bring him a cup of coffee as he slid into the booth across from Reuben. They were meeting at the IHOP on the interstate, which was fine by Ethan. He hadn't eaten since lunch the day before, and he needed some time to touch base with reality after only a few days in that antiquated little town.

His search of the possible hangar hadn't turned up anything concrete, but it was enough he felt the need to let Reuben in on what he'd seen. When he'd called his friend late last night, Reu had suggested they meet here.

"Man, you've been a busy dude already," Reuben said. He grinned as he raised his coffee cup to take a drink.

Ethan nodded. *You have no idea, buddy.*

The waitress set his coffee in front of him, along with a glass of ice water, then took their orders and disappeared into the kitchen.

"I don't know that I have anything useful. Only speculation."

"It's more than we had, so we're grateful. Thanks for

meeting with me. Sometimes these things are better discussed in person."

Ethan suspected Reuben was as much interested in doing a welfare check on him as his friend was meeting in person to discuss what might be potentially pivotal information. Ethan didn't bother with the niceties, but jumped right into what he'd seen last night, knowing it didn't amount to much. Unfortunately for him, he had to start at the very beginning for any of it to make sense. He was only a short way into his account when his friend held up a hand to stop him.

"Hold on, there. Are you telling me the daughter of the woman who leased us the house showed up at the same time, unannounced?" The expression on Reuben's face perplexed Ethan. His friend should have been frustrated that it might put Ethan's mission in jeopardy. Instead, he looked amused.

It occurred to Ethan too late that Reuben might insist on her leaving. As much logic as that held, Ethan couldn't quite bring himself to want the same thing. He'd managed to avoid her for almost twenty-four hours now. And he didn't like it.

"That's right." He studied his friend, still not convinced he wasn't being played.

"The Lord sure does work in mysterious ways."

"What's that supposed to mean?"

"You'll see ... eventually." Reuben moved his cup to the side as the waitress began depositing plates of pancakes, eggs, fried ham, and hash browns in front of him. "May I have some Tabasco sauce too, please?"

She nodded, then disappeared, returning with Reuben's requested choice of self-torture and Ethan's omelet with a side of pancakes and bacon. The men ate in silence for a few minutes. Ethan debated whether or not he wanted to continue his retelling. Next up on the big reveal was the questionable part about how the somewhat notorious Levi

Hollingsworth showed up with his dubious story that set this whole thing in motion.

Ethan shook out a generous amount of salt, followed by double that amount of pepper on his eggs, then bit the bullet and poured out the rest of the story. The only thing he held back was the truth that Shayne Wright had him flummoxed.

When he finished, Reu leaned back, pushing away from the table, and whistled. He stared at Ethan for a long moment, then busted out laughing. "You've got to be kidding me? We've been trying to find a way in without drawing attention for months now and you just walk up, and it all falls in your lap."

It felt more like it fell on his big toe, but yeah, Ethan supposed that was about the sum of it.

"And the ranch where all this supposedly took place is the Rancho de Chela?"

"Yeah, that's what they're calling it now."

Reu's expression sobered. "The Lord does indeed work in mysterious ways." He wadded up his napkin and tossed it on the table. "Can you keep your house guests quiet?"

"There are things I could do."

"Not like that. We're not Special Forces anymore."

"Honest answer?"

"Of course."

"No idea."

"I'm not asking you to cross any lines, but do the best you can." This time Reu winked and grinned before taking another sip of coffee. "What's she like?"

Ethan watched the waitress refill their cups. "Just another opportunity to get myself in trouble." He grinned for his friend's benefit. He wasn't smiling on the inside.

After they'd paid their tabs and walked outside, Reuben pulled out his phone. "Have you met the sheriff in Turnaround?"

Ethan shook his head.

"Well, you're about to."

CHAPTER TWENTY-THREE

"Nice sermon, son." Sheriff Griger walked up before Shayne had a chance to respond to Conner's remark that someone was asking about her. Which was fine since she really didn't want to know.

"But don't get any ideas about a career change. The Academy starts in seven weeks, and I'll drag you there in handcuffs if I have to." Sheriff Griger didn't have to convince them he meant it. The flint-like expression he wore told them he wasn't in the mood for any argument.

Conner dipped his head, one slow, sure nod to show he not only understood the words, but grasped the meaning behind them as well. "Got it. And don't worry. I sat in on a committee meeting before church and trust me, I'd rather have a job where I'm allowed to be armed in hostile situations."

"What? You've always had those ladies eating out of the palm of your hand. Did you forget to flash them those adorable dimples?" Maribel asked. She batted her eyes, teasing him. "Besides, I thought the Spirit of the Lord was your sword?"

"Neither the Spirit of the Lord nor adorable dimples stand a chance against a room full of gray-haired church ladies and over seventy years of 'we've-never-done-it-that-way-before.' I don't even think pepper spray and a cattle prod would be enough for that," Conner said.

"I saw Bryce Leech in church today, so something good must be happening. And according to Mrs. Nabors, he made a generous contribution to the mission fund." Maribel patted Conner's arm.

"I saw him, but the 'Only One Promotion Left' Sunday School class was giving me a critique of my sermon, so I missed him. Then, anyway."

Shayne sensed his attention and looked up from the menu.

"He stopped me in the parking lot on my way over. He was curious about our visitor today," Conner said. He arched a meddling eyebrow as he stared at Shayne.

"Why'd he think she was a visitor? He never comes to church either," Maribel asked.

Conner shrugged. "Lucky guess. But he wasn't asking who Shayne was. He recognized her. Just wanted to be sure, and said he was sorry he didn't stay to say hello. Said he didn't realize he knew you until he was almost to his truck. That's where I met up with him."

"We should have invited him to join us for lunch," Maribel said.

"I offered, but he said he needed to get back to his horses."

Sunday was fried liver and onions day at Momma Mae's. Shayne had forgotten how strong and unpleasant the smell of that dish cooking could be. Like when someone who with no reason to starts asking around about you. Her finger settled onto the silver ring, but she didn't twist it. Instead, she let her fingertips glide back and forth over its smooth surface.

"He wasn't our only unusual visitor." Conner turned to address the sheriff. "Did you notice Jimmo Cleese in church this morning? I didn't realize he was out of prison already."

"Yep. Got out a couple of weeks ago. His momma says he found the Lord while he was in the second time." Griger edged his words with a trace of doubt, expressing enough mercy to withhold final judgment and enough prudence to say watch out. "Time reveals all secrets, so I guess we'll have our answer soon enough."

Shayne shifted in her seat, drawing a glance from both the sheriff and Conner.

"Who's Jimmo Cleese?" Maribel's forehead wrinkled at a name she evidently didn't recognize. "And what did he do to warrant such notice?"

"Jimmo was a dealer. And not a nice one." Conner thumped the edge of the table. "As bad as I was and as much trouble as I found to get into, my stuff was child's play compared to Jimmo's."

"Got locked up for selling marijuana laced with PCP," Sheriff Griger added. "The worst kind of the worst, the ones that'll trick their friends to get 'em hooked ... or get 'em killed. But the first trip to prison wasn't enough to keep him from going back for a second stay. We'll see if the lesson sticks this time."

"I remember that night like it was yesterday. I thought Tom was going to die," Conner said. He studied the empty tabletop as though that night scrolled across it in high-definition memories, his mood so somber it pulled the rest of them in with him.

He glanced up at Shayne. "I think you were there that night, but you must have left before that happened. I remember wondering what brought the nerd—uh, bookworm —out of her cave." The grin he flashed her held a note of melancholy. "Levi was there. He and Tom were hanging out with Jimmo. I had a bad feeling about it, which was weird. I wasn't known to have bad feelings about too many things back in those days."

"Good Lord must have been watching over you. Jimmo was dealing wet weed to his buddies. Nice friend to have," Sheriff Griger said, practically growling the words.

"Wet weed?" Shayne asked. She remembered that night no matter how fervently she prayed to forget it. She, too, had been concerned when she'd seen Levi hanging around with Jimmo. It had unnerved her to see Levi smoke pot, something she'd never known him to do before that night. The fight he'd had with their father earlier that day had been one of the worst. It put Levi in a disposition unreceptive to her words of caution. She shuddered, the warmth of the cafe disappearing as the cold of those memories seeped in.

"Marijuana joints dipped in formaldehyde. Jimmo was lacing them with the hallucinogen PCP and not telling anyone what they were getting." Sheriff Griger nodded at an older couple as they entered the cafe, then turned back to their booth. "Dang near killed Tom Bradley. It's a wonder no one else got hurt that night."

Shayne wrapped her arms around her middle and looked away. *Yeah, a wonder.*

But what if it had been Levi instead of Tom? She should've done more to save them both that night. She should've made him leave. Instead, she waited, not wanting to disappoint him and not wanting to leave him. She adored her brother and trusted him, even when what he was doing terrified her. So she'd separated herself from the misdeeds she wanted no part of. Not wanting to observe her brother's behavior, she'd ventured past the row of trees to watch the full moon rise over the ridge.

Because nothing really bad ever happened in Turnaround, right? Stupid.

"They'd been smoking weed all night, and suddenly Tom starts having seizures and acting like he couldn't breathe. A couple of us tried to get him in the car, but he was freaking out, screaming stuff about demons. That little dude was strong. Like he was feeling *no* pain—literally. I'd heard of people reacting like that, but never witnessed it before then. Scariest thing I've ever seen. Someone must have called nine-one-one, though, because an ambulance showed up not too long after that." Conner sobered considerably as he recounted the story to Maribel. "We're lucky he didn't die, but he's not been quite right since."

"You know Levi's the one that turned Jimmo in, don't you?" Sheriff Griger turned to Shayne. "He didn't remember anything about that night, but a few days later he showed up at my house one evening, told me how he and Tom had both bought joints from Jimmo the night it happened. Thankfully, his only made him black out."

Shayne pressed her lips together as she felt the blood draining from her face. She tensed, trying to still the telltale rocking her body engaged in when emotions she couldn't show became too strong. Hidden beneath the table, her fingers spun her ring in rapid motion. *Absolutely, thank goodness no one got hurt.* "I didn't."

"He had to testify in the trial, but I never told anyone he was the one who tipped me off."

"We're lucky any of us survived that summer," Conner stated, his gaze on a memory no one else could see.

"Y'all were one of the worst bunches to come through Turnaround High, that's for sure. Made me work harder than I wanted for a few years."

"Look at us now, Sheriff. I just preached a sermon to a born again Jimmo Cleese. I guess you did something right back then."

Sheriff Griger grunted. "We'll see about that," he said.

"Now all we need is to get Levi straightened out and on the right path again." Conner clamped his teeth together and sucked in a breath through his still open lips. "I'm sorry, Shayne. I didn't mean anything bad. It's just, I hear the rumors."

"No, you're right. Life has not turned out well for him." Shayne answered as civilly as she could, forbidding herself to say that his life had turned out exactly as he'd chosen to make it. He deserved no better. Or did he? She stopped spinning the ring and pressed the etched compass into the soft pad of her thumb.

Ten years ago she'd run as far and as fast as she could, packing her things and leaving her bewildered grandparents standing confused on their front porch. She'd gone straight to the one place her mother and brother couldn't touch her—her dad's house in Houston. She understood now—probably understood then, but wouldn't have admitted it—that moving in with their dad was meant to hurt Levi. His relationship with their father had never been peaceful. It only became worse the older Levi got and the more he exercised his independence. Her father's hysterical new wife added another layer of insulation for Shayne by deliberately keeping distance between the scattered family.

Shayne was welcome to live in their house as long as she paid her own expenses.

It was a condition Shayne was pleased to accept, especially since it also came with the privilege of coming and going as she pleased without anyone asking questions. It was the perfect set-up for her senior year transformation. Looking back now, she realized there was nothing perfect about it. She had needed people then.

She looked at the people gathered around her. She needed people now as well.

"Well, speak of the devil," Conner said, his voice lowered for only them to hear.

Shayne looked up to see a large, heavily muscled man, tattooed arms bulging from the sleeves of a Got Jesus t-shirt a size too small, making his way to where they now sat in anxious silence. His buzz cut, broad shoulders, and scowl gave him the appearance of someone you didn't want to meet in an alley—or the produce section of the grocery store. Anywhere, really. Jimmo Cleese.

"Sheriff." The man acknowledged the law enforcement official first and with a respect that lessened the tension that had mushroomed in the small booth.

"Jimmo," the sheriff responded, nodding.

"I've been wanting to stop by and see you."

Sheriff Griger frowned as if Jimmo wasn't going to get any sympathy from him. "What's on your mind?"

"Nothing, really. Just wanted to apologize for roughing up your county back in the day. Let ya know things have changed." Jimmo had tucked his hands in his pockets, shuffling awkwardly as he spoke.

"And some things have stayed the same." Sheriff Griger worked his jaw as though he wanted to spit.

"Fair enough. But you won't get no more trouble out of me. You have my word ... for what it's worth."

"I'll hold you to it," Griger said. He extended his hand and Jimmo shook it. The sheriff's phone buzzed, and he pulled it from his shirt pocket. His frown deepened. "Now, if you all will excuse me. I got work to do."

They watched the sheriff walk away, phone pressed to his ear, before starting up the conversation again.

Jimmo let out a laugh. "Yes, sir, I believe some things have stayed the same." He swung his head from side to side as though astounded by the unexpected reality of his current circumstances. "But look at us, Conner. Don't you know Frogface Phelps would have a heart attack if she saw us now."

"*Mrs.* Phelps was our Biology teacher." The look on Conner's face said Jimmo's choice of name was one he wanted to agree with, but his conscience no longer allowed. He shot a look of apology to the women. "And I believe the correct phrase would be that she would roll over in her grave seein' as how she died last year."

"Hmph ... didn't know that. Anyway, just wanted to tell ya I appreciated the message this morning. I work most Sundays. Got a job doin' ranch work at the Rancho de Chela, of all places." He added some form of an indistinguishable accent and rolled the words out as though the name had a fancy meaning. "Just goes to show you the good Lord has a wicked sense of humor."

"I'm not sure about that," Conner replied. "But it must be a little strange working there after all that happened?"

"That's an understatement. But the strangest part is working for Leech. He was a hired hand when the Tackmores owned it. Not sure how I feel about all that, but I needed the job and opportunities are slim when you have any part of the word convict next to your name. Anyway, the big boss is a little strange, but Leech treats me fair enough." He shrugged as if to say it is what it is. "Swing by the house if you want to talk Bible stuff sometime. I'm missing the fellowship with others we had back at the unit."

"I might just take you up on that," Conner said. "By the way, this is Maribel, and I'm sure you remember Shayne."

"I do, although she was way out of my league." His cheeks rounded up, revealing a row of crooked teeth in various shades of yellow and tan. Still, the expression radiated nothing but innocent respect and happiness. Being born again could wash away one's sins and restore their innocence, but it couldn't restore their teeth. "Say, you don't know where

I could find Levi, do you? I have a bit of unfinished business with him."

Shayne's heart sank as quickly as it had risen. He must know Levi was the one who turned him in.

"I haven't heard much from him lately," Shayne answered, her voice little more than a guilty murmur. It wasn't an answer to his question, but it wasn't exactly a lie either, even if it felt like one.

"I gotta get going. But if you do talk to Levi, you tell him Jimmo's looking for him." He turned to walk away.

Shayne's conscience wrestled with the questions inside her. Engaging Jimmo in further conversation didn't appeal to her, but there was a question that wouldn't rest until she asked. "Did you say you are working at the Rancho de Chela?"

"Yep. Just a hired hand who needs a paycheck. I shore wish they hadn't changed the name, though I reckon calling it the Tackmore ranch after the Tackmores were gone didn't seem right either."

"What's wrong with the new name? I like the sound of it. It sounds Spanish. Although I'm pretty sure I've been mispronouncing it," Maribel said.

"I didn't want to mention it, but yeah … you've been calling it the Ranch of Beer, but it was so cute I just couldn't tell you." Conner shook his head, grinning as he corrected her.

Jimmo scratched his head. "I don't know about that, but I do know chela means scorpion's claw. That little pincher thing. Remember that much at least from biology class. Guess you was absent that day, Conner," he said, then laughed at his joke.

Conner gave a sheepish shrug and a-you're-probably-right grin.

Shayne stared out the window, frowning.

There was something making her skin clammy in the suddenly thick air of the booth. Something in the words of the man at the accident moved around in her brain, escaping her grasp.

CHAPTER TWENTY-FOUR

The porch swing slow danced in a graceful arc that rocked Ethan's soul. Or maybe it was the unassuming beauty of the woman in the swing. With only the subtle twitch from the tip of one foot touching the wooden planks beneath her, she moved the swing in its lazy arc. Was this a picture of what Sunday afternoons should feel like?

He parked his truck beside her SUV, leaving just enough room he could continue to watch without seeming obvious.

Wrapped in a quilt, the soft amber light of the setting sun glowing around her like a painting of a mystic being, to Ethan she was the picture of tranquility that pulled him in.

He drew in a slow breath, letting the moment linger, taking in as much of the unfamiliar peace as he could.

Shayne was a whisper of hope that something honorable still existed, that a better life existed than what he experienced all around him.

He'd hoped she would have left today. Correction, he told himself he should hope she'd have gone back to whatever perfect life awaited her. The truth was something much less encouraging to think about. He didn't want her to leave.

But why *was* she still here?

He killed the engine and sat. Why did life have to be so difficult? All human interaction was love or war, and by far the majority was war.

What they had here certainly wasn't love, but it hadn't spiraled into an all-out war. Best to leave it exactly where it was. When she found out what was about to happen, that was likely to change, anyway.

Shayne was the first woman he'd been attracted to since he'd found Alexa cheating on him. He couldn't explain why he felt any attraction at all. Besides, if Alexa hadn't been able to live with his demons, there was no way anyone as tender as Shayne could handle them. Alexa was a fiery, passionate woman who ran headfirst into trouble—and into the beds of his buddies, apparently. Shayne appeared to be tenderhearted, full of mercy, and from the little he'd seen, one who'd rather avoid conflict than face it head on.

So what was with his attraction? It scared him to admit it went far beyond the physical.

All it would amount to was more self-inflicted suffering on his part. Hands that had done things his hands had done should never touch something as virtuous as what Shayne offered.

But it gave him insight into why scientists were drawn to study galaxies far beyond their own.

As if she sensed his attention, she turned to him, her head tilted in question. Any resolve to do the decent thing dissolved into ... well, something about as dedicated to one course of action as a puppy in a room full of shoes.

Reluctant feet carried him to the porch. He wanted to hang on to this moment as long as possible. His thoughts were so tangled it was a wonder he wasn't walking in circles. Had he done the right thing?

"Where's Levi?" he asked, lowering himself into the rocking chair near the swing.

"Sleeping." Her eyes held fast to his. In them he read the mixture of wanting to know and fearing she didn't. "He told me where you went yesterday."

Ethan gazed at the weathered barn fifty yards away without commenting. He knew what was coming, but felt no compunction about answering a question she hadn't yet asked.

"Did you find anything?" The softness of her tone confirmed she suspected his answer might not be one she was eager to hear.

The worried lines of her tight face annoyed him. Was it concern for a girl in danger or for Levi? He hesitated before responding, cutting his eyes to the curve at the top of the driveway where it first appeared through the wall of trees. "I don't know."

"That's not much of an answer."

"Sorry. It's all I got for now." He watched her for a response, wondering what it was she really wanted, but her only action was to sit there, running her finger over the pattern of stitches holding the quilt together, almost as if it was what held her together as well. Finally he asked, "So what's the deal with you and Levi? Family's gotta stick together, guard each other's backs? That why you're hiding him from the sheriff?"

A concealment Ethan had just blown, but she'd discover that soon enough.

He regretted it the moment the words were out. It was none of his business, and he needed to distance himself from these feelings that might carry him head on into more trouble than he wanted. Plus, the sarcasm was unnecessary. *Jealous much?*

Besides the nagging concern about whether or not it had

really been gas Levi went there for, he was her brother, for Pete's sake. Any possessiveness on Ethan's part amounted to a line he shouldn't cross. It wasn't his territory—she wasn't his —to protect.

The directness in the look she gave him sliced through his male hubris, wounding him with its honesty. It expressed hurt and disappointment. He'd earned it.

"Just the distant past and lives that took two different roads."

Let it go, man. It's not your problem. But Levi was one of those smooth-looking types with little depth and probably even less compassion, a mile wide but only an inch deep. Even if it was only in the realm of typical family dysfunction, it pained him to think Levi had hurt her somehow. It stirred the urge to punch the guy in the face.

"So why not just leave it that way? Why put yourself through this for that worthless piece of—."

"What is wrong with you?" The sharpened stare she pinned him with—again one he'd earned—splintered his male pride into a thousand shards. Jealous or not, he'd gone too far.

"I apologize. That was uncalled for." He ducked his head, chewing on his bottom lip and staring at the wooden boards beneath his feet. He had to get himself under control. She wasn't Alexa, and he couldn't make her the target for that anger.

"Thank you." Her soft answer drew his attention. Her lips entertained a brief smile, forced as though she was trying to be friendly while she quietly but firmly closed the door in his face. Unfortunately for him, even though it was a forced and troubled looking smile, it was dazzling.

It was a smile he couldn't live with. She needed to go. The last five minutes had already proven he couldn't trust himself around her. He would not risk having his heart shredded again, and if he asked her for what he wanted, he'd only end up shredding hers. "I thought you'd have headed out already."

She refused to meet his stare as she twisted the ring on her finger. Caution warnings marched up his spine. What wasn't she telling him?

"So about that ... Would it change your mind about staying here if I told you I had accepted a temporary teaching job at the school? I'll need a place to stay ... and here makes the most sense, of course."

"Of course," he said, his stomach clenched in a fervent hope she was kidding, "but no."

"No it won't change your mind?"

"Not even a little."

She sat up a little straighter, clearing her throat and fidgeting with the edge of the quilt. "Well, the thing is that uhmm ... since I have to stay somewhere ... and it can't be with a man, especially one I don't even know ..." She glanced at him before lowering her eyes back to the quilt. "It'll only be for a couple of weeks, and I can pay you for the rent while I'm here."

He stared at the flustered woman now moving the swing as if she were attempting to launch herself through the roof above. An agitated motion replacing the peaceful swaying of moments ago. "You broke into my house while I was taking a shower. A little late to worry about modesty or gossip now, don't you think?"

She opened and then closed her mouth as though struggling to decide what to say. "Why do you ..."

"Why do I what?"

"Never mind. I'm needed—" She paused and looked away. "They asked me to help a girl train for the state cross country championships ... and keep her out of trouble. She's the young waitress at the cafe. That's actually something I can do. I'll be filling in to teach a few classes as well. Just for two weeks. Will you please just consider it?"

"No." He crossed his arms, refusing to give in. If he did, she might decide he was a decent guy, someone she could count on, or even worse—trust. He couldn't be that man, maybe not for anyone ... but certainly not for her. Innocent and uncorrupted by the world, she held his last hope that goodness still existed. He desperately needed to believe in that right now, and he wouldn't be the one to extinguish that light.

Plus, he had his own commitments to fulfill. The mission was his priority. It had to be.

Shayne tucked a strand of hair behind her ear before bringing her hands together in her lap. If not for the firm set of her mouth, it would be a picture of defeat. His response seemed to frustrate her, but hers frustrated him. How could she be so headstrong and forceful at times, yet so timid and uncertain at others? Why wouldn't she just fight like a normal woman?

Truth hit like a rocket in the middle of his gut. She was only headstrong and forceful when fighting for someone or something else. When it came to standing up for herself, she crumbled.

"That's it? You're just going to give up, not stand up for what you want?"

"I'm not giving up. I just don't like to argue or fight, if that's what you mean."

"It's not. I'm asking why you don't stand up for yourself more often?"

"Sometimes there are more important things than claiming your own rights."

"I don't agree. I mean, it's obvious you aren't happy to have your brother here. Yet here you sit, for whatever reason, as if he had a greater right to be here than you do."

"That's none of your business."

"It became my business when you both invaded my house." Ethan leaned forward, resting his elbows on his knees. He cocked his head back slightly to look at her, his stare unwavering. "I don't actually think you even like him, which is what perplexes me why you're protecting him?"

"It's still not your house." She glanced away. "And just because I may not ... like someone doesn't mean I have a reason to be mean, to withhold compassion."

"Well, we'll agree to disagree on that one, then."

"Then let's agree you can't stay here." Flames of anger danced in her eyes.

Apparently, she could catch fire if he used the right spark.

"Oh ... there she is." Ethan cocked an eyebrow, secretly both pleased and irritated. "But still not happening."

"You just said I should stand up for myself, so now I'm saying I want you to leave."

The higher pitch of her voice as she tripped over the word *want* revealed the truth. When she touched her nose with her finger, he was certain. Shayne Wright was lying when she said she wanted him to leave.

And that was a problem. "No you don't."

"I beg your pardon."

"I said you don't really want me to leave, do you?"

"Of course I do." The blush racing up her cheeks said otherwise.

He clasped his hands behind his head, leaning back with his eyes glued to the curious woman in front of him. "Liar."

She glared at him, eyes narrowed. That she uncharacteristically held his gaze surprised him. That her beauty enthralled him terrified him, sizzling through him like a lightning bolt.

He'd come close to drowning once. It had felt like he'd swallowed hot coals. The sensation roared back at him, reminding him of the desperate panic that followed. It was a moment that drove a man to surrender all for just one more breath of air, pushing him to the point of forgetting who he was and what he stood for. This moment with Shayne set off a similar instinct for survival.

He wouldn't go down this path. He smiled a crooked smile and winked suggestively. "What's it worth to you if I let you stay?"

But how low would he stoop in order to drive her away?

Chagrin over his actions fluttered into his thoughts. He swatted it away. Ethan McGregor would not fall for this woman. Correction. He already had. All he could do now was eliminate the possibility she might return those feelings.

"Why are you going through so much effort to be cruel?"

A half laugh, half huff of breath escaped from Ethan. "It's really no effort at all." Conviction and remorse kicked him in the gut. This wasn't who he was. He didn't go around looking for opportunities to hurt people. But it was who he had let life make him. "So you're asking if you can stay here with me? I got no problem with that. Might be rather cozy."

He'd started his roll downhill with no stopping himself. It occurred to him he could tell her the truth about the things he'd done, but he didn't. Somehow, it was less painful for her to believe him a lecherous clod than a bloody warrior. She'd never understand the wickedness he'd seen in this world, and it would destroy everything innocent in her if he tried.

Shayne swallowed, the flush on her cheeks heightening her beauty. She refused to make eye contact with him, but pulled the quilt even tighter around her. "Chilly is the word you need, not cozy. But I will reimburse you financially. So I can stay?"

He rose and leaned on the porch post, his back to her as he faced out into the darkness that crept over the hill to find them. There was no one to blame but himself now. He was the one who'd just challenged her to stand up for herself.

Hating himself for taking the low road with what he was about to say, he said it anyway. "Sure. I've always had a thing for schoolteachers."

"Stop it. I know what you're trying to do. And please, stop. I have no interest in whatever it is you're implying. I ... I will keep my door locked."

"Suit yourself. But just remember the lock on your door and the chair jammed under the knob can't protect you if I break the doorknob off."

"You wouldn't."

Ethan rubbed his beard. Sighing, he faced her. "No. I wouldn't. But you shouldn't ever take your safety for granted. You need to go back to wherever you came from. It's not right or safe for you to stay here."

"It couldn't be more right since this place is more mine than yours. And I'm not afraid of you. You aren't that kind of person."

He was pretty sure she was bluffing when she claimed she wasn't afraid of him. "Don't be too sure of that."

Her lips parted, expressing doubt, but it was her eyes that pierced his heart. Fear, but not a fear of the unknown.

The glazed, broken look in her eyes ...

Understanding detonated in his chest. It was a specter from the past—not him—that captured her thoughts and brought a look of recognition, a look that told him she knew more than she should have about the evilness of this world. What that was, he could only guess, but an immense rush of protectiveness engulfed him.

A remorse so cold it burned through his gut seized him, followed by a confident knowing. If he ever found out who had hurt her, he'd extract a heavy amount of vengeance.

CHAPTER TWENTY-FIVE

The crunch of gravel announced the approach of a vehicle. The sheriff's truck eased into view at the top of the hill. Ethan braced.

"What did you do?" Shayne's head spun to Ethan, distrust sharpening her words.

"I'm the only one here not stitched up, and I'd like to keep it that way." His mood shifted, taking on a sternness he didn't fully intend, a posture ingrained in him so deeply it came about without conscious thought.

The sting of betrayal radiated from her body.

Ethan's jaw twitched as he chose his words. "There's some evidence that something might have happened in the barn where Levi said he had gone." He still hesitated to accept all of Levi's story. But in honesty, it was his protective nature that moved him to shelter her from the ugly truth.

"Such as?" Shayne asked, her brow furrowed in concern. Exactly what he didn't want.

"There are elements of Levi's story that check out."

"What elements? What aren't you telling me?"

He met her stare as if looking deep enough into hers

could transport them to a time when they might've had a chance to take whatever this was he felt for her a little further. He'd promised Reu he'd find a way to keep her and Levi quiet. Looking into her now stormy eyes made him thankful he'd enlisted the sheriff in that part of his agreement. Whatever emotions—and to be clear, there were many swirling in the depths of her eyes—gripped her now came together in an expression of haunting vulnerability that magnified his guardian instincts.

"I may have found some blood where he said I might." He didn't bother glancing at her. He knew what her next question would be.

"Levi's?"

"Possibly." He shrugged. "I can't say for sure if it's even really blood."

"But you believe him? There was a woman held hostage there?"

"Something happened there recently, but if it was what he told us about, they've gone through some effort to clean up."

"But you saw blood? They didn't clean that up?"

"They might've missed it. Or it could've been from a bird or animal. Hard to say without testing." He stalled, maneuvering around what his gut told him was true. Judging by where he'd found the blood, it wasn't likely it belonged to a bird or animal.

Ethan watched the rise and fall of her chest, her breathing shallow and rapid. It was like watching water come to a boil. He knew what was coming, just wasn't sure exactly how long it would take to get there.

"You knew this last night, but you went to the sheriff first, even after I asked you not to."

And there it was.

The anger in her speech sparked his own. He was trying to protect her as well as do what he'd come here to do. Her lack of trust, under other circumstances, would have been perfectly reasonable, but right now with his heart on his sleeve reaching for her like a child reaching for a forbidden toy, it riled him. He pressed his lips in a firm line. He'd not take a chance on unwittingly exposing his true feelings.

Unwelcomed feelings that made no sense.

The sheriff's vehicle rolled to a stop behind his truck. The man Ethan had spent the last few hours with climbed out, settled his Stetson in place, and headed toward them.

"Evening, Ethan. Shayne." Sheriff Griger stopped in front of the porch steps. He nodded at Ethan, then tipped his hat as he shifted his gaze to Shayne. "It's good to see you again. How's that shoulder doing?"

"A little sore, but I've felt worse." Her answer came out too bright and chipper, but Ethan detected the tight, clipped quality of someone working to hide emotions they didn't want to admit.

"Just don't overdo it," Sheriff Griger said. He turned to Ethan. "The Hickorys were sure 'nuff good folk. Too bad you never got to meet Frank and Hazel, but I can tell you, their character lives on in this one. I think she got all the best of both of them." He nodded toward Shayne. "I sure do miss having your granddad out here. Your grandmother too." He rubbed his midsection. "Good people. We need more like 'em."

Shayne's shoulders dropped as though the realization deflated her. "I miss them too."

"Hope I'm not interrupting your evening, but I need to have a visit with Levi. He still around?"

Shayne nodded, giving Ethan a sharp glance.

"I also want to let you know we're still waiting on fingerprints for positive IDs on the men in the wreck. What we do know is they have tattoos connecting them to a Mexican drug cartel and jail time. They were not good people, and I'm sorry some of their misfortune fell on you," Sheriff Griger said.

Shayne's face said she'd already assumed as much. The confirmation drained the color from her flushed cheeks. It was the complete opposite of the blushing effect he usually enjoyed, but its affect was even more powerful in terms of his heart.

"You told us one of them mentioned some money. You remember anything else ... any little detail, no matter how insignificant it seems?" Sheriff Griger watched Shayne with a compassionate yet scrutinizing intensity in his eyes.

Shayne looked down, then covered her eyes with her hand. When she lowered her hand, her gaze met the sheriff's. "He was just talking in bits and pieces. He said something about money and finding a girl. And I'm not sure, but maybe something about a scorpion."

Ethan exchanged a pointed glance with the sheriff, his blood starting to sizzle in his veins. But the level of coincidence needed for both her and Levi to stumble into the middle of something like this seemed unreal. He crossed his arms. He'd operated under less favorable and likely odds and been surprised by what he'd found. Frowning, he studied Shayne. Probably the effects of the two stressful situations confused and intertwined the events in her mind.

"Did he say anything to indicate who this girl was or why she needed finding?" Sheriff Griger asked.

Shayne shook her head.

"And you don't have any idea who took a shot at you? You'd just come around that corner where the shooter must've been standing. Do you remember seeing anyone or anything out of place?" Sheriff Griger continued with his questions, asking them without adding a note of offense. Ethan could take some lessons.

"I'm ..." Shayne's brow wrinkled. "No. There was no one

there. I'm sure I would've seen them. The only person I saw close to the time of the accident was the motorcycle rider who ran me off the road."

The sizzling in his veins increased. Was this important? Maybe. Was it worth looking into? Definitely.

"Why didn't you tell us this before? Describe the motorcycle and the person on it." Ethan regretted the order as soon as he said it. This was Sheriff Griger's domain, and the sharp glance the man sent him confirmed it. Shayne also wasn't a subordinate to be ordered around. Her eyes narrowed in suspicion. Or was that just animosity?

Yep, he could definitely use lessons in tactful interrogation techniques from the sheriff.

The expression on Sheriff Griger's face said he'd let Ethan's interruption slide ... this time.

"My apologies for being a bit more focused on the fact I'd been shot than on recording traffic violations," Shayne responded. She glared at Ethan, her look hostile, her words caustic. He was only trying to help her, but if she couldn't see that, then he'd be more than happy to leave her to help herself.

He probably should have let her in on why he'd gone to the sheriff before the man actually drove up. Would that have made her sense of betrayal a little less ferocious?

Her attitude was more compliant when she addressed the sheriff. "It might've been a dirt bike. It wasn't a big one. The driver was wearing black, and his helmet was black too ... I think. I was more intent on avoiding a wreck than on taking down a detailed description of the other driver. If I'd known someone was about to start shooting at me, I'd have done a better job."

"Well, every little bit helps. You keep thinking, and let me know if anything else comes up. Cindy told me what you're doing for her niece. Nice of you to stay around and help. Just what I'd expect from a member of the Hickory family." Sheriff Griger placed a foot on the porch, leaning in and resting his body over his bent knee.

He cleared his throat. "'Course every now and then there's a nut that rolls a bit. Guess I better have a talk with your brother now."

"Nut tree sums up this family pretty well," Ethan said. He mumbled the words under his breath where only she could hear.

It earned him another hostile glare as she stood. "Why don't you come in, Sheriff? That's if it's all right. Ethan made sure to tell me I'm trespassing. Are you here to discuss that as well?"

A puzzled expression came over the sheriff's face as his eyes shifted from Shayne to Ethan.

Ethan gave the sheriff a who-knows look and pulled the door open, waving the sheriff through first as the trio entered.

He seized Shayne's elbow as she stepped near, stopping her from entering as he leaned close and whispered. "Bit dramatic, don't you think?"

The smell of her shampoo wrapped around him as she jerked her arm away and stomped into the house. The wake of vanilla-scented wrath pulled him in behind her.

A lamp on the end table cast a yellowy glow in the room, offering barely enough light to create shadows.

"What the—oh hey, Sheriff," Levi said. His groggy, startled voice spilled up from the couch. "You'd suppose my roommates could have given me a little warning."

Ethan flipped the overhead light on, making the shadows disappear.

"Levi," Sheriff Griger said. "Need to ask you a few questions."

"Oh, yeah, sure." Levi winced as he shifted into a seated position.

"Don't get up. I'll just have myself a seat over here." Sheriff Griger extended his hand for Levi to shake, then seated himself.

"So you know about ..." Levi's words trailed into an unfinished question.

Ethan's distrust clicked up a notch as he watched Levi sidestepping any admissions to possible wrongdoing on his part. There was just something about Levi he wanted not to like. *Never admit to a crime no one yet knows you've committed, right Levi?*

"What you say you saw and what you say happened to you? Yeah, Ethan filled me in, but I'm going to need to hear it from you," Sheriff Griger said. He leaned back, tapping his hat on his knee.

"Why? What'd you find? Was she there?" Levi was fully alert now, his eyes pivoting from the sheriff to Ethan as the questions poured out.

"Easy there, son. You sure you don't need to see a doctor?" asked Griger.

Levi exhaled and stared down, running his tongue around the inside of his cheek. "Yeah, I'm sure." He looked up at the sheriff, "But could someone tell me what's going on?"

Sheriff Griger halted his hat tapping. "I reckon you're the one needs to do the talking."

Levi looked around the room, struggling with a decision.

"Ethan says you thought you saw a man wearing a badge?" Sheriff Griger reached into his coat pocket and pulled out a piece of paper. He unfolded it to show pictures of his department staff to Levi. "Any of these the one you saw?"

Levi shook his head. "I didn't get a good look at his face. All I can tell you is he seemed kind of stocky, not too tall, and he was solid as a rock. I'm thinking he could have a stellar career as a cage fighter. I only said I *thought* he had a badge clipped to his belt."

Sheriff Griger chuckled as he refolded the paper. "That lets off most of my men. The only stocky ones aren't what you would call 'solid as a rock.' The only cage fighting any of them has ever done would be trying to get eggs out from under a setting hen. So now, you want to talk to me here, or shall we take a little trip?"

"Right here's good with me, then," Levi answered. He shrugged and recounted the story the same way he'd told it before.

Sheriff Griger let a silence linger, bloating like a water balloon filling with a watery, apprehensive unease. "Thought you were on tour in South Texas?"

A smile flickered over Levi's face, as though he were proud to know the sheriff kept up with his schedule. He sobered quickly, erasing the smile. "Had to take a little break. Some time away to clear my head."

"And you believed coming here would do that for you?"

"Just needed to come home, that's all," Levi answered.

"Don't we all," Sheriff Griger said. He rose, swatting his hat against his leg, replacing the motion of tapping it on his knee. "Well, it looks like you're not the only one in the family with that idea." He smiled at Shayne. "Welcome home to the Wright twins."

Ethan caught himself before he staggered at the sheriff's statement. Twins? He didn't know why it mattered. A brother was a brother, after all. But somehow the omission resonated like a lie.

"I guess we're about to add another fella into the family, too. What do you think of your future brother-in-law? He worthy of your sister's hand in marriage? That was a mighty big rock I saw on her finger the other night." Sheriff Griger winked at Shayne. He may not have noticed the color emptying from her face, but Ethan did.

Ethan's shoulders squared, going ridged with stoicism, his expression one of forced indifference. The vein in his forehead throbbed. He had no doubt the look he gave her was as hard as the muscles he felt contracting in his shoulders and midsection. Another lie.

She hadn't actually lied, but she hadn't been honest with him about it, either. Same thing, right?

He caught the quick, frightened glance Shayne shot him. Well, good for her. Maybe she did have a face for poker after all. She'd kept this secret like a pro.

Not that it mattered to him anymore. He'd played with fire like that before. He was tired of getting torched.

CHAPTER TWENTY-SIX

Levi did a quick job of offering a brotherly and suitably sarcastic remark in answer to the sheriff's statement. Shayne didn't catch the exact words, though. Ethan's reaction held her attention. His dark glare shredded through the tattered remnant of the deceit she wore like a cloak. She bristled. She may not have told him the truth, but she hadn't exactly lied to him, either.

The condemning look he wore—which wasn't a look at all, but the absence of one—told her he didn't see it that way.

But what did she care?

She didn't need him inserting himself into her problems as though he might help. He'd have to do a lot more than just look at her with a tender empathy if he wanted to gain her confidence.

"Last thing I'm going to ask," Sheriff Griger articulated his final words in a fashion that said it wasn't really going to be a question, but an order, "is that this all stays between the four of us for now."

He threw in a speech about the "ongoing nature of the

investigation." Shayne was too busy denying the raw feeling of betrayal, as though there should be something more. She'd been shot, and her brother had been beaten and threatened. But now they were supposed to act like nothing happened. The unfairness of it all crashed around her.

Breathe in. Hold. Breathe out. Again.

Rational thought seeped back in. What the sheriff asked was only for their protection.

Ethan followed the sheriff out the door, leaving his animosity to linger like a fire-breathing dragon.

"I asked you not to go to the sheriff yet." Levi pinched the bridge of his nose, closing his eyes as though seeing her would be more than he could stand. "The least you could have done was give me a little warning."

"I didn't go to the sheriff," Shayne said. Her words snapped like a rubber band, stinging her tongue although it was him she tried to wound.

"Ethan?" He opened his eyes slowly, as though everything would look differently if he took his time seeing it.

"Yes."

"I guess I should have known he would." Resignation settled over him as he sank back against the couch. "There's another reason I didn't want to drag the sheriff into this yet."

"Besides allegedly being beaten by a man with a badge? I'm sure there is, and I'm equally sure I could guess what it is."

Levi shook his head. "I'm sorry. That didn't come out the way I meant. I'm not mad at you. I'm just ... mad." He cursed, clenched fists pounding the cushions.

She should walk away. He wouldn't dare follow. She didn't need to hear anymore.

He sighed. "I meant it when I said I'm trying to change, to get my life cleaned up. I'm supposed to be in a treatment facility right now—court-ordered, but I skipped out early. If

Sheriff Griger figures that out, he'll probably have to arrest me."

"So skipping out on treatment will help you change? Typical Levi. He'll fix his problems all on his own," Shayne said. She crossed her arms. Like mixing too many colors created black, too many emotions mixed within her, verging on out-of-control rage.

"No. Not exactly, anyway." Levi looked at her, pleading for her to not only listen, but believe. "One thing they taught us was that our addiction is always rooted in a heart issue. Until we know what that is and deal with it, treatment won't help."

"Great. Thanks for telling me this. Now you've made me —Ethan too—accomplices to ... whatever crime you're committing."

He looked around the room, taking in everything but his sister. "I had to come here. This is where the answer is, Shayne. I don't know how and why, but it is. It always has been."

"What do you want me to do for you, Levi? Oh wait, I remember. I just lie back and take it as long as you're getting what you want." She might have sprouted fangs for all the venom in her speech, for all the poison she felt shooting through her veins.

"What are you talking about?"

The sound of the door closing as Ethan returned silenced them.

Truths she didn't want to deal with whirled within her.

Why God? Why now?

She was here to find her own answers, not deal with Levi's. But he was right. The answer was here. It always had been.

Shayne spun and hurried through the kitchen out the back door, snatching the quilt from the recliner on her way.

"Where do you think you're going?" Ethan called,

following her out the door. The vexation she heard confirmed this was another conversation she didn't wish to have right now.

"Not now, Ethan." She charged down the hill into the last waning light of day—into a growing darkness that not only crept over the landscape, but over her heart as well. If only she could outrun it. She couldn't forgive her brother, even though she was the one choking on poison.

Ethan's fingers clamped around her arm, jerking her to face him. He pulled her close, and she saw the sparks of wrath flashing across his face. Wrath aimed at her.

That he'd grabbed her uninjured arm was not something she overlooked. He was trying not to hurt her.

Fear filled her still. Not of physical harm, but of something more painful and permanent. She feared being seen. Her outburst had broken down a wall. Now she lacked what she needed to put it back in place. She desperately wanted to let it all go, to scream at the injustice. She wanted to see those who had hurt her suffer.

She wanted violence.

But to what avail? The question sucked the anger from her marrow, numbing her. What she really wanted was to step out of the grave and into living again.

Or for it to fill in on top of her, burying her at last. The living in between was too painful.

"Yes, now." His order was little more than a growl as he guided her firmly to the stone fence and seated her. "You're going to explain to me why you never mentioned he's your *twin* brother, or that you have a fiancé."

Ethan scowled at her, hands on his hips, when she didn't answer. "What the blazes is going on here?"

Shayne shook her head. But that was a lie. She knew. She just didn't want to admit it.

"Don't try me right now." He glanced away for a moment,

as if trying to control his anger. "I don't even know why I'm bothering to ask, but what's up with all the lies? You have some sort of problem with telling the truth? I didn't take you for a pathological liar, yet the list of things you haven't been honest about just keeps getting longer."

"I never lied to you. Besides, what difference does it make? It doesn't concern you."

"Hiding the truth is the same as telling a lie. And it started concerning me—" He stopped short of finishing his statement. The look he gave her exploded in her heart. He wasn't judging. He was seeking, seeing, reaching out.

Her grip on the quilt she held relaxed as he lifted it from her lap to wrap around her shoulders.

What if he wasn't just pretending to be on her side? What if the need to protect that she sensed radiating from him was real? What if she could trust him?

She wanted him to prove to her she mattered. She wanted it in a way that opened a hollow ache deep within her chest and caused her limbs to tremble. *Why does it concern you? Say the words Ethan. Please say the words and show me I matter.*

Instead, he looked away. "It started concerning me when you both made yourselves at home in my house." He shook his head. "Not one thing has made sense since you showed up. I'm beginning to think your entire existence is a lie."

Despised tears she couldn't stop ran down her cheeks for the second time today.

"Oh, no you don't. You don't get out of this by crying," Ethan said. He tried to sound angry, but there was a wavering in his voice that confessed something softer.

"I'm sorry. I'm not crying on purpose. You'd be the last person ..."

"The last person what?" The anger came back, his sharp tone piercing her heart.

"Never mind."

"So then, answer my question. What's going on here?"

"I don't want to talk about it."

"I didn't ask if you did." His stare bored into her, daring her to ignore him. There was no chance she'd win an argument right now. She felt herself drowning, but refused to let go of the anchor weighing her down just yet. She didn't trust the lifeline he extended.

He lowered himself to the stone wall beside her and exhaled. "Okay, let's start with an easy one. Why didn't you tell me Levi Hollingsworth was your twin brother?"

Shayne wiped at her cheeks and stared up at the stars as if they might align themselves into the answer she needed.

"Okay then, neither of you go by Hickory, so what's with the different last names? Talk to me, Shayne." His words wrapped her in a thread of tenderness, like the swirling stitches securing the quilt.

A safe place for her heart to heal. Wasn't that what she wanted? How would she find it if she didn't try? She looked into eyes that watched her with genuine warmth. *Catch my heart, Ethan.*

"Hollingsworth is our grandmother's maiden name. Levi's relationship with our dad wasn't a good one, so he uses it for performing."

"I might have an idea why you wouldn't want people to know you were related, but I'd like to hear it from you. Why wouldn't you tell me?"

She bit her lip. Maybe it wasn't that she cared whether others knew. She just wanted to forget the fact for herself.

The change in Ethan's voice, a subtle understanding and compassion, stirred a new excitement within her, energized by the tenderness reflected in his eyes. She didn't need light to recall the cinnamon chocolate warmth of the eyes staring back at her.

Her senses took in the smell of bacon and coffee and manliness clinging to him. His nearness drew the air from her lungs.

Truth hung in her chest like a breath that couldn't move. He was right. Everything in her life was a lie. It was the lie that was burying her, and she wanted to break free. Setting herself free would be the only way to release the painful air still caught in her chest. And the only way to breathe again. In this moment, she knew her life depended on taking a new breath.

Without considering the consequences, she let the moment free her, leaning into the feel of freedom until her lips found his. A zing of fiery, unfamiliar electricity shot through her as the taste of his masculinity soaked into her senses. Every long-withheld emotion seemed to flow out of her on the electrical current of that kiss. A volcanic eruption couldn't have released any more pressure—or wreaked any more destruction.

At first he didn't move, then his arms found their way around her, his grip neither tender nor rough. He stood, pulling her tight against him, wrapping her in his arms. Something within him released, as well. The kiss he returned intensified, its heat joining them together like molten ore. An honest mingling of two souls who didn't understand the moment, but weren't willing to risk missing it.

Shayne froze, pulling back sharply. "I'm sorry. I don't know what just happened. I didn't mean to ..." The shock she experienced caused the words to tumble out as she tried to step away. Shame devoured her from the inside, intensifying at the expression on Ethan's face. She had never initiated anything so bold. Even with holding hands, she'd never been the first to reach for Nick's.

Nick. What had she done? Her hand flew to her mouth.

For what seemed an eternity, neither moved. While the blistering heat of desire still lingered, each retreated into the cooling pool of stunned uncertainty.

A throat clearing from the yard near the house spun them around. "Shayne, I ... uhmm ... believe you have a visitor."

CHAPTER TWENTY-SEVEN

What was he doing here? Even in the pale light spilling from the kitchen window, it would be impossible not to recognize the uptight body that stepped through the back door to stand beside Levi.

"Nick?"

Ethan tensed beside her.

Her world of lies finished imploding around her, sucking her back into the grave as she desperately searched for a reason to hang on.

A liar and now a cheat. She deserved no less than a complete burial. But how much had he seen?

Since returning to Turnaround, everything about her had been built on lies. Much like everything had since she left.

"What's going on here, Shayne?" Nick asked. The patronizing tone of his voice pierced her with accusation.

Nick Turner in his slouch beanie and dark jeans that bordered on being too tight, cuffs rolled up over clunky black hiking boots that had probably just seen the most ground they ever would. Everything about him looked out of place in her world.

Her world? That's where she was now, wasn't it? The truth rang through her like the Liberty Bell.

"I wasn't expecting you," Shayne said. It was a stupid and obvious thing to say, and she hated herself for it.

"Obviously." Nick's glare took in both Ethan and Levi. He pressed his lips together as though something unpleasant had touched his tongue, then shook his head. "Unbelievable."

He shall cover you with His feathers, and under His wings you shall take refuge. If only it were that easy, Lord. She felt fully exposed.

Shayne clasped her hands in front of her, careful to conceal the finger with the missing engagement ring.

"Someone want to tell me what's going on here?" Ethan's voice was dark.

"I find you alone with my fiancée, and you're the one asking for an explanation?" His tone hinted at a subtext that wasn't hard to grasp.

A shaky exhale stumbled from between her lips. He hadn't mentioned the kiss.

Ethan slipped closer, angling himself between Shayne and Nick. "Choose your words carefully."

"And you mind your own business." Nick put his hands on his hips, elbows splaying outward.

"Nick, let's go inside and talk about—"

"I wish I could say I'm surprised, but I've always known there was something not quite right with you." He spun away and back again, as if a second look might make things better. "This isn't going to change anything, though. We can fix this. I will not let you ruin the future I've worked for. Get your things. Let's go."

"I ..." Shayne floundered, wanting to diffuse the rising tension, and painfully aware there were no words to justify what she'd done. Even if Nick didn't yet realize the extent of her betrayal, she knew.

And Ethan knew. The realization of what that meant plummeted like a stone to the bottom of her stomach.

"I didn't ask for your input. Get your things, and get in the car," Nick said.

Shayne took a step backwards, offering the only defense she could think of. "But I gave them my word."

"Your word? How valuable that must be." Nick sneered, pulling his wallet from his back pocket. "How much, Shayne? Is that what it is? We need to reimburse for services not rendered. How much did they pay you? We'll refund their money, and they can go find another wh—"

Ethan's hand shot up, planting itself firmly against Nick's chest. "I warned you to watch your mouth."

Nick's words struck her like a fist, punching her heart. This was a side of Nick she'd never experienced before. And it was her fault.

Levi had crept closer, standing beside her opposite of Ethan, thumbs tucked into the front pockets of his jeans. His breath came in a deep, steady rhythm, a sense of control radiating from him.

"I'm so sorry. I am. I ..." Shayne didn't want anything to end this way.

"It was my fault. I was trying to take advantage of the moment. Whatever it is you think you saw, it was all me." Ethan lowered his hand to his side. "It wasn't her fault."

"Not her fault? From what I saw, she didn't look like she objected. If she hadn't been here playing the harl—"

Ethan jabbed his finger into Nick's chest. "I told you to watch your mouth. One more time and I'll make it so you don't have to worry about it."

"I don't believe we've met?" Levi extended his hand, his lazy drawl a drastic change from the heated words coming from the other two. "Name's Levi Hollingsworth."

Nick froze, lips parting as though confused by this information.

Finally, a use for Levi's notoriety. It could only make things worse, but at least it distracted Nick, giving Shayne a moment to recover.

"Levi Hollingsworth? You're kind of a big deal on the Texas music scene." Nick eyed Levi's outstretched hand for a moment before shaking. "Of course. I should have recognized you sooner. Now I'm really curious why you're here."

"Well, you know what they say, curiosity killed the cat." Levi winked at him. "Besides, a man's gotta be somewhere, right?"

Nick laughed, a tight false sound. "I guess that's true, but it's not exactly an answer to my question."

"I'm having myself a little sabbatical."

Nick smirked, his eyes taking in the bruises and cuts still fresh on Levi's face. "A sabbatical with my fiancée."

Levi didn't react. His lackadaisical demeanor never flinched. "Like I said, a man's gotta be somewhere. The lucky ones always understand where they're wanted." He sniffed, giving his head a quick jerk. "And where they aren't."

Nick's eyes narrowed. "I'm not sure what you're implying. But I'm not happy to find you here with my fiancée. I'd wonder how your fans might feel about that, but then those with morals aren't really the ones you attract."

Shayne braced, ready to duck when Levi swung. To her surprise, he laughed, then pressed his hand against his side, wincing. "Easy man. No need to be so territorial. She's all yours ..." he looked at Shayne, "if that's what she wants."

The expression he wore shattered her heart. "Is it Shayne? Is that what you want?"

She kept her mouth closed for fear she'd say something she'd regret. Where was this version of her brother ten years ago?

"Who are you to be asking the questions? We can settle this ourselves. Thank you for your help." As usual, Nick answered for her, his words curt.

Levi gave her a questioning look. "Does he not know? You really didn't tell him?"

Shayne shook her head, unable to speak.

"Know what?" Nick asked.

"You got it wrong. Shayne and I aren't *friends*." Levi grinned and draped his arm over her shoulders. Shayne recognized malicious pleasure aimed at Nick. "This here's my twin sister."

Despite the distance between them, she could feel the tension grinding through Nick's body as he considered Levi's announcement.

"Yeah, right." Nick turned to Shayne.

She nodded.

"He's telling the truth?"

Another nod.

"Why didn't you tell me Levi Hollingsworth was your brother?" Nick's eyebrow arched in accusation.

"Yeah, Shayne, why didn't you tell him? You know, secrets don't make friends." Levi's words teased, but she sensed the wounded quality that lie beneath the surface.

"I just ... I didn't want to sound like I was bragging," she said. Levi's expression told her he saw through the lie.

"Would y'all give us a moment, please?" Shayne asked. She looked at Levi and then at Ethan.

"Sure thing." Levi raised his hands, arms wide as he stepped back, then turned to the porch. "I'll just go sit myself on the porch and watch for falling stars."

She sensed Ethan's eyes on her, checking for confirmation, but she couldn't face the judgment she would see there. Rubbing her arm, she looked away. Finally, he walked off to join Levi.

Nick waited until Ethan moved away before speaking. Without Ethan and Levi there to shield her, his words turned hateful. "I don't know what's going on here. I can't even trust you to tell me the truth. Do you have any idea how it feels to find my fiancée—"

"Don't you dare! I never said yes, so we're not engaged. You have no right to make accusations. This is only ... a misunderstanding." She stopped short of saying innocent. Her feelings about what she'd done were anything but that.

"I caught you alone with another man, and I got the impression it was anything but innocent." Tiny droplets of moisture landed on Shayne's cheek as he leaned in, spitting the words out in his anger. "Now get in the car. We're leaving."

"Leaving?"

"Seriously? You're lucky I'm still willing to marry you. Now you're going to come home and plan a wedding. For God's sake, you have a reputation to at least pretend you care about. We'll have to deal with some damage control once people find out Levi Hollingsworth is your brother, but that might work to our advantage, anyway. Maybe we can lead him to salvation. A little good publicity that would play well with our membership."

His words sickened her. Her brother's salvation was not something to be used as a publicity stunt. She allowed herself a brief glance at the porch to see Levi sitting on the step, watching them. Ethan leaned on the porch post next to him like a guard dog waiting to be let off the leash.

He wanted to defend her, was ready to engage in protecting her at the slightest sign that he should.

In this moment, she wanted to run, only this time it wasn't from, but to. She wasn't sure to what, but for the first time in a long time, she was sure it was out there if she had the courage to go for it.

Kissing Ethan had somehow been a foothold on her climb from the grave. She refused to regret it.

Still, when you've been buried as long as she had, learning to live in your own soul again is a scary thing.

"I can't leave. I've given Kindley and the school my word."

"What about giving me your word? Let them find somebody else." His eyes darted to the men on the porch. "Someone more suited for this kind of environment."

"They won't be able to find anyone on this short notice. It's only for two weeks to help someone in need. And I never gave you my word."

Nick laughed. "You're going to help? That's pretty rich, Shay. You can't even find your way around Austin in the dark."

"I do fine. You just won't let me." Shayne gripped her hands in front of her, pulling them close as though she held on to something that needed protecting. "I didn't know my mother had leased the house to Ethan when I stayed, and neither did Levi. But that's all there is to this. I won't let you make it into something it isn't."

"I'd say there was a bit more to it," Nick said. The degrading tone in his words curdled inside her. A dark look shrouded his features, revealing more than Shayne wanted to see and making her shiver.

He reached for her, grabbing her wounded arm. A small cry of pain slipped out as she jerked her arm from his grasp.

"Don't play the victim card with me. Get in the car." The words were ground out between a jaw clenched in rage.

"Is there a problem here?" Ethan strode toward them, Levi at his side. "And that's a rhetorical question, because clearly there is."

"My fiancée gives me some sob story about how the school needs her, and she's going to save the day by helping them out. Then I show up to find her alone with two men I've never met, and she certainly didn't bother telling me about. No problem at all. But the party's over. Get in the car, Shay."

That Nick refused to acknowledge their lack of an engagement, treating her as though she were some sort of property to possess, alarmed her.

When she failed to obey, he leaned closer, spitting his next words with a vehemence she'd never seen. "I can't believe you're even arguing with me over this after what I just caught you doing."

"I can explain." Could she? A twisted understanding of something she felt in her gut more than reasoned in her head worked its way into her thoughts. The intensity of Nick's anger flowed from a guilt of his own. That was the explanation, but it stung just as smartly as the accusations he flung at her. Shayne stared at the ground as another truth broke through her. Thanks to her lies, Ethan wouldn't be there to catch her heart now.

"I don't need an explanation. My eyes work just fine. I've always known you were a little selfish, but how stupid could I be that I never realized what a self-centered little tramp you were?"

Ethan moved within inches of Nick. "You need to leave."

"Maybe you need to mind your own business. This is between me and her."

"When you started talking to her like that, you included me." Ethan seemed taller and broader than normal.

"I will not stand here and be lectured by a man who doesn't care that he's carrying on with another man's fiancée." Nick was too furious to understand the peril he was putting himself in. He'd probably never dealt with a man like Ethan before. "Was it your idea or hers to take off the engagement ring? Did that make it easier on your conscience if you couldn't see it?"

"What did you say?" Ethan's eyes held a murderous glint.

"Nick, please, you're overreacting. I took the ring off to clean because it's covered in blood. There is nothing going on here. It really is just a big misunderstanding." Shayne didn't want to watch Ethan beat him to a pulp, which was the direction this would go if Nick didn't shut his mouth.

"He didn't know, did he? You really are playing the harlot." Nick continued, not bothering to ask about the cause for a blood covered ring, and oblivious to the danger he put himself in.

Ethan's hand shot out and grabbed a fistful of Nick's collar, lifting him to greater height.

"I said, watch your mouth. She's telling the truth. There's nothing going on here. Trust me, there's zero interest from me in that department." He shot a condemning glance at Shayne. "Now, I'm not asking. I'm telling you to get in your car and take a drive. Come back tomorrow and we can talk this out."

Ethan released Nick with a shove. "Or better yet, never cross my path again."

Nick staggered. "I'll do that. But if you think we're just going to pretend this never happened, you're wrong." He spat the words at Shayne as he backed away. "You don't get to ruin my plans or my reputation. This church plant committee expects a married couple, and that's what they are going to get."

Ethan turned abruptly and moved away, leaving the distance between them to feel like a million miles. Levi gave her a curt nod without meeting her eyes. He walked back to the porch and reclaimed his seat on the steps. The expression on his face said he, too, was a million miles away.

Unable to move from her spot, Shayne shook as she watched Nick leave. It was several minutes before she trusted her legs to move again,

She didn't bother looking up as she headed up the steps into the house.

"Yep, he seems real nice," Levi said, letting his West Texas drawl stretch the words beyond their normal limits.

"Is this all a joke to you?" Shayne asked.

"No one's laughing, are they?" Levi swallowed and continued staring into the night. "I don't like him. I overheard your conversation with him on the phone and saw the way you became a cowed puppy after talking to him. That's not who you are, Shayne."

"Not who I am? Isn't it exactly who you made me?"

"Is it? Hang it all, I wish I knew."

"What do you want from me?"

They were yelling now, their angry voices spilling into the night.

Levi closed his eyes, his breathing suddenly heavy, forced, his words little more than a whisper. "The truth, Shayne. That's all I want. For once, just tell me the truth."

The despair in his voice ripped through her. She squeezed her eyes shut to stop the memories, but they kept coming.

They'd covered her eyes with her own shirt. But sight was the only detail of that night she didn't have.

The feel of the gritty concrete scraping against her back, her knees, her elbows. Her perspiration dampened hair clinging to her sticky body. The touch of cruel, rough hands that smelled of unwashed human flesh and motor grease. The sound of their laughter scuttling about in the small space like feral rodents. The sharp hiss of metal zippers and work boots scuffling over the concrete floor. Breaths rotten with the stench of stale garlic and warm beer. And the sickening odor of the joints they'd smoked right outside the door clinging to their clothes and hair.

And the consuming fear she'd never draw another breath free from the nightmare that trapped her.

Unable to stop the memories dragging her back into the hell of that night, she trembled. Nausea roiled through her. She reached for the rale to steady herself.

"Say it, Shayne. Just say it. You've avoided me for all these years. I was so high that night I don't remember. Not one moment of it, so for God's sake say it." Levi was on his feet, his face inches from hers.

She shrank away from the intensity burning in his eyes, scorching the air between them as he demanded from her what she didn't want to give.

"No." Her throat tightened, making it hurt to swallow. If she said it, if she spoke the words out loud, then she could never again pretend it was only a horrible nightmare. What good would it do? "Leave the past in the past."

The fierceness of his look made her lean away as he took hold of her arms, forcing her to look at him. "You haven't left it in the past. You hate me so much now you can't even stand to talk to me. Don't you think I have a right to know why? To hear you say it."

Ethan rammed his hand against Levi's chest, releasing Shayne from her brother's hold as he shoved Levi back against the house.

"What happened? Tell me now! Please." Levi's plea heaved forth from a broken spirit as Ethan held him pinned in place. His breathing came in ragged jerks as he dragged his fingers through his hair. "You were raped that night, weren't you? And I let it happen. I was too wasted to even know or care what was happening to my sister." Levi sagged against the house, consumed by grief. "Who was it? Who did this to you?"

Shayne shook, every inch of her body reliving that night until she felt nothing but hollowness. "I don't know who *they* were."

"Oh, God," Levi sobbed, his body slumped against Ethan's

muscled arm. His fierce but tear-filled eyes came up to meet hers in the dim porch light. "I may have let them rape your ... your body, Shayne. But I'm not going to let a man like Nick rape your soul. That's what you're letting him do."

"You son of a—" Ethan crushed Levi against the wall, his fist drawn back.

"Stop! Please, just stop." Shayne grabbed Ethan's arm before he could launch his fist into Levi's face. For a moment, nothing moved, not time, not people.

Then Ethan ground Levi against the wall as he released him and stepped back.

"You're bleeding again." Shayne nodded toward the small patch of red spreading over Levi's shirt.

He yanked his shirt down by its hem, his eyes boring into Ethan as he thrust his chest out in defiance. "You want to punch me? Go ahead. It's not like I don't deserve it. I've been knocked down by a lot worse. My old man, in fact. Let's see, I blew a baseball scholarship by getting a DUI. My music career is in the tank. I owe more money than I'll make in a lifetime. And I destroyed the life of the one person I ever cared about. The one person who saw nothing but good in me. And I don't remember a thing about it."

Levi's voice was hoarse as he taunted, as though he wanted the punishment Ethan could give. "For the love of all things holy, did you hear her? All she can think to worry about right now is that I'm bleeding again. You think anything you can do to me matters? Go ahead." He pointed at his chin. "Let me see what you got."

"Just stop." Anguish choked her words as Shayne spun, racing off the porch to disappear into the dark.

She'd spoken those words before and no one had listened then.

CHAPTER TWENTY-EIGHT

Vito stood at the window overlooking the Margolis Social Club below. Hands clasped behind his back, he stared at the growing crowd filling the room. Occasionally, a few of them cast anxious, eager glances at the window where he stood, but they couldn't see him through the one-way glass.

Perhaps they felt his eyes on them because they never looked long. He believed he had that kind of power.

They were wondering when the next course would be offered. The Margolis Social Club was well known for the *something extra* it could provide.

He inhaled the satisfying power of it all. He loved his view from above. What it must feel like to the gods when they looked down on the futility of men.

The little matter of the other night's fiasco would be resolved soon. He'd find a way. The buyer still expected the girl to be delivered, but there was the rest of his payment to consider first.

The wreck troubled him. He felt no sympathy or remorse for the loss of two lives. Their reckless driving had put everything in jeopardy. He had no tolerance for those who couldn't do their jobs well. But it niggled at him about that beast in the road. Fate he believed in, coincidence not so much.

He twisted the gold pinkie ring he wore. This place was starting to bore him, anyway. As a child growing up in the orphanage, he'd dreamed about being a cowboy. His loosely fisted hand tapped the ring against the Texas Star money clip he wore over the front pocket of his starched jeans. It lent credibility to his good ol' boy and proud citizen of the Lone Star state image. He'd played the role admirably, he thought. First with buying the ranch and bringing in high dollar cutting horses. The freedom to move his merchandise around in the back of a horse trailer without raising suspicions had been exhilarating at first. Until it became too easy.

Having a capable, if slightly sociopathic, foreman to front the place worked well. Leech had his appetites, and Vito had his. The arrangement was mutually beneficial ... for now.

That Leech was withholding something from Vito still prickled in his thoughts.

Vito sighed. It was time for a change.

He was tired of wearing denim. The first thing he would do when he stepped away from this charade was purchase a new wardrobe of Brunello Cucinelli.

Tedium with life. That was the problem with genius. One found themselves bored far too quickly and far too often.

The milksop of a man seated at the bar caught his attention.

Soon bored with that as well, Vito glanced at the Breguet watch on his wrist. The clear watch face revealed the inner mechanisms, all moving with intricate precision. Watching the minute movements of each miniature cog and part, all working together in perfection, soothed him.

Either someone had known about the exchange and the money secreted in that truck, or there was a crooked cop with sticky fingers.

His thoughts circled back to the notion that someone knew beforehand. If so, then they would have needed knowledge of the route being taken down to the exact time. They would have had to follow the truck without being noticed, which seemed unlikely. Or they would've had to have been waiting, knowing exactly when and where the accident would take place. Meaning it was no accident.

If the traitor came from within the cartel, they'd take care of it. He'd most likely be out his money, but that was the chance he took in dealing with those sorts to start with. But if the traitor was within his association, that was another matter. He smiled.

The list of possibilities there was short. Only one person was aware there was an exchange about to happen, but Vito had made sure he lacked the intricate details as to time and place. No matter how much he relied on his employees, he kept them on a need-to-know basis.

If the wreck was a staged event meant to supply the opportunity to steal his money, someone would have had to access the files on Vito's computer in order to plan it. Bryce had the skills, but Vito had left him no opportunity. The only ones who had any possible time alone with his computer were the crew of misfit ranch hands they employed. Cleese had done time in prison. Perhaps Vito needed to pay him a bit more consideration.

His attention wandered back to the man at the bar.

It annoyed Vito when people stumbled into the Margolis Social Club, thinking it was something as common as a bar. A backwoods hole-in-the-wall for the drinking of cheap beer and wallowing in sorrow brought on by their ineptitude.

The Social Club was a place where intelligent urbanites from the cities came to play cards. They came to test their mental acuity against one another and hone their skills of deception in the anonymity of this pothole of a town. And if they knew the right word and flashed the correct card, to enjoy something a little more exciting. It was Vito's one attempt at cultural diversion while he played with the persona of Texas horse breeder and upstanding citizen.

Yes, there was a bar, but he served only the finest of brandies. And only to those who played cards and knew the word.

The troubled young man sitting at the bar for the past half hour piqued Vito's curiosity. Most often, when people didn't find what they expected, they politely excused themselves and left. But not this one. He'd claimed a seat at the bar, appearing completely unconcerned no one had served him. Whatever had brought him through the front door clearly consumed his thoughts. But his presence here was wearying Vito.

It was no hard thing to see he was a poser, all image. Like dandelion fluff, to be easily destroyed with one puff of breath. Well, as luck would have it, Vito needed to exhale.

Unhurried, he descended the stairs from his office, his steps following the slow, steady ticking of his watch as he slipped into his current identity as easily as a snake slipped out of its skin.

He stepped behind the bar and approached the man, offering him a drink, "on the house for first-time visitors."

The man hesitated, then, to Vito's surprise, accepted. He slid the crystal snifter containing beautiful and expensive burnished brown liquid in front of him.

Uncertainty flickered over the young man's features, confirming what Vito already knew. He wasn't here for a drink. In fact, the man shifted uncomfortably, as if the idea of alcohol was slightly distasteful to him. Out of amusement more than desired fellowship, Vito poured himself a drink, lifted the glass and toasted. "Here's to life and love." He raised the glass to his mouth and savored a sip. One did not toss back his brandy like a shot of cheap whiskey.

He suppressed a smirk as the man first watched him, then looked around the room before copying Vito. The man flinched, his eyes watering as the alcohol burned his throat. The warmth a man always felt as that first sip hit his gut, settled the look the visitor wore into something a bit more appreciative. And mildly astonished by his liking. Not an uncommon reaction to one's first taste of fine liquor.

"You like?" He asked, as he poured another round into the empty glass without waiting for a response.

"Might as well." This time, the man downed the liquid with a speed that grated on Vito's nerves. The flavors of such a fine beverage were not to be appreciated by gulping it down like boxed wine. But Vito wasn't interested in stimulating culture in his guest. He was bored and, at the moment, the sad looking excuse for a human sitting in front of him was the best diversion available.

"You are here to play cards?" Vito asked.

The man looked around as if aware of the card games going on around him for the first time. "Just need directions out of here. No idea how people function in this hayseed hole-in-the-wall place without their GPS working."

Disgusted, the man shook his head, then returned to staring at his phone screen as though he'd like to smash the device. But the picture on the screen led Vito to believe the lack of an accurately functioning GPS wasn't the object of his hostility.

A smiling couple stared up from the device. Vito repressed the amusement he felt on the inside. At least half of that couple wasn't smiling right now.

Ah ... but the woman next to him in the picture. Now there was some potential for piquing the interest of a man like Vito.

"Your girl?" Vito made sure he looked appropriately interested. No more, no less.

The man hesitated again, then angled the screen for him to see. Vito made quick work of observing the photo, portraying only a casual curiosity that hid the truth while thoughts of what he might do to her sent fire through his veins.

His mouth watered. Her eyes made her absolutely tantalizing. She was guarding something. There behind the—brown, he believed, but hard to tell from the picture—eyes, was a secret. This one wore her mask on the inside.

The eyes truly were windows into the soul.

Oh, those eyes. What would they look like in that moment when realization came, and fear replaced the strength he saw there now?

He inhaled a slow, almost ragged breath as the tip of his tongue slid between his lips. His desire had nothing to do with a physical attraction. It was the psychological thrill of breaking her that set him aflame. He could almost taste the moment. His fingers tightened around the decanter he still held.

"Problems with your woman?" he asked.

The man snorted as though the question wasn't worthy of an answer.

"I'm Vito." He extended his hand. "And if you don't mind my saying so, I've had plenty of problems with the women myself."

The man eyed him warily before shaking his hand. "Nick. What makes you think there's a problem?"

"It happens all the time. Women, eh." Vito had already taken in the fact that Nick was without a wedding ring. That made him even more vulnerable. Being legally married gave a man certain rights with his woman, rights a single man still had to claim the hard way.

Nick's shirt sleeve rode up to reveal a silver bracelet with some sort of religious message on it.

Vito smiled. This just kept getting better. He propped an elbow on the bar and leaned toward Nick. "So tell me about it. What'd she do?"

Nick shifted in his seat, refusing to meet Vito's stare.

"Another man, perhaps?"

"No." His defense came a little too rapidly and a little too passionately.

He was lying. This one was prideful, and Vito had just insulted his fragile manhood. He pushed it further. "Ah, so it's what she's not doing, eh?" He quirked an eyebrow suggestively.

Nick's eyes dilated. Vito knew he had seen inside the man's hidden thoughts even as he watched him press his lips into a thin, pale line.

Quickly shifting his telltale eyes away from Vito, Nick pursed his lips, a fleeting grimace that was replaced with an uneven smile. "I don't know exactly what it is she's not doing, other than she's *not doing* it with me."

Indecision and distrust flickered in Nick's eyes before being replaced with anger and defiance. He leaned Vito's direction, lowering his voice. "I mean, I watch some stuff, but it's not like I expect any of that from her yet. She's pure. Our wedding night will be her first time. That's how a good wife should be, right?"

"Ah," Vito leaned in slightly, mirroring Nick's posture, encouraging him to continue without verbally asking.

Nick's nostrils flared, and Vito noted his breathing had become slightly shallower. "She should save herself for me. That's what a godly woman does, right? If she's not pure ..." He clamped his mouth shut, a flash of regret sparking in his eyes. "You'd think she'd be more appreciative of all that I'm offering her. I'm going to pastor a mega church one day, and my wife needs to be spotless."

"The spotless bride," Vito said, tilting his head sympathetically. "Sounds like you got a problem on your hands then, friend. How about I offer you a bit of distraction, eh? Name your pleasure." He cut his eyes toward a closed door at the back of the room, making sure Nick followed his gaze.

"Are you suggesting...?" Nick licked his lips as tiny beads of sweat formed along his brow, but he didn't finish the question.

"A man should not be afraid of his needs. Nor should he be denied. And sometimes looking just isn't enough, eh?"

Nick shook his head, looking as much disgusted as he was frustrated. "Look man, I watch some stuff, but I'm not paying for sex."

"An honorable answer for a man seeking to serve the Lord." Vito refilled his glass and waited while Nick downed it again, refraining from knocking it out of the heathen's hands. "You want a little advice?"

Nick didn't answer, but Vito took the glance he gave him as a yes.

"You must make sure she knows you're the man. You must be in charge—always. Let me ask you, whatever this thing is she is or isn't doing, did you make certain she knows what your wishes are?"

"She was supposed to come home after that old lady's funeral."

"I'm guessing she has failed to comply." Vito's fingers curled into a fist before he reclaimed neutrality in his demeanor. It wouldn't do to give away his increased interest.

Once again, the gods were sent to honor Vito Slavin.

Nick sneered. "She decided to ..." He trailed off and Vito understood the truth was hard for someone like him to accept. "She said he was her brother, but she'd never mentioned anything about him to me before. You'd think she would have mentioned that her brother was Levi Hollingsworth." He mumbled as if speaking only to himself, then to Vito, "Now she's saying she made a promise to help coach some girl for a cross country meet."

"So there is another man." Vito weighed his words, careful not to give away the fact that man was exactly who he sought to kill. And now he had all the information he needed. There were few places where a runner trained for cross country and even fewer times when they might, thanks to the short days of winter. "I see you are a god-fearing man. The requirement for your fiancée, soon to be a wife, is obedience. It is biblical, no?"

Not that Vito concerned himself with anything of a biblical nature. The book itself had been an interesting read, full of far more violence and sinfulness than most people knew or admitted they knew. It was practically an instruction manual for wickedness. That was one thing he could have admired about the ancient Hebrews. But he also could have taught them a thing or two. In his opinion, they ruined the whole thing when they began preaching the weak thinking of love and mercy and forgiveness. Those things would never happen in this world. Power and fear were the only things this world understood.

"She's just ... she's not following our plan. We had everything settled exactly the way I wanted it, the way it should be, until she came back here."

Good for her, Vito thought. The poser in front of him lacked the backbone to keep his woman at home or in line. That he was willingly admitting it to a total stranger disgusted Vito. Nick spun the empty glass on the bar top, the sound rasping on both Vito's nerves and his patience.

The timing of her arrival here heightened his interest in her beyond the desire to torment the pitiful excuse of a man in front of him. The money—his money—was still missing. He didn't intend to overlook any possibility of finding it. This was the second time the subject of an old woman's funeral had come up in a conversation. And the second time a young woman had been mentioned there as well.

Now this new piece of information struck him like a tent stake through his temple. The female in question was the sister of the man Vito had caught with his merchandise. Once again, Vito would place his bets on fate. Coincidence, not so much.

Even more troublesome was the fact Leech had mentioned a woman being shot at the accident where his money had disappeared. A woman who had been back in town for a funeral. A woman about which Leech hadn't told Vito everything he knew. Vito's grip on the smooth curve of the bar's edge tightened. If he discovered Leech was involved in double crossing him, he would see to it his death was slow and excruciating—his and anyone Vito found with him.

"So you just want her to come home. That is all?"

"Yeah. Come home and we'll forget all about ..." Nick cut his eyes to Vito, then looked away, "this little episode."

Vito thought about following Nick from town and putting him out of everyone's misery, but he wasn't worth the effort. Besides, he could enjoy himself more knowing Nick would have to live with the consequences of what he was about to agree to.

"I wouldn't say this to just anybody, but you are wanting to serve the Lord and I can see Satan is using her to bring you grief. Let me do you a little favor." Vito held his hands out as though he were offering himself personally.

"How exactly do you think you can help? She's not going to—" color crept into Nick's face, but he kept his eyes averted, "talk to a man she doesn't know."

Vito wanted to chuckle. *Oh, she'll speak to me ... in begging and pleading and the submission you aren't man enough to demand from her.* "I wouldn't have thought otherwise, but I wasn't planning to have a conversation. There are other ways to convince her she needs to be at home where she belongs."

Nick seemed to contemplate the offer, as though some part of him realized he was making a deal with the devil, but pride won out.

"What do you have in mind?"

CHAPTER TWENTY-NINE

Levi hadn't lingered outside after Shayne stormed off. Ethan, however, had remained stationed like a paid bodyguard. Or perhaps he was more like a personal guardian. Shayne had waited long after the fire of her emotions burned out in the hopes he'd move. The last thing she wanted this evening was another confrontation. Ethan had as much right to despise her as everyone else did. Maybe more so.

Finally, the cold had driven her back to the house despite his waiting presence on the porch.

To her relief, he hadn't said a word or even glanced at her as she slipped up the steps and into the house. It was what she thought she'd wanted until it was what she got. Not knowing what he was thinking or where she stood with him now consumed far more of her thoughts than what she'd done to Nick.

A fragile ray of light from the early morning sun eased across the room to settle on her phone. Shayne looked at the screen. Still no message from Nick. Had he driven all the way back to Austin last night? She regretted the guilt-ridden message she'd left him before going to bed, but that didn't mean she wasn't worried about him too.

Their relationship was over, but there were still things that needed to be said.

Like I'm sorry. Both of them needed to speak those words. And delaying the inevitable was probably the cause of their current distress.

That and her lies, both the ones she told herself and the ones she told others.

Nick was in love—if that was even what she'd call it now—with a fraud. A fraud that didn't love him, only what he could give her. And after what she heard in his words and felt in his actions last night, that was all she was to him as well.

Not wearing the ring hadn't meant to be a deception. It wasn't her intent to appear single or available. She only wanted to experience herself as Shayne Wright one more time before Nick took that away from her. She covered her eyes with her hands, but there were no more tears to cry.

Even the words in her head were all wrong. Nick wasn't taking her identity from her. She was giving it away.

A stitch of panic needled her. Staying here was a mistake. Agreeing to a job that kept her here was a disaster in the making. Was this the result of cold feet? Her fingers went to the silver band she wore, pausing when her gaze landed on the compass.

Unless this was what she really wanted. Resolution bubbled within her.

Resolution for everything except Ethan. She didn't yet understand why her heart kept inserting him into her head. Everything about him was all wrong.

Except for the kiss.

Kissing Ethan ... she still didn't regret it, but she did plan to avoid him this morning and pretend it never happened.

She slipped down the stairs, planning to grab an apple on

her way out the door and hoping to go unnoticed. She had a job to do today and with her swollen eyes, she already looked like a questionable choice for teaching teenagers.

The smell of fresh coffee was the first thing that met her as she stepped into the kitchen. The broad back of the man she was trying to avoid was the second. Ethan stretched the tape measure across the counter-top and jotted down a measurement on the notepad beside him.

Stopping in the kitchen doorway, she frowned. "What are you doing?"

"Measuring." He didn't bother to look at her.

"I can tell that, but I want to know why."

"Then next time ask why," he glanced her way, "instead of what."

"Is there anything that could make you a less obstinate person?"

"Probably."

"Such as?"

"Not having foolish—or pointless—conversations first thing in the morning."

She wrapped her arms around her, drawing her shoulders in. Then she recalled the kiss, and her mouth went dry. *Please Lord, let him be as eager to pretend that didn't happen as I am.*

Ethan paused, staring. The intensity in his eyes as they took in everything about her made her feel analyzed. No doubt what he saw and the conclusion he reached confirmed his estimation. Just another foolish, hysterical woman ... every bit the fraud he called her out for.

"I didn't mean to be foolish," Shayne said.

"I didn't say *you* were foolish. I said the conversation was."

"Only because you made it that way by being obstinate."

He didn't respond, just stared for a moment. A slow grin crawled across his face, and he laughed. "Possibly."

Shayne couldn't stop the traitorous blush that she felt

taking over her cheeks. Irritated that a man who didn't like her could fluster her so easily, she clamped her hands on her hips, elbows out and spine straight. *But did he just laugh?*

Ethan turned back to measuring, extending the tape measure.

"All right then, why are you measuring the cabinets in my grandparents' house?"

"It's a necessary part of the remodeling process."

"Remodeling? Who said you could remodel?"

"No one ... yet."

"I'll save you some time. Stop. This house is not being changed."

"Hmmm." He let the yellow strip of metal tape race back into its container, the zinging sound it made mimicking the one Shayne heard in her heart.

"What does that mean?"

He turned to face her, fisted knuckles planted on the table as he leaned toward her. "It means you really don't talk to your family much, do you?"

Shayne frowned.

"I spoke to your mother—" Ethan said.

"My mother! You didn't tell her I was here. She doesn't know about Levi, does she? What did you—"

"Relax. I told her I had some thoughts on remodeling and repairs if she was interested in updating the place. Your name never came up." The accusation in his eyes said he had an opinion on the subject he'd keep to himself for now.

Shayne exhaled.

Ethan peered at her. "From what I've seen so far, there a number of things around here about to fall apart."

———

Ethan chided himself for trying to draw her into an argument. He enjoyed watching her get riled more than he should. But darn it all, he'd seen her come out from behind the wall she'd built a time or two, and it never failed to quicken his pulse. Which was a clear sign he should stop.

But what was a guy supposed to say after everything he'd heard last night. He had proved himself to be a callous jerk by the things he'd said to her. His ignorance of what had happened to her didn't excuse him for being a first-class cad.

He wasn't sure how to make amends for that, so teasing her into a state of annoyance seemed the most logical choice. She'd understand the meaning behind his aggravating her, right?

To say she was a mystery would be an understatement, but then when had he ever understood any female? If he could forget the kiss, he might manage to walk away. And that alone would be an impossible *if*.

But he'd never forget those eyes. And he'd never understand what they saw in Nick Turner.

She was too good for a man like Nick. How did she not see that?

He turned back to measuring the cabinets. Everything male in him wanted her to understand Nick wasn't the one for her. And yet he knew he had no right to tell her and no reason she'd believe him.

"We'll see." She wasn't giving in, but she also wasn't fighting. She stepped around the opposite side of the table and reached for an apple.

"Life is hard on a ... home, especially when it's left empty and untended. If you don't address what needs repaired, it'll all fall down around you. It's not healthy to pretend problems don't exist."

She stared at the countertop. Lines of worry written on

her face failed to reveal to him what she was thinking. But whatever it was, it must have troubled her.

He saw something else, too. Fear. She was afraid of letting go. Of what, he didn't know, but he was well enough acquainted with fear to recognize it in her eyes. "There's plenty of coffee if you'd like any."

"No, thanks," she said, clearly distracted. Judging by the level of tension radiating off her, the distraction had nothing to do with coffee or remodeling.

"There's something we still need to discuss." Technically, Ethan didn't plan to discuss it. It was his place to make the call. He just wanted to see what she was willing to agree to before he told her she could stay. After that unexpected kiss, he needed to know what the rules of engagement were going to be. She'd come as close as possible to turning him into the same person Alexa had been. It was a line he wasn't willing to cross.

Shayne glanced at her watch. "I need to get going. There'll be papers for me to fill out this morning, and I can't be late."

Ethan rested back against the counter, arms crossed. "That's what we need to talk about. After meeting your fiancé —a rather untimely meeting, I might add—I've wondered exactly why you're doing this?"

"Nostalgia, I guess." She busied herself searching through her purse. "They asked for my help."

"Uh hmm." He scratched his beard. "I think you're lying, and you just don't know it yet."

"Well, you're wrong. And I need to go now." She pulled her keyring from the purse. Her eyes darted to him, a flicker of defiance sparking there.

"Nostalgia doesn't make you take a job you weren't looking for and don't need. It doesn't make you walk out on your fiancé. And it certainly doesn't make you take up residence with a total stranger."

"If you want to accuse me of something, then please, just say it." A hint of anger noodled its way into her challenge.

"All I'm saying is that for someone who didn't plan to stay, you certainly packed a lot of clothes." He picked up one of the apples she'd bought, shined it on the t-shirt he wore, then took a bite before turning to take another measurement.

Her angry steps thumped across the wood floor to the front door.

"What? No goodbye kiss?" Ethan called after her, then realized he was only half joking. Yep, he was in over his head.

CHAPTER THIRTY

Shayne pulled into the school parking lot without the normal tingly sense of anticipation. Instead, she was gripped by the churning waves of too many other emotions. Dread, self-doubt, shame.

Anger at herself.

What if they found out? How could she stand in front of a class full of teenagers if they knew what had happened to her? Or what she had done last night? She never should have agreed to this.

Perhaps this was just another in her long list of poor decisions.

She stared at the two-story sandstone building that housed the school. A relic from another time, with multiple additions over the years. Each section was a witness to the decade that had contributed to its existence. Walking through the halls was like architectural time travel.

Her mother and father had gone to school here. High school sweethearts who had found that life outside of Turn-around didn't delight in their love story as much as they did. The divorce had been brutal, and her father had become a rare and random figure in Shayne's life until she'd moved in with him her senior year. Thanks to his job as an attorney at a prestigious law firm, he'd still been a random figure in her life, but at least he seemed glad to have her around.

What was she trying to prove by coming here now?

A sensible person would drive straight back to the man who promised her a safe future.

Two things kept her from it.

First, she was tired of being sensible. What she craved was to feel alive, to feel real. The reckless action that had led to the unforgettable kiss had broken open a well of yearning for things that spoke of daring adventure. A life fully lived.

I have come that they may have life and have it abundantly. Jesus spoke these words although Shayne couldn't recall the verse exactly. What she did know, though, was that Jesus had chosen death nailed to a cross so she could have that life. Did she really have the right to throw that away?

The second thing keeping her from going back to Nick was that she wasn't really sure that was the course of action a sensible person would take. She'd witnessed another side of Nick, and what she'd seen scared her. She couldn't quite blur the lines to make it work anymore.

A few minutes later, she stood in the empty front office wondering if she'd come too early. A harried woman with an armload of papers charged through the door, teetering slightly off balance as she swerved to avoid colliding with Shayne.

"I'm so sorry," she said as she deposited the stack on the desk. She ran both hands over her hair, flattening the wayward curls, then turned to greet Shayne. "How can I help you?"

"I'm Shayne Wri—"

"Oh, yes! Thank goodness." The young woman laughed, clasping her hands in front of her as she rocked up on her toes. "Our new—well, temporary, but still—English teacher and cross-country coach extraordinaire. I'm Lacy, the school counselor. The secretary is out today, but she had me pull some papers for you to fill out." She sifted through the files she'd just heaved onto her desk.

"Here they are. You'll have to forgive us. I was at a training for school counselor's last week. Things around here are a mad house today, what with the funeral and all. You know about the funeral, right?" she asked.

Shayne shook her head.

"It's not really a funeral per se." Lacy did that funny laughing, hand clasping thing again. "I'm really not sure what you call it when it's for a cow."

"Buster wasn't a cow, Lacy. He was a steer." A male teenage voice resonated from beneath the desk.

Shayne smiled. The voice was right, and Lacy clearly wasn't from around here.

"Anyway, Buster *the steer* got out and someone ran over him last week. And he's a bit of a big deal around here—of course you probably already know that—anyway, they're holding a ceremony to bury him at the park this morning."

"I'm familiar with Buster."

"Oh, good, then you already know it's kind of a major upset to folks around here. You'd think the mayor died—no disrespect to Buster. People are more worked up over that animal than they are the two men who died in the accident."

"They were drug dealers, Lacy," the voice from beneath the desk interjected again.

Lacy leaned close to whisper, "Please excuse him. One of his jobs was taking care of Buster to help earn some money. Our parents sent him here to live with me after he got into a little trouble last year, and... well, it's going to be awhile before he gets his debt repaid. He still has his other jobs, but I'm not fond of those."

Shayne nodded, understanding that jobs for teenagers in small towns could be hard to find, especially if you were a new kid. "I think we're lucky no one else died. There was a motorcycle that must have just missed the accident. He ran me off the road right before I came upon the wreck," Shayne said.

A thump sounded against the desk, followed by the sound of something clattering to the floor.

"See Collin. I told you motorcycles were dangerous," Lacy said, then continued, "So you're the one? Nobody said. Well, not officially, but ..." Lacy blinked, biting her lip as though she suddenly thought better of finishing her statement. "Collin, you need to stop messing with that and get to class." Lacy handed the folder to Shayne. "Collin's my baby—"

"I'm six foot one, Lacy. I'm not a baby anything."

Lacy rolled her eyes. "He's my younger brother and a technical genius. Which is how he got into trouble at his last school when he used his talent to hack into the school's records. He's trying to set up a second monitor for me now. I'll ask one of the other teachers to assist you with wrangling your class to Buster's funeral. Of course, second period you have the juniors. They're usually pretty tame. Collin can show you where your room is, and you can drop the papers off later."

The teenager climbed out from under the desk and Shayne recognized the boy who'd had her phone that first morning at the cafe.

The unexpected animosity she felt radiating from the youth beside her only helped reinforce her doubts that there was anything good to be gained by being here.

Students always expected the worst from their substitute teachers. Especially when they've hacked into their phones and scrolled through their personal information. Shayne arched an eyebrow as he glanced at her.

"A technical genius, huh?" She attempted to make conversation as she followed Collin down the hallway.

"So they say." His tone made it clear he wasn't interested in conversation.

Shayne lacked the energy to keep trying.

As she followed the sullen teenager down familiar hallways, she acknowledged even more than the feeling there was nothing to be gained, that maybe a more accurate perspective was that she had nothing left to lose.

———

The day narrowed down like a funnel, draining Shayne back to the inevitable return to the battlefield ... or home, as she used to call it. The classes and students had been a pleasant diversion during the day. Then she found she'd actually enjoyed the challenge of coaching Kindley after school.

Convincing someone to believe in their potential required a mental strategy, not unlike a game of chess. One didn't simply walk up to a teenager and announce the truth, expecting they'd believe it. Truth was more often discovered by sight rather than sound.

Kindley had potential. What she didn't have was a heart for running. Running gave her something to do for which she could garner some attention. That was what she wanted most of all.

Not ready to go home, she stopped by the Buffalo Nickle Dime Store, then found an out of the way place to park on a side street by the church. Shayne was ready to indulge in a sugar fix, as she ripped open the bag of Reese's peanut butter cups. The sensation of chocolate on her tastebuds relaxed her. Life wasn't all bad. She ate three before closing the bag with finality and setting it in the passenger seat.

The sun slipped lower, casting the shadow of the steeple

across the pavement before her. A gust of wind carried a parade of rust and golden colored leaves down the pavement. A rare contentment settled over her. Maybe the place she'd run from was the place she'd been running to all these years.

All about perspective, Ethan's voice crowded into her thoughts.

She rolled her eyes, finding it exasperating that Ethan was the one who spoke the most truth into her life now, whether he realized—or intended—it.

That much she had in common with Kindley. Shayne needed to see the truth, not just hear it.

Ethan was an angry, unhappy, arrogant person. The bitterness in his words still stung. *Zero interest*.

Sure, he'd returned her kiss in a way no man had ever kissed her and held her like no man had ever held her. And he'd defended her against Nick, lying to say he was to blame for initiating the ... moment of passion. She had no other words for it.

Then he'd brushed her off like an offensive piece of lint clinging to his shirt. Or had he?

Waiting in the evening chill for her to come back inside suggested otherwise.

Still, *zero interest*. His acting as a gentleman didn't have to equate to an interest in her personally.

She'd given him plenty of reason for his animosity. Once he'd discovered the truth ... well, it really shouldn't surprise her if he didn't want anything more to do with her. Their conversation this morning had skated dangerously close to the edge of something she wouldn't want to hear.

There's something else we need to talk about ... like why're you doing this?

Memory of his statement gave her no incentive to hurry home.

She sneaked a fourth Reese's and retrieved the folder of

poems Maribel had given her from her purse. She let the chocolate and sugary peanut butter dissolve in her mouth as she studied the rubric for grading.

A half hour later, she pressed back in the seat, arrested by the words she'd just read. She'd muddled through a half dozen collections of juvenile contemplations expressed in lines of elementary rhyming words, but this one had stopped her. Perhaps the creation of a vivid imagination, or perhaps, as Maribel had said, a window into a tender, hurting heart. It was the latter possibility that concerned Shayne.

There would be more to rescuing Kindley than she had imagined.

Someone Kindley's age should be to innocent to write about something so dark. How was it possible?

She closed her eyes, willing the tears not to come. She knew how.

Lost in Kindley's words, Shayne jumped at the tap on her window. Bryce Leech bent down to peer through the glass.

She'd let her guard down, but the usual panic didn't overwhelm her. Even now, Kindley's words clung to her thoughts, distracting her from the possibility of danger.

"I'm sorry," he said. He held his hands out, palms exposed. "I didn't mean to startle you."

Shayne lowered the window a few inches, stopping short of being enough for him to get a hand through. "Can I help you?"

He shook his head and chuckled. "I was about to ask you the same thing. I noticed you sitting here when I came by earlier, and when I saw you still here, I was concerned something might be wrong. Everything all right?"

Shayne relaxed, remembering good Samaritan-ship was still the norm in places like Turnaround. "I'm fine. Just," she held up the stack of papers, "enjoying some quiet time and grading papers."

"Good. I mean good that you're enjoying a moment to yourself, but not good that it's apparently not quiet where you live."

"Understatement," Shayne replied.

"I haven't introduced myself. I'm Bryce." He extended his hand but switched to a small wave. "But I see we will not be shaking hands."

Shayne toyed with the idea of fully lowering the window, but he continued before she reached a decision. There was no reason to tell him she remembered him from so many years ago. After all, they'd never actually met. And she wasn't sure how she felt about his conversation with Conner concerning her.

"I wanted to introduce myself yesterday, but I'd just returned from an extended trip and was anxious to get back and check on my mares. One was about to foal."

"Was she all right?" Shayne eased the window down, deciding it was better than trying to talk through the glass.

"Everything went well." His gaze moved down the street to a black SUV parked at the corner, his eyes narrowing as if he saw something he didn't like. It was the same one Shayne had noticed driving past the school during her cross-country practice with Kindley. "Well, if everything is okay, I guess I'll be going now. But I would feel better about this if I knew you weren't going to keep sitting here alone in the dark. It's not safe." He glanced to the black SUV down the street again.

Shayne thanked him for checking on her, assuring him she didn't plan to stay much longer.

He took a few steps, then stopped, turning back to face her. "I was hoping to visit with Reverend Stapleton about a charity I'm interested in helping with, but he's still out of town. Now I find myself with a little extra time. You wouldn't want to join me for dinner, would you?"

Shayne eyed the man, clean cut, tall, and attractive. And

an amiable smile. The complete polar opposite of Ethan. "No, thank you. I should probably get home now."

"Well, don't hold it against a man for hoping." His smile radiated charm. "Maybe some other time. I'm sure we'll be seeing more of each other soon. Small towns, right Miss Wright?" The wink he gave bore a suggestive undertone. Or possibly she'd consumed too much sugar.

An unreadable glint in his eyes hinted at a secret promise.

Unable to decide how best to respond, Shayne remained quiet.

The look disappeared, leaving Shayne wondering if she'd only imagined it. Then he winked, the action carrying no subtext other than *it's been a pleasure*. "Until next time, Miss Wright."

CHAPTER THIRTY-ONE

Filling his lungs with crisp fall air, Ethan stomped back from the river bottom in the lengthening late-day shadows. With the pretext of scouting out a good fishing hole as an excuse to wander around for the past two hours, he'd hoped to enjoy some therapeutic time in the outdoors. Maybe clear his head and organize his thoughts about what Reuben had told him. They were ramping up the investigation on their end, but needed him to stay close by in case.

He was in a holding pattern. And Ethan didn't do well in inactivity.

The head clearing he hoped for hadn't happened.

Where was she? School had ended a couple of hours ago. How long did cross-country practice take? Surely they didn't run in the dark. They weren't training for a combat mission.

Not that he wanted to see her.

Lie. He wanted to *not* want to see her. But that wasn't the case. He'd heard of the phantom pains a person felt when they lost a limb, but was it possible to have a phantom pain caused by a single kiss? A single illicit kiss of betrayal.

Recognition of the man Nick was grated through him, but

didn't erase her deceit. Ethan couldn't overlook the fact that she was no different from Alexa. Promises meant nothing to her.

Only she was different in every way. She completely captivated him.

He huffed, reminding himself not to confuse captivating with bewitching.

Was he really that much different? An honest evaluation of himself—the kind a man gets while wandering through the woods—said no. His faults might be the exact opposite of Nick's, but they were still faults.

Back at the house, but still in need of a distraction, he snagged the toolbox from his truck, pausing for a moment to stare at the damage she'd already done in his life.

The house was empty. Good. He'd had enough time with Levi when he'd taken him to get his truck this morning. Even without talking, the somber weight of Levi's thoughts had pressed into Ethan's mood. The revelations made last night proved to be a brutal burden for them all, albeit for different reasons.

Ethan set the toolbox on the counter and pulled out his notepad and tape measure. He didn't know why he was doing this, other than he couldn't think of anything else to occupy his thoughts.

The back door opened as he stretched the tape measure across the windowsill. The unwanted hope it was Shayne rose like a hot air balloon in his chest. He would have seen her drive up, though.

The balloon popped, torpedoed by Levi's appearance in the doorway.

Carrying a small box in his hand, Levi staggered in as though only half aware of his surroundings.

Ethan ignored him and began measuring the windows.

Levi stopped to watch. "Uhm ... what're you doing?"

"Measuring."

"So I see. Why?"

"It helps with the remodeling."

Levi let out a long, slow whistle. "She is not going to like that."

"It's not her call." A small stab of regret nicked at his heart, knowing Levi was right. She'd already made that perfectly clear.

Levi slouched onto the couch, dropping the box beside him. "You like her? And before you answer, let me remind you I was witness to that rather passionate moment between you two. As her brother, I thought briefly about punching you."

"I wish you would've tried."

"No doubt. But a part of me also thought good for her. So, do you like her?"

"She's engaged." Ethan kept his back to Levi, taking longer to read the tape measure than he needed.

"I'm not too sure about that, and that wasn't my question."

"Doesn't matter." He gave Levi a warning look meant to put an end to that discussion.

"I think you're wrong." Levi leaned forward, elbows coming to rest on his knees, letting his forearms dangle as he ignored Ethan's warning. "You see, twins have this special connection. Like sometimes we sense the same things the other one is feeling."

Ethan jotted measurements on the paper and moved to the next window.

"I don't want you to take this the wrong way, but I'm pretty sure she likes you." He shook his head. "And I promise you I am not enjoying being a part of this shared feeling."

Ethan attempted to glare Levi into silence, but drew a cavalier grin and a shrug from him instead.

Levi rocked back, thumping his fist on the cushioned seat

beside him. "Look, I'm being serious, man. She deserves better than Nick."

"I'm not what she needs."

"You're exactly what she needs." Levi licked his lips and shook his head. "I don't think you understand what happened last night. My sister never dated. Throughout high school, she was the good girl, innocent. She always knew what she wanted and claimed she wasn't interested in dating until she found it."

Levi swallowed as though his mouth overflowed with a bitterness that might choke him. "That night ... I don't remember a single thing other than talking her into going with me so she could drive me home. I was mad at our old man and planned to get wasted. I never once considered what kind of danger I was putting her in."

The confession may have been cleansing for Levi, but it fed into Ethan's simmering wrath.

"I think somehow maybe I've always known—that stupid twin thing—but hearing her say it last night ..." His words trailed off as his eyes filled with pain. He thrust the box to Ethan. "Here. I want you to get rid of this for me."

Ethan eyed him warily. "What is it?"

"Open it."

Ethan hesitated, then took the box from Levi's hand and lifted the lid, exposing an assortment of drug paraphernalia and a few dime bags filled with weed. "Get rid of it yourself." He flung the box back into Levi's lap.

"No, man, you don't understand. I've been clean for thirty-three days now, but ...I'm asking you to do this because I need someone who'll bust my chops if I ever even think about it again. And you're frankly the scariest person I know who won't actually kill me."

"What makes you so sure I wouldn't?"

"Because you care about her." He pinched the bridge of

his nose. "I know what my heart issue is, and I don't want to do this anymore. I need you to hold me accountable—for her."

Levi cut his eyes up to Ethan, the intensity burning in them, pinning Ethan's conscience to his heart. "And I want you to save my sister."

CHAPTER THIRTY-TWO

Shayne deposited the sack of groceries onto the passenger floorboard, then walked around to the driver's side and climbed in, glimpsing herself in the rearview mirror as she did. In the words of Grandma Hazel, she looked like death warmed over. Being shot might have a little to do with that. Working as a substitute teacher definitely did.

The sugar crash after devouring half a bag of Reese's Peanut Butter Cups didn't help.

She had devised one last excuse to delay her return to the house—a quick trip to the grocery store to purchase the ingredients she'd need to make chicken noodle soup for Levi. A home cooked meal would counter the effects of all the chaos and misfortune. Cooking was therapy and food was medicine, or so Grandma Hazel always said. Of course, she'd also said the way to a man's heart was through his stomach— and that was a journey Shayne didn't plan to take.

That she'd bought enough food for three was purely an act of hospitality. Nothing more.

Perhaps she should've taken Bryce up on his offer of dinner.

Bryce—the man who managed the ranch where Levi supposedly saw a woman being held against her will and where someone tried to kill him. But Maribel had said he was generous in his giving at the church, and he had been in town this evening to talk to Mack about a charity he wanted to help with. Plus, Jimmo said he treated him fairly as an employee. If he gave all his attention to his horses, he might be unaware of anything like that happening on the property. Or maybe Levi was wrong.

Ethan must not think so, or he wouldn't have gone to the sheriff.

Ethan McGregor. Not handsome, but made attractive by some compelling quality she hadn't yet identified. The kiss last night still tingled through her body, forcing her to resist the urge to touch her lips all day. But it was the intensity in his eyes when he looked at her that touched her broken places, covering them in the belief restoration was possible. He looked at her as if he saw something whole, something intriguing, something of value.

His smell had lingered in her senses all day too, twisting itself up in the image she had of him. He smelled of assurance, as though he was confident in himself and knew exactly how to handle everything that came his way. Of course, she'd already seen that wasn't the case. But it didn't change the fact the scent of him warmed her all the way to her toes.

She couldn't deny the intuition telling her Ethan suffered from his own form of unhealed wounding, too. She might not know the source, but the sadness in his eyes revealed its presence. Plus, he'd made it abundantly clear he had no interest. The binding connection that embrace had stirred in her—like two copper wires soldered together beneath a smoldering heat of compassion—was not mutual.

Zero interest echoed in her head again.

She'd never do anything so bold and heart-wrenching again.

Ethan made her believe in something she didn't think existed anymore. He'd almost made her feel … worthy. To watch it all dissolve into nothing more than an ugly memory was too painful to contemplate. Best to retreat into that protective shell while she still could.

If she still could.

She pulled out of the parking lot and headed home with the wheels on her car turning much slower than the ones in her head. Ethan, Levi, Kindley, could she actually help anyone? As she wove her way out of town, she turned to the last place most people went when they finally realized how lost they were. She prayed, asking God to show her how and where.

The last orange arch of the sun rested low on the horizon as though stuck for a moment before dropping from sight. Its rays lingered, painting the sky in swaths of purple, pink, and vermilion, and lining the asphalt with the long shadows cast by leafless trees. The ice storm had rent all but the most tenacious of foliage from their limbs. The wind had stripped the stately oaks and elms of their coverings, until they stood exposed, nothing hidden. No secrets. The ability to stand uncovered and exposed while still looking noble was a trait not everything—or everyone—possessed.

The events of last night had left Shayne exposed, and there was nothing noble about it.

One of Peg's favorite sayings blew through her mind.

Good timber does not grow with ease. The stronger the wind, the stronger the trees.

A vehicle on the side of the pavement ahead drew her attention. She slowed, recognizing the white truck, its hood raised in the universally understood expression of *this day just took a turn for the worse*. Her stomach tightened, regretting her prayer, as the man hunched over the engine straightened to step into the beam of her headlights. Bryce.

This can't be the way, Lord. This can't be the how and where.

But there was no denying she'd just asked God for an opportunity to help someone.

And there was no way to avoid the man now standing in the middle of the road.

She eased to a stop and lowered the passenger window as he moved to the side.

Maybe if she hadn't just had a friendly conversation with him less than an hour earlier when he'd checked on her. Ignoring him now? That wasn't the way folks handled things in Turnaround.

He leaned down to look in the open window, grinning sheepishly. "Well, this is awkward. I stopped to check on you because I was concerned something might be wrong with your car, and now here I am, stranded while you stop to check on me."

"Is it serious?" Stupid question. He was bent over his truck engine in the near dark while temperatures dipped toward freezing. Of course it was serious.

"Everything I do is serious." His lips curved upward, parting to reveal a row of straight white teeth accentuated by the dimples that dug into his five o'clock shadow covered cheeks.

He drew in a long breath, followed by a sharp exhale. "I think it's the fuel pump."

She understood enough to know that wasn't good. The truck wasn't going anywhere until he replaced the faulty pump, or someone towed it away. "Yeah, that's ... not good."

She bit her lip as a daring idea pulsated in her thoughts.

"It's not optimal. Unless I consider it has given me another chance to see you. I was, uh, about to start walking home." He rubbed his hands together and blew on them, hunching his shoulders in the cold.

"Did you call someone?" An unexpected note of hopefulness lifted her voice, making her cringe inwardly. Could she trust that this was an act of providence? A divine appointment orchestrated by God, offering her the opportunity to help. Wasn't that what she'd just prayed for?

He held his palms out and shrugged. "I'm not very good about keeping my cell phone with me ... so no."

Rubbing the back of his neck, he ducked his head and looked up at her, a timid, hesitant smile this time. "This is not the first impression I would have liked to make, but ..." he glanced down the road in the direction he wanted to go, "it's a long walk and a chilly night. I don't suppose I might talk you into giving me a ride?"

Shayne sank her teeth into her lip, shifting her gaze out the windshield to hide the whirl of emotions her eyes would give away.

And an unhealthy bravado pushing her to do something ... big. To do something that proclaimed her no longer a victim, but a victor.

She didn't want to ever set foot on that property again.

But just enough of her conscience whispered, *what if ...*

It was possible Bryce wasn't a part of what Levi had seen. He said he'd been away for a while. It seemed impossible that someone capable of that level of wickedness could show up in church and no one would suspect him of anything questionable. What if he was the nice guy he seemed and really just needed a ride home on a cold night?

Levi said he'd seen a girl held captive. Now she either had to choose to believe him, or look the other way.

What if she might learn something that could help the girl Levi claimed to have seen? She had pepper spray, a cell phone, and control of the car.

She glanced at Bryce, still standing outside her car, waiting for her answer. Because what if …

What if she was tired of running, tired of pretending, tired of holding on to fear? What if the impression she'd had as she walked through the school hallways this morning was right, and she really had nothing else to lose?

What if one more wasted hour meant an eternity of terror for a woman still trapped in a nightmare?

A breath of the crisp night air filled Shayne's lungs and propelled her heart. "Of course, … I mean, I assume it's not too far, right? I …" even though she knew exactly where he wanted to go, she pointed to the bags in the back, "have groceries that need to get home."

"Farther than I want to walk, but not far enough to be done with good company by the time we arrive." He smiled, then hurried to close the hood and lock his truck doors.

Shayne seized the moment to hastily dig through her purse. She found her cell phone and opened the alarm app. After a quick glance to see Bryce's back still turned, she set the alarm, clicking the screen off just as Bryce opened the door.

She set the phone in the empty cup holder. "Texted my brother to let him know I'd be a few minutes late."

Hoping her smile looked more lighthearted and confident than she felt, she reached to lift the purse and package of chocolates from the passenger seat. A stab of pain shot through her arm.

"Here. Allow me." He lifted the purse from her grip and settled it on the back seat. Then he turned to study her. "Is your arm okay?"

Her hand went to the bandaged shoulder before she could stop it. She looked away, shifting under the intensity of his stare. "Yes. I must have pulled a muscle … somehow."

"I see." He tilted his head to the side, that same peculiar

glint in his eyes as before. "As humbling as this is, I really do appreciate your help."

She fumbled to move the folder of poems, unable to stop a few papers from sliding out.

He shuffled them back together before Shayne could reach over. "Ah, poetry. An English teacher, I take it?"

"Yes." She took the papers from his hand, noticing the slight tremor as she shoved them back into the folder. Bryce settled himself into the seat as she hurried the folder into the back.

With the passenger door closed, the space inside the car seemed much too small, much too warm. The scent of his cologne wafted around her, a tad heavy-handed, although not an unpleasant fragrance. It mixed with a faint aroma of someone who spends a lot of time with horses.

"What brings you to Turnaround? I haven't seen you around in a long time." He stared ahead, appearing not to notice her unease.

"I came back for a funeral." She chanced a glance in his direction. "And you?"

He laughed. "Ten years and people can still tell I'm not a local. There are aspects of that for which I am grateful."

"I think that's understandable. We—they—are an interesting lot, for sure."

"That's one way of putting it. But in answer to your question, I just drifted in and never left. I like that it's away from all the crowds."

"No crowds here, although Turnaround isn't exactly a place someone would choose if they were looking for privacy. Not too many things stay a secret around here." The end of her speech came out cracked. She cleared her throat.

"And what would someone as fair as you know about secrets?"

Shayne focused on the pavement ahead, thankful for the

dark that hid the blush warming her cheeks. "It was just a ... fact of life in rural America." Only the secret she kept was proof it wasn't.

"So only visiting but also teaching? I'm both confused and curious."

"It wasn't the plan when I came back, but yes. Temporarily."

"This might come as a surprise to you, but I was actually a pretty good English student. I enjoyed it, though I found I was not in the majority there. I will admit, however, my poetry was probably not very different from the papers in your folder. Unimaginative." He shifted, angling himself toward her. "But then something happened that gave me a new perspective. Shortly after that, I discovered what I think may have been the greatest literary genius of all time. And ever since I've tried, no matter what it is I'm doing, to never again be unimaginative."

The subtle shift in his tone hinted at a subtext she couldn't grasp ... or didn't want to. Chills skittered up her arms. Shayne cut her eyes to him and found him gazing out the window.

She glanced at the phone resting in the cup holder. *You can do this. We're just discussing poetry. How much more innocuous of a topic could there be?* "Greatest literary genius of all time? That's big praise."

"Indeed it is. His was the first poem I ever memorized for the pure pleasure of reciting it." His tongue traced a slow trail across his lips. He squinted in thought, as though trying to recall the words.

> *It was many and many a year ago,*
> *In a kingdom by the sea,*
> *That a maiden there lived whom you may know*
> *By the name of Annabel Lee;*

And this maiden she lived with no other thought
Than to love and be loved by me."

His words thickened as he spoke, taking on an overtone of familiarity. She felt his gaze on her as he spoke the last words. "Do you know it?"

"Annabel Lee by Edgar Allan Poe." She found it too dark to be one of her favorites, although she wouldn't deny it held a certain macabre poetic charm.

"A beautifully moving poem of undying love," he said, watching her. "But you don't like it?"

"I didn't say that. I'm just not sure I find poeticizing about sleeping with a dead body to be very inspiring ... or romantic."

Bryce laughed. "No. I don't imagine most people would. But as for the romance, it's all about perspective, I suppose. What of the dark angels that cause her death because they're jealous? Do you ever wonder if a jealous desire might drive a person to do something reckless in order to win that love? I wonder if unrequited love might warp a man's nature into pursuing a love that isn't even love at all."

Shayne frowned. She'd seen the darkness people possessed. "That's possible, but I believe it's often selfishness and greed that warps men's hearts."

"Hmm ..." He studied his hands, rotating them from first backs to palms. "But I think perhaps selfishness and greed are the byproducts of living with unreturned love. Everyone wants to be loved, don't you agree? That's what it's all about, isn't it? All the striving for money or fame or success. It's all about earning love."

"But that's a delusion. Love doesn't work like that," Shayne said.

"All right then, would you agree there are some people who must be shown how deeply they are loved—perhaps even with the sort of love that would make a man lie down in a tomb just to be close to his bride—before they will understand?"

Shayne couldn't breathe, but she didn't trust her hands not to give her away by trembling if she reached for the dials to adjust the air. *Help me, Lord. Give me some wisdom.*

In her heart she heard, *Love never fails.* She frowned.

That's it? That's all the wisdom you have for me?

"Of course, those are still the lucky ones. There are some people who just never can be loved."

Although she wasn't sure Bryce's intent was for her to ponder the Father's love, that was the answer to every question. "God's love is the only perfect and unending love. And it's available to everyone. No one has to go unloved unless they choose to." She risked a quick glance at Bryce before continuing. "So, I don't agree. Everyone can have that love. It's only when we make ourselves our own god that we satisfy our desires at the expense of others."

"Your faith becomes you. But while your perspective is generous, although I fear sweetly naïve, I see things a little differently. I believe selfishness wants for itself, while the wickedness of a dark soul desires for the other not to have. And every one of us may become one or the other. In the end, the question is, which? After all, there is no one good. Not even one."

That's a statement of need for grace and mercy, not an excuse to be evil. She kept the thought to herself. The fickle sense of calm crept to take a seat in the rear of the dark theater of Shayne's psyche. The twilight had fully slipped away, settling them in a blanket of darkness. She drove a little faster than usual.

"No offense, but that's pretty deep thinking for a cowboy," she said when the silence grew uncomfortable.

He threw his head back and laughed. "Now I'm convinced you must join me for dinner sometime. This is what I've been missing. The chance to engage in enlightened conversation with a beautiful woman in this intellectually deficient county."

He reached up to touch the cross that hung from her rearview mirror. "Now, I wouldn't really call myself a cowboy. Cows are such big, dumb creatures. But I do like that I can surprise you. Perhaps even make you think I'm a bit mysterious. I do like mysteries.

"I think that's why I enjoy poetry. The poet never says exactly what they mean. Instead, they hide it in the words they string together. Poetry teaches us to think and explore. To risk."

Her fingers tightened around the steering wheel as tension steeled itself through her body. She was officially removing poetry from the list of harmless topics to be discussed with strangers.

"Of course, poetry isn't the only interest of mine that might surprise you. I also love to fly small aircraft, work crossword puzzles. Perhaps the second most unexpected thing you might discover about me is that I write gaming software."

The unexpected revelation caused Shayne to look over to see if he was teasing.

"It's true. I'm a gamer. I love the worldbuilding aspect of designing new games."

"If that's the second most unexpected thing about you, I'm curious about the first?" Shayne asked.

"That will be something I leave for you to discover at a future time." His soft laugh floated on the night. "Perhaps it will make you curious enough to want to see me again."

She jumped as the alarm she'd set triggered the sound of her phone ringing. Snatching it away from his view, she answered as though taking a call, then engaged in a pretend conversation about why she was going to be late getting home, complete with the details of Bryce's presence beside her and where she knew he'd ask her to take him. If this turned out badly, the mock phone call wouldn't help anyone find her. She hung up and gave him an apologetic smile. "My brother can be very protective."

"As he should be." Bryce's tone took on a clipped edge.

She breathed a prayer of thanks when he shifted the conversation to his horses. He had no shame in pointing out the irony of calling himself a cowboy, since he was by training a computer engineer. In the lightened mood of his enthusiastic description of his horse breeding operation, Shayne relaxed. The atmosphere inside the SUV shifted as though a different person now occupied the seat beside her, making her wonder if she'd been overreacting before.

The warmth from the heaters fed the lethargy that followed the sugar rush she'd experienced after her snack.

"You should turn here." He nodded to a gated opening in the pipe rail fence.

She swerved into the driveway with a sharp turn of the steering wheel, failing to recognize the entry to his property. The abruptness of her turn caused Bryce to lean her direction, brushing her shoulder with his.

"Easy there," he said, but he was slow to right himself.

The giant spur that had once arched over the gravel road was gone. In its place was a small, but elaborately crafted metal sign that read Rancho de Chela. She could ask about the meaning, but the conversation with Jimmo yesterday told her alone in the dark with a stranger wasn't the time she wanted to discuss anything that might be scorpion related. There was something she was missing, though. She was certain of it even though the sugar crash confusing her thoughts kept her from grasping exactly what.

The paved drive wound in and out of trees to a house and a series of barns hidden from the main road by a thick wall of brush. The drive split, but she didn't need him to tell her to head left. She was well aware of what resided at the bottom if she went right.

"So, how many ranch hands do you employ? I remember the Tackmores had so many children, they supplied their own work force."

It was hard to tell in the dark that surrounded them, but Shayne thought Bryce tensed a little at her question.

"I handle the horses myself." A satisfied pride resonated in his voice. "You could say I'm very particular about the way things are handled when they belong to me. I made a mistake once with something valuable. I won't make that mistake again." His breath took on a raspy, labored quality, as though some unnamed emotion nipped at it.

He hadn't answered her question. From the corner of her eye, Shayne watched as the smug angle of his jaw sank lower, a sharp contrast to his moments ago self-confident demeanor. "Stop near the barn if you don't mind. I'd like to check on the foal again tonight. He's a handsome little guy. Jet black. As dark as sin. I have a feeling you would like him. Why don't you join me?"

"Maybe some other time. I have the groceries still ..." Her words tapered off. She nodded to the bags piled behind her but kept her shaking hands tight against the steering wheel.

"Of course. Well, thank you for rescuing me." He tapped his hand against his knee while he smiled at her. "Let's see ... *For the moon never beams, without bringing me dreams of the beautiful Annabel Lee.* How was that? Do I remember accurately?"

"Yes," Shayne said, working to conceal her growing dislike for Poe's poem.

He reached over, covering her hand still gripping the steering wheel. His thumb stroked the compass ring she wore. "I wish you'd relax a bit. If you keep biting your lip like that, you'll make it bleed." The husky quality in his voice jangled against her nerves.

He moved his hand away. The touch was brief, but he might as well have brushed acid across her knuckles for the burning sensation it left.

"You have to let me make this up to you somehow." The look in his eyes sent cold shivers down her back.

He opened his door and climbed out. After glancing up at the night sky, he leaned back into the open car door.

> *"And the stars never rise, but I feel the bright eyes*
> *Of the beautiful Annabel Lee;*
> *And so, all the night-tide, I lie down by the side*
> *Of my darling—my darling—my life and my bride,*
> *In her sepulcher there by the sea—*
> *In her tomb by the sounding sea."*

"I was right when I told you we'd see each other again soon." He winked as he swung the door shut. "Until next time. May it be sooner rather than later."

The timbre of his voice as he'd finished the ending lines lingered in the SUV, making her skin prickle.

The drive home couldn't go fast enough as she checked the rearview mirror for the hundredth time.

Something was wrong, but it was possible that something was just the memories she had of that place.

In her tomb by the sounding sea. There's more than one way to bury a person.

Of all the ranches he could have managed, that his was associated with the old Tackmore place was one of the cruelest ironies God had ever brought her way.

He couldn't know, could he?

CHAPTER THIRTY-THREE

He'd give Ethan credit. His suturing job was holding up well to the strain Levi was putting it through. He braced a hand against the wall while the other clutched his side as another round of coughing tore at his lungs, threatening to rip apart the stitches.

He blamed the frigid swim and subsequent hike through the ice storm for the fever that kept him shivering, refusing to contemplate the possibility of an infection taking up residence in his wound.

More troublesome was the fact he felt worse every day. Maybe he did need to see a doctor. Just not yet. Besides the possibility his unwanted new friend might be watching, there was the concern they might prescribe a medicine that would send him right back down the path he was struggling to leave.

When the coughing stopped, he continued down the hall. Shayne's door was closed. He'd heard her leave earlier this morning. He'd hoped to talk to her last night, but the weight and cadence of her steps on the stairs convinced his better judgement to forgo the talk. For whatever reason, she'd come home in the mood that said she didn't want company—certainly not his.

He'd avoided her this morning for an entirely different reason. He didn't want her to see him in the condition he awoke, feverish and shaky.

Not taking the cold medicine she'd brought him had been difficult and painful. The alcohol content would be too big a temptation, a gateway back to the low road he was trying to escape. If he was going to suffer now, he might as well suffer all the way. Pain could purify, right?

He didn't blame her for not knowing. He hadn't let anyone know how bad his problem really was.

In the kitchen, he filled a glass with water and downed it before heading to the shower. He'd finally realized how to help, because sitting here doing nothing was making him crazy.

Or maybe the guilt and shame made him crazy. He'd chosen not to see once before, and nearly destroyed his sister's life. Even though it hadn't been his intent, he'd put her in danger, then surrendered his ability to protect her by fogging his brain with drugs. Another reason he refused to take the medicine.

He also wanted his head clear when he drove to the sheriff's office and asked—no, demanded—to start what would probably be a tedious process of searching the missing persons database. Sitting in front of a computer screen staring at faces of missing people was bound to carry emotional consequences. But doing nothing carried worse. And that was all he had to go on—the terrified face of a woman he'd never seen before.

Fear soured his stomach at the all-too-real possibility it was a face no one would ever see again.

Ethan pulled a convenience store sandwich from the plastic bag. The unopened potato chips and a Moon pie lay on the truck seat beside him.

It wasn't yet lunchtime, but the fish weren't biting. He might as well eat the sandwich before it slipped any further past its expiration date.

He was still in the holding pattern Reu put him in while the team gathered the necessary intel. The waiting made him antsy.

And he needed out of the house.

Time on the riverbank wasting bait was still preferable to hanging around where he might run into bewitching blondes who kissed like Delilah and were just as trustworthy.

A promise was a promise. It should mean something. But was she really promised to Nick? He'd only heard it from Nick's mouth, not hers. Levi seemed to doubt it.

Great. He'd become so desperate to believe he had a chance with Shayne that he'd sunk to trusting Levi's opinion.

He bit into the sandwich—tasteless ham, wilted lettuce, and cheap, waxy cheese mashed together between soggy slices of bread. He'd doused it in mustard, hoping to improve the taste. A foul mood fermented its way through him as he wadded the wrapper and tossed it onto the floorboard.

He had a house full of unwanted guests and an itchy feeling that one of them wasn't as unwanted as she should've been. That was a feeling he didn't like.

The notion of booting them out and reclaiming what he had the right to held a decent amount of appeal. But somehow having the right didn't make it right.

Would you rather be right or righteous? Her words snagged at the edges of his conscience. Another reason she should go. He didn't need a woman with an overly tender heart confusing his seared-over conscience.

Save my sister.

The agonized, desperate look in Levi's eyes when he'd made the request wouldn't leave Ethan alone.

Ethan saw Nick for what he was. He'd known too many men like him. It pained him to think of her, or any woman, committing her life to such a self-involved weasel who didn't have a clue how to treat a woman.

As if Ethan was any better. He might not be a cowering, conniving little rodent, but he was a hard-hearted blackguard. He knew how to treat a woman, but rarely cared enough to try. Hands that had done the things his hands had done should never touch anything as beautiful and pure as Shayne.

And man, did he want to touch her, to wrap her in his arms, to experience that kiss all over again and let it take them so much further.

That he was coveting what might belong to another man confirmed more about his character than he wanted to acknowledge. Nope. She might marry Nick, but Ethan hoped Shayne never *belonged* to anyone.

What kept her out so late last night? The idea she'd met up with Nick plagued him, escalating the churning of his sour mood.

He chewed on the sandwich, washing it down with a gulp of tepid water. Physical attraction to a woman didn't scare him. He knew what to do with that emotion. What scared him was being way beyond just physically attracted. He had somehow slipped off into the pool of those brown eyes and found himself drowning in the intense longing to wander through her thoughts.

What made her so meek at times and yet so fiery and headstrong at others? An interesting quirk that her emotional pendulum always seemed to swing in the opposite direction from what was actually helpful in the moment.

His thoughts wrestled with what they had done to her, fueling his rage. But his rage wouldn't help her now.

And that was an angle he hadn't considered before. She didn't need someone to avenge the wrong that had been done to her. She needed ... to see herself as the amazing woman she was.

He ceased chewing as the truth resonated, demanding all his attention. Shayne Wright had hidden herself, possibly for so long even she didn't see her real beauty.

What did she believe about herself because of what had been done to her, and could he make it right?

Did he dare even try?

If ever he was going to trust in God again, it might just be through the goodness he saw in her eyes.

He gnawed off another chunk of sandwich and ruminated. He couldn't make it right, and it was a stupid thought. She wasn't some old house to be remodeled and restored. He couldn't just rewire the electrical system, put fresh paint on the walls, and change the appliances.

Make a plan, execute the plan, mold the circumstances and situation to meet his needs. He'd been good at his job, but this wasn't the Army, and he wasn't maneuvering against hostiles now.

His lips twitched. Well, she did get a bit hostile when he pushed the right buttons.

The Army seemed like a lifetime ago. Too bad those days didn't also seem like a dream he could wake from and return to a normal life. The memories weren't as easy to take off as the uniform was.

He'd done what he had to. He'd fought for his country and protected his men. But it had taken something from him he would never get back. It had made him someone he wasn't sure how to live with. Every time he had pulled the trigger to take a life, he'd shot a hole in his own heart until there wasn't enough left to give away. Or worse, there wasn't enough left to hold anyone in. Perhaps Alexa hadn't betrayed him so much as he'd let her slip out of his heart.

The coldness of that thought constricted his veins, shriveling what little hope he held onto.

Was he capable of loving someone? Would he ever be?

If not, then he was no better a man than Nick.

And that was something he would never accept.

He chunked the rest of his sandwich out the window and leaned back against the seat.

With his eyes closed, he let his thoughts go back to that day four years ago, to that split second when he'd had to decide to pull the trigger in order to stop the woman approaching the position his men held. A suicide bomber. If what he'd observed of her behavior hadn't been enough to convince him, the explosion when his shot found its mark had.

There was no way he could have seen the small child clinging to her burka behind her. He'd played the memory over in his head a million times.

He hadn't seen. Not until the infinitesimal fraction of time when muscle memory was already engaged with the trigger of his rifle.

Even if he had seen, what could he have possibly done differently? It was an impossible situation. One he hadn't forgiven God for putting him in.

If Ethan were honest, he'd like to punch God right in the face. He'd heard the story of Jacob wrestling with God. Ethan wanted his turn as well.

Sheriff Griger's truck rolled to a stop beside him. The window lowered and Griger greeted him with a nod. "Your new friend Levi said I might find you here."

Ethan wasn't sure he'd call Levi a friend, but didn't bother to say so. Ethan hadn't rid himself of the suspicion Levi might not have shared everything he knew yet.

"Showed up at the station with the idea he might help with the investigation," Sheriff Griger continued.

"How so?" Ethan doubted how much the sheriff would tell him, but no harm in asking.

"Wanted to look through the missing person's database for the girl he says he saw."

"Think he'll have any luck?"

"Doubtful. But I reckon it's worth a try. It'll be worth it if it keeps him out of trouble and out of your hair until this thing is settled. Levi always had a knack for finding mischief if he had too much time on his hands. At least this way I can keep an eye on him. You and your buddies don't need him meddling in this right now." He leaned out and spit. "And neither do I. If this is going on in my county, I want it stopped ... yesterday."

Ethan stared at the shallows just up from where he'd been fishing, watching the water ripple over the riverbed. The agitated water turned from the dull mossy green to a glassy white. If only the hard places in his life could do the same. "I won't judge his propensity for trouble. The Army was probably the only thing that kept me from the same."

Sheriff Griger grunted. "I took you for a vet."

Ethan bristled, the sheriff's tone unreadable. "The blood stains on my hands that obvious?"

"For scarcely for a righteous man will one die; yet perhaps for a good man someone would even dare to die. But God demonstrates His own love toward us, in that while we were still sinners, Christ died for us."

"I'm not much of a religious man, Sheriff."

"Good. Neither am I. But I know my Savior ... and He knows me. How about this one ... Greater love has no one than this, than to lay down one's life for his friends?"

"Yeah ... the problem with that is I'm still living."

"You sure about that?" A long silence settled between

them, only the gentle hush of the water rolling through the shallows below filled the air. "I don't know your story, but I can see your character. I reckon you did what you had to do, and you did it for the right reason. Sometimes you gotta take life for what it is, know you did the best you could with the mess you were given, and move on. It was a compliment, son. Take it as one."

Ethan released a breath and watched the river flow past. All about perspective, right?

"Anyway, came to ask you for a favor."

"Fire away." Ethan pulled his attention from the water to look at the sheriff.

"This work you're doing and where it's got you looking. Some bad business went on out there about ten years ago. Bad business involving both your current housemates." Sheriff Griger twisted an antacid from the roll he pulled from his pocket. He tossed the green disc to the ground and popped a purple one into his mouth. He crunched on the antacid.

Ethan shook his head. "I don't follow."

"Ended up sending a man to prison for dealing drugs, but something else happened there that night. Never could get to the bottom of it, but my gut told me. I've never been able to forget it."

Ethan took a drink of water. He was too frustrated to enjoy guessing games with the sheriff right now. "I'm not sure what you're asking of me, Sheriff?"

"Whatever it is you're on to might dig up some old skeletons as well." He stared ahead, not looking at Ethan. "I don't know what you're planning to do with your houseguests, but you need to handle her with care. And to do that, you're going to have to handle him that way too."

"Then you got it all wrong, Sheriff. I'm not a shrink. I don't plan on handling either of them."

"Maybe not, but I imagine you've seen enough and learned enough about life to want to protect what's good." Sheriff Griger pinned him with a hard stare. "Ten years ago, that girl was a breath of fresh air and a force to be reckoned with. She had a heart of gold and the compassion of a saint. I'll make this as clear as I can for you. She was one of a kind," he paused, his look hardening, "and that kind is special."

"No doubt." Ethan wasn't certain where this was headed, but he didn't like it.

"A decade ago, I investigated a party where there was a bunch of drugs and minors. A kid nearly died that night. Bad drugs and I sent the man who dealt them to prison."

"And?"

"And the day after that party, Shayne Wright left town. Just up and took off without a single explanation to anyone. That wasn't like her, and it took a toll on her grandparents."

"I still don't see what you're getting at." Ethan tried to keep the annoyance out of his voice. He wasn't dense, but the sheriff was tap dancing around whatever it was he wanted to say. It was about to wear a hole in Ethan's already thin patience.

"What I'm getting at is I suspect there was more happened that night than the drugs and a boy nearly dying. That girl you may think you're having trouble with—well, it ain't the same Shayne Wright I knew back then."

Ethan swallowed the bitterness that had crept into his mouth while the sheriff talked. This wasn't what he needed or wanted. "What do you want from me?"

He directed his question to the sheriff, but it was God he wanted to hear from.

"Like I said, you just be careful how you handle her." He rolled his window up an inch or two, then stopped to add one more bit of information. "I failed her and her family back then. Don't you do the same."

Ethan knew what had happened to Shayne that night. Understanding that the sheriff didn't actually know, only suspected, didn't help, but it wasn't his place to tell—yet.

What he didn't appreciate was confirmation that his instinct was right. Shayne was as good as he suspected, as good as Levi said, and too good for a man like Ethan McGregor.

And so help him, if he found out who had hurt her, he'd kill him with his bare hands.

"By the way, what happened to your truck? You might want to run that over to Horn's Auto Shop and have it fixed."

Ethan answered the question with a peevish shake of his head as the sheriff pulled away. What happened to his truck felt an awful lot like what was happening to his heart right now.

He was an experienced combat soldier, a trained sniper who could hold his position in the worst of conditions for days at a time, yet he felt his position with her crumbling around him as he tumbled helplessly into an abyss.

I need you to save my sister. Levi's words echoed through Ethan's head as the memory of brown eyes fluttered through his thoughts.

Yeah, well ... He'd love nothing more than to do just that, but it wasn't going to happen.

Ethan McGregor wasn't the one.

CHAPTER THIRTY-FOUR

Ethan's truck wasn't parked in front of the house when Shayne returned home after cross-country practice. School had been a blur today—an Edgar Allan Poe laced blur—and she still hadn't heard from Nick.

Her sleep last night had been fitful. She'd even awoken at one time thinking she smelled smoke. Cigar smoke to be exact.

Once in the house, she headed straight to the kitchen. Despite the ache in her arm, her hands needed a job to do that would keep her mind occupied with something less dire.

In the kitchen, she pulled out the ingredients she'd bought the day before. Taking a Dutch oven from the cabinet, she filled the pot with water before setting it on the stove and adding the chicken.

Her grandmother's chicken noodle soup recipe had healing powers. If Grandma Hazel had been here, she would have already had Levi eating it. But Shayne had needed time *to lick her wounds* first, as Ethan so eloquently stated it. She hadn't forgiven Levi yet, but neither did she wish him dead.

The sound of the cutting board sliding from the narrow

gap between the stove and the cabinet ushered her back to a more carefree place and time. She set the wooden board in the sink and turned on the hot water to give it a thorough scrubbing. Her grandmother had kept an immaculate house, but Shayne trusted the space between the cabinets much less than the space inside them.

She rubbed the hand-crocheted dishrag back and forth across the wooden board, staring out the window as she performed the routine task of cleaning. The steaming hot water reddened her hands.

A cardinal perched in the bare limbs of the pecan tree at the corner of the yard, his red feathers in sharp contrast to the muted tones of winter around him. Grandma Hazel had taught her the song they sang was *cheer, cheer, cheer*.

It sounded a lot more like *cheater, cheater, cheater* to Shayne's ears now.

Desiring a love that's not really love at all. That was what she had offered Nick—a love that wasn't really love at all. In exchange, she never had to risk her damaged heart.

Ah, but selfishness wants only for itself. Again, Bryce's voice mocked her thoughts.

"You're going to rub a hole in that thing if you keep going at it like that." Levi's groggy voice caused her to jump.

She didn't respond, but continued rinsing and drying the board. With measured hostility, she chopped the celery and carrots she'd set out. She couldn't help but take care of Levi. She loved him still. But that didn't mean she wanted to have a conversation with him. They hadn't spoken since the night of Nick's visit. She was fine keeping it that way.

Only that wasn't true either. She wasn't fine. She was scared.

"Kind of aggressive with the knife, aren't you? What'd the veggies ever do to you?"

She placed the knife firmly on the counter and turned to face him. "Is there something you want?"

"Not really." He seated himself at the table, then nodded toward the pot on the stove. The aroma of the chicken cooking filled the kitchen. "Let me guess, chicken noodle soup?"

"Yes."

"Please tell me you're not also going to put vapor rub all over me and stick me in footy pajamas, too."

The image of a grown Levi in footy pajamas teased out a faint smile she couldn't help. Like it or not, they shared memories no one else would understand, and most of them were of sweet and blessed moments. If she shut him out because of the bad ones, what happened to the good ones? "I think we're out of vapor rub, so you're safe," she replied. She returned her attention to slicing vegetables.

"So ... are we ever going to talk about ... about what happened?"

Shayne froze, the knife in her hand hovering above the celery as if she debated the vegetable's fate. "No."

"Is it because you don't believe me? Or do you just want to hate me for the rest of my life?"

"I don't hate you." She resumed slicing the stalk of celery with slow, deliberate motions.

"But you don't believe me?" Levi's voice had taken on a flinty quality. "Look at me Shayne, please."

She closed her eyes and inhaled. *Don't let the memories come, please God. Don't let me remember the look in my brother's eyes when he saw me there with those men, and he didn't even know who I was.*

But it was too late. The memories came with their filthy hands, grabbing her, dragging her back to the dark of that night. A violent sob wrenched free from deep within, causing her shoulders to shake. Bringing the knife down hard against the cutting board, she stabbed the sharp point deep into the wood.

"I begged you. I begged you to make them stop, to take me home. I loved you. After Dad left, I looked up to you. I trusted you. I counted on you." Hot tears raced down her cheeks as the sobs shook her. When she had spent all of her energy, she faced him. What she saw was a broken boy with tears of grief that matched her own.

He rested his head in his hands, his tears dripping onto the tabletop. The need to mend, to heal, to take away his hurt came unexpectedly. It rose, overpowering her own hurt and the anger she harbored. It was who she was, and she couldn't stop herself from going to him.

She rested her hand on his shoulder, whispering his name.

Her touch drew him from the chair. He lunged into her embrace, his sobs shuddering through them both as his arms wrapped around her so tightly she couldn't breathe.

"I'm sorry. I'm so sorry." He repeated the apology over and over, as though it were a mantra for erasing the pain of the past. His wet cheeks pressed against her, dampening her hair with his tears.

Finally, she pushed against him. "Levi, I can't breathe."

With a weak and ragged laugh, he released her.

"I love you, Shayne." His husky, cry-worn voice covered her in a balm that hinted healing was possible.

"I know you do." Her own words caught in her throat. "And I'm sorry, too. I shouldn't have shut you out. But ..."

"I understand how much I hurt you. I understand it's going to take time. And I'm okay with that." He took her hand in his. "As long as you promise not to shut me out again."

She nodded, a fragile smile whisking over her features. "Look at us. Grandma Hazel would say what a fine mess we are if she could see us now."

Levi smiled, his eyes lingering on her like the brother she used to know. A coughing fit seized him. Shayne filled a glass with water and handed it to him, then touched his forehead. "You have a fever and you're as pale as a ghost. You should probably go back to bed. I'll call you when the soup is ready." She went to the stove to stir the boiling pot. "Now if I can just remember where those footy pajamas are."

He headed to the stairs, then paused, looking back. "Why didn't you ever say anything? You just disappeared. I understand why you wouldn't want to talk to me, but why didn't you tell someone?"

His eyes met hers, tentative and uncertain. In them Shayne saw the boy who had been her best friend, instead of the monster who had offered her up on the altar of his own ego.

And she saw the wounded man Levi had become. Like a cold, hard fist, understanding pounded against her chest. She wasn't the only one in the room left wounded by that night. With no explanation, she'd left him with only his fears about why she'd abandoned him and their mom. All this time, she told herself she was fighting to protect her family from the devastation of knowing what had happened to her. They'd only just found their way after the divorce. Her father would blame Levi. Her grandparents would charge in to defend him, and her mother would play the peacekeeper while trying to shelter Levi from their father.

And every one of them would have treated her like a hapless victim. She'd never disappointed anyone in her life. In all they'd been through, she'd been the strong one—the steady one.

No, she hadn't been fighting to protect her family as much as she'd been running to protect herself.

It's all about perspective. Ethan's words played in her head. And maybe she'd just found the one she needed. The life she'd built wasn't the life she wanted. But was there a perspective that could change it?

If so, it might be the act of saving Levi. "I'm sorry," Shayne said.

"You're sorry? You're not the one who needs to be apologizing. All I can think about now is how much I've taken from you. How much I failed you." Levi looked everywhere but at her, then stopped. His eyes moved to her with certainty. "I wasn't worth it. I wasn't worth you giving up even one of your worst days, Shayne."

Shayne's throat burned with rawness as understanding filled her. "You were to me."

The torment that darkened his eyes, making them glassy with the moisture of pain wrenched open her heart even more. "I don't remember anything about that night, Shayne. Nothing after hitting the blunt I got from Jimmo. I swear I never would have ... would have ... let anyone hurt you. Please believe me."

"I believe you." Her voice was barely more than a whisper, but the truth resounded within her. She believed him. He reached for her hands, but hesitated, waiting this time for her to accept his touch. She paused, then placed her hands in his.

"Then believe this too." He finally spoke. "I will make it up to you. I don't know how. I know what I did can't be undone, but I promise you, Shayne, I will make it up to you somehow."

She stared at their hands still clasped together. He was right about one thing.

What had happened couldn't be undone.

But maybe it could be redeemed.

CHAPTER THIRTY-FIVE

Another day, another return to the house that more resembled a pressure cooker. Shayne hesitated beside her car. The November sun settled warm against her face as it tiptoed down the horizon, leaving a sky filled with wisps of mare's tails dipped in orange.

Kindley had ended her practice early today under the pretext of having a test to study for. Shayne had her doubts. The girl had seemed happier than a person heading to prepare for an exam.

Her phone rang.

Leaning against her car to continue watching the sunset, Shayne listened while her new friend, Maribel, invited her to dinner. Although a return trip to town to be the third party with Maribel and Conner wasn't ideal, it appealed to her more than returning to a house where who knew what might happen. The normally predictable routines of the farm she'd grown up with were nowhere to be found in its current reality.

The call ended, and she reached for her purse, knocking it from the hood of the car to dump its contents on the ground.

She bent to scoop up the items, hoping to return them to her purse without adding any grass or gravel. An unfamiliar case caught her attention. She picked it up to find a tube of lipstick. Slipping the lid off with care, she found the contents in unused condition. Considering the color, she understood why. The bright red resembled blood too much to be attractive to anyone but a vampire.

She slid the lid, a crown made of crystal, back in place, and studied it, trying to recall if she'd ever seen one like it or how it had found its way into her possession.

Her purse stayed stored in her desk while at school, and she didn't see a reason or an opportunity for Kindley to have put it there after practice.

The only explanation seemed to be that it had accidentally been put in her purse when she'd shopped for groceries a few days before. She had no idea by whom or why? But it would be easy enough to confirm with a quick stop at the store on her way to meet Conner and Maribel.

A half hour later, the puzzle was still unsolved. The cashier at the grocery store had looked at her like she'd sprouted an extra nose when she'd offered to return it.

She and Maribel arrived at Momma Mae's cafe at the same time, walking in together to find Conner ensconced in the usual booth. The mystery of the misplaced lipstick slipped from her thoughts as Shayne sank into the booth across from the couple.

"You must have gotten here early." Maribel glanced from his almost empty glass to the basket of crumbs left from an order of chips and salsa.

"Too early. He's about to eat us out of chips and salsa," Cindy said as she walked over, drinks for the girls already in hand. "Carl's talking about having to put a limit on the 'all you can eat chips and salsa.'"

"I'm pretty sure that is illegal in the state of Texas."

Conner smiled at the waitress. "But then I guess we'd have to send the sheriff over to investigate. Might take a long time to interrogate. Shoot ... might even have to lock you up and give you a—"

"Conner Pierce, if you even think about mentioning a pat down, I will see to it you've eaten your last chip in this establishment." Cindy socked a hand on her hip, eyes narrowed in warning.

"Just trying to help."

"Tend to your own business. Seems to me you're taking your sweet time in asking Maribel to marry you. Oh ... don't either of you look so shocked. Everybody knows it's coming."

"A man's gotta ... well, you know ... there's things that can't be rushed." Conner stuttered out a response before looking past Cindy. A devilish grin replaced the flustered expression on his face. "Isn't that right, Sheriff?"

"Isn't what right?" Sheriff Griger stalked into their midst like a man on a mission.

"That there's a certain way a man's got to do things before he expresses his intent with a woman, don't you agree?" Conner's eyes danced with mischief as he rubbed his chin in contemplation. "How would you go about it?"

Shayne covered the lower half of her face with her hand to hide the smile she couldn't repress.

"I ain't got time to court a woman," Sheriff Griger answered, scowling at Conner.

"But if you were going to, what would you do?"

Cindy shot Conner a glare made of razors while Maribel elbowed him in the side, neither of which kept him from basking in thoughts of his cleverness.

Sheriff Griger placed his boot on the edge of the bench where Shayne sat, resting his arms over his bent knee as he leaned forward. "I can tell you what I wouldn't do. I wouldn't mess in someone else's affairs while I was sitting right next to something better than I deserved. No sir, I'd be afraid someone might sneak in and steal her. Or even worse, she might figure out just what kind of idiot I was." His lips twitched as he almost smiled.

Conner looked down, chagrined but enjoying his moment. He thumped the glass in front of him a few times and nodded. "Point taken."

"Good. Now, if it's all right with you, I'd like to order my dinner." Sheriff Griger straightened and headed to the counter.

Cindy gave Conner one last unspoken warning, then whisked herself off in pursuit of the sheriff's food.

"You need to quit playing matchmaker," Maribel said. She jabbed him in the ribs to emphasize her warning.

He twisted a lock of her hair around his finger and gave a gentle tug. "I just want everyone to be as happy as I am."

Maribel rolled her eyes. "Well stop. I don't have time to pray for all the victims of your good intentions."

He pressed a hand to his heart in mock agony. "I'm hurt. I thought what we had was special."

"It's special all right. Just not sure everyone enjoys your brand of special as much as I do."

He sighed, then looked at Shayne. "How about you? Anyone special in your life?"

"Before I answer, am I about to become a victim of your *good intentions*?" Shayne laughed, but it came out hollow. She clasped her hands in her lap, rubbing the place where her engagement ring should've been. She still hadn't heard from Nick, but in her heart, she knew what she needed to tell him.

"Yes. Don't answer that. Let's order." Maribel opened her menu and went to work reading what Shayne was certain she already knew by heart.

Cindy returned to take their orders, and the conversation drifted over safer ground.

"So did my niece tell you she's wanting to quit cross country?" The tight lines around her lips and deep furrows between her brows said she wasn't happy.

"No. She can't quit this close to the state meet?" Shayne said, surprised by the news.

"It's a boy. He took her to a steak dinner over in Margolis and gave her some fancy bracelet. Now she imagines she's in love." She shook her head. An equal measure of frustration and concern filled her voice and pinched her features in worry. "If I figure out how he makes enough money shoveling horse poop to take her out for a steak dinner and buy her expensive jewelry, I might just switch careers myself."

She sat down next to Shayne. "I don't know how much longer I can do this. Carl's got me working overtime until we can find another full time waitress. And it's going to take an army to keep that girl out of harm's way."

Shayne studied the places on the tabletop where scratches and rubs had stolen its shine and made it seem ... worn. No one considered replacing it because it was, well ... still a table. The superficial damage hadn't robbed it of its purpose.

Kindley needed to hear some hard truths about life. Maybe the secret Shayne had kept didn't need to be a secret any longer. She wasn't sure she could share it. She wasn't even sure it would matter, but something told her she needed to at least consider it. "I'll try to talk some sense into her tomorrow."

Cindy reached over to pat Shayne's hand. "Thank you."

"So who is this steak dinner and jewelry buying Romeo?" Conner asked.

"It's Collin, Lacy's little brother. He seems like a nice boy, makes good grades, and is never in trouble after that one incident at his previous school. Although I'm not a fan of the motorcycle. I'm probably upset for no reason. I mean, his sister is the school counselor, so Kindley is safe with him, right?" Cindy looked from one face to another, clearly hoping to find some reassurance.

Shayne watched as the waitress rose and walked away, certain she hadn't found the encouragement she needed.

Wrapped in thoughts that made her nose and eyes burn, Shayne stared out the window, hoping no one would notice.

For such a time as this.

"Hey, Ethan," Conner's words yanked her from her worries about tomorrow, depositing her in a much more immediate concern.

She turned to find Ethan standing near the counter. His eyes fastened on her for a moment before shifting to Conner. "Evening."

"Why don't you join us, and I'll introduce you."

"Thanks, but I don't want to interrupt your evening." Ethan waved the offer off. He cut his eyes to the sheriff seated on the stool nearby. Something flickered between them, a brief exchange that puzzled Shayne.

"You won't be interrupting. You'll be saving me. I'm outnumbered and not getting much mercy from these two," Conner said. Eternally social, Conner refused to give up.

"This better not be more of your attempts to victimize innocent people," Maribel whispered under her breath, casting Shayne an apologetic glance—and warning.

"Of course not. Just bein' neighborly. I met Ethan this morning when I went for a run. He was fishing down at the bridge by the camp. Aren't you the one always lecturing me on how hard it is to be the new kid in town?"

Ethan was a lot of things, but kid definitely wasn't one of them. She glanced his direction and saw the playful gleam in his eyes that always made her pulse dance. It never quite took away the sadness, but she always understood the change to be a respite for his soul, however, brief it might be.

It didn't help that he wore the same green hoodie she'd

first seen him in. The bright green one that emphasized the cinnamon hue of his eyes, causing her to hunger for his gaze.

They hadn't talked since she'd left for school the morning after that kiss. Maybe he'd understand how awkward it would be to start now ... in the company of others.

"I might as well. If you're sure." He smiled as he addressed Conner, then pinned Shayne with a look meant only for her. "It's not like I have any other *engagements*."

Nope, he definitely understood. It just didn't bother him. Tension ran through her body like the hardening of quick-dry cement as he seated himself next to her, claiming more of the vinyl covered bench than his fair half.

She moved her purse into place between them, discreetly crowding herself against the window. She didn't need to see his face to know he was smiling. A mischievous pleasure radiated off him like atomic waves. That he had the nerve to smile while her insides twisted in apprehension only made the twisting that much tighter.

If the school knew she was living with him—dear Lord, that's the conclusion everyone would jump to—she'd be done. It wouldn't matter that she wasn't technically living with him. They were just ... sleeping in the same location. That was a completely different thing, especially since Levi was there too. Now that Levi had made himself known by his appearance at the sheriff's office, it was no secret he was here. The realization gave Shayne a small amount of comfort.

Conner began his introductions. "Ethan, this is Maribel. She's taken, so don't get any ideas. And this is Shay—"

"We've met." Shayne cut him off before he could say anything she'd regret.

Ethan turned to her with a grin that told her exactly what he was thinking. He opened his mouth to speak, but to Shayne's relief, Cindy descended on the table with more chips and salsa.

"Already met, huh?" Once again, Conner wouldn't leave it alone.

Desperate for a distraction, Shayne reached into her purse and retrieved the lipstick. "Oh ... before I forget, is this yours?" She held it out for Maribel.

"No. Why do you ask?" Maribel examined the elaborate case.

Conner pulled it from her fingers and plucked the cap off. He let out a low whistle. "Now that is some red lipstick."

Maribel took it back from him and returned the lid.

"And so you don't get any notions otherwise, I like your lips just the way they are." He leaned toward Maribel with a look that smoldered enough even Shayne could feel the heat.

"Here." Maribel handed the lipstick to Shayne, blocking Conner's romantic advance as she pressed her other hand against his chest. "Why did you think it might be mine?"

"It's weird, really. I found it in my purse. At first I thought someone had accidentally put it in there while I was at the store the other day. The girl bagging my groceries seemed pretty distracted. The EMT who treated me at the accident came in and stopped to ask how I was doing. She was a bit focused on gaining his attention."

"Sounds like she wasn't the only one." Ethan dipped a chip into the salsa and shoved it in his mouth.

Shayne pressed her lips together with a slight pause before responding. "Anyway, I set my purse down while we were talking, so yes, I was distracted as well. But when I tried to return it to the store today, they told me they don't sell ninety-dollar lipstick at the Goodson Grab-n-Go."

"Ninety-dollar lipstick? It must make you one heck of a kisser," Conner said, disbelief that such a thing existed intensifying his words. Recovering from the shock, he winked at Maribel. "Still not needed."

Ethan rubbed his beard and glanced at Shayne, devilment

sparking in his eyes. She was more than grateful it didn't also come out of his mouth.

This wasn't the sort of diversion she'd hoped for. "I just can't figure out how it got in my purse."

"What about the kids at school? Although who could afford to pay that for lipstick is beyond me. Who else has access to your purse?" Maribel asked.

"No one. It's locked in my desk at school and in my car when I'm not."

"Anyone else been in your car lately?" Ethan asked.

"Only Bryce. I had to give him a ride home night before last. And I highly doubt he left his lipstick in my car." Their conversation had been uncomfortable in a way she couldn't explain, but she was still certain he hadn't deposited unused lipstick in her purse.

"You gave Bryce a ride home?" Maribel asked, eyebrow lifted.

"Yes. His truck broke down, and he didn't have his phone with him."

"He sure didn't waste any time," Conner said. He winked at her as he raked another chip through the bowl of salsa.

Beside her, Ethan's normally tense body seemed to take on a new level of rigidity, something she sensed more than saw.

"He was concerned I might be having car trouble earlier and stopped to check on me. Then on my way home, there he was. I couldn't really just leave him there."

"Convenient," Ethan mumbled under his breath.

"What did you think of our resident cyber geek cowboy philosopher?" Maribel asked.

"I believe that would fall into the category of gossiping," Conner said. "And as your acting pastor, it is my responsibility to protect you from an eternity of damnation."

"Seriously, you just flirted with me like you were hitting

on a buckle bunny at last call," Maribel replied. "You can't lecture anyone about the possibility of eternal damnation right now."

"Absolutely not. I stated pure facts and honest-to-God truth. Have you never read the Song of Solomon? My feelings for you are incredibly biblical."

Maribel actually blushed, turning a shade of red not too far removed from the color of the mysterious lipstick. "We'll discuss this later."

"I look forward to it." The wicked delight in Conner's smile made Shayne squirm.

She drew her leg closest to Ethan up to tuck beneath the opposite leg, then folded her hands beneath the table. The Song of Solomon was only a reminder of something she'd never have. Kind of like the relationship she witnessed between Conner and Maribel.

"Back to the question at hand," Maribel ignored him. "An objective analysis is not gossip. He's an interesting character. There's something enigmatic about him. Although, I'm not sure I would have wanted to give him a ride alone ... in the dark."

"Says the girl who believed I was the next Ted Bundy when we first met. I'm not convinced we should trust the intuition of anyone who could be that far off the mark."

Maribel grinned as though she'd been busted. "I recognized my mistake before it was too late."

"Only because I had persistence. There's a difference between enigmatic and creepy. He gives me an odd feeling. He's weird." Conner narrowed his eyes.

"What you mean is he's smart to the point of being awkward," Maribel said, giving Conner her best attempt at a lecture. "The man did make a sizeable donation to the Girls' Home Fund at church on Sunday. Besides, you think everyone who knows how to turn on a computer is weird. What about you, Shayne?"

"About people who can turn on computers being weird ... there may be some truth to that."

"No. About Bryce?"

"He was polite ... and poetic." She deliberately kept her true feelings about her time with Bryce hidden, not wanting them to know the full extent of how uncomfortable he'd made her feel. She'd gone back over the evening and their conversation. Her discomfort seemed unfounded in the light of day.

"Who's Bryce?" Ethan looked around the table.

"He's a man whose hired hand was just Care Flighted to John Peter Smith Hospital for a drug overdose," Sheriff Griger said, his voice booming as he stalked up the table.

"Just got off the phone with my deputy. Jimmo's mom called. He's in a coma. They think he's stable now, but not sure when he might wake up. Unfortunately, when she got home tonight, someone had trashed her house." He pinned Conner with a glare. "Now you want to tell me why she's asking for you?"

CHAPTER THIRTY-SIX

Conner's expression revealed both confusion and concern. "I met with Jimmo yesterday, and I thought he was doing good and staying clean. I have no idea why she'd want to talk to me."

"Well, today's a new day. Now you're coming with me. Mrs. Cleese insists she has something to say, but she won't talk to anyone but you."

"But I ... Sheriff, I'm kinda on a date here." Conner looked at Maribel, his eyes scanning her face for her reaction.

"Now you see why I don't court women," the sheriff said.

"It's just ... are you sure you need me?"

"I'm quite sure I don't." Sheriff Griger dug some money from his pocket and laid it on the table. "Jimmo's mom requested you come. Said she has something to tell you. So you're coming with me on the remote chance you might make my life a bit easier for a change."

"I'll come too." Maribel scooted out of the booth, following Conner.

Sheriff Griger frowned. "I'm not running an Uber service here."

"Are you sure you want to do that?" Conner asked.

"Yes. Apparently, if we're ever going to have a date, I'm going to have to be flexible in what that means. If this is going to be a taste of how our life is about to be, then I want to see what I'm getting into. Besides, Mrs. Cleese might need a woman around. You two don't exactly ooze empathy."

"Okay then. We'll follow you in my truck, Sheriff."

The trio disappeared, leaving Shayne alone with Ethan. He slouched back in the seat, spreading his already large presence into as much of her space as he could, as if he'd never known a greater contentment.

"Do you mind?" She motioned to the other side of the booth as she leaned away, preferring the touch of the cold glass to risking a chance contact with Ethan. It might be a childish response, but he was doing no better with his immature bullying.

"Not at all."

Shayne reached around him, attempting to catch Cindy's attention. "I'm going to get my order to go."

"Stay where you are. I'm moving."

"What if I don't want to eat with you?"

He stared at her before leaning closer to respond. "It would make me wonder how you plan to stay in a house with someone you can't even eat a meal with." He rose and reseated himself across from her. "Much less how you could—"

"Fine. I'll stay." Shayne moved to the center of the bench.

Her hand wandered up to tuck her hair behind her ear. Maybe this would be less awkward if they just addressed the elephant sized emotional misstep of the kiss head on. "So, about what happened, I want to apologize."

He settled into his seat and crossed his arms. "You'll need to be more specific. Apologize for what? Breaking into my house while I was taking a shower? Running your car into my truck?

Bossing me around in the house I have legal possession of? Nagging me into helping your brother? Forgetting to tell me you were engaged ... or is there something else on your mind?"

"I did not nag you to help my brother. I appealed to your sense of decency and compassion."

Ethan laughed as he scratched his forehead. Then he sobered and peered at her with a steady, intrigued gaze. "You are the most confusing woman I have ever met. And that's saying a lot."

"I'm sorry. I'm just—"

"There it is. Stubborn enough to argue with a fence post one minute, crumbling and apologizing the next." His look bored through her. "Makes me want to get inside your head for a moment and see what really goes on in there."

Shayne looked down. "No, you don't."

Their food arrived, filling the space with the aroma of the freshly baked rolls that came with the meal. It put a welcomed pause on further discussion as they hurried to butter the hot bread. The ensuing silence as they dug into their meals was a pleasant side dish. It was just too small of a portion.

"How's school going?" Ethan swiped a slice of Texas toast through his gravy and stuck it in his mouth.

"Good. I enjoy teaching." Shayne swirled her straw in the glass of iced tea. "I'm a little worried about Kindley and the state meet. Which is probably stupid since I hardly know her. She's lost her focus. She's thinking about quitting because of a boy."

"You're right. No good can come of that." He tore off another piece of toast. "And your gut feeling tells you there's something more wrong?"

"Yeah."

"Always go with your gut."

If only everything were that easy. She licked her lips, working up as much courage as she could. "What I wanted to apologize for earlier was ... kissing you."

Ethan arched an eyebrow. "I'd appreciate it if you didn't. Apologizing makes it sound like you regret it. That was not a kiss a man regrets, nor forgets. And he certainly hopes the lady feels the same."

Shayne swallowed, the heat returning to her cheeks. "I mean, I know it was wrong. I'm in a relationship with another man ... sort of."

"The correct term is engaged to."

"It's not the term if I haven't yet said yes."

"Have you?"

"No. But I wasn't honest with you or him."

"No, but maybe you were honest with yourself. In fact, I think that kiss may have been the most honest thing you've done in a long time."

Shayne glanced away, a small smile toying with her lips. Maybe it was.

Ethan sliced a piece of steak and stabbed it with his fork. "I reckon we all have our moments when we wish things might have gone differently."

Her eyes stutter-stepped up to meet his. There was no mocking in what she saw, nothing but an understanding she didn't like. A kiss wouldn't change the truth between them.

"For what it's worth, my answer for Nick is no." Remorse settled around her, but it was a thin weight compared to the dread brought on by thoughts of a yes.

The grave clothes were coming off.

Her smile drew a questioning look from Ethan.

They finished their meal in a heavy silence seasoned with occasional small talk. When it came time to leave, Ethan insisted on paying in spite of her protest. And when she reached for her coat, he lifted it from her possession to help her into it.

"Guess I'll see you at the house later, then," Shayne said as she dug her car keys from her purse.

"You're not done seeing me right now. I'm walking you to your car. Gentlemen still do that for a lady." His hand brushed against her back as he ushered her through the door.

They walked down the sidewalk in a quiet that did not reflect the growing storm of longing inside her chest. She wasn't exactly certain what the longing was for, but the freedom to long was exhilarating.

"So no one ever really said, who's Bryce?"

"I don't really know much about him other than he's the ranch manager for the Rancho de Chela."

Ethan's shoulders twitched back so subtly Shayne thought it might be only her imagination. He added, "And he turns on computers and recites poetry. Sounds like a weirdo, all right."

"That's the kind I attract, it seems."

"I wouldn't say that. You have some distinct potential in the—"

"In the *what?*" She eased from the longing to the edge of an actual hope.

"Never mind. Doesn't matter. Tell me again when you found the lipstick in your purse?"

"After practice today."

"It wasn't there before today?"

"I can't say for sure. It's a big purse and there's a lot of ... important stuff in there. I might have just missed it."

"Important stuff. I see. Well, red isn't your color, so I'd probably get rid of it." He kicked a loose stone on the side-walk. "And just my opinion, but your kiss was darn—" He gave his head a sharp shake, grinning, "just fine without it."

A flustering warmth crept through her as they stopped

beside her car. Fitting the key into the lock with suddenly unsteady hands proved to be a challenge.

Ethan reached out, slipping the keys from her fingers into his steadfast hands. For Shayne, time froze for just a moment, an interminable blink that spun the world in slow motion. Unvarnished truth shot up her arm and into her heart at his touch. He knew the worst about her, and he saw her the better for it. He hadn't looked away. If anything, he looked deeper.

She didn't regret that kiss. He was right. It was the first honest thing she'd done in a long time.

Words she might speak tangled up in her emotions to stick in her throat. She wanted to hold on to this time, this feeling, for as long as possible.

His dark eyes seemed to soak her in until his gaze was more than a look. For the first time in a long time, someone saw her.

"Ethan, I ..." Tears she didn't want pooled in her eyes, making her angry. If only he could feel what she did, to understand what she couldn't say, but how could he? She looked away.

His fingers brushed against her cheek, drawing her gaze back to his. When he spoke her name, it stirred a desire within her. The sweetness of the moment was almost more than she could bear. "Shayne, I don't know everything that has happened, but I know you're hiding from it, from life. You're even hiding behind Nick. Why?"

She placed a hand against his chest. She didn't want to go there. Not tonight, not in this moment where she could almost pretend she was whole again. "Please. I don't want to talk about it. It happened. That's all. I just want to forget and move on."

"Only you aren't. Pretending it didn't happen isn't forgetting. And from what I've observed, you're not moving on.

You're giving up. I don't know what God's plan for you is, but I'm pretty sure it's not a life hiding behind someone like Nick."

"So, God's plan for me was to be ... to ..." The magic of the moment fell away, shattering at her feet like glass.

"Raped, Shayne. Say it. Call it for what it was. You act as though your life has to be lived as some sort of penance because of something that wasn't your fault. It's like you've given up on life."

"I'm not a victim. I made my choices that night. I shouldn't have gone with Levi, or I should have tried harder to leave." A strangled sob broke free in her chest. "Why didn't I try harder?"

Ethan pulled her close, and she melted into the sanctuary of his embrace.

"Shhh. It's not your fault." He murmured words of comfort, his breath stirring her hair as his words stirred her soul. "Why did you try to carry this all by yourself for all these years?"

Why had she? For years she'd kept this secret. Even the counselor she saw for panic attacks didn't know. So why now? And why Ethan?

Tears that had fallen in secrecy for ten years now flowed unstoppable as she buried her head in the safety of his shoulder. A safe place for her heart to heal. Maribel had found it, not in Conner but in Turnaround. Maybe it was here for Shayne as well.

In the arms of a stranger beneath the streetlamp on a sidewalk in her hometown, she let herself surrender to such a hope.

CHAPTER THIRTY-SEVEN

Rock Griger pulled the nearly empty roll of antacids from his pocket. Not eating supper left him hungry. His angry stomach revolted with a bubbling fluid that burned his throat. He peeled away the next section of wrapper. Cherry. Well, at least that had gone right.

The chalky tablets crunched between his teeth, filling his mouth with grit. It was not unlike the feeling of trying to get information out of Arabella Cleese. Maybe Conner would have better luck, although he doubted it.

The woman righted a flimsy plastic chair and seated herself, waving her e-cigarette around like a magic wand. It gave off an aroma smelling like a mixture of Christmas potpourri and the trash dumpster behind the cafe. The casual frown Rock wore slid into an expression of unconcealed aggravation.

Conner placed his hands on a newly built section of the porch rail and gave the fresh, still yellow lumber a tentative shake before leaning against it.

"Jimmo's been helping me fix the place up." Arabella flicked her hands at the partially replaced rails. The new lumber made a stark contrast to the decaying boards around it. Jimmo still had a decent way to go before anyone could consider this place *fixed up*. "He always was good with that sort of stuff. I sure could use his help."

Mrs. Cleese stuck the offensive device between her shriveled lips and inhaled until her cheeks caved, giving her a cadaverous appearance in the shadowy light of the front porch. When she released her breath, a cloud of white hovered in the night like an apparition.

Rock's eye twitched, but he wasn't going to give her the satisfaction of seeing him fan the unsavory smog away.

Maribel stood beside the seated woman, resting a sympathetic hand on her shoulder. Mrs. Cleese sniffed and reached up to pat Maribel's with a wrinkled hand, complete with purple age spots, turquoise nail polish, and an excess of gaudy rings that rattled around her bony fingers as she patted.

"I just want to see my boy."

Rock looked at the decrepit car parked on the hard-packed ground beside the house, doubting the car could make the hundred plus mile drive to the hospital. He also doubted the woman was any more road worthy than her car. Arabella Cleese had worked at Lemcky's Bar and Grill over at the county line for as long as he could remember. She and the grease in Lemcky's fryers had probably gone to work there at the same time. And both were well past the age of needing to be replaced. The grease probably knew it. Arabella Cleese, in her cut-off shorts and black Harley Davidson tank top, did not.

She failed to grasp the concept that time marched on, whether you marched with it or not. Rock didn't want to be that person.

"You're sure nothing was taken?" He asked one more time, wondering how anyone would ever know. Housekeeping wasn't a skill Arabella possessed. But after waiting tables all day, who could blame her?

Although Cindy waited tables all day and still kept her stuff neat as a judge's drawers.

"Not a thing." Mrs. Cleese took another puff from her e-cigarette. "'Course somethin' might turn up I forgot about."

Sheriff Griger licked the inside of his mouth, chasing down the remnants of his antacid tablet. He shifted his stance in that special way he'd learned when he needed to remind someone his patience only stretched so far.

Conner glanced at the sheriff for the go ahead before speaking. "You said you had something you wanted to talk to me about?"

Mrs. Cleese looked at the sheriff, then back at Conner. "I'm not sure I should say anything in front of him." She jerked her head in Rock's direction.

"Anything you can say to me, you can say to him." Conner pulled a second chair over, tested its sturdiness, then seated himself, drawing her attention away from Rock.

Her head wobbled side to side, as her bottom lip edged out over the one above it. She wrung her hands, the clacking of her rings grating away a little more of Rock's patience. "It's just, I don't want to get Jimmo in trouble. If he was to talk to you, it'd be confidential, right? You bein' a preacher and all."

Conner shook his head with a soft chuckle. "I'm not a preacher, so I'm afraid that's not the way it would work. Jimmo knows that, so if he needed to talk to me, he must not have been worried about that sort of thing. Why don't you tell us what's on your mind?"

"I don't wanna say nuthin' that might get him sent back to prison's all."

Rock rested a hand on his holstered gun and looked away. Seems like the first thing a mother should be worried about was getting her kid back home from the hospital alive. "A mite premature to be worrying about that," he mumbled.

Arabella sniffled again, and Rock resisted the urge to roll his eyes.

"Just tell us what you know, why don't you?" Conner glanced his way, then rested his forearms across his knees as he leaned closer to Arabella.

"It's not much really, but when he was leaving this morning—he's been repairing some fence for that man who bought the Tackmore Ranch—anyways, on his way out, he told me he had to find you before he came home. Said he wouldn't be home until he had talked to you and for me not to keep his supper warm. Course, I usually bring him something from the grill."

Rock's stomach soured a little more at the thought of what a cold, greasy meal that must be. It would probably give prison food a run for the money, so maybe Jimmo didn't mind.

"He didn't say why he wanted to speak to me? I was out here yesterday, and we had a good visit. Maybe he wanted to ask me a question about something we talked about then."

"That's what I thought at first. But then I got to thinking about it and remembered he started acting kinda strange last night. A friend of his came by, and they talked for a long time outside. He acted different when he came back inside. Real quiet, like he was upset, but not mad, more like preoccupied." She hesitated, inhaling again from the device in her hand, before releasing another apparition into the night. "And I think he was scared."

"Who was it he talked to?" Rock asked, causing her to shoot him a look meant to remind him she wasn't talking to him. She addressed the answer to Conner. "I don't know. I couldn't see in the dark. All I know is he was riding a motorcycle."

"And Jimmo didn't tell you anything else?"

She worked her lips together in an odd contortion, shaking her head in remorse. "You promise me you won't let him get in no trouble for this, but he did mention he was afraid something bad was about to happen. But he promised me it wasn't because he was doing anything he wasn't supposed to. He swore he was clean." She glanced at Rock, then raised her voice to finish her statement. "And my Jimmo never lies to his momma."

Rock doubted the veracity of that statement. Perhaps if Momma Cleese hadn't kept her blinders on when Jimmo was growing up, the boy's life wouldn't have taken him where it had. But then again, there were some folks bent on learning everything the hard way.

He thought back to what he'd seen inside the ramshackle house. Somebody had been looking for something. With Jimmo, chances were fair it might be drugs or drug money.

What were the odds the big guy would OD on the same day someone who didn't care what kind of mess they left searched his house? Jimmo was a lot of things, but suicidal had never been one of them. A deliberate overdose seemed unlikely, but an accidental one was always a possibility.

Something didn't sit quite right with Rock this time.

CHAPTER THIRTY-EIGHT

"Want to let you know that I'll be staying at the Wagon Wheel Motel for a couple of weeks until you lea ... until you're done here," Ethan said. He didn't make eye contact as he held the SUV's door while Shayne slid into the driver's seat.

His casual statement steam rolled over the moment of hopefulness.

It was what she'd wanted—what she'd practically begged for. It was for the best. So why did the unexpected disappointment feel like a hammer against her heart? "You're ..."

"I'm trying to be a gentleman and do the right thing. Let's not make too much out of it, or I might change my mind." His lopsided grin hinted at a deliberate attempt to lighten the moment.

Shayne looked away, praying he didn't notice the fresh tears—stupid tears—as she clicked the seatbelt in place and turned the key. It was the morally right decision for him to make, and it was borderline immoral that she suddenly regretted it.

His phone chirped from his coat pocket. He pulled it out and stared at the screen. His brow furrowed. "I need to take this. You head on out to the house. I'm going to stop by the hotel and make reservations, then I'll be right behind you." He pushed the door closed, his attention already shifted to the phone in his hand.

She pulled away from the curb, watching in the rearview mirror as he pressed the phone to his ear and turned away.

The loneliness that captured her as she stared at his back while driving away was irrational. Nothing had really changed. But there it was, hanging onto her heart and pulling her mood even lower. Even though it was temporary this time, it was a taste of what the future would be. It surprised her to find how much she dreaded it.

The house was dark when she returned. Levi had traded the sofa for his bed upstairs. She stood at his doorway and listened to the congested snoring. He hadn't left a mess in the kitchen for her to clean, so there was no real reason to tarry around awaiting Ethan's arrival. A part of her wanted to wait for him—to see him again—hoping to reclaim a bit of what they'd shared tonight. Friendship? Maybe. A truce? Something more?

The part of her that feared knowing it was over, a moment meant to pass and never be recaptured, won out.

She pulled a cookbook from the shelf, doubting sleep would come soon, and carried the book to her room. Studying recipes and imagining the meals she'd like to prepare for others soothed her when her emotions were too raw.

She kicked her shoes off and curled up on the bed, tucking the quilt around her. She sighed, realizing she'd picked up one of her grandmother's collections from the 1800s. Reading about rendering chitlins and wringing chickens' necks might not put her to sleep, but it would definitely be a distraction.

Touching the aged pages connected her with a past she hadn't lived. Was it possible she could touch a future she couldn't see?

For such a time as this.

The book rested heavily in her lap. Generations of hands had held it before her. Hands that had witnessed the horrors of the Civil War and everything that came after.

Stories she'd heard as a kid came back to her now. The one about her great-great-great grandmother, who'd been taken by the Comanches from this very county as a child, had always been a favorite. She'd spent three months living with the nomadic tribe before being ransomed and returned to her family. What courage and resilience she must have had.

Shayne remembered her great aunt who'd lost both her husband and her son in World War II, and her grandmother who had served as a nurse in Vietnam.

Generations before her had lived through the Spanish flu, the Great Depression, and more wars than most people wanted to admit.

They'd all known tragedy, some much worse than what she'd experienced.

She didn't know what it was, but even Ethan had walked through something that left its mark upon his heart.

One thing remained constant. Life rolled on.

She let her mind drift into new possibilities as a contented sleep drew her under. It was a sleep filled with dreams of the future instead of nightmares from the past.

———

Loud pounding at her door startled her. The cookbook

thudded to the floor as she fought to untangle herself from the quilt. How long had she been asleep?

"Shayne!" Ethan burst through the door without waiting for her response. "We have to get out. The house is on fire."

He grabbed for her hand, but she jerked away, confused.

"What do you mean? A fire ... where?" Shayne stood beside her bed, paralyzed, unable to make sense of his words. She recognized the words he spoke, but her sleep-dazed brain couldn't make sense of them.

"In the kitchen. We have to go before it blocks the stairway. Now!" He didn't wait for her to comply, but threw the quilt around her shoulders, scooped up her shoes, then snatched her hand and yanked her through the bedroom door.

A thick curtain of smoke met them as he hurried her out of the room. She coughed as the acrid smoke hit her lungs. Panic shot through her as Ethan pulled her down the stairs. He led her through the backdoor, and she gulped in a fresh breath of the crisp night air.

Halfway across the yard, reality set in. She dug her feet in, pulling back and trying to break free of his hold. "I need to get the quilts, the cookbooks, the pictures. I can't just ... I have to go back."

Ethan's grip tightened as he held onto her. "It's just stuff. The fire department's on the way."

This couldn't be happening. This was her safe place. The only thing in her life that reminded her of who she was. Her legs gave way, and she collapsed. Ethan caught her before she hit the ground. She kicked, pushing against him as he carried her further from the house to the stone wall.

"It's just stuff, Shayne! Let it go!" He pinned her down against the wall.

Just stuff? she wanted to scream. It was all she had left of

... she stopped, her thoughts calming. All she had left of what? Her family, her identity, her past?

Her life? She'd been wrong walking down the halls of school just a few days before when she'd felt she had nothing else to lose. She still had all that mattered.

Then it hit her. "Levi! Where's Levi?"

Ethan stared at her, his breath coming hard. "He wasn't on the couch when I came in. Where did you last see him?"

"He was asleep in his room when I got home."

"Stay here." Ethan thrust her shoes into her lap and grabbed her shoulders. She flinched as his grip arced pain through her still sore arm. "Promise me you won't move." He stooped lower, demanding she look him in the eye.

Shayne could only nod.

"I'm going to get him. Don't move." He didn't take his eyes off her as he backed toward the house, his look questioning if he could trust her. Finally, he turned and ran back into the burning structure.

Her hands trembled as she fumbled to put on her shoes. She had to be ready if they needed her, right?

She wrapped her arms tight around her middle, swaying back and forth as she reminded herself. *It's just stuff, but Lord, please get Ethan and Levi back out safely.* She repeated the words over and over while she watched the orange flames licking up against the side of the house. Her fingers twisted the silver ring she wore, worrying it around her finger.

A freedom came in knowing nothing mattered to her now except having Ethan and Levi out safely.

Nothing.

It was going to be okay. Ethan would see to it they both got out.

"And the stars never rise, but I feel the bright eyes ... hello Shayne." Chills skittered down her body like an army of spiders as the soft, melodic voice carried through the crackling growl of the fire in front of her.

A hand clamped over her mouth before she could scream.

Terror slid down her legs as he whispered in her ear. "For the moon never beams, without bringing me dreams of the beautiful Annabel Lee."

CHAPTER THIRTY-NINE

Ethan pulled his shirt over his nose, trying not to choke on the smoke as he and Levi scrambled to the staircase. He stopped halfway down. The flames were too intense, the smoke too thick. His eyes burned, blocking his vision. "We can't go this way. We have to find another way out." He pushed the now fully awake Levi back up the stairs.

Racked by coughing, Levi doubled over as he moved, his already afflicted lungs struggling against the smoke.

Ethan didn't pause to think. Any thinking that needed doing had to be done on the move. He shoved open the door to the third upstairs bedroom, lunging to the floor and dragging Levi with him as the fire below rushed up to devour the fresh supply of oxygen. He prayed his instinct was right as heat fanned over their bodies.

He lunged up and scrambled to the window. This room was on the far corner from where the fire raged, the window facing toward the front of the house opposite where he'd left Shayne. He jerked it open, stuck his head out, and gave a small shout of victory. He waved Levi to him, pointing at the roof of the porch directly below them.

"The fire hasn't gotten this far on the first floor. The roof here should still be solid." He gave Levi a grim smile. "You first. And try not to break a leg when you slide off the roof."

Levi's expression said he'd already contemplated the possibility and wasn't looking forward to it. Still, it was better than sticking around here to end up barbequed. He started coughing again. "You sure?"

Ethan helped him to the windowsill. "Yeah, but don't let it go to your head. This is strictly for Shayne. You don't sound like you'll last much longer if you don't."

"I knew you liked her," Levi said, giving Ethan a cocky grin.

He dangled from the window ledge for a second, then dropped onto the tin roof. The sharp angle made it impossible to secure his footing. He sprawled face down on the metal. Unable to stop himself, he slid unhindered toward the end of the metal roof. The last thing Ethan saw were Levi's fingers curling around the lower edge before all of him slipped from sight.

Ethan counted the seconds, waiting until Levi's lanky form appeared limping away from the house. He gave Ethan a thumbs-up and a lopsided, pain-filled grin as he gripped his injured side with his other hand.

Seconds later, both men stood on the ground watching the ominous orange glow growing as flames ravaged the old house. Sirens filled the night as fire trucks rushed to the scene.

"Where's Shayne?" Levi's voice held a frantic urgency.

"She's waiting out back," Ethan said, already hurrying to where he'd made her promise to wait.

He rounded the house, but didn't see her. His eyes raked across the yard, sifting through the contorting shadows cast by the fire. "Shayne!"

Levi jogged up beside him, clutching his side, winded and gasping.

Ethan called again, running his fingers through sweat soaked hair despite the cold of the early morning. "She's supposed to be right here."

The morning sun lit the landscape beyond in a soft light that did not match the darkness raging through Ethan's veins right now.

Both men turned to look at the house in unison. Ethan started that way, but Levi's hand on his arm stopped him. "Don't. She's not in there."

Ethan jerked away.

"She's not in there," Levi repeated, staring at the stone fence where Ethan indicated he'd last seen Shayne. He bent to retrieve a small shiny object. Gripping it between his thumb and forefinger, he held it so the firelight illuminated the silver band. Levi's eyes met Ethan's. "You know that twin thing I was telling you about? Something's wrong, and here's her message."

Ethan dragged frustrated fingers through his hair again, disbelief rattling through his words. "She lost her ring, and you think it's a message?"

"She never takes this ring off. Haven't you noticed the way she's always fussing with it?"

"What're you saying?" Ethan asked, the flames consuming the house paling compared to the one devouring him from the inside.

"I'm saying someone took her," Levi said.

Ethan's mind raced through the possibilities, but in his gut he knew who had done this.

The phone call he'd received when leaving the cafe had been Reuben. They'd found a link between the Rancho de Chela and the Margolis Social Club. It had some digging, but they'd found an airplane registered to the same company that owned both. By themselves, none of this amounted to anything criminal. Together with the other rumors, they aroused suspicion. Add in Levi's story and what Ethan felt in his bones, and they set off all the bells and whistles.

Ethan had a bad feeling about this Bryce Leech guy ever since he heard the name. That the man associated with the ranch where possible human trafficking was occurring had finagled a ride with Shayne kindled a white-hot fire in his blood.

The expression Levi wore said that even without the benefit of what Ethan knew, he was thinking the same thing.

"Where would he have taken her?"

"Only one place I can think of." Levi was already in motion as he answered.

Ethan overtook him as they sprinted to his truck.

Shayne had been asleep by the time Ethan had gotten home. His conversation with Reuben had taken a while as they discussed how best to proceed. All that was out the window now.

He'd planned to pack his bags and head back to the hotel, but something had kept him from leaving. After carrying half his stuff to the truck, he'd found his heart wasn't ready to carry out the rest. Stalling, he'd picked up a Bible on the dresser, surprised to see it contained old letters and notes tucked between the pages. He hadn't read any of them, but the notes written on the onionskin-like pages of the book he'd treated as free game. At first, it had been the pull to draw closer to Shayne, anything that gave him a connection to her. He'd flipped through the pages, taking in the handwritten prayers and dates of important events scribbled in the margins.

But then he'd started reading the actual text. It had felt like a conversation, not a book of rules.

He must have fallen asleep, because sometime later he'd awakened, still dressed, unpacked suitcase beside him, with the Bible open against his chest. And the faint smell of smoke out of place in the lemon furniture polish and moth-ball scented room.

God, if this was your hand holding me here tonight, thank you. As they climbed into his truck, Ethan realized he was long overdue for a conversation with the Lord.

The truck raced up the driveway, swerving to avoid running head on into the firetrucks headed in the opposite direction. Ethan tossed Levi his phone. "Call the sheriff."

A call to nine-one-one would go through dispatch and they might not be as confident of the information Ethan had to share. Sheriff Griger would take him seriously.

One other thing troubled Ethan. Reuben had told him the plane in question had been fueled and prepped for an early take off. It would be less than a thirty-minute flight. If, as they suspected, this was its target destination, it could arrive less than half an hour past dawn. Then what?

He jammed his foot down on the accelerator. He didn't want to contemplate the then what.

CHAPTER FORTY

The fluorescent bulbs hanging above her cast a harsh glare inside the metal building. A surreal fog clouded her thinking, blocking out all but the strange feeling of déjà vu.

When he'd bound her wrists with a zip tie before bringing her here, a ferocious calm had filled her. She knew where he'd take her. And she understood she'd been naïve and unprepared for the last time. Not this time. She might not win, but she planned to take a little bit of him with her when she lost.

But Conner was wrong.

Bryce Leech wasn't just creepy. He was depraved.

Not knowing if Ethan and Levi had survived hurt the most. Nothing else mattered.

"The stars never rise, but I feel the bright eyes of the beautiful Annabel Lee." Bryce was standing behind her, too close, his breath warm and moist on her skin as he brushed her hair away from the back of her neck. His lips moved slowly down the vertebrae in her neck. "I've dreamed of this moment for a long time, dear. I thought I'd lost you when you ran off and didn't come back." He placed his hands on her shoulders. The scent of the diesel that clung to his skin stung her nose.

He'd started the fire that destroyed her home and possibly the lives of two people she cared about. Her pulse throbbed along the vein in her neck as anger vibrated in every cell of her body.

Replace fear with anger, her self-defense instructor had said.

Done. If any harm came to Ethan or Levi because of Bryce's actions, she'd happily die returning the favor.

"I'm disappointed you aren't wearing my gift," he said.

His words made no sense. Reasoning with an insane person wouldn't work.

"The lipstick. It would be so beautiful, like crushed cherries against your pale skin. Delicious. It would be just like the first time when I fell in love with you."

Shayne offered no response, but stared straight ahead.

"Do you know when that was?" His thumbs rubbed back and forth over her bare skin.

It took everything in her not to cringe, shrinking away beneath his touch. Shayne fisted her hands still bound in front of her. The sharp edge of the plastic sank into her flesh. *Breathe in. Hold. Breathe out.*

"You remember the night? I know you do." He traced a fingertip along the side of her neck and across her shoulder.

The urge to shudder threatened to ripple over her body in a way she refused to let him see. The overhead lights created a shadow on the wall in front of her. The dark lines they formed fell on the wall in the shape of a cross.

"You were so patient, waiting for your brother, the dutiful, loving sister. Loyalty is a rare virtue." He scooped her hair into his hands and pressed it to his face before letting it slide through his fingers. "Tell me you remember me like I do you. I'd just started working for the Tackmores that summer. I remember that night so well. You looked perfect sitting in the moonlight all by yourself. You must have wanted me to follow you that night, but I was too shy."

Cold seeped through her body, tightening her muscles. Had he been one of them?

"*For the moon never beams, without bringing me dreams of the beautiful Annabel Lee.* I didn't know it then, but later, as I watched what happened, I realized you are my Annabel."

He inhaled deeply, as though satisfied by his memories. His hand cupped her neck. "Tell me you love me, Precious."

Shayne licked her lips and tried to slow her racing pulse. It was getting harder to repurpose her fear into anger, much less to think.

"I think you love yourself enough for the both of us. Weren't you the one who said selfishness wants for itself?" she asked, surprised by the bold, calm quality in her voice.

He chuckled, then tugged her head back, his lips brushing against her ear. "While wickedness desires for the other not to have. You were paying attention. See how good we are together?" He released her hair, letting his hand slide down her back until he no longer touched her, then moved to face her. "But I wasn't selfish or wicked that night. I was disappointed that they got to you before I did. My fault for waiting ... for wanting to take my time and savor the moment. All I could do was watch as they did such vile, yet fascinating, things to you."

His breathing grew erratic. "You bit your lip so hard it bled." He reached into his pocket and pulled out a tube of lipstick identical to the one she'd found in her purse. Removing the cap, he reached to brush the waxy, blood red substance against her lips.

Shayne jerked her head away.

"If you only knew how very seductive the sight of that bright red was against such pale, soft skin. You can't imagine how difficult it was for me to watch, knowing I couldn't have a taste." He laughed. His hand shot up, vice like fingers gripping her jaw and turning her to face him as he held her still and traced the contours of her mouth with the lipstick. "There now. No need to be shy."

The lipstick felt vulgar against her lips.

"Watching wasn't all bad, though. You never cried. You wanted to. I could tell. But you didn't." He stepped back, his gaze caressing her lips with a look of such hunger she feared he planned to bite her.

"Do you know why you didn't cry?"

She didn't want to look back. She wanted to look forward. Instead, she stared into the eyes of a maniac. A strength that couldn't have been her own filled her.

Bryce moved around behind her once more, his hands coming to rest on her shoulders as he leaned close. "You didn't cry because you refused to give that part of yourself away. It was the one thing they didn't take from you then." He inhaled again.

That's right. She hadn't cried. *Focus, Shayne.*

Fight.

"You were the first time I'd ever experienced those kinds of thoughts. I hadn't yet learned what they meant or how to handle them. Somehow, even then, I understood it wasn't yet our time." He kissed her neck.

"I've practiced since then. And I tracked you down. Oh yes, I had an ulterior motive for developing those computer skills I told you about. I don't like Nick, by the way. You'd never be happy with him. But there was something about the possibility of watching you plan a wedding, even if it was with him, that I found so irresistible. Like the beautiful and tragic Annabel, lying in her tomb in her gown of white. I wouldn't have let you go through with it. I would have come for you. But now you've returned to me." He wove his fingers in and out through her hair, inhaling. "A hint of smoke, but we can take care of that."

Shayne swallowed, trying to push her breath deep into her lungs.

"You don't need to be afraid. Everything will be perfect." His lips toyed with her ear as he whispered the words.

The vulgar touched steeled its way through Shayne, triggering a determination that surprised and strengthened her. There was no room for fear now. She would survive. That is how she saw herself.

But she needed a plan, some idea of what to do. Seizing his momentary distraction, she surveyed her surroundings. Could she get to the door, open it, and get out? With her hands bound, probably not. Her eyes searched for another way while her heart searched for something supernatural.

In all your ways acknowledge Him and He will make your paths straight. Shayne wanted to scream at her subconscious. It wasn't Scripture she needed right now. Her gaze went back to the shadow of the cross, and then she saw it. A misplaced ax handle rested across two buckets on a shelf, forming the vertical beam of the shadow.

I am the way, the truth, and the life. There was only one way through all of life. Jesus. Not her perfection, nor her purity. Not her family, friends, or even her faith. It was Jesus and nothing else. Jesus, who died a horrific death on a cross to save her.

She'd known it all along, but had run from it anyway. No more.

The morning sunlight crept in through a crack on the far wall to land at her feet. She wasn't alone and unseen. She never had been.

And she wasn't alone now.

A faint hum filled the morning as sunlight erased the last of the shadows. Bryce turned to the sliding doors that opened to the field as the sound grew louder. Walking over, he lifted a metal latch, then put his shoulder to each, pushing them apart.

Shayne used the moment. Gritting her teeth, she braced for the pain. She raised her bound wrists high above her head, then brought them down as hard as she could to strike her midsection, thrusting her elbows backwards in one fierce movement. The momentum created enough pressure to release the locking mechanism on the zip tie, freeing her hands. Who said watching videos on the internet was a waste of time?

She bit her lip as pain screamed down her arm when the stitches from her healing wound ripped apart. She lunged for the ax handle.

Bryce was quicker, spinning toward her with a gun he pulled from beneath his coat before she reached her objective. He aimed it at her, his eyes wide and breath shallower than before.

"Aren't you the clever one?"

He fidgeted, his motions jerky now as his eyes darted to the smaller walk-through doorway behind them. Apprehension ghosted across his face as though something that frightened him might come through that door. Despite his words, it was obvious he didn't feel in control at the moment.

The buzzing grew until Shayne recognized the sound of an approaching airplane.

A smile edged in relief inched across Bryce's face.

He grabbed her arm, wrenching it as he pulled her toward the open door.

What were her odds of escape? If she could get close enough to the door, then maybe.

"I don't want to hurt you, but it will be for your own good if you force me to." His words were chilly and full of a promise she didn't question.

Numbness rendered her legs unsteady, making her stumble as understanding consumed her. If she got on this plane, there was little chance she'd escape.

You survived before when you thought you wouldn't.

Bryce jerked her up until she regained her footing.

Yeah, well, I'm not a cat. The nine lives thing isn't going to work for me.

Again, curiosity about the thoughts her mind was capable of under such circumstances astounded her. And again she shoved them away to ponder later.

If there was a later.

The small plane touched down on the distant end of the field. A faint hope it would bring a rescue fluttered through her, but the reality of her circumstances ground it to bits beneath the cruel heel of truth. Her subconscious understood what her mind refused to acknowledge. The plane wasn't coming to help her.

The landing carried it alongside the barn, bouncing over the uneven ground as it slowed. At the far edge of the field, it turned, heading back to where they stood just inside the open barn doors. Bryce jammed the gun into her ribs. "Move."

She swallowed the metallic taste of fear filling her mouth as the gun barrel dug into her side. He pulled Shayne close in front of him and stepped out, waiting for the plane to stop.

The pilot's door swung open, exposing an irritated man who cursed at Bryce. "What the ... this isn't the deal. That's not the girl, and I don't deal with you. Where's Vito?"

In one fluid motion, Bryce swung his gun around and pulled the trigger. The man toppled from the cockpit, bouncing from the small step attached to the main leg to the ground. Shayne screamed as he landed in front of her.

"All aboard," Bryce said, shoving her over the body as if it weren't there.

Unable to catch her breath or think beyond the man

sprawled at her feet, she obeyed. Her foot found the step attached, but slipped on the bloody surface. Her shin banged against the metal, causing her to gasp. The pain shattered through the shock, breaking its hold on her thoughts. She pulled herself up and spun, hoping for enough room to plant a solid kick to Bryce's head, but he was too close.

He smiled at her. "It's almost as if I can read your mind, isn't it? We do make a great team, *don't we?*" He shoved her across to the co-pilot's seat, then seated himself where the pilot had been. He slammed the door and turned to her. "For however long we live."

Within seconds, they were taxiing across the field. Determined to keep him from taking off, she considered lunging at him. She was as good as dead either way, right?

Again, he must have read her mind. He brought the gun up, then smashed it across her cheek.

"You should probably buckle up, dear." His words flowed like black oil as the world blurred.

CHAPTER FORTY-ONE

Vito cursed. Such an ugly word. Hearing it from his own lips only heightened his anger.

He paused, inhaling deeply as he adjusted the cuffs of his shirt sleeves. Then he rolled his neck.

He would not let such a little thing as a flat tire have control over him. His failure to find his money or uncover who to blame for that fiasco nagged at him. Not that he planned to give up. That wasn't the way Vito conducted his business.

No. The greater source of his ire was that his foreman had proven himself untrustworthy. He'd known it as soon as he'd watched him stop to talk to that woman, Shayne Wright.

Yes, Bryce Leech held some sort of connection to the same woman who'd been at the accident where Vito's money went missing. A fact that Leech had failed to disclose to his employer.

Vito would see to it he atoned for that omission. But it would have to wait.

Today, he was moving his other merchandise to a new

location. There was already one person who knew she was here. Another loose end Vito hadn't yet tied up.

He wanted his payment, but the lead he thought he had with Shayne Wright perplexed him. He'd watched her come and go from the school and as she wandered through the aisles of the grocery store. He'd even watched her sleep one night. Nothing she did hinted that she kept a significant quantity of stolen money hidden away.

Perhaps it was time to press her a little harder, and a little more intimately. It, too, would have to wait until he'd taken care of his other problem first.

All these untidy problems had given him a headache. He'd awakened this morning feeling tired, wrestling with the unpleasant sensation there was something he was missing. It had caused him to take longer getting ready than he'd planned. But finally he'd written it off as a test from the gods. They wanted to see if he could persevere when these pesky problems arose.

They didn't know Vito if they thought something this trivial would stop him.

He'd packed his leather travel bag with only a few essentials he didn't want to part with. He didn't plan to waste precious time to refuel the plane once it landed. Less weight meant less fuel required and would ensure they made it across the border into Mexico. He'd turned off the lights to the apartment he kept over the Margolis Social Club and made his way down the stairs for the last time. He'd be back one more time to take care of the unfinished business, but it wouldn't be as respectable business owner Vito Slavin. It would be as a menace in the night no one would ever see.

He stepped out to discover a flat tire. Again, the gods offended him if they expected such a small thing as this would disrupt his plans.

He looked at his watch and calculated how much time he

had left before the plane arrived. He'd still need a few minutes to retrieve the woman from the place where he'd hidden her.

Something unusual snagged his attention. He leaned closer, squinting to see the slash in the wall of the deflated tire.

Vito let another foul word escape.

Bryce Leech. His gut told him the man had double crossed him. Vito had no doubt Bryce and Shayne had something that belonged to him, and now they were interfering with his plans to move the girl. Perhaps they were even planning to take the girl and sell her themselves.

As he changed the flat tire, the smell of the blood he planned to spill filled his nostrils in a way that soothed and satisfied him.

Leech was as good as dead. And so was Shayne Wright if he found her with him.

———

The sun had moved several degrees up from the horizon when they crested the hill overlooking the Rancho de Chela fifteen minutes later. Ethan had Levi call the sheriff and then Reuben. There was nothing more he could do but drive. Neither man had spoken it, but both understood where they were headed.

"Stop!"

Ethan stomped on the brakes, sending the truck sliding on the loose gravel road as Levi pointed to the field at the bottom of the hill.

In an instant, he saw the same thing as Levi. In the open field, a plane taxied away from the barn. He knew instinctively it was preparing to take off. And he knew Shayne was on that plane.

Jamming the truck in park, he jumped out and swung open the back door, pulling his rifle case from behind the seat.

He swung the rifle up and peered through the scope. The position of the early morning sun made it hard to see. He squeezed his eyes closed, then opened them again, narrowing his focus. The harsh words he spoke sliced through the air. He could make out the outlines of two people inside the narrow fuselage, but the angle kept him from knowing which one was Shayne, or if it was for certain her.

The plane was only taxiing. It would have to turn and come back this way for its takeoff. But would he have any better shot then? What if Shayne was too close, the viewpoint was wrong, or he missed?

Sweat raced down his hairline and soaked his sweatshirt despite the cool morning temperatures.

He glanced at Levi. He might not get a crippling shot in, but he could send Levi down the hill. He'd have to drive like the demons were chasing him to make it, but it might be their only other chance.

"Take the truck!" He jerked a revolver from its holster at his back and thrust it into Levi's hand. "Go!"

Ethan scrambled to the edge of the road and swung the rifle to his shoulder.

Could he stop the plane if it meant risking her life?

As Levi sped, bouncing away in his truck, Ethan started that long overdue conversation with God.

CHAPTER FORTY-TWO

Shayne squeezed her eyes closed, pinching the tender space between her thumb and forefinger as she fought against the black tide pulling her under. The side of her head where Bryce hit her stung as the force of the impact hammered through her skull. The foul taste of blood, like a mouthful of old pennies, filled her mouth.

Something thumped against the plane. A knocking sound she couldn't identify.

The grim expression on Bryce's face told her something wasn't right. His fingers around the control column turned white as he pushed back against the seat, fighting against an aircraft that seemed to have a mind of its own.

Ethan's truck bounced into view, speeding downhill toward the open field. It fishtailed on a slick spot of still damp ground before shooting in front of them. The driver locked the brakes, jerking the steering wheel, spinning the truck around to face the opposite direction. An arcing fin of grass and earth sprayed behind it.

Bryce pulled back on the control column. The plane hopped, going airborne for a few feet before striking the ground again. Shayne's shoulder banged against the frame, sending revived waves of agony along her injured arm as the warmth of fresh blood from the torn stitches soaked her shirt.

The truck raced head-on for the plane.

What was he doing? He was going to collide with the out-of-control airplane. Shayne braced herself and prayed he missed as the aircraft bobbed as though unable to balance itself.

The truck rammed the fuselage just in front of the pilot's side door. The scream of shredding metal ripped through the air as the propeller sliced through the hood of the truck.

Bryce didn't move. Blood seeped from a gash on his forehead.

The passenger side door—her only way out—angled up to expose more sky than earth. She found the latch, then heaved the door open, wedging her body into the space before the door could slam shut. Wiggling through the opening, she tumbled out, falling head-first toward the ground. A pair of strong arms broke her fall, catching her before she landed.

Levi scooped her into his arms, moving her away from where fire already licked up around the disabled aircraft.

"Where's Ethan? Is he ..." She couldn't finish.

"He's fine. He was the one helping steer the plane with his special form of remote control." Levi didn't slow his pace despite the pain carrying her must cause him. The strain in his voice confirmed it. "I knew he had special skills. Thank goodness those skills include being a topnotch sniper."

Relief flooded through her, bringing with it restored energy. "Put me down. I can do this myself."

"Before I hurt myself, right?" Levi asked, teasing her with her own words from that first night. He set her gently on her feet, watching her face for proof she wasn't lying.

"Are you okay?" she asked.

"I will be." His words seemed to carry much more depth

than the simple answer he'd given. "But let's get out of here before we discuss the matter more thoroughly."

With her hand in his grip, he set off toward the barn.

For such a time as this.

"Wait!" Shayne pulled on his sleeve. "I know where she is."

Levi faced her, a lack of understanding on his face. Then knowledge thundered in his eyes. "Did you see her? Where is she? Is she okay?" The questions sped from his lips until Shayne squeezed his jaw to silence him.

"I haven't seen her." Shayne swallowed a knot of memories in her throat. "But I know where they might keep her."

His eyes met hers with a flint-like determination that spoke volumes about his heart. "Let's go."

Shayne headed toward the stone house on the far side of the barn, running on legs that wanted to carry her away from —not to—the pain. Pausing at the locked door, she froze as flashbacks from that night leaped from the shadows to taunt her. *In her tomb by the sounding sea.* Fear engulfed her. They had to get the girl out.

Levi checked the pad lock, but it didn't budge. "Wait here."

He disappeared around the barn, while Shayne stared at the stone walls uttering the sort of prayers from deep within that only God could hear. He came back carrying a length of pipe. Shayne recognized that he had found a t-post driver, a pipe filled with the added weight of cement ranchers often used to drive fence posts into the ground.

The lock gave way after three solid blows, and he swung the door open.

She reached out to touch the cold stone walls, their grit pressing into her palms. It was just a building. The demons couldn't live here if she didn't let them.

"Shayne?" Levi's soft voice spoke over her shoulder, and she shook her head.

"For such a time as this."

"What?" Levi asked, confusion written on his wrinkled brow.

"I'll explain later." Maybe.

She followed him into the building, a single room, only ten feet by ten feet. And in the middle of the cement floor was a steel door that led to hell itself.

Shayne swayed, a low moaning sound from deep within filling the space. Levi reached to steady her. "Are you sure you're okay?"

She would not let them win. Not this time. "I'll be fine. Hurry and open it."

He raised the door, the well-oiled hinges making little noise.

A low whistling sound he probably didn't even know he'd made slipped from his lips. "All these years and I never knew this existed."

He eased himself down the metal ladder into the dark, hollowed-out bunker.

The sound of a click was followed by a faint glow radiating up from the dark hole.

"She's here." Levi's lowered voice was raw with emotion.

"I'm coming down," Shayne said, lowering herself through the opening, refusing to let the memories paralyze her.

The girl, her dark hair tangled, curled in the corner on a crumpled blanket. A half empty bottle of water lay on the floor beside her. The world seemed to give way beneath Shayne until Levi's arm caught her. "You can't fall apart now. You just saved this girl's life, but not if we don't get out of here soon."

Shayne focused on the girl. The dazed look in her eyes did little to hide her fear.

"I think she's been drugged." Levi moved closer to her, his steps slow. She didn't respond when he spoke to her. He tried again in Spanish, and Shayne saw a glimmer of recognition behind the terrified eyes.

He lifted the girl in his arms, grimacing as the added weight pulled against his still sore side. "Can you help me lift her up from above?"

Shayne was halfway up the ladder before he'd finished asking.

Together, they hoisted the girl up. Shayne scanned the girl's thin frame, searching for injuries. A few bruises externally. The actual damage would be inside and take years to overcome ... if she ever did. The girl swayed, unsteady in her drugged condition. Levi once again lifted her into his arms.

The morning sun blinded them as they left the building. With Levi carrying the girl, they headed around the old smokehouse, away from the wreck and fire now marching across the field.

An all too familiar whine split the air a fraction of a second before the bullet hit the stone wall behind them, sending sharp chips of stone to sting Shayne's skin. Ducking back into the shelter of the stone building, they waited as more shots came.

Shayne looked around. They'd be trapped if they stayed here.

A pained growl came from Levi as he repositioned the girl, heaving her limp body over his shoulder. She'd passed out, and Shayne knew that only made it harder for Levi. With his other hand, he pulled a revolver from his pocket. Shayne recognized the thirty-eight special Ethan had pointed at her the first time they met.

Keeping the girl covered by the wall of rock, he leaned out just enough to send two rounds zinging into the space

Bryce had fired from. They waited for return fire, but none came.

Fire swept across the pasture. He yelled loud enough for Shayne to hear him over her pounding heart. "In the barn."

They darted through the narrow gap, leaving them momentarily exposed before swinging through the sliding doors and into the barn. Ducking behind a pallet of boxes, Levi lowered the girl to the floor just before another shot thudded into their short wall of cardboard concealment.

The almost deafening whir of blood rushed through her body.

"You're making a mistake, Shayne. What you really want is to be loved by me." His voice grew as he moved inside the barn. She heard the gritty sound of his slow steps when they met the concrete. "I love you too much to let you do something you'll regret. You need to trust me."

Without warning, Levi stood up and aimed toward Bryce's voice. His shot was wide, pinging off the metal with a sinister screech. He fired another round before sinking down beside Shayne. "I never was any good with a handgun."

The smell of smoke wafted in to mingle with the pungent scent of gunpowder.

Shayne checked the girl's wrist for a pulse, then turned to Levi. "Her pulse is too weak. You've got to get her out of here."

"And leave you? Not a chance."

"It's the only chance. I can't carry her. It has to be you. We won't all three make it. Someone has to distract him. I'm the one he's fixated on, so it needs to be me."

"I'm not leaving you again."

"If any of us are going to get out alive, you don't have a choice. Go! Please. Get her out of here."

"Shayne, I can't leave—"

"Give me the gun and go! You said you wanted to make it

up to me for what happened. Then save her." Shayne reached for the gun, struggling to show no fear lest he waver.

The storm in his eyes reflected the emotional turbulence they both felt. It was an impossible situation with little hope they'd all survive. The bitterest part might have been that they'd only just started on the path to healing their relationship. Shayne stared, willing him to make the right choice.

"I'm coming back for you. I will." He let her take the gun from his hand, his doubtful eyes still asking for her forgiveness. His gaze settled on something she hadn't noticed. A clump of gray dirt clinging to the surface of a box. A dirt dabber's nest. He broke it off from its lodging. He stared at Shayne and shrugged. "It's not much, but I'll do the best I can."

Their eyes locked in understanding.

She knew how to use the gun she now held, but could she look at a person and pull the trigger? She'd have just one moment to decide. One moment or they might all die.

He secured the unconscious girl against his shoulder.

"I love you." It was all she could say, but if this was her last chance, those would be her last words.

Levi nodded but didn't speak.

"Shayne, I'm waiting, *my darling, my darling, my life and my bride.*" Bryce was getting closer. "Come with me, and I'll let your friends go."

Smoke filled the opening, blown in by the breeze that built as the sun crept higher in the sky. Shayne coughed, then took one more look at Levi. His eyes confirmed her own fears. This was a long shot, unlikely to meet with success. She knew he would have stopped her if his hands weren't already full. But if they kept waiting, it'd be too late. She had to trust he'd follow through on his part with that pitcher's arm that had earned him a scholarship.

"I'm here Bryce. Don't shoot, please. I'll go with you." She stood, shifting to the side of the boxes, drawing his attention, while keeping her right hand and the gun it held shielded from his sight. Pain wreaked havoc on the injured muscles of that arm. She hoped she'd have the strength to pull the trigger when the time came. "You and I can be together. Just let them go."

Bryce laughed. "Oh, my darling, we'll be together, anyway. In the sepulcher by the sea. Remember?"

Levi lurched up from hiding, launching the hapless insect's nest forcefully against the far wall. Bryce jerked his weapon around and fired as the clod of dirt crashed against the metal. His action gave Shayne the opportunity she needed.

Her shot clipped his shoulder. She steadied her aim, concentrated on the front sight, and pressed the trigger with a smooth, controlled press of her finger. She pressed her finger against the trigger one more time and heard the click of an empty chamber.

The look of disbelief and confusion on his face morphed into a rage as he swung his gun up.

A spray of pink mist exploded from the side of his head as another shot boomed inside the metal building. Shayne opened her mouth for the scream that never came. Unable to make her lungs work as Bryce collapse.

A figure stepped from beneath the stairway, moving through the thickening smoke. Ethan had saved her.

Only it wasn't Ethan that stalked from the shadows.

CHAPTER FORTY-THREE

"Hello, Shayne."

"Who are you?" She straightened, bolts of warning zinging through her. Any hope this nightmare was over evaporated. There was nothing but menace in the man who approached her.

"Nick is very upset about what you're doing to the beautiful future he had planned."

Shayne's thoughts reeled. "Nick? No, he wouldn't have anything to do with this." She looked into the stranger's eyes. "Or you?"

He laughed. "He has much to do with this. But let's not trouble ourselves with concerns for him."

He stopped and ran his eyes over her, a salacious smile on his wicked face. "Oh, that we might spend some time together. But alas, business before pleasure. I should like very much for you to tell me where my money is now."

Shayne shook her head, confused. She contemplated raising the revolver she still held, knowing it was useless.

The smoke stung her eyes, and she blinked, glimpsing movement overhead. A bird must be trapped in the building, unable to escape through the haze. She sympathized with its plight, acknowledging it might actually survive while she probably would not. "I don't know who you are or anything about any money." But she did. The memory of the man's words from the accident sounded in her thoughts. The girl, the money, it all came together now. She took a step back.

"Ah, but you do know about the money. I can see it in your eyes." He tilted his head as though he found her amusing.

With nothing but an empty gun, the only weapon she had was her ability to bluff until she sorted out a better plan. She wasn't optimistic about the success of either.

She raised the empty gun, pointing the muzzle at his head.

"Is that how you're going to play it now? That's okay. Vito Slavin is well known for liking it rough. The tougher you are, the more delicious our time together and the sweeter the occasion when it all becomes clear."

Do not shake. Convince him you'll kill him.

Again something flickered at the edge of her vision ... something in a shade of green that didn't belong in the rafters of a barn. It wasn't a bird trapped above her. She refused to take her eyes off Vito, though, knowing if she blinked, if she hesitated, if she gave him one ounce of opportunity, he'd be a greater threat than the unknown entity above her. The splash of green moved with a predatory stealth, crouching in her peripheral vision but unmistakably human. Ethan.

But what could he do?

Vito was directly beneath him, sheltered from above by the stairs and overhead rooms. If she lured him out, then maybe. But would Ethan risk a shot in here—risk the possibility it might ricochet and hit her? Shayne felt her lip twitch, determination steeling its way through her body.

So what if it ended right now? She'd saved a girl's life. Wasn't that enough?

She could do this. She could stand firm and not show fear. Shayne Wright could fight. Just let him come a little closer.

Sliding back a half step, she hoped he'd think she was considering running. Well, she was done with running.

Vito, leering and emboldened, stepped closer.

"I will shoot you," Shayne said.

"But alas, I won't shoot you. Not until I have what I want." He tucked his gun away and held out his hands, showing her she didn't frighten him. "Can we not discuss this like mature people?" He took another step toward her. He was almost in the clear.

"Stay back." She said the words, hoping he didn't obey. She inched another step backwards. "I will shoot if I have to."

"No you won't. And why would you? So you could go back to your pathetic fiancé. He isn't man enough to satisfy a woman like you. He will bore you. That's how I know you won't shoot me. You clearly don't recognize your worth if you will settle for the prison he'll keep you in. Your strength doesn't come in fighting. It comes in sacrifice. You, my dear, will always sacrifice yourself in order to prevent another from suffering. Even if that someone is me. You can't help yourself. It's who you are."

He stepped closer, his cat-like eyes mesmerizing her. "You don't want to hurt me, now do you? The thought of that troubles you. Perhaps even makes you a bit queasy, eh? You don't hurt people. You help them, save them." Vito moved closer, but still wasn't clear from the protection of the loft. She dared not glance up and give Ethan away, but how much closer must she allow Vito to come?

Ethan probably didn't realize the gun in her hand was empty. Would he hesitate to jump if he thought she might shoot him? Doubtful.

She braced herself, feet wide, arm muscles tense, and let the fury flow through her veins, morphing itself into a strength that could only come from a supernatural source.

"I'm not afraid of you." Her words came out strong, determined.

Vito beamed, seemingly pleased by her words. "Not yet, but you will change your mind. It's what you want. You want to feel. All this caring for others, guarding their secrets, it has left you numb. You've been numb for too long, haven't you, Shayne? I understand. I have been there myself. And you see, fear, it is the strongest and purest of feelings. You want to feel afraid. That is why you are pushing me now, testing my patience. I can help you. I can make you know a terror you never imagined possible. It is the only way to feel alive again."

"I'll take my chances with love instead," Shayne said.

He laughed and stepped toward her. "Suit yourself."

"Don't come any closer. I mean it. I will shoot. I'm not scared to see you die."

"You're right. You aren't afraid of what you'll see. But you are afraid of who you'll be. That is the secret, is it not? Go ahead, pull the trigger, Shayne. Kill me. Oh, the blood that will be on your hands. You've already taken one life today. How many will you kill before you call yourself a killer? You'll never be able to look at your own hands again and not see what you really are."

Vito became bolder as he moved closer.

Shayne didn't back away.

"Has anyone ever told you how beautiful your eyes are when you're afraid? Fear brings out so many lovely colors." Vito's words twisted around her, slithering over her, but she refused to react.

He stood close now. So close that if he lunged for her, he'd be upon her. He stared at the gun she aimed at his forehead as though it were no more dangerous than a toy.

"I'm not afraid, but you should be." She squeezed the trigger. For one split second, Vito faced death. And in that instant, the curtain parted, revealing his own fear before he realized the gun was empty.

The flicker of fear gave way to a moment of recognition, as though he sensed he'd just made a terrible mistake.

Ethan landed on top of him with the fierceness of a wild animal. The men crashed to the floor in a rabid heap of arms and legs. Ethan came to his knees, swinging his fist into Vito's face. Vito twisted, exhibiting more agility than Shayne expected, knocking Ethan off balance. Ethan rolled clear of the kick Vito aimed for his head.

Vito lunged for Shayne, but Ethan pulled his legs out from under him, collapsing him to the floor. Equally matched in strength, Vito was still the more limber of the two. As they wrestled, he managed to get his hands around Ethan's throat. And once there, he held on.

Shayne brought the gun down against the back of Vito's skull. Ethan had a fraction of a second after the impact to break the man's hold on his neck. He shoved Vito, sending the man sliding on the cement.

Vito lunged to his feet, a predatory cat with a thirst for blood. He grabbed for Shayne, but before his fingers closed around her, she raised her hand, then swung it down with all the fierceness she possessed, connecting the side of her open palm with the side of his neck. Vito crumpled to the cement, unconscious. Ethan stripped the man's gun from his side holster, jamming it into his own before turning to Shayne. Her feet felt anchored in place. She could only stare at the violence she'd just took part in.

Ethan stared at her, his expression unreadable. Then a smile of never-before-seen proportion broke over his features as he wagged his head from side to side. "Nice brachial stun, Wright."

Shayne looked from Ethan to Vito and back again. Vito wasn't the only one stunned at the moment. "I took some self-defense classes," she said, her voice barely above a whisper as the reality of what she'd just accomplished sank in.

Then his arms were around her, wrapping her in his fierce protectiveness. His words tumbled out in broken questions, desperate to believe she was really okay. An intensity had replaced the familiar sadness in his eyes.

"I'm okay." She placed a hand against his beard. For once, she meant it.

She rested her head on his chest, letting his strength intertwine with her own.

"For such a time as this," she murmured into the steady beating of his heart.

CHAPTER FORTY-FOUR

From her vantage point a safe distance away, Shayne watched the bedlam that followed. Seated on one of the Volunteer Firefighter's tailgates, she could almost pretend this didn't concern her.

But it did in every way.

Despite all that had happened in the past few hours, she noted the easy rise and fall of her chest. Free. Was this how breathing was supposed to feel? Because if it was, she could get used to this.

Someone had handed her a bottle of water and a rough gray blanket. She inhaled, settling the blanket over her shoulders. Warmth soaked into a body she hadn't realized was cold. Exhaling, she released the tension tightening her body, like a silk scarf carried away in the morning breeze.

She relaxed, not because everything was right. The surrounding turmoil proved it otherwise. She relaxed because, alone in the barn with a madman, God had reminded her of a valuable truth. He was with her always. She saw herself and the world around with a clarity she'd been incapable of for a long time.

Today, the men she cared about were okay. They'd rescued a young woman. And two wicked men had been stopped.

She relaxed because she could trust God's promise that one day all things would be made right.

But until then, she'd fulfilled her *for such a time as this*.

The morning breeze whispered in her ear, *Nevertheless, not My will but Yours be done*. Jesus' words as He prepared to go to the cross when He asked His Father to take the cup from Him.

Did that mean what happened to her ten years ago was God's will?

Shayne's gaze settled on Levi, watching as Conner gripped his shoulder, their heads bowed in prayer.

It wasn't God's will. It broke her Father's heart.

But He'd redeemed it once she allowed Him to. And then He'd used her to save another, probably more than just one with Bryce dead and Vito in custody. How many more women would they have destroyed with their wickedness if it hadn't ended today?

It may have seemed a small part to play in God's larger story, but she'd been here to play it. If all of her life had been leading up to this very moment, would she have changed a thing? Would there be more moments in her future for which her past might become her destiny? It was a lot to think about, and she would one day soon. Amid a morning filled with sirens, smoke, and second chances, the peace that covered her in this moment was enough.

She'd received the news about her grandparents' house. The fire had devoured the one-hundred-year-old structure with a voracious appetite for the dry wood. The firefighters had never had a chance against the blaze. And they'd shown up here exhausted, but determined. The grass fire had been no match for the intensity of their determination not to be defeated by two fires in one morning.

Shayne knew she might grieve the loss eventually. But for now, she could let go of the past and embrace the sense of contentment. This day could have turned out much worse.

She looked around for Ethan, finding him near an ambulance, scowling and fidgeting impatiently while an EMT wrapped his bloody fingers. He'd busted a couple of knuckles pounding Vito. When his gaze met hers, his mustache twitched in something that tended toward a smile.

The paramedic clipped the roll of tape as Ethan walked away.

He strode over to her, and she reached for the hand still trailing a measure of adhesive tape. She smoothed the tape in place as he fit himself between her knees, removing as much distance between them as the metal tailgate where she sat allowed. His hands slid around her cheeks, cupping her head in his bandaged palms.

He ran his thumb over her lips, wiping away the last of the red stain left by Bryce's hateful lipstick. "Hey there, Hero. Hard to imagine what you should do for the rest of the day when it starts out like this." His eyes traveled from her eyes to her lips and back again.

"Not really." Shayne felt everything inside her softening in the affection of his gaze.

"Oh yeah?" Ethan angled closer, quirking an eyebrow.

"So you two sure made a wreck of my morning. You have any idea how much paperwork this is going to create?" Sheriff Griger walked up and glared, hands on his hips.

Ethan dropped his hands and took a step back, grinning as Shayne blushed.

Griger's face broke into a smile, and he extended his hand to Ethan. "Looks like we took at least one piece out of your traffickers' puzzle today. And it was bigger than we realized. Discovered a half dozen other young women being forced to live in the basement over at the Margolis Social Club. Victims of sex trafficking. Tell your team how much I appreciate what they're doing."

"And the girl here? Is she going to be okay?" Ethan asked, his concern melting into Shayne's heart even as the sheriff's comment stirred questions in her mind. *His team?*

As if he could read her mind, Ethan glanced at her, his look promising answers later if she'd trust him now.

"I expect so ... physically, anyway. We know who she is now. Marjorie Elizondo. Her father's a prominent attorney in Mexico City. Apparently, she was being used as a pawn in some sort of power struggle between two of the cartels." Sheriff Griger shook his head. "If that kind of nasty business can turn up way out here in this little dust mite of a county, it can turn up anywhere."

He turned away, a rare note of emotion thickening his words.

Ethan shifted to stand beside Shayne, his hand slipping over hers, capturing it in his tender grip. "And the women at the club?"

"Abused in ways I'd rather not discuss, but safe now." Sheriff Griger cleared his throat. "Also got the prints back on those men who died in the wreck. Turns out the DEA had flipped the one you tried to save. He was working for our side. He wasn't supposed to be involved in this, but looks like he had a personal connection to the girl. They're not saying whether he'd gone back to his old ways, but I'm believing for the best." He cut his eyes between Ethan and Shayne. "Everybody needs a good love story to believe in, right?"

"So those men were on their way here for her? But the money? The man at the accident mentioned money, and Vito asked me where his money was," Shayne said, her brow lined in deliberation.

"He must have been the one expecting it in exchange for Miss Elizondo." Ethan leaned back against the tailgate. "And it makes me think there's still one more person we need to find."

"We, huh?" Sheriff Griger dipped his head toward Ethan, then reached up to scratch his stubble covered cheek. "I've been thinking about your motorcycle friend, Shayne ... the one that tried to run you off the road. The timing of his presence interests me. Anything at all you can remember would be helpful?"

"Sheriff, you need to see this." Before Shayne had time to answer, the investigator walked up with a box of baler twine in his hands. He turned it over to reveal a bullet hole in the opposite side, a slip of green poking out. He opened the cardboard box to reveal not rolls of twine, but stacks of currency. "And there are others just like it."

"Well," Sheriff Griger said, "looks like we might have found our missing money. Now the question is, how did it get here?"

The surrounding conversation droned into a static hum. Her thoughts worked to follow the trail of implications, but it led her nowhere. There was some nugget of information hovering just beyond her reach, something she should remember.

The officer disappeared back into the barn with the box.

"If it is the missing money, it was right here under their nose the whole time. That's a pretty big risk for someone to take." The sound of Ethan's voice pulled her from her fruitless search for the answer.

Sheriff Griger's countenance hardened. "Yes, it is."

"Any chance Bryce put it there?" Ethan asked, but his voice held more hope than belief that might be the answer.

"I don't think so," Shayne said. "He didn't mention it and apparently wasn't planning to take it with him. He didn't seem interested in anything but ..." She shuddered unexpectedly. Ethan slipped his arm around her shoulders until the solidness of his body pressed alongside her own. Shayne leaned into the reassuring warmth of his touch.

Sheriff Griger pulled the antacids from his pocket and offered them to first Shayne, then Ethan. "Y'all had any breakfast yet?"

When they graciously declined, he tossed the first one he took out, green, onto the ground and popped the next one, orange, into his mouth.

"And we still don't know who shot me. Do you think it had something to do with the money?" Shayne asked. She looked from Sheriff Griger to Ethan.

"I got a hunch it had to do with the money *and* the motor-cycle," Griger said. He placed a thick hand on her shoulder and gave a gentle squeeze. He said nothing more, but the expression he wore carried a burden of empathy and remorse. "I don't know how you and your brother stumbled into opposite ends of this deal, but maybe it'll help you start walking a little closer together."

Something nudged her inside. She could give him peace about the unsettled concerns lingering in his eyes. "There's something I should probably tell you. Something I should have told you long ago."

CHAPTER FORTY-FIVE

The beginning of the end. Was that what the next few hours would bring? After only recently finding the courage to make a new beginning, it seemed unfair.

Still, Shayne smiled. She had no desire to judge the fairness of life right now.

She took her seat in the booth across from Maribel at Momma Mae's, but didn't squeeze herself against the window. This time the narrow gap between them was Ethan's to claim. And she desperately hoped he would.

Even if this was the last time. He'd answered some of her questions about what he was really doing here and promised to answer the rest later. But he'd said nothing that hinted at the future.

Shayne's fingers found the silver ring Levi had returned to her. It had only made a partial turn when she stopped. She'd found an alternative source of comfort, or rather, rediscovered the true source of comfort. It had always seemed the compass had been Peg's way of beckoning her back here. Now she understood it pointed to something much bigger. Peg had meant for the ring to point her to Jesus.

Trust in the Lord with all your heart and lean not on your own understanding. In all your ways acknowledge Him and He shall direct your paths. Proverbs 3:5-6.

That had been the note she'd slipped in the box with the ring.

All right, Lord. I trust you. Lead me onward. Shayne rested back in the seat. She stretched her fingers out to examine the ring and couldn't help but smile.

Levi had gone back to the rehab facility, ready to face whatever punishment he had coming. Letting him go had been harder than she imagined. The feel of his arms crushing her in his brotherly hug of goodbye still lingered.

Nick had finally taken her call, but she was pretty sure he wished he hadn't. The words that had come out of her mouth had been a release of something kept bottled up for too long.

He'd tried to deny having ever met Vito, but Shayne refused to be lied to. At first, the truth about Nick had made Shayne ill. But it was the truth about herself that hurt the worst. No question, what had happened to her had been horrific, but she'd let herself hide in the shadow of that pain for so long she hadn't recognized the truth about Nick.

She was going to be okay now. It would take some time and effort, but she believed it would happen.

She'd let her parting message to him be a plea that he get help.

Ethan slid into the booth beside her.

She was going to be okay, even if not everything turned out the way she wanted or expected. But she'd learned to believe God's plan was bigger than anything she could imagine.

It didn't surprise her when Sheriff Griger walked in and headed straight to the counter where Cindy worked to ring out a customer. He understood where his true north was, even if he didn't know he knew it. One day God would help him see ... God or Conner. Shayne laughed.

"What's so funny?" Ethan asked. He studied her with curiosity twinkling in his eyes.

"Life, I guess."

He raised both eyebrows. "You sure have a strange sense of humor, then."

Ethan continued to stare at her as though he saw something that thoroughly fascinated him. The heat in her cheeks skyrocketed beneath the intensity of the unspoken message he conveyed. A new gleam had replaced the sadness in his eyes, although she couldn't quite name what this new look signified.

"So, what have y'all two been up to today besides escaping fires, crashing airplanes, and engaging in gun fights? And that was all before breakfast. I can only imagine what you have on the agenda for tonight" Conner said, as he walked in carrying the quilt Shayne had taken from the house. He handed it to Shayne then slid in beside Maribel. "I found this out behind the house after the fire. It's the only thing that wasn't damaged. I figured you'd want to have it."

Shayne was unable to speak, but the moisture in her eyes revealed her emotion more clearly than anything she could have said. She ran her fingers over the double wedding ring pattern, then set it on the seat beside her.

His bloodshot eyes attested to the time he'd spent fighting the blaze this morning. "If it's all right with you two, though, I'm tuckered out. If y'all could keep it kinda boring for the next few hours, I'd appreciate it."

Maribel swatted at his arm, as though to remind him sensitivity was needed.

"I am sorry about the house, though, Shayne. We tried, but there wasn't any way we could save it. Are you okay?"

"I am, and thank you. It was just ... stuff I've been told." Shayne looked at Ethan. "And he was right."

After what seemed like hours of answering questions for the sheriff, Maribel had mercifully whisked Shayne away for a shower and a meal—although she couldn't remember what she'd eaten—and clean clothes. At least, what little she had that fit Shayne's tall frame. She'd ended up borrowing a pair of Conner's sweatpants in order to have anything long enough to cover her legs.

After that, she'd somehow slept for a few hours.

"Are you going to tell them?" Maribel elbowed Conner.

"Jimmo woke up this morning." Conner's expression said there was something more to this than the relief of knowing Jimmo was alive.

"How is he?" Shayne asked.

"He's a little agitated and groggy, but he's going to be fine." Conner leaned back against the vinyl seat. "And I finally know what he wanted to talk to me about. I think we may have the last piece of this puzzle."

A soft sob from the counter drew Shayne's attention. Cindy stood, her face against the sheriff's shoulder, as he held her.

"It was Collin, Kindley's new boyfriend." Conner's tone sobered at the sight of Cindy's grief. "Jimmo found a handgun in his truck. If the sheriff had found it, Jimmo would have gone back to prison. Apparently, Jimmo had given Collin a ride home from the ranch the night of the accident."

"My deputy called and said they found the motorcycle hidden in some brush at the ranch." Sheriff Griger walked up, his arm still around Cindy.

"When Collin offered Jimmo money not to tell anyone about the gun—a lot of money—Jimmo figured Collin was into something he shouldn't be. He just didn't know what, and he wasn't sure how to go about telling the sheriff with no proof. That's why he was coming to see me."

"I'm so mad at myself I could spit nails." Cindy wiped her hands across her cheeks. "I let Kindley accept gifts from that boy. I trusted him."

"Now, now, you did what any of us would have. No one had any reason to suspect what he was up to." Sheriff Griger patted Cindy's shoulder, pulling her closer in a way that radiated protectiveness.

The front door opened and Kindley burst in. Spotting Cindy, she ran into her aunt's hug. Tears smeared mascara across the girl's face. "They told me about Collin. I'm so sorry, Aunt Cindy. I didn't know."

The waitress led her away, the two of them disappearing through the kitchen doors.

Shayne's heart hurt for both of them, but it also beat with a hope this lesson, harsh though it might seem, would be enough to keep the girl on the right path.

"So Collin had the missing money? How did he know about it to begin with?" Ethan directed his question to the sheriff.

"Hacked Vito's computer while working for him. Says he did it for fun, but when he realized what he'd found, he ran with it. When he saw which road they'd be taking, he arranged for the accident."

"Poor Buster," said Maribel.

"So is he the one who shot me?" Shayne thought back to the morning she'd found him with her phone, and his surly attitude both at the cafe and at school.

"Said he was afraid you'd be able to identify him after seeing him on the motorcycle. Claims he didn't really want to hurt you, he panicked. Same reason he tried to kill Jimmo. Fortunately for Jimmo, his system has built up a bit more tolerance to drugs than Collin allowed for."

"That doesn't change the fact she could have died." Ethan's angry words ground out the truth.

Shayne closed her eyes and inhaled. She opened them again. "But I didn't."

"You could have ..."

She placed a hand on Ethan's arm, silencing him. "But I didn't. Let's focus on the positive. A wise man once told me we can never move forward if we're always looking back."

Tension ebbed from his clenched muscles beneath her touch.

"Let's focus on some food. I'm starving." Conner reached for the menus.

Night settled in long before anyone thought about leaving the fellowship of their booth or the security of the cafe. Shayne would stay with Maribel, thankful she wouldn't have to make any more decisions for the day. When Conner offered Ethan his truck for the night, Ethan insisted on driving her there.

After the others left, Ethan and Shayne still tarried in the warmth and privacy of their corner booth.

She was still trying to wrap her head around what Ethan had told her. Her mother had purposefully leased the house for free, to the group Ethan was working with. She'd approached Reuben after hearing him speak at a women's luncheon at her church, planning to donate to their cause. In casual conversation, she'd mentioned her hometown and her fears about what might have happened to Shayne ten years ago.

Shayne swallowed the guilt that filled her with remorse. All this time she'd been hiding it, but her mom had known, or at least suspected, anyway.

But it was her mother's fears that drove her to get involved with his organization. With the area already on their radar, they both readily acknowledged God's providence in bringing them together.

Cleansing tears fell when Ethan relayed the story to her. Then she'd called her mother to apologize. Apparently, it was Shayne's father that had silenced her mother's inquiries, convincing her that Shayne was getting help, and it was best if her mother didn't bring it up. The truth was he'd been considering a run for State Representative and didn't need the possibility of scandal.

Someone had run after her, but Shayne had pushed them away and unknowingly allowed her father to close the door.

Cindy was sweeping the floor, tipping chairs up on the tables like tucking children in at night, when Ethan pulled Shayne from the booth.

He captured her hand in this strong, warm grip as they walked beneath the streetlights. They stepped around a corner, and Shayne pulled him to a stop in the shadows.

She didn't know if this—they—would go anywhere, but she couldn't forget the way it felt to kiss this man. Boldly and unabashedly and recklessly. What if tonight they went their separate ways, never seeing each other again? After all, that could be the reason he wanted to drive her to Maribel's alone, so he could say goodbye. He didn't owe her anything. They hardly knew each other. Still, the possibility burned in her throat with a pain so fierce she wasn't sure she could endure.

But if this was the end, then what she wanted, against all reason and decency, was one more kiss.

There were no guarantees in this life. Maybe she would find another to love, and someone who would love her back, but if not, then she would have this moment of honest emotion. "Remember when you told me life is all about perspective?"

Ethan nodded without speaking, his eyes never leaving her face.

"I understand now." Shayne brushed her hands against his chest, letting them come to rest as she felt his heartbeat. "There is one perspective, though, that I think I'd like to try again."

He arched an eyebrow over eyes that seemed to grow warmer with each breath. "And that is?"

"Kiss me, Ethan McGregor." Shayne swallowed, desperately hoping he wouldn't refuse. "Thoroughly." The kiss they'd shared before had been one of only partial knowledge. There had still been too many secrets. And the moment had come with an unfortunate interruption the last time.

Her words stilled him, his dark eyes going even darker. He looked away. "I'm not sure that's a good idea."

Her heart splintered into a thousand shards, shredding through her insides. "So this is goodbye then."

He leaned toward her. "I didn't say that."

"But you don't want to kiss me."

"I definitely didn't say that." The nearness of his body sent heat shimmering through her despite the cold brick wall pressing against her back. The faint scent of smoke still lingered in his hair.

"Then maybe you'd better explain yourself better. If you're worried you'll break my heart, don't be. It was already broken. You've just allowed the mending to start." She met his stare, opening her heart with vulnerability under the light of his gaze. "I realize what I'm asking, and I accept the consequences."

"You don't realize what you're asking. I heard what Vito was saying about having blood on your hands for the rest of your life. He was right. My hands are not innocent hands."

"I think you're forgetting someone else who had blood on their hands." She looked at him with her heart, understanding what it was Ethan needed to grasp. "Blood ran from Jesus' nail-pierced hands. It ran for you, Ethan. It ran for me, and for Levi, for those girls your friends rescued today. It even ran for people like Bryce and Vito if they'd only let it."

He looked away, staring into the darkened alley.

"For such a time as this, Ethan." Shayne spoke the words softly. "How many more girls might have died at the hands of that monster today if you hadn't been exactly where you were?"

Ethan shook his head and looked down for a long moment. Shayne longed to know where his thoughts were, but she didn't ask. She waited for him in his own time. When he looked back at her, there was a tender humility in his eyes. "I guess I need to do some talking to the Lord, then."

She tapped the button on his shirt with her finger. "Speaking from experience, it only makes the hurt last longer when you don't."

They stood, no one moving, as their breaths mingled in the crisp night air.

"So about that kiss and my willingness to accept the consequences ..." Shayne's eyebrow arched in challenge.

"That's just it. I still don't think you fully understand the consequences." He leaned closer, finally erasing the last of the space between them. He traced her cheek with his finger and her lips with his gaze. "You see, when a man is asked to kiss a woman like you *thoroughly* ... well, that doesn't happen in a single kiss."

His lips brushed against the place where her neck curved into her shoulder.

A nervous giggle escaped.

A giggle! She was a grown woman for the love of Pete. *Grown women don't giggle.*

But perhaps those who've just discovered the tender truth of a first love could let the moment sweep them back into the innocence lost before its time.

He pulled back, grinning, then found his place and started over.

A moan of delight vibrated from deep within her.

"Shayne?"

"Hmmm ...?"

"You're not giggling anymore." He murmured the words against her skin, his whiskers softly tickling, his breath warm and full of something she wanted so much more of.

Her hands slid up his chest to slip around his neck. "Are you going to kiss me or not?"

"Thoroughly?"

"Mmm hmmm."

"Might take a lifetime." His lips fluttered against her cheek as he spoke.

"I think I can handle it." Shayne closed her eyes, letting everything fall away, intent on remembering the feel of this moment forever. Perhaps it was time to read the Song of Solomon again with a fresh perspective.

And then his mouth was on hers, the kiss slow and tender, deepening until he pulled away abruptly.

Doubt and disappointment burned her eyes.

"But not like this." He rested his forehead against hers. "You, Shayne Wright, are worth so much more. I want to do this right." A look that pressed upon her the seriousness of his message settled on his face. He lifted her hand and kissed her fingers. "I *will* do this right."

"I don't understand."

"And that's a problem, because you should understand." He pulled her back into the glow of the streetlamps, leading her along the sidewalk once again.

"I want to know everything there is to know about you, Shayne. I want to know exactly how you like your coffee, why on earth you want to teach literature to teenagers, and exactly what your record holding cross country time is. I want to know how long you take in the shower, which one is your favorite shirt, and what in the world is up with all the quilts. I want to know why you think you're better at fishing than I am—"

"Fishing? We've never talked about fishing. What makes you say I think I'm better than you?"

"Because you do. I can see it in your eyes."

"We've never even discussed fishing."

"But still you think it. Don't lie." He brushed her hair away from her face. "I found a picture in your grandfather's Bible. It was an adorable, although I'm guessing precocious, little girl holding a fish and a trophy. The pigtails were cute, by the way."

"I was only nine! But I did win the entire tournament, not just the youth division. Even beat Sheriff Griger out."

"Perhaps we should head to the river tomorrow and see if you've still got it."

"For the record, I do. So, are you asking me to go fishing with you?"

"You're welcome to go *fishing* all you want. I plan to go *catching*." Mischief twinkled in his eyes.

Say something profound, witty, or at least semi-intelligent. "Oh." That was all she had.

"Shayne Wright, I want you to know the truth about yourself. You are a remarkable, dazzling, one-of-a-kind woman. I want to discover everything there is to know about you. And then ..." He leaned back to look her in the eye. "And then, well, I do believe I could see myself spending a lifetime kissing you the way a woman ought to be kissed."

ACKNOWLEDGMENTS

It may not take a village to write a book, but it certainly helps to have a community. These are the people who patiently talk you off the ledge while suffering through innumerable readings of the same thing. They are the ones who enthusiastically help plot mayhem or worse for your characters. They catch your mistakes and challenge you when you aren't risking yourself to make enough of them. They are precious and priceless, and I've been blessed with an abundance of them.

Although I'm sure to overlook someone, here's my attempt at expressing gratitude to the people who make this possible.

Always first and foremost, the humans I treasure most in this world: Joe, Emily, Austin, Jeff, Sabrina, and Tucker. Without their support and encouragement, I would have given up long ago. And without their unending supply of new material, I might run out of things to say.

Some writing partners become irreplaceable friends. The list of these people in my life is long, but I'd like to give a special thanks to Donna Nabors, Kelly Goshorn, and Lori DeJong for keeping my feet moving on the journey God has me on. I'm beyond grateful for my Living Write Texas family: Deb, Karen, Sharon, Michele, Laura, Becky, Leslie, and Donna. I couldn't ask for a better set of cheerleaders and role models. Early readers are brave souls who sacrifice a lot to make a book become all that it should be. For their willingness to do this for me, these people have a special place in my heart: Susan, Carly, Deena, and Angela.

Technical assistance in covering the topics where my knowledge is lacking is a priceless resource. My special thanks to Austin and David for sharing their expertise and understanding in regard to law enforcement and police procedures, and to Gareth for providing me with a wealth of information on everything related to my Cessna airplane and how to crash it. Any mistakes in the writing are all mine.

If this work shines in any way, it is because of the editing wisdom of Yolanda Smith and the eagle-eyed proofreading skills of Donna Nabors.

ABOUT THE AUTHOR

Lori Altebaumer is a writer who only half-jokingly tells others she lives with one foot in a parallel universe. With her boots on the ground, head in the clouds, and heart in His hands, she is a wandering soul with a home-keeping heart in search of life's best adventures. Lori loves sharing the joys of living a Christ-centered life with others through her writing. Her first novel, A <u>Firm Place to Stand</u>, was a finalist for both the Selah and the Director's Choice awards. In addition to being a regular contributor to The Word on Wednesday, Crossmap, and other online devotions, she blogs irregularly from her website. She currently serving as the 2024 Vice President of the Faith, Hope, & Love Christian Writers. Lori also cohosts the My Mornings with Jesus and Joe podcast with her husband.